HE JUMPED FIRST

A NOVEL
TIM BAKER

NORMANDIE PRESS

ISBN: 979-8-218-83485-2 (Paperback)

This is a work of fiction. Names, characters, places, and incidents either are the product of the author's imagination or are used fictitiously. While the historical sinking of the RMS Titanic and certain public figures of the era are portrayed, the central narrative, main characters, and their personal stories are inventions. Any resemblance to actual events or locales or persons, living or dead, beyond those of the public historical record, is entirely coincidental.

CONTENTS

"The past is never dead. It's not even past." - William Faulkner

"Man is least himself when he talks in his own person. Give him a mask, and he will tell you the truth." - Oscar Wilde

SOS...CQD...MGY

CHAPTER 1

B en Howell was awake.

High above the mountains that watched over the still-sleeping City of Angels, dawn's fingers combed the horizon. Hues of lapis and periwinkle spilled into the warmth of amber, fuchsia, and vermilion. Rays scattered to the earth, kissing the treetops, the rooftops, and finally the lonely streets—still deserted at this early hour.

Ben Howell was *wide awake.*

The dawn crept closer. Up the avenues, down the boulevards, until it reached a row of industry-money mansions lining a showy block of Sunset Boulevard. Each house felt itself better than the rest—proudly ostentatious in scale, haughtily lavish in appointments. High walls of brick and stucco shielded them while wrought-iron gates stood guard like centurions.

One such house, just as presumptuous as all the others, yet decidedly withdrawn, the wallflower of the party, shrank back from the sun's caress, not wanting to be touched. The light tried again, bounding the high walls, splashing over emerald grass, climbing the vines to the second level of the ivy-clad facade. It stopped at a pair of tall windows looking into the master suite, lingering as if waiting for permission to enter.

Ben took no notice.

Wrapped in a cocoon of fine linen and silk jacquard, his bedding felt more like a straitjacket than luxury. Comfort was a luxury he could no longer afford. This morning, like every morning, his mind churned with unrest. *Thoughts of what had been. Thoughts of what should be but never would be again.*

Beside him, Adelaide slept. Sleep had always come easily for her, and he resented that. She must have remembered the bliss they'd once called their happy marriage, but those days—like the last of their four children—had left them alone years before.

Tendrils of sunlight finally broke through the gap between the window sheers, reaching deeper into the room until everything became awash in a sea of fragile blue.

Through the dim glow, his eyes found the reality of the room that trapped him. The suite—a tastefully decorated mausoleum—reverently housed its hosts. Both were living, though one only by definition.

"It's six o'clock, sir," the old man whispered. Ben, startled, hadn't heard him enter, but that was his way. Always there to serve, but never to intrude.

"Thank you, Gil," Ben replied, in a matching whisper.

The butler stealthily set about the silver tray and fine bone china on the small table across the room, before imparting, "Enjoy your breakfast, sir." And with that, he split the door ever so slightly, poured himself back into the cheery glow of the warm hallway, and closed the door behind him, all as silently as he'd entered.

After listening a moment or two for the gentle snore of his wife, he quietly sat up, lowered his legs over the side of the bed, then dug his toes into the plush carpet, before rising like a ghost from the grave and floating to his breakfast across the room.

He sank into the sofa, raised the cup to his nose, and inhaled the rich aroma. The scent of the finest Belgian chocolate, married into a molten sweet cream, delighted his senses. Hot cocoa had been his daily breakfast since childhood, something which his father had never approved of—which only delighted Ben further. Forty years after the death of his father, Ben still cursed his name.

Next came the first sip. Then Ben closed his eyes and, in an instant, was transported back in time. First it was just the gentle swell of strings, music from a nearby orchestra; then he could see the large, bright room. Rich plasterwork stretched from floor to ceiling, every inch of it blazing with light. Beautiful women and handsome men, dressed in the finery of a bygone era, reclined into green leather chairs and carefully choreographed every moment as they ate their breakfast. Dainty fingers, silent sips through sturdy pursed lips, carefully muted chuckles and conversations, all the result of the airs of pedigree. They stopped at once and all eyes fell upon him. Smiles greeted him from one end of the room to the other, and he could feel their anticipation. They'd been waiting for him. *They were waiting for him.*

"Go on, Benji, take another sip," she said.

Across the table sat a stunning woman, so regal she might've been a postcard; hair piled perfectly atop her subtly painted features. She gave an encouraging smile. "Are you enjoying your breakfast, darling?"

"Yes," Ben said aloud, the sound of his own voice bringing him back to reality. All at once the bright room was gone, replaced with the coldness of his bedroom. Ben started at the shift, then realized it had all been in his mind. Not a dream, but a flashback to a moment in time, a former life. He had slipped between these realities for years, but it was becoming more and more frequent these days; harder to control.

Adelaide sighed in her sleep. Ben, relieved his subconscious outburst hadn't woken her, took one final sip of cocoa, replaced the cup to its saucer, and moved into the dressing room.

He selected the navy suit with the fine pinstripe—tailor-made in Paris last summer. Despite nearing sixty, he'd long possessed a reputation for style. In his fashion choices, his homes, his cars, Ben Howell was a man of impeccable taste. These old-money sensibilities were the one thing that still united him and his wife, though unlike him, she hadn't been born into that world. She simply had a natural sense for it.

After showering, shaving, dressing, combing his hair, and placing his signature hyacinth blossom in his lapel, he finished his routine with a glance in the mirror. Sure, the ritual was used to track the signs of aging—new gray hairs overtaking the brown ones, fresh wrinkles that hadn't been there yesterday. But more than anything, this was his chance to practice smiling. His last chance to remind himself the world didn't want to see his scowl. The first smile always felt awkward. The second, nearly as uncomfortable. But by the third, then the fourth—there, that's it—he could manage it with ease. He could make it convincing.

"Goodbye, my love," he whispered, kissing his sleeping wife's forehead. She didn't stir, but she smiled, peaceful. He took this to mean some part of her knew that despite the distance between their lives, between their hearts, he still loved her. And she, him.

He closed the door silently and descended the stairs, passing a row of framed movie posters lining the walls. They told the story of the last thirty-five years—the highs and lows of success that had built this stately home, initiated a relationship and then a marriage, put four children through Ivy League schools and given them trust funds. Success that was no longer enough to distract him from the past.

"Morning, Mr. Howell!" the guard's voice was hearty for this early hour.

"Isaac, how was your Easter?" Ben asked.

"Fantastic! First one with my little guy. The missus and I hid eggs and everything. Of course, we had to be the one to find them, but it's the thought, right?" he laughed.

"That reminds me," Ben reached into his glove compartment and then turned back to the guard, holding out an envelope.

"What's this?"

"You can open it."

Isaac opened the envelope and saw a card that read, *Congratulations on your newest addition!* Along with a check for a thousand dollars. The man's eyes went wide.

"Mr. Howell, I *can't*—"

"You *can*. I insist. Think of it as a start towards his college fund. Or use it as you and your wife see fit."

"Thank you, Mr. Howell, this is so very generous. I wish I knew what to say, but I'm afraid I just don't have the words right now," the man was on the verge of tears.

"Think nothing of it."

And with that, Ben's car passed through the open gate and onto the studio lot.

Even though he was early, as always, work on the lot was already underway after the lengthy three-day weekend. He waved at the carpenters working on the sets outside of sound stage 12. This was Ben's domain. It was his safe place. Outside these studio walls there was chaos. Wars raged. Murders went unsolved. Famine and recession took out entire family lines. But, in here, everything had a script, had a timeline, had a budget. Sure, things could run off the rails, but you always had a contingency plan, a fail-safe. Within these walls, Ben could control his world, and that made him breathe a little easier.

"Good morning, Mr. Howell!" the secretary looked up from her typing.

"Edith, how was your holiday weekend?"

"Not much of a holiday. I don't think anyone told the folks at 20th Century-Fox that it was Easter."

"Mr. Klein forgets that not everyone in this town is Jewish, I'm afraid," Ben chuckled.

"He's already called three times this morning, that's in addition to the dozen calls this weekend, and at least ten messages."

"And? What did you tell our dear friend?"

"I told him to piss off!" Edith laughed.

"You didn't," Ben said, half believing her.

"Of course I minced words just a bit." She sat down at the desk and read aloud her last reply, "*Mr. Howell continues to be appreciative of your consideration for this upcoming picture; however, he is currently booked through the year, and unable to take on any additional projects. Should his schedule free up, his office will be in touch. Until then, warmest regards, et cetera, et cetera, et cetera—*" she drew out the last word for dramatic effect.

Ben laughed. "We'll make a writer out of you yet."

As he turned to step into his office, "I should warn you," Edith called out.

"*Yes?*" Ben asked, turning back to her.

"The sharks are circling. They've been here for an hour already."

Ben drew a long sigh.

"They can sense the blood," she continued.

"Ugh. Thank you, Miss Blake." He turned to leave once more.

"Should I come in and rescue you?"

"If I'm not out in fifteen!" his laughter rang down the hallway as he left.

"Ben, my boy! It's about time you showed up," Geoff said in the same, cheeky tone that a father gives their teenager when they finally roll out of bed on a lazy Saturday.

"Hope you're ready to hit the ground running this morning. We've got lots to talk about. Lots. I took the liberty of bringing us some breakfast," Larry stretched out a hand to the pile of donuts and bagels at the center of the conference table.

Ben took a seat. "Thanks, but I've already eaten."

"You don't know what you're missing," Larry began spreading cream cheese onto a bagel. "These are from Mentz's, the best bagels outside of New York."

"It's the saltwater, you know"—Geoff took one for himself—"you Gentiles just don't get it. It's all in the saltwater—"

"I'm sorry, did you two say that you had something to talk about this morning? I'm sure you didn't come to gnaw my ear about bagels," Ben said.

"*Oy vey.* Fine, forgive me for trying to bring a little conversation into the morning before we get down to brass tacks," Larry folded a sliver of lox onto the cream cheese, then took a bite.

"Two pictures"—Geoff took over the reins—"that's what we've got to cover this morning. Both promise to be quite the windfall if we go about this right." He rubbed his fingers together, signifying money.

"I'm listening," Ben said.

Geoff continued, "Alright, picture this, two broads, both knockouts, one brunette and one blonde..."

"But not just any blonde. *The* blonde!" Larry interrupted.

"Lana Turner?" Ben asked.

"*Turner?!* What is this, the *'30s?*" Geoff laughed.

"*Monroe!*" Larry said.

"Monroe?" Ben thought aloud.

"*Marilyn* Monroe! Surely you know about *Marilyn!*" Larry said.

"Our boy's a mensch, you know that, Larry," Geoff chimed in. Then, after opening a folder, he placed a black and white photograph of a beautiful blonde in front of Ben, and went on, "Body that just won't quit, this one."

"And that *ass!*" Larry said.

"Keep it in your pants," Geoff chastised. "But, she is a real up-and-comer. Audiences are asking for her by name. And we've got her."

"What's the premise?" Ben asked, still not sold.

"A romantic comedy, this girl, and her best friend, the brunette, are obsessed with finding husbands. One looking for love, the other looking for money. Great script. Lots of laughs. They're calling it *Gentlemen Prefer Blondes*," Geoff said.

"*And...*" Larry added, "it's right up your alley! Whole thing takes place on a ship!"

Ben looked up with a start. His partners, not meaning for the jest to be taken seriously, realized that it had been. Just as Geoff feared they were losing him, he said, "We'll come back to this one. Let's talk about the other picture. The opportunity of a lifetime. Something they'll be talking about for years to come."

"Millions," Larry said, "it's sure to bring in *millions!*"

Ben sighed, then reluctantly came back to the conversation. "What kind of picture is it?"

"An epic!" Larry said. "A historical drama. Big names already attached, Clifton Webb, Barbara Stanwyck..."

Geoff broke in, "CinemaScope! The entire thing will be shot in CinemaScope! Just think of it! Nothing like this has been done before!"

"What's the title?" Ben asked.

"They're offering a million-dollar budget!" Larry deflected.

"The name!" Ben demanded. "What is the *name?!*"

His partners looked at each other, hesitant, then turned to him, and, in unison, said, "*Titanic.*"

The room began to grow dark around Ben. Tunnel vision to start, then that murkiness that comes with opening one's eyes while underwater. The sounds too became distorted. Became distant. *Groaning.*

In an instant, though awake, Ben was transformed to a familiar moment. A nightmare that he'd wrestled with countless times. But he wasn't asleep, not this time. This time it was the mere mention of that word, Titanic, and he was back there. He could hear the groans of a dying monster, a monster which held him trapped in its belly. There was a rushing of water. The massive room lay in total darkness, until, *FLASH!* Pulses of light came and went as the monster was trying to revive itself; it wanted to live; it was fighting to hold on. In those faint glimpses of light, cast in a sickly, eerie green glow, like the glowing of light from beneath seawater, he could see her. The lovely woman who sat across from him at breakfast. She was dressed in that familiar, Edwardian opulence, but she no longer smiled. Her face was wrapped in horror, the extent of which made her features almost inhuman. Her eyes, her mouth, stretched to the extreme as only sheer terror can demand. Those eyes penetrated him. They pleaded for him to help her, to save her.

"Benji!" she screamed.

Then, all at once, another groan gave way to an ear-splitting tear. The sharp twisting of metal. The floor vibrating and lurching beneath his feet. Again, her face appeared before him in that haunting glow. This time her scream was louder than ever, her fear, her anguish palpable, *"BENJI!"*

"Ben!" Geoff said, as he gently patted Ben's face.

"Here, drink this," Larry handed Ben a glass of ice water.

Slowly the brown paneled walls of the boardroom came back into focus. The sounds of hammers and saws filtering through the window, as the carpenters and builders constructed their sets out on the lot below.

"Are you with us, Ben?" Larry asked.

"I... uh..." Ben stammered.

"There he is. Alright. We're alright now. Everything's going to be alright," Geoff assured.

"Take a drink, Ben. Can you do that for me?" Larry took Ben's wrist and raised his hand, which held the glass, to his face. Ben took a sip. "That's it. Easy does it," Larry continued. "Enough business for today."

"Yes," agreed Geoff. "We can circle back around to this next week."

"No," said Ben, resolute. His voice was so sure, and so authoritative, that both men who'd been tending to his wounds were shocked at their partner's sudden fervor.

"You're not up to it, Ben," Geoff began.

"You're right," said Ben, "not now. Not tomorrow. Not next week, goddamnit! This picture is *not* happening! At least not with my name attached. You two can knock yourselves out, but I'll have no part of it!"

"Ben," Larry began, "you're not feeling well. Let's not discuss—"

"Forty years," Ben closed his eyes, as if recalling some deeply suppressed memory, then his eyes opened, blazing with anger. "I haven't spoken of this for forty years!"

"Then isn't it time—"

"No, Larry! It's not time! It'll never be time, until I, *and I alone*, say so! You want my take on the *Titanic* disaster, you can read about it. My words were a front-page exclusive in *The New York Times* when I was eighteen. I said all that I had to say then, and I haven't a thing more to say now. Not to you, nor to Mr. Klein at 20th Century-Fox, not to anyone! Do I make myself clear?!"

Both men looked at each other in silence.

"Do I make myself clear, gentlemen?!" Ben thundered.

"Yes," the men said in unison, their tones weak and quiet.

And, with that, Ben stormed out of the boardroom, slamming the doors behind him, and leaving the men alone in shock and silence. After a moment, Geoff mocked Larry's earlier delivery. "It's right up your alley. *Whole thing takes place on a ship!"*

Larry slapped his partner smartly in the back of the head.

For the second time today, Edith looked up from her typing at the sound of her boss's footsteps approaching. This time, however, they were different. Different than they had been this morning. Different than they'd ever been. They sounded angry. Unbridled. Dangerous, even. Words that she never would've used to describe the actions of her boss. Mr. Howell was timid, reserved, even withdrawn, so who was this man? The man who burst back into the room where she sat at her desk and began pacing back and forth across the small lobby, fuming. For a moment, she didn't know what to say, until, "Edith, I'll be out for the rest of the day," he said, refusing to look in her direction, refusing to allow her to see the red in his face.

"Uh, yes, sir," she stammered.

"Please, don't forward any calls, or messages."

"Should I tell them that you'll be back tomorrow?"

"No. I'm not sure how long I'll be, but I won't be back in tomorrow. I just... I need some time. *Away*."

"Of course, sir. I understand. I'll be discreet."

"Thank you, Edith," his words were barely above a whisper. Still refusing to look at her, he began once more for the door.

"Ben!" the secretary called after him by name, a gesture not lost on either of them. Ben stopped dead in his tracks and finally turned around to face her. His eyes were wet, not like he'd been crying, but clearly he wanted to.

Edith reached into a lower desk drawer. "Since you're going to be gone tomorrow, I suppose I should give you this today." She reached out to present a small box, tied with a scarlet ribbon.

"What's this?" Ben stepped forward to take it from her hand.

"I know you don't celebrate birthdays"—she stopped herself, choosing her words very carefully, then went on—"you know there are those of us who'd like to celebrate you, even if you don't celebrate yourself. I just wanted to make sure you knew I didn't forget you. That I won't forget you, ever. Because you matter, very much."

For a moment they stood there, eyes locked. Each wondering just what the other was thinking, what they would say to each other in this moment if they were being honest, truly honest, with each other, with themselves.

"Anyway," Edith said, breaking the spell, "it's just a little something for you to open later."

She turned and went back to her desk, back to her typing, as if all were back to normal. Ben stood there, looking at the small gift box in his hand. Contemplating the kindness of the gesture. Feeling unworthy of such a selfless display. Once more, he turned for the door. Just before the door opened, he turned back to face her. "You know, Edith, you're right. Birthdays aren't my thing, but I think that, today, we might be able to make an exception," he smiled.

"You mean it?" she said, beaming.

"Just this once," he playfully insisted.

"Of course," she replied, equally as playful. "Is there anything I can do? If you'd like me to book a venue, make reservations, a guest list, I can—"

"Thank you, no. That won't be necessary. Nothing big. I think," he thought to himself, then went on, "A simple day, doing all of my favorite things, no phone calls, no meetings, just going wherever the road takes me. You know?" he smiled, so genuinely, that Edith realized it may have been the first genuine smile he'd given her, the first one in the three years they'd known each other.

"That sounds... *perfect*," she said.

The sexy Art Deco silhouette of a 1938 Bugatti 57SC Atlantic tore across several lanes of Hollywood Boulevard, then onto Los Feliz, bound for Colorado Boulevard in Pasadena. Ben's foot kept the accelerator glued to the floor as his angst surged like gasoline through the chambers of the straight-eight, supercharged engine. Horns honked as he weaved in and out of lanes, often without looking. He had to get away. This felt *good*. For the first time in years, he was allowing himself the freedom to live in the moment; *honestly live*.

The first stop was the Pasadena Post Office, then the Huntington-Langham Hotel; just in time for their famous high tea.

After entrusting the Bugatti with the valet, Ben was led to the back terrace which overlooked the Olympic-sized swimming pool.

"Will this table do, sir?" the waiter pulled out a chair.

"Mr. Howell, welcome back," the head waiter intercepted the pair and took the reins of the conversation. "We have your usual table all ready for you." He led the men to a small two-top close to the railing, with the best views of the pool and the gardens. "Here we are, sir. David is new, so I'm afraid we haven't properly broken him in yet, but I assure you he'll remember next time. David, this is Mr. Howell, one of our favorite guests here at the Huntington."

"My apologies, Mr. Howell," said the waiter.

"No harm done," Ben smiled. "David? Please, call me Ben." He offered a warm handshake.

"I've already given word to the kitchen, sir. Your order will be out momentarily. David? Let's give our guest his privacy."

Both waiters bowed, then backed away, leaving Ben alone with his thoughts.

Once the coast was clear, Ben slipped a journal out of his bag, opened the cover, found a fresh page, and began writing.

Shadows fell across the page as the sun was slowly falling into the west. It was only just after two o'clock. The sun wouldn't fully disappear for another five hours or so, but the twinge of an early April chill could easily be felt in the bony fingers of shade that quietly crept over the fleeting afternoon.

Onlookers watched as the famed producer scribbled feverishly, then paused, pen to chin, deep in thought, only to burst back full-force into his writing as soon as the inspiration struck. Lost in his own world, far removed from reality, far away from the fragrant smells of pastries, coffee, and the perfume of Spring flowers abloom on the grounds of the hotel, the audience wondered what he must be writing. Perhaps his next big script. *Yeah, that surely must be it.* With such vigor, the onlookers surmised that this must be his magnum opus.

"Here we are, Mr. Howell," David lowered the items from his tray onto the table, one by one.

"Thank you, David. And, don't forget, you may call me Ben."

"Of course, sir; I mean, *Ben.* Is there anything else I can get for you?"

"No, thank you. That will be all."

And with that, the waiter left the table, as Ben carefully tucked his journal back into his bag, arranged the items strategically about the table, and began to sip his espresso.

A few yards away, safely out of earshot, a group of waiters watched their patron. One of them called out to David as he made his way back to the kitchen.

"First day on the job, and he gets Mr. Howell's table. How's that for beginner's luck, eh?"

"Mr. Howell? Who is he? Why's everyone makin' such a fuss about him? I mean, he seems nice enough and all, but—"

"The nicest. And don't you forget it," one of the waiters said.

"And you're certain to get at least a twenty-dollar tip," said another.

"You're kidding?" said David.

"Benjamin Howell is a big-time movie producer. You seriously haven't heard of him?"

All of them turned to watch Ben, his back to them, as he, unaware of their gaze, conducted his routine. Strangely, he looked as though he might've been talking to someone, yet he was alone at the table. His movements were slow, almost dreamlike, or as though he were moving underwater.

"Poor guy," the first waiter said.

"Whataya mean?" asked David.

"I think he's lonely," replied one, ignoring David's question.

"I think he sees things that aren't there," said another.

"You mean, like he's crazy? Or maybe drugs?" said another.

"Maybe *both*, you know how this town is," said the first.

"That's enough, all of you," the head waiter walked into their conversation. "I know you're not talking about Mr. Howell in such a manner. A man who's been more than generous to each and every one of you."

"No, sir," "Sorry, sir," came the stammered replies of the waiters.

"I should think not," their superior said. "Well then, let's get back to work."

In a frenzied swell, each of the waiters straightened themselves, regained their composure, and set back to matriculate amongst their guests.

"David?" the head waiter motioned his newest to stay behind.

"I'm really sorry, sir. I wasn't—"

"Ben really is a wonderful man, son. You'll come to learn that. I'll admit some of his habits seem a bit odd, but he really is kind, and very generous."

"Odd?" David asked. "How so?"

"Well," he spun David around to watch his patron once more, "every time he comes in he orders the same thing."

They watched Ben slowly sip his espresso, then, even from behind, he gave a noticeable wince, as though he didn't enjoy it.

"It's always two espressos. One which he drinks, the other he leaves sitting across the table."

Next Ben picked up a knife and began to slice the pastry in half.

"And one chocolate croissant, which he cuts in half. Half he eats, the other half he leaves on the plate."

"Maybe he's just watching his weight?" David suggested.

"No, son, it's nothing as simple as all of that. There's a deeper reason behind it."

"Have you ever asked him about it?" David asked.

"Certainly not!" the superior snapped. "Son, look at me."

David turned to face him.

"Many of our clientele may act peculiar, even downright crazy. But you must never, **never**, question them on it! You mustn't talk about it. This town, the industry, relies on a level of professional discretion. Your place here relies upon your ability to keep your mouth shut. Do you understand?"

David nodded his head.

"Good lad. Now, go see if Mr. Howell, I mean Ben, needs anything, huh?"

"Yessir."

He watched as the young waiter walked away, then his gaze shifted to Ben, who seemed to come back to reality as David approached his table.

Ben, Ben, Ben… who's hurt you? the head waiter thought aloud.

It was nearly four o'clock when Ben left the hotel. Only minutes later he found himself at his favorite haunt in Pasadena, The Huntington Library. On this visit, perhaps due to the onsetting coolness of the late afternoon, he found, to his delight, the gardens were sparsely speckled with people. Here he'd done some of his best writing, and the tourists were always a loathsome distraction.

Nestled in his favorite spot, the open lawn of the statue garden, near the fountain, Ben nestled himself into the soft carpet of emerald grass, once more withdrew his journal, opened back to that unfinished page, and began writing once more. With the backdrop of the flowing water, cascading from the pinnacle of the fountain beside him, inspiration came easily. Each line he wrote would inspire another, then another. Faster and faster he worked, his hands hardly able to keep up with the sharp wit of his mind. Just as the onlookers at the hotel had imagined, the words being poured out onto these hungry pages would indeed become Ben's magnum opus.

A gentle, crisp breeze carried the sweet scent of Hyacinth to Ben's nose. The scent perked his senses at once. It had long been a comforting, familiar friend; hence the reason he often tucked a blossom of it into his lapel, as he had that very morning. He closed his eyes and breathed it in, deeply.

"Benji?" he heard a man's voice say.

"Yes? It's *me*. I'm *here*," Ben said, although this time it wasn't said aloud.

"Where are you? Are you still here?" the man's voice called again.

"Yes! I'm here, please don't go, I'm here!"

In his mind's eye, Ben could see the man's face, blurry like a cloudy night sky.

"I'm here, please! Stay with me!"

And, just like that, the vision faded, and the gardens around him slowly came back into view. Another breeze, colder this time with the setting sun, stung his face where the wet streaks of tears had left their marks upon his cheeks.

"Please, *don't go. I'm here*," Ben cried silently.

Ben wanted nothing more than to stay in this moment. To stay here, to bid the specter of his thoughts to return. But he knew it wouldn't return. Not here. Not *ever*. It had left him for the last time. *It'll be dark before long*, he thought.

Gathering his things, Ben arose from his nest and ventured back to his car, intent on fulfilling every task that he had on his to-do list for the day.

Before leaving Pasadena, he returned once more to the post office, then it was back down Colorado Boulevard and on to his final destination.

The Bugatti secured a private spot near The Griffith Observatory, a spot that may as well have been hand-picked for the view of the sunset. Here, between the showy Art Deco building and the Hollywood sign, Ben sat in his car with panoramic views of the Western sky. No one around. No onlookers. No tourists. No one. Just Ben, alone with his thoughts. Alone so that he might drink in this, perfect sunset, without wasting a single drop.

Just as the sunrise had been this morning, the colors plumed and danced above the point where the black mountain peaks met with the horizon. So warm, so lush, so vibrant, back was the warmth of amber, fuchsia, and vermilion, but this time they were fighting to maintain their position of center stage while being extinguished by an ominous sea of deep indigo sky.

As he watched, Ben relaxed into the seat, a speechless spectator sitting front-row center; the best seat in the house.

Almost in a trance, eyes fixed, unmoving from the show, he reached across the car's cabin and opened the glove compartment. As he reached inside, his hands fell upon a familiar shape, something he'd been saving for this moment. Withdrawing his hand, he held the small box, with the scarlet ribbon, given to him by Edith earlier that morning. Holding it between the sunset and his own face, the box became the only invited guest to this intimate party. Ben smiled and gently tugged on the ends of the bow, releasing the ribbon's grasp from the small box. Next he tore the paper and opened the box.

Inside, a small chocolate cupcake waited to surprise him. A single candle was pushed carefully into the center of the chocolate frosted dome of the cake. Again, Ben couldn't help but smile. How sweet of Edith to remember him, on a day, a date which he himself had chosen to forget. How sweet of her to remember his fondness for chocolate. His entire family likely wouldn't make a move to recognize him on his birthday, and, sure, he may have directed them to keep quiet about it; but Edith chose to defy him, to defy his fragile wishes not to be recognized. She alone could see just how badly he needed to be recognized.

"Happy Birthday to you," he sang in a whisper. *"Happy Birthday to you. Happy Birthday dear Benji, Happy Birthday to you."*

Then he mimicked blowing out the unlit candle on the cake. For a minute or two, lost in the moment, he remembered how to smile. That genuine smile he'd unlocked earlier in the day. The genuine smile that he'd only recently remembered how to use.

His eyes floated back to the glorious sunset which loomed seemingly just beyond the hood of his car. A deep breath in and out.

Then, once more, without taking his eyes away from the sky, Ben reached into the glove compartment. This time his hand was searching for something different. Perhaps another familiar friend, but not one that was as friendly as the gift box. This one was cold to the touch. Silently, his hand withdrew.

The colors were in their final throes now, losing their fight against the looming darkness hanging over them.

A metallic *click* pierced the silence.

Ben drew one more deep breath in, held it, then let it out.

That's it, Ben. Relax. This is a perfect day. Your perfect day.

As the colors began to fade and drop out of sight, Ben dropped right along with them, sinking deeper and deeper into the comforting embrace of the leather upholstery of the driver's seat.

His eyes glued to the sky, counting down the seconds until darkness.

Happy Birthday, Ben.

BANG!

The reverberations of a tightly wound spring, recoiling after being held against its will, rang out through the car's interior.

Outside, one would've only heard a muffled crash; perhaps seen a flash of light, then all would be silent.

Inside though, fragments of bones and teeth, hair and flesh flung themselves about the car's interior, becoming shrapnel, embedding themselves into the car's headliner, before raining down upon the lonely cabin. For a moment or two, chaos reigned unchecked, then, all was silent once more.

Both outside and inside, Ben's car was still once more.

Deadly still.

Ben Howell was *dead*.

CHAPTER 2

The whirling of engines, that's the first thing I remembered; the first thing that brought me out of my distant thoughts, my waking sleep.

Allow me to introduce myself, my name's Will. Well, technically, it's William Sutherland-Howell, but Will is sufficient. My students call me Mr. Howell, but that's not my choice; the way I see it, Mr. Howell is my father. *Was*, he was my father. You see, the words you've read up until this point have all been mine, told from his perspective, using his lush, whimsical style, to the best of my ability. I suppose I owe him that much.

Benjamin Sutherland-Howell II, Hollywood royalty, beloved by millions, but not by me. Don't get me wrong, I respect the incredible body of work that he brought to life. And, it's not as though I hated him; how could I? I barely knew the man. For thirty years I've shared a family name with him. Twenty years I shared a roof with him. Despite all of this, I can safely say, he might as well be a stranger.

So, why am I here, on this plane, taking two weeks away from my job as a public school teacher in New York City, to go to Los Angeles for the funeral of a man that I didn't know or care about? Simple, my mother.

The extent to which I felt my father was distant, my mother, my sweet, hopelessly optimistic mother, was convinced that he was the greatest man who ever lived. She loves to tell my siblings and I about the days that my father was a doting, jovial man, a man who loved to shower his family with kisses and affection. As the oldest child, I am the only one to recall fleeting visions of him, or someone, acting like the person whom my mother describes.

"Oh, Will," she'd say, "if only you'd known him as he once was. You were the apple of his eye. Even though he can't show it, he still sees you that way. You mean the world to him. We all do. Your father may be quiet, but I promise you, he does care. I hope and pray that we'll see him like that again."

Sadly for her, my mother never got her wish. The man remained an enigma, locked in his own silence for the remainder of his life. As I've been told, he took his life the night before his fifty-eighth birthday and left no note. There were no signs. None of his business partners, nor his secretary, sensed that anything was terribly wrong. It was all just a sad end to a sad man. A man which the world mourns, even though they never knew him; just as his family never knew him. Perhaps in that regard, we're one and the same, his family and the world.

"Wait'll you see the Grand Canyon from here. There's nothing else like it," came a familiar voice from the seat behind me.

In an instant, I knew that voice. Not just because it was familiar to me, to my family, but literally everyone in the world knew that voice.

"Mr. Hope, it's so good to see you," I mustered with a smile. It felt weird to be so formal. I'd grown up around this man, around many celebrities. To me, he'd always been Uncle Bob, but as a thirty-year-old, it felt even more awkward to address this man, no relation, as Uncle Bob.

"Willy, how ya doin', son? How's your mom?"

"She's taking it pretty hard. We all are," I lied. Sure, mom was, but my siblings and I, we couldn't really care any less.

"Poor lady. Your father was a good man, no, a great man, son. You remember that."

"Yessir. I know," again, I lied.

"When I heard the news, I hopped the first plane to LA. I wouldn't miss paying my respects, not for the whole world."

"Thank you, that really means a lot. I know it'll mean the world to my mother too."

"You betcha, Willy boy. If you or your family need anything, all you have to do is ask."

With that, he patted my shoulder, then reclined back into his own seat and gave me my space.

Once again I welcomed the dull roar of those engines. I welcomed the view, even if it were only an endless sea of cottony clouds. All of it was something which

I could use to take my mind away from the fact that I was heading home to my grief-stricken mother. A woman whose soul was spun from pure gold. A woman who didn't deserve to be selfishly abandoned by the basket case of a husband she had spent years championing, defending to their own children, and ultimately, trying to fix.

What's more, she didn't deserve to have me, her oldest son, merely returning home in the wake of his father's suicide out of an act of duty. She didn't deserve to have me lying to her, telling her how sad I was about my father, about how much I'd miss him; what's more, I didn't deserve to have to lie about it. The man had been dead to me for as long as I could remember, so what's left for me to grieve? The way I see it, he's been gone for pretty much all of my life.

But, I suppose that wouldn't make for a very moving eulogy, would it?

Shortly after the plane touched down in Los Angeles, I waddled down the aisle, bags in tow, and emerged from the plane and down the air stairs, wondering just how clumsily I might manage to get my circus of bags to the car rental counter. Suddenly, another man's familiar voice rang out,

"Master William! Welcome home, son!"

In the fierce sunlight, with my eyes still adjusting after five hours inside of a dark plane cabin, I could barely make him out. Five-foot-nothing, silvery hair, waving his arms like he were signaling the plane itself to sidle up next to him and the black Lincoln Town Car he'd brought right out onto the tarmac.

"Gil!" I shouted over the raucous spooling down of the exhausted propellers, before hurriedly making my way over to hug his neck.

The embrace was warm, partially because it'd been nearly three years since I'd seen him, and partially because despite being a servant, this man—this wise old sage, made up of chicken noodle soup and bedtime stories—possessed a heart that beat just as strongly for me as it did for him. As if that heart were enough for both of us to live. He was the closest thing I'd ever had to a real, true, father figure.

"It's good to see you, son."

"You too, old man."

"Come on, then, in we go." He opened the rear door of the car and bade me inside. After closing the door behind me, he managed to scoop both of my bulky bags with a free hand, waltzed to the trunk and, in one fell swoop, gingerly arranged them in place and closed the lid; all as if he'd rehearsed the choreography for months. But, to him, it was second nature. The man had made a life doing the mundane tasks that others deign to do; and yet, somehow, making it look regal, important, impressive, even.

"Alright, then, are you all settled in?" he asked, slipping into the driver's seat.

"All settled," I said.

"Seatbelt?" he asked, eyeing me from the mirror.

"Uh-huh," I replied.

"Seatbelt, sir. Or we can keep sitting here."

"*Fine,*" I relented-clicking on the seatbelt. "Still can't get anything past you, eh old man?"

"*Never,*" his eyes sparkled in the rearview.

And with that, he shifted the car into gear, and we slowly began our drive home. You know, there's a saying about the fact that, no matter what changes, the weather in LA always stays the same. It's actually pretty true. Several years spent on the East Coast and I'd forgotten just how great it felt to have such warm, sunny days, even in mid-April.

Welcome home, Will, I thought to myself. The traffic buzzed, the palm trees waved, and the two-story billboards blazed with electricity, while trying to steal focus from the scenery of blue skies and lush mountains.

"There's the new Hollywood sign," Gil said with a gesture.

Huh, sure enough. When I left town, the sign was an eyesore, an eyesore that spelled out, 'Hollywoodland.' Back then, there were missing letters, poorly faded paint, graffiti, and I'd heard the city was looking to take the sign down, but, later, the parks department wanted to rehabilitate it and keep the Hollywood dream alive. Fancy that, a parallel to real life. Things in this town are mostly all broken, faded, and masked with a cheap coat of paint every now and then to keep them attractive and shiny. I guess it's not just the weather here; *some things just never really change.*

The front door opened, revealing a statue of a woman, juxtaposed in masculine femininity. She donned an oversized blazer with broad shoulders which was unbuttoned to reveal a relaxed button-down shirt. A pair of high-waisted trousers tamed the tails of her shirt, their legs draping to the floor in wide cuffs, just barely revealing a smart pair of peep-toe pumps. Her chestnut hair had been carefully touched up, quite recently, and her hand sported a long cigarette holder, fully loaded, which she balanced perfectly between her index and middle finger as if it were merely a prop.

"Hello, Aunt Maggie," I said.

"Oh, Will. I'm so glad to see you." She stepped into my realm then pulled me into hers. My aunt had always possessed such a hearty embrace that I sometimes forgot she was actually my father's twin sister. The two shared no similar qualities. My aunt, who loved to tease and joke, to play games, to laugh until her stomach hurt; I often wondered, being twins, if she got all of the personality, and my father was left with, well, a business acumen, I suppose. At least the man could make money.

We walked into the living room where I found my siblings already holding their charge, waiting for me to relieve them.

"Will," my sister Claire was the first to hug me, "oh, isn't it just awful?" She and I were closest in age. Claire had always had that sort of victim mentality and a flair for drama. Even if the circumstances did not involve her, she'd always find a way to make herself a part of them; to make herself a victim.

"Yes," I said.

"How was your flight?" June, my youngest sister, was next in line with the hugs.

"Fine," I said, keeping the replies short and sweet. Lord knows we'd all have more than our fair share of fumbling words this week, why waste them this early in the game?

"New York treatin' you okay?" Louis, my younger brother, was perhaps the most aloof. If I were effectively masking the lack of grief I felt over my father's passing, Louis, clearly, wasn't even trying.

"Yeah, it's okay," I said, extending a handshake since the men in my family didn't hug other men. That just wasn't something you did.

I turned to face my siblings collectively. "How's mom holding up?"

"She's pretty shaken up, still," June said.

"Hasn't left her room; not for days," Claire added.

"But," my aunt swooped in, "I know that she'll be so glad to see you. Why don't you go up and let her know you're here, huh?"

My siblings all dropped their heads at the suggestion, unwilling to look me in the eye. *Was it really that bad? Did they know something I didn't? I knew I'd be on damage control detail, but just how much were we talking about here?*

"Uh, yeah, sure," I said, hesitantly.

Nineteen. That's how many steps there were to connect the foyer to the second level of my parents' house. I know, because I counted them, almost pausing for dramatic effect as I mounted each one. At the summit, I looked down to the foyer; suddenly it felt like I was in a different world. By climbing those nineteen stairs I'd left the warm land of the living, and I was now venturing into the cold, dark void. The hallway to my parents' bedroom grew darker with each step. Even with the high windows of the foyer behind me, no sunlight was welcomed this far into the house; it likely hadn't been allowed in for quite some time.

One by one I passed the garish barrage of framed movie posters, trophies of my father's success, their top-billed faces all watching me with menace as I crept past. Ironically, it was at this very moment that I realized I couldn't tell you a single title on even one of them. I'd walked by them on a daily basis for years, yet I hadn't cared enough to even stop and glance at one; *not one*. For the first time, I felt selfish. Sure, my father hadn't been an active part of my life, but the fruits of his labor, his passion were all around me, and I hadn't stopped to take notice.

I paused outside of the door to my parents' room, preparing myself for whatever might lie inside. *Would my mother be hysterical? Could I remember the lies I'd practiced on the plane? The lies about how much I loved my father? Would she believe them?*

Alright, Will. Let's do this. You can do this.

As if it were made of glass, I gently turned the doorknob and silently opened the door.

A small, old film projector sat on a table just inside the room. The sounds of the reels spinning in their deliberate cadence, winding and unwinding their film, lilted like an old Model T in the otherwise silent sanctuary. The bright light of the projector could've brought life into the room, were it not locked behind chains of celluloid, sentenced to sit on the sidelines, while the grainy images it projected took center stage on the far wall across the room.

On the bed, silent, motionless, sat my mother. Entranced by the flashing silver screen that flickered before her, in silence, save the sounds of the projector. The silent film, an old melodrama, with over-the-top acting, lavish sets, large hair and costumes, appeared to be some sort of French Renaissance plot; perhaps Marie Antoinette. She was so lost in the film that, for a moment, I thought she hadn't even noticed that I'd come into the room. She just continued sitting there, eyes fixed, without blinking, holding a cigarette with an ash trail at least an inch long.

"Mama, I'm home—"

"*Shhh...*" she cut me off, "this is the best part."

I looked up at the screen. The love interests, both in their powdered wigs, their powdered faces, their painted lips, were about to exaggerate their undying love for each other in a performance that would be better suited for vaudeville. Then I looked back at my mother. I watched her face as she studied the screen siren. Her lips quivering as if she knew what the actress was really saying.

Quietly, I sat down on the bed next to her, trying my best to be a part of this moment with her; even though I didn't understand why this was important to her, I could tell that it was. If this was her way of grieving, I'd do my best to be a part of it, if she wanted me to. Without tearing her eyes from the screen, she reached out and took me by the hand, finally signaling that she was indeed happy to have me here, by her side.

"I thought I'd never see you again," she said, in perfect timing with the woman on the screen. "You know that I would never leave you," this time she delivered the man's lines.

"You know all of the lines?" I said. "You must've watched this one a lot."

"This was the first film your father cast me in," she said, her eyes still straight ahead.

I stopped dead in my tracks.

"Wait, what? This is you?" I asked in amazement.

"A long time ago, in another lifetime, it seems, I came to this town with big dreams. Dreams to be a movie star," she laughed. The sight seemed so peculiar with mascara tears staining her face.

"You've never told me this story," I said, trying my best to continue this light-hearted moment she'd latched onto.

"After a year, I was broke, I'd been all over Hollywood and no one wanted to cast me, nothing except for background," another smile brought her back to life, "then your father called me in for a chemistry read. The producers didn't want me, they said I was all wrong for the part. 'She's just not star material,' one of them said," another chuckle—it was so wonderful to hear her laugh, to see her smile—"but then your father, who was directing, told the producers, 'That girl will be my leading lady. Either you cast her, or I'll quit the entire picture!'"

"And?" I asked.

"Well, that's me up there, isn't it?" she laughed. The moment was fleeting, as her face fell, and her mood shifted back in an instant. "Oh, Will, my darling, your father really was a remarkable man. You know that, don't you?"

She looked at me, pleadingly. What else could I say, but...

"Of course, mama. I know that."

We both turned our attention back to the picture.

"My father was a great man," I lied.

CHAPTER 3

T he world stopped turning so that all might pay their respects to my father. On Hollywood Boulevard, the lights dimmed on every theater marquee, while the letter boards gave their regards to Hollywood's *'Greatest Man.'*

The weather, as if on cue, as if the studios themselves made arrangements with God above to fit the stereotypical, somber funeral scene, traded those famous, sunny LA skies for a smoky gray. A light mist floated amongst the atmosphere, giving each of us a tangible sense of heaviness.

Likewise, the mourners, a sea of black cloaks, like a depressing costume parade, encircled the lakeside corner plot of the Hollywood Forever Cemetery. Their wardrobe may've been comprised of understated tones, but their faces could not be ignored. The guest list, or perhaps cast list would be a more appropriate term, to describe the celebrities who attended my father's graveside service.

Of course there was Bob Hope, or *Uncle Bob* as I'd address him in front of my mother. Then there was Vivien Leigh, Katharine Hepburn, Clark Gable, Mae West, John Wayne, Desi and Lucy, Judy Garland… I could write a chapter on the actors alone. Then there were the producers, studio heads, everyone who kept the film mills churning, spewing their candy-coated propaganda pieces to distract the rest of the world away from their problems for an hour and twenty minutes at a time; all while pretending that they were gods, creating life itself, or even more pretentious, those who actually thought they were creating art.

Okay, I guess I should come clean about something. I've mentioned the fact that I'd never taken an interest in my father's work, which may make me seem like a hypocrite. I mean, sure, his financial success, due to the industry, has afforded me many privileges. Most don't grow up eating caviar with the silver spoon they'd been born with. If they did, they would have the pedigree to know you never use a metal utensil for caviar; you should always opt for bone. They don't waltz right into Yale without having to go through the tedious application process, the interviews, the letters of recommendation; only requiring a simple phone call from their father's office. Or even calling celebrities, people like Bob Hope, names like Uncle Bob. I get it, I'm a lucky guy, and Hollywood's the reason.

But, it didn't come free. There's always a cost...especially in Tinseltown. In my case, it was at the expense of my father, the man that I'm standing here, amongst the royalty of the film industry, pretending to care about. If I had one regret about my father, it was that I never knew him. The man was so lost in his drive to be the biggest, the best, the richest, that he forsook everyone around him. My mother. My siblings. Me.

The funny thing is, there was a time that I wanted to be just like him; a writer, just like my old man. Those were the days when I still saw him smile, days when he'd still hug me, bounce me on his knee, tell me that I was his son. But, as I grew, I saw a change in him, and thus, a change in me. The more he desired to win, the less he desired to be a father, a husband, and the less I desired to be like him. By the time I was in school, my love of writing remained, but my desire to follow it as a career path had already faded. I saw how it had destroyed my father, how it had destroyed my mother, whether she admitted it or not. I wanted no part of that for myself.

So, if I didn't want to focus on writing as a profession, I'd find a profession that allowed me to dabble in it as a passion. That's what led me to teaching. English Lit. Instead of selling my soul for a few bucks, crafting cheap stories for the masses, I could write about things that matter and help others to do the same. And you know what? I couldn't feel more fulfilled. Does it make me rich? No. Do I regret giving my trust fund to charity? Not one bit. Why? Because looking around at this crowd, today, looking at this gathering of the richest, the most beloved faces in the world, they couldn't look more sad. I can see who they really are. They're not just sad because my father is gone; they're sad because they see themselves in him, in his tragic end. They see the unhappiness that led him to take his own life, to make his escape when he got too far in. They're worried that a similar fate may await each and every one of them. That's the cost of selling your soul.

That said, as a man who controls his own life these days, I couldn't be more rich. No amount of money can replace that.

My mother sobbed silently as the pastor recited that familiar 'ashes to ashes, dust to dust' scripture. I pulled her in, gently. Despite all of this, all of my bitterness for my father and his world, I pitied my mother more than anything. Don't get me wrong, she is a strong woman; she'd have to be to maintain her sanity through the past thirty years. But, as someone who's given nothing but love, strength, her absolute best and asked nothing in return, she's suffered more than any of us. Every time she told me that my father was doing better, I hoped, for her sake alone, that she were right.

Later that evening, after my father had been placed into the ground, after the procession of a thousand movie stars had passed by with their gentle kisses, their scripted condolences, safely inside the candlelit glow of the dining room in my parents' Sunset Boulevard castle, now a haunted house, we sat around the table recounting the poignant highlights of the day, trying our best to weave a plausible narrative about the infallible character of my father. Aunt Maggie, Claire, June, Louis, my mother, and myself, each playing our roles as they'd been written for us.

"You know," my aunt began, "your father used to say to me, 'Birdie, I've written some real doozies in my life, but no matter how desperate I get, I'll never, *ever* write a *Western!*'"

Everyone laughed. Everyone, of course, except for my mother. The entire evening she just sat there, hands in her lap, silently looking down at her untouched plate. Each of us tried our best to keep the mood light. Each of us recounting the funnier, happier moments we could remember about our father; admittedly, most of them were a stretch, but we were trying our best.

"Oh! I've got one!" Claire piped up. "Remember that time we got a Christmas tree that came with an unexpected surprise in it?"

"The squirrel!" June laughed. "I can still hear Dad saying, 'Get that goddamn rodent before he burns the house down!'"

Again everyone laughed. Again, everyone, except my mother.

"Did anyone read the piece about Dad, published in the *LA Times* today?" I asked. "They told the story about the time Dad discovered Paul Henson, remember the guy who played the mob boss in all Dad's film noir pictures? He was working as the Santa Claus at the Farmer's Market in Fairfax. Dad waited in line for over an hour, he gets up to Santa, and Santa asks, 'So, young man, what do you want for Christmas this year?' and Dad says, 'I want you to be in my next picture.'"

Once more, light-hearted laughter made its rounds at the dinner table.

"That never happened," scoffed Louis.

All laughter abruptly stopped, and all eyes turned to my brother, the youngest, and perhaps the most cynical of all of the Howell children.

"Of course it did—" Claire was cut off by my brother.

"No, it didn't, and you all know it. It was a puff piece, nothing but fucking lies. Orchestrated by the studio. You know that everything in this town is designed to cash in on any measly opportunity they can find. If they can't find one, they'll create one. Case in point, making our father look like some sort of benevolent Daddy Warbucks!"

Everyone went quiet as Louis went on.

"Dad was a fraud and you all know it! He barely spoke to any of us. He was barely capable of looking at us. I mean here's the proof! We're having to rely on other people's stories to recount moments with our father. That's because he was never a father. He was a ghost. And we're sitting around telling ghost stories, trying to pretend that they're true. They'll never be true!"

"Stop it!" my mother stood at once, slamming her hands on the table.

Everyone snapped their gaze to her.

"Your father did love you! All of you. Just like he loved me. His family was so important to him. How dare you, sitting around, trashing his memory like this.

You should be ashamed of yourselves!" Losing her composure, my mother fled the scene, weeping uncontrollably.

My aunt rose to her feet, primed to chase after her.

"No," I stopped her. "I'll go," I began, "but she's right, you know," I looked at my siblings. "We should be ashamed. No matter how we might feel about our father, this isn't about us, it's about Mom. If you love her, you'll shut the hell up and be there for her. She needs us."

I left them alone and ventured that long, lonely path to my parents' bedroom.

I found my mother, face down on the bed, fists clutching the covers in a death grip, back heaving as she wept. I now understood the depth of her despair. It wasn't just the fact that my father had left her alone. It wasn't just the fact that his death had been by his own hands, his own design, his own script. It was that her years of fighting to exonerate him, to revive that human fire within him, to convince everyone, including herself, that my father was not lost, that the man she loved and had once loved her would return; but in this moment, it was clear that all of that was lost. My father, the man, the dream, the eminent return, none of it would ever come back. My mother was all alone.

"Mama," I whispered as I gently stroked her hair.

"Willy, oh my Willy," she looked up at me, those thick mascara tears slicing her face once again. "I know you don't believe me, but your father did love you. He loved us."

"I know that, Mama. I know..." I said, surprised by the sincerity of my own voice. *Was I believing my own words, or were the stakes of this moment so high that I discovered myself a believable actor?*

"You do? Really?" her voice brought the first bit of hopefulness I'd heard since my return to LA.

"Well, I mean, I have these vague memories, more like flashbacks, but—"

"Tell me," she pleaded, "what do you remember?"

"I was very small, very little, but I remember looking up at a man's face, a man that I believed to be my father, and him looking down at me. Then he smiled, the biggest, warmest smile."

"His smile was the best. Oh, Willy, when your father smiled—"

"Then he said, 'Willy, my boy, you're gonna change the world someday.'"

My mother's eyes lit with the light of a thousand suns; it's a cheesy cliché, but I can't think of a more genuine way to describe the light I saw ignite within her gaze in that moment. She was living for these words, these memories. My recount of my father, the man he once was, the man he still could've been beneath all of those cold, distant layers of apathy, in this moment he still existed; he was still here with us. All we had to do was talk about him, and he was still here.

"Even as a young kid, I remember believing him. The honesty of his smile, his tone, his words, made me believe that he was right. I would change the world. With him believing in me, telling me it was so, there'd be no stopping me."

"Willy," my mother cried, cried happy tears, then embraced me.

And, no more was said between us in this moment. Nothing else needed to be said. I had given her what she needed. And, yet, somehow, I'd planted seeds of doubt in my own mind. All of these years, thinking my father had passed the point of no return. All these years thinking that my mother was hopelessly optimistic. Now, remembering the feeling I had as I bounced on my father's knee, being near him, feeling that warm, loving energy... that was him. *That was real*. My father was human. Some part of him, even the man that was now lying six feet under, was a loving, caring, warm-blooded human. And, some part of me had loved him. *Some part of me still loved him.*

CHAPTER 4

The room was cold. I remember that. Not just the temperature, but the tension. Between the mahogany-paneled walls, thick wainscoting, and the dark leather furniture that wrapped around the walls of the conference room, there sat an attorney and his assistant, my mother, my aunt, myself, my siblings, and, rather curiously, my father's secretary, Edith.

All of us took note of the attractive twenty-something whom my mother had often referred to as a teenager, but Edith looked more seasoned, more capable than I had remembered when I met her a few years ago when she first came to work for my father.

"Let us begin," the attorney's voice was gruff and all-business. "To start, let the record reflect that we are here to disclose the last will and testament of one, Benjamin Sutherland-Howell II, and furthermore, to account for the dispersion of the assets of his estate, as recorded in said will. Before we begin, are there any questions?"

All sat motionless. *Silent.*

"Then, we'll continue."

My mother retreated back into her almost catatonic state, looking at her feet, or possibly the floor. *I wondered if she were even listening.* I tried my best to remember all that the attorney said in his droning dirge, just in case I needed to relay it all back to her when she regained her consciousness.

"...and, now, we come to the assets bequeathed to my closest friends and family," the attorney sounded almost relieved after going over the rather exhaustive list of charities my father had selected to honor with a few thousand. "To my loving wife, Adelaide, *my forever leading lady,* I give half of all of my estate. I leave this without conditions, so she may utilize it however she sees fit."

My mother began sobbing, quietly. I placed my arm around her, glad to know that she was indeed listening to the proceedings. The attorney went on.

"As for my beloved sister, Margaret, my Birdie, and to my four children, I leave each of them an equal amount of five million dollars, each; again without condition."

I could feel the eyes of my siblings as they exchanged glances. Satisfied at our good fortune, but still trying their best to conceal their giddiness behind an air of solemn grief.

"And last, but not least," the attorney continued, "to my right hand, my assistant, Edith Blake, I leave one million dollars, as well as the entirety of my business contacts, my accounts, and my unfinished works; so that she may use them to begin her own business practice, and plant roots in the system."

All eyes looked at the secretary, Edith, who tried her best not to notice, though one would have to be an escape artist to bob and weave without drawing blood from the daggers that were thrown in this conference room.

"Once again," said the attorney, "these assets are given without conditions."

And that was the end of my father's estate. His wealth shelled out upon the few and faithful, or at least the customary connections of family.

After leaving my mother in the care of Aunt Maggie, I stepped out of the stuffiness of that room, away from the palpable excitement of my greedy siblings, and ventured outside to soak up some of the warm sun and unwind with a cigarette.

To my surprise, I could hear someone following me. Down the hall I heard their footsteps keeping time with mine. Down the stairs, across the lobby, and then out the front door. As I bounded the front stairs of the office building, then gained a few steps on my pursuer as I hit the sidewalk, I turned to see just who had been tailing me so closely, so intently.

"Mr. Howell?" she said, almost whispering, as though the others, the vicious snakes from the conference room, might still be listening.

"Mr. Howell was my father," I said. "Call me Will. And it's Miss Blake, isn't it? Or, perhaps, Missus?"

"Edith. And it's *Miss*. But I'd prefer Edith."

"Alright, Edith. Do you mind telling me why you stalked me out here?" I laughed to lighten the tension.

"Sorry about that. I didn't realize how creepy that may've looked."

We shared a laugh this time.

"Well," Edith began, "I know this must all be very awkward for you and your family."

"Awkward? How so?" I asked.

"You don't have to pretend," she rolled her eyes. "I mean, I'd be suspicious too. Your father's young secretary, inheriting a large sum of his estate. I'm sure your mother thinks that I'm some girl Friday who did more than just organize your father's schedule."

"Well, *did you?*"

"Wow. Just cut right to the chase, didn't we?" she said.

"I mean, my father was a very private man. I know he must have secrets."

"No. It was nothing like that. Your father trusted me. You've mentioned that he was private."

"I think the term is elusive," I said.

"Complicated would be a more appropriate term," she scolded.

"Well, you're the writer," I said. Whether I was being sarcastic or flirtatious, I couldn't tell. *Maybe both?*

"That I am," she smiled. Apparently she picked up on the subtext too. "And, from what your father told me about you, writing is something we have in common."

"Nah, I teach it. You know the saying, those who can't *do, teach?*" I laughed. "So, Edith, you still haven't told me why you stalked me out here. Was it to kill me, so you can take my share of inheritance too?" I was definitely flirting now. My sarcasm was unbridled, unabridged, scathing, because I knew she could handle it. We spoke the same language, Edith and I.

"Yes, I've got a nail file in my purse with your name on it, buster. Any last requests?"

"Just your number?"

"Cheesy!" she laughed. "I expected more from you. Maybe your father did talk up your writing abilities just a little too much."

"Is that so? Maybe, in the right setting, we can discuss it further. Give me a chance to redeem myself. Dinner?"

"Oh, no, I'm sorry, I don't eat," she said.

"Playing hard to get, huh?" I smiled.

"But a drink," she said, "I could *definitely* go for a drink right now."

CHAPTER 5

"I'll Walk Alone" by Dinah Shore was playing as Edith and I cozied up to the bar. The room was dark. Small tables, with warm lamps, were scattered about the abyss; each built for two, held faceless couples who were lost in their own world, or maybe, like the two of us, hiding from it.

"What'll it be?" asked the bartender.

"Bourbon, neat," Edith said. The bartender looked just as shocked as I was. Suddenly, the chardonnay I was about to order didn't seem sturdy enough.

"Uh, make that two," I blurted out.

"Coming right up," he said, before peeling away.

"*Definitely not a girl Friday.* I've never seen one of them that can drink Bourbon," I joked.

"Now you believe me?" she asked.

"I'm coming around. So Edith—"

"*Edie,*" she interrupted, then before I could respond, "my friends call me Edie."

"Oh, so we're friends now, huh? Goddamn we move fast."

"Will, look," she turned serious, "all jokes aside, I did bring you here to discuss something. It's something important."

"Okay."

"Your father, he, he did love you. Your mother. Your entire family. Very much. He'd talk about you all the time."

"My father? We're talking about the same guy here?"

"I'm serious, Will. He..." she trailed off in thought.

"He what?" I brought her back.

"He had trouble talking about his feelings. But that doesn't mean he didn't feel them."

"How do you know?"

She reached into her bag and began setting out a bunch of papers on the bar.

"I've been going through his office, and I found these. Your father loved to express his feelings, his innermost thoughts, in the best way he knew how. His writing."

I began to comb through the stack of pages, some of which were scraps of paper, torn corners from larger pages, any haphazard fragment he had within arm's reach, he'd use to record his thoughts. I took one to read aloud.

"I heard from Will today. He says he's going to become a teacher. Not just any teacher, an English teacher. Teaching writing, the appreciation for good literature to young, impressionable minds. To nurture them. To cultivate them. To prime and inspire the minds that will forever change the world; just as he's doing. I couldn't be more proud to call him my son."

"He really was so, very proud of you, Will. He'd talk about you constantly."

I said nothing, but stared at the bar, trying my best to look right through it. To focus on anything but her words. Her words of affirmation confirmed what my mother had always believed. What my own faded memories had me questioning just days ago. My father was human. My father loved me.

"Will?" she took my face in her hands, "your father left something for you."

She reached back into her bag and retrieved a thick, padded envelope.

"What is it?" I asked, taking it from her.

"I dunno. He didn't tell me. It's not for me to know. It's for you and you alone."

I now stared down at the envelope, which lay atop the stack of my father's string of thoughts, spilled out across a mess of torn pages. *Now what?* I wondered to myself. *Do I open it? Do I wait until I can be alone? Do I tell the others? Do I even want to know what's inside? Do I even care?*

"Will, I know this is a lot to take in. As you know, your father was a complex man. But, as you now know, and you'll come to know more as you read over these, he loved you and your family so very much. I wanted you to have these so that you can finally understand, and then help your family to understand, just how much you all meant to him. Please don't pass by this opportunity. No matter how much you may've felt betrayed by him. No matter how much you think you don't care. I know that you do. You and your family need this closure. Your father needs this closure too. He's gone, but he's not. His presence still lingers with you. With your mother. With your aunt. They need this. You need this. Does that make sense?"

I decided to wait until I could be alone to open the envelope. I trusted Edie, sure. She'd already seen me cry over my father, a man whom I thought, up until a few hours ago, that I hated. Even though I no longer hated him, I didn't understand him. But, I felt like the envelope he'd secretly left for me might just hold the key to that understanding.

After dinner that evening, after putting my mother to bed, after sharing a bit of small talk and even smaller conversation with my siblings about the reading of the will that afternoon, I called it a night and ventured up to my room.

There, in the room I'd grown up in, the room that had been mine since childhood, the room that still had my superhero posters on the wall, old toys safely stored in toy boxes, all of my effects carefully maintained just as I'd left them-at the direction of my mother, I was about to learn the truth of my father. *Who was he? If he loved us, why did he abandon us? Was his ghost still here, watching us fight over his memory, his legacy, his fortune? Had he somehow orchestrated every moment after his death to bring us to discover the truth about his life, a truth that he never had the courage to willingly tell us?*

"Alright, Dad, here goes."

I sat on the bed, holding the thick envelope between my fingers, sliding them across the surfaces on both sides, my mind's eye trying to envision what was inside. Then, after a few deep breaths, it was time to rip off the Band-Aid. Time to see what was inside. Time to find out who my father really was. Time to find out what he had hidden away all of these years.

The vast marble lobby of the Pasadena Post Office was impressive. With the polished, solid surfaces that seemed to stretch for miles, not only wall to wall but also floor to ceiling, every sound, every footstep was amplified tenfold through the echo chamber. Trying my best to move quietly in my conquest, I looked about for my target. To my left, a counter, complete with a queue of customers awaiting the help of the attendant, buzzed with quiet activity. To my right, aha! There they were. The rows upon rows of mailboxes; their gilt doors, their slim glass windows, all stacked on each other like the bricks of a cathedral.

I looked down at the contents of the bizarre envelope, which I now held in my hand. The small, brass key, with the plastic tag which simply said, 'Pasadena Post Office' on the front, and '401' on the back. I took a breath to prepare myself, then ventured over to find box 401 and finally see what lay waiting for me within.

There it was. Since the numbers were all easily arranged in numerical order, 401 caught my attention almost instantly. One more deep breath, and I'd finally be ready to put an end to this mystery.

But, to my surprise, the key didn't want to fit into the lock. I tried it this way. I tried it that way. Beads of sweat stung my back as I felt almost embarrassed by my clumsy attempts to insert the key, as though everyone were watching me try and fail. I double-checked the number on the keychain: 401. The number matched the box in front of me. And this was the Pasadena Post Office, was it not? Was there more than one? No, there wasn't, I was sure of that. I had no choice but to ask for help. Before I knew it, I found myself in the queue of patrons waiting to see the postmaster.

"Next," the old woman called out as she jotted down a note from the previous transaction. I stepped forward, prompting her to look up. Her eyes immediately softened. Suddenly I was questioning what it was about my appearance that had caught her eye. *Was it my hair? Had a gust of wind caught my mane and tangled it into a mess?* Nope, a quick smoothing of my hand confirmed that my hair was fine. *Maybe it was my nose. Maybe I had something dangling from my nose.* The sting of sweat hit my lower back once more as I weighed the odds that this woman might be about to laugh right in my face, because *this entire time I'd been standing here, looking like a booger-touting idiot.* Then, I noticed the tears in her eyes.

"Well, I'll be. You're...you're Ben's boy, aren't you?" She nearly leapt over the counter to hug me. If I hadn't felt like an idiot before, I surely did now. Me, a full-grown man, standing in a line of customers with a complete stranger embracing me, and my face clearly revealing that I had no idea who she was.

"I'm so sorry," she said, pushing herself away. "I didn't mean to be so forward, but you look *just like him.*"

It wasn't the first time I'd heard that. Apparently I could've passed as my father's twin, albeit decades younger.

"I'm sorry, I'm afraid I don't know—"

"Oh my goodness, where are my manners?" she caught herself. "I'm Mabel. Your father was a regular in here. Nearly every day, he'd come in. When he stopped coming in, I knew something had to be wrong. Then I read about it in the papers. I'm so very sorry. Your father...he...he was a great man."

"Yeah, I've heard—" I caught myself, "I mean, *yes*, he was."

"What brings you in?" she asked.

"Well," I pulled out the key, "he left me this key, but I can't seem to get it to fit the box over there."

She took the key from me.

"That's because this isn't a mailbox key. It's a key to a safe deposit box. Here, follow me."

As her partner took over the queue, Mabel led me down a long, marble corridor to a massive steel door. This door opened into a room with yet another steel door, this one larger, more sturdy than the first, the type you'd see in a bank's vault. A procession of turning gears, the falling of latches within, then, the titanic door slowly swung open, and the old woman led me inside.

The room had even more boxes than the lobby. They wrapped around the walls, stacked in rows ten high, no windows to hint at their contents, no gilding to make them more attractive; these were strictly utilitarian. These boxes were used to hold secrets. Their loyalty, their strength, their discretion was unquestionable.

At the center of the room, a large table, complete with hard-wired reading lamps, the sole sources of light in the dark chamber, and a lonely telephone, took up residence; the desert island in a treacherous sea.

Mabel took the key and walked directly to the steel box, labeled '401.' The key glided in effortlessly, the tumbler released its hold, and the door dutifully opened.

"Here we are," she said.

Then she pulled the long, steel box out of the wall and placed it on the central table.

"I'll give you some time," she said, pausing to suggest asking for my name.

"Will," I replied, picking up the hint.

"Will. If you need anything, you just pick up that phone. It'll automatically call my desk."

"I will. Thank you, Mabel, for everything," I said.

Her eyes moistened once more, but before she could lose control of them, "Alright then. I'll leave you to it."

And with that, she disappeared, locking me in the vault as she left.

Okay, Will. No more setbacks. No more excuses. You have the key. You have the box. Time to finally uncover what it is you're doing here.

Slowly, carefully, I opened the lid of the large, steel drawer.

CHAPTER 6

My dear Will,

If you're reading this, it means I'm gone. I know that in your mind, I've been gone for years. I won't pretend I was the father that you, your siblings, or your dear mother deserved. You have every right to judge me, but my hope is that this journal will help you understand the man I became. The tragedies of my life have a long reach, and they long ago stripped me of the will to fight for my own happiness. If you're reading this, then I've lost that fight for good.

I leave this to you, son, in the hopes that you can make sense of it all in a way I never could. Please, read it with an open mind.

To begin, you need to understand that my story is inextricably linked to my experience on the *Titanic*. You know I sailed on the ship when I was seventeen, and you may have even read the newspaper account. But that was a curated version, the cherry-picked details I chose to share with the world. These words—uncensored and vulnerable—are the full truth about that fateful voyage. Words I've never shared with anyone.

The story of the *Titanic* has become an oversensationalized melodrama, and it's often difficult to sift the facts from the bullshit. So, before we go on, allow me to clear a few things up.

Let's start with the first piece of bullshit: that the *Titanic* was a marvel of engineering unlike anything the world had ever seen. The truth is, she wasn't. While large and luxurious, she was not the "most" anything, because the *Titanic* wasn't unique. She was one of three sister ships—the Olympic-class—all built from the same set of plans by the White Star Line.

The real revolutionary was her older sister, the RMS *Olympic*. She was the first. Nearly every interior photograph you've seen labeled as *Titanic* is actually the

Olympic. By the time *Titanic* sailed a year later, she was essentially a carbon copy with a few minor improvements—just enough to claim the title of "Largest Ship in the World" from her sister by a mere technicality.

To understand why these ships even existed, you have to understand the bitter rivalry between Britain's two main passenger lines: the established Cunard and the ambitious White Star. In the early 1900s, the American tycoon J.P. Morgan, seeing the immense profit in transatlantic travel, bought White Star, injecting it with American capital and the infamous American desire to be the biggest and the best.

Not to be outdone, the wholly British Cunard secured a government subsidy to build two revolutionary ships: the RMS *Lusitania* and RMS *Mauretania*. These ships were built for one thing above all: speed. They were designed to outrun enemy warships and easily capture the coveted Blue Riband for the fastest Atlantic crossing.

White Star gambled on a different strategy. Instead of speed—which often meant an uncomfortable voyage—they focused on unparalleled size and luxury. What Cunard offered with two fast ships, White Star would counter with three colossal floating palaces, offering a weekly service across the Atlantic.

This brings us to bullshit number two: the claim that she was unsinkable. I never once heard the phrase "God himself could not sink that ship" before I sailed. The term used was "practically unsinkable," and it was a common marketing phrase for any modern ship built with watertight compartments. The idea was that if the hull were breached, watertight doors would close, containing the flood and keeping the ship afloat. This design was put to the test about six months before my voyage, in September of 1911, when the *Olympic* survived a major collision with a warship. With two of her compartments flooded, she safely returned to port, which seemed to prove the merit of her design. White Star leaned into the publicity, selling safety.

But the good press was short-lived. Not long after she was repaired, the *Olympic* suffered another setback, losing a propeller blade mid-crossing. To get her back into service quickly, the company made the obvious move: they took a propeller intended for the still-under-construction *Titanic*. This decision pushed my ship's maiden voyage back by several months. These repeated incidents with her sister ship put immense pressure on White Star to ensure *Titanic's* debut was a flawless, headline-grabbing success.

Lastly, while we're debunking myths, let's talk about the lifeboats. The papers after the disaster screamed about the lack of them, but the truth is, *Titanic* actually carried more lifeboats than was legally required. The regulations were simply archaic, written for smaller ships in an era when it was believed no modern liner could sink so quickly. Lifeboats weren't seen as vessels for long-term survival; they were seen as ferries to shuttle passengers to a nearby rescue ship. The tragic flaw in that logic was that on April 15th, 1912, no other ship was close enough to help in time.

So, that gets us to April 1912. After the setbacks and repairs to her sister ship delayed her maiden voyage, the *Titanic* sat docked in Southampton, a hive of activity. Her designer, Thomas Andrews, a man for whom these ships were his life's work, walked her decks, notebook in hand, cataloging every minor detail that could be improved upon for her and her third, still-unnamed sister. He worked alongside every department as the final touches were made, ensuring that every detail, for both passengers and crew, was as close to perfect as humanly possible before she set out to sea.

CHAPTER 7

About two hundred miles away from *Titanic*'s Southampton port, in the shipping port city of Liverpool, where White Star had maintained their offices up until five years prior, Bruce Ismay sat in the parlor of his secluded mansion, reading aloud a London newspaper article which referenced the upcoming maiden voyage of his newest ship.

"*Titanic*, the largest ship in the world, will transport millionaires across the Atlantic Ocean in style. First-class passengers can dine sumptuously in her titanic-sized Dining Saloon, enjoy haute cuisine in her à la carte restaurant, or take in lighter fare and afternoon tea in her Veranda Café and her Café Parisian; a feature unique to *Titanic*. This Paris-inspired, sidewalk café, features seaside views, espressos and pastries, all day long, so guests may dine on their schedule."

He took a pen and began making notes on the newspaper.

"That really was a stroke of genius on your part, Bruce," his wife, Florence, draped herself over the back of the chair so she could read over his shoulder.

"Well, in all fairness this was Tommy's idea, not mine. But, yes, the B deck promenade was a rather waste of space, I suppose." He continued making his notes.

"What are you doing?" she prodded.

"*I'm working,*" he said without looking up at her.

"You're *always* working," Florence sighed. "I'll be so happy when this week is over and *Titanic* is out of England, then I can have you back again."

Bruce looked up at her, slightly dejected.

"My love, you know how important this is. I've got a lot on the line with these ships. I have to see them through 'til the end."

"The responsibility isn't all on your shoulders, Bruce. You've got a team of people who care about this ship too. Let them do their jobs."

"Florence, please. I can't think," he waved his hands as if shooing her away. Florence stood, looking down on him.

"Bruce."

No response.

"Bruce!"

He stopped writing, but didn't look up.

"What?"

"Your father is *dead.*"

"I know that. What does he have to do with—?"

"Everything."

Florence knelt down and took her husband's face in her hands.

"Your father was a cruel, bitter man, who didn't see how incredible you are."

"Florence, please—"

"You do not have to prove yourself, Bruce!"

Bruce stood abruptly.

"You have no idea what you're talking about!" he said, before storming for the door.

"Bruce, stop!"

He stopped at the door, but he refused to look at his wife.

"You're using these ships to try and live up to his expectations. And what's more, you're using them to escape."

"Escape from what?" he turned to her.

"Me."

He said nothing.

"Us," she continued, "you've been using them for years to give an excuse to be distant. First *Olympic,* now *Titanic,* and soon it'll be...what did you call it, *Gigantic?*"

"Britannic," he sighed.

"Bruce, I'm sorry that I haven't been the most supportive—"

"Darling, it's not that—"

"No, it is. You don't have to pretend. You should've known better than to marry an American. We're all crazy," she chuckled, ironically. "Things haven't been easy for us since we left New York. I don't fit in here, I know that. Your English friends, your family, I know they talk about me behind my back. But I'm trying, Bruce, I really am trying…"

"Florence," he walked over and embraced her. "I know that, and I love you for everything you do for me, for us. Please believe me when I say, this really has nothing to do with you. I promise. J.P. has been very vocal about the expense of these ships to the line, to the company, and it's my job to make sure they deliver the profits that he expects. Like you said, Americans are crazy; and I answer to the craziest one," he laughed to lighten the mood.

"You're sure that's all it is?" she asked.

He kissed her.

"You know what? *Titanic* sails next week. I've gotten her ready for her maiden voyage; I think I'm due for a vacation."

"Really? You mean it? Just the two of us?" Florence beamed.

"What do you say? The Isle of Wight? Rome? Hell, we can go to Australia if you want. Your call."

"New York?" she said.

Ismay looked at his watch.

"Pack your bags, my dear. I'll send a wire to book us the finest suite on *Olympic*. We'll have to hurry, but she departs tomorrow at noon."

Florence nearly shrieked with excitement.

"Oh, Bruce," she kissed him, "thank you. I need this trip. We need this trip."

This time, he kissed her.

"I'd do anything for you, darling; for us. Please remember that," he said. "Now, we both have our marching orders. You start packing and I'll send a wire!" he laughed.

And, with that, Florence left the room to summon her maid to help her pack for a month-long excursion to her native New York.

Bruce stood silent in the room as his wife left. He wouldn't tell her the truth. He no longer loved her, and it was becoming more apparent to both of them. He'd managed to avoid the collision today, but he was playing on borrowed time.

How much longer could they navigate these troubled waters before one of them was pulled under?

At the very same moment that Florence was trying to decide how many pairs of shoes she'd need, and Bruce was sending a wire to the White Star offices in Southampton, securing passage for him and his wife on *Olympic*, another ship was about to leave its British port, bound for North America, by way of New Orleans.

This ship was not large. Nor was she luxurious. In fact, she wasn't even a devoted passenger ship, but rather a cargo ship that sometimes carried passengers. On this voyage, however, she would carry no passengers. In fact, on this particular voyage she'd been slated to carry a large shipment of sweaters and blankets. The peculiarity of her manifest would later become the subject of multiple conspiracy theories.

Her name was *Californian*. She was a small steam ship that had been in service for about a decade, and she was owned and operated by one of the steamship companies that J.P. Morgan held in his portfolio, The International Mercantile Marine Company.

As the crew were testing lines, checking gauges and levels, setting up their berths, and making general preparations for the day's departure, the ship's captain, Stanley Lord, was at his post on the ship's bridge, overseeing the final particulars before they cast off. He'd been chatting with one of the ship's officers when voices rang out from the forecastle deck below.

"I don't care who you are, I told you, no bloody buggar is going to set foot on this vessel without the captain's orders!" a seaman's voice rang loud and clear to the bridge.

Captain Lord and the officer scurried to the lower deck to see who was disrupting the work of his crew. As the men arrived on the scene they saw two strangers, gentlemen in formal dress clothes, coolly asserting an air of dominance in the face of the seaman.

"I already told you," the gentleman's voice was laden with haughtiness, with condescension, "my orders come from—"

"What's all this then?" the captain asked. "Why are you bothering my crew? We've got a tight schedule."

"Ah, you're the captain, I presume?" the man stuck out a handshake, which Lord did not accept.

"Captain Stanley Lord, commander of this vessel. As I said, we've got a tight—"

"Of course, Captain. The last thing I'd like to do is hold you up. So we'll just finish our business and you can be on your way."

"What business?" Lord demanded.

"They's sayin' they have orders to load more cargo, sir," the seaman chimed in, "but we've already signed off on the manifest. All complements are already aboard."

"So we have," the captain agreed. "I'm sorry gentlemen, but rules are rules. Leave word with our offices and we'll accommodate you on the next vessel that departs."

"*Actually, Captain,*" the stranger began, "my orders come from *your* offices. They've already cleared us to bring our cargo aboard." He held out a folded piece of paper, which the captain took and silently read.

"They don't make the orders," said the seaman. "Captain Lord gives the orders 'round here, and he said—"

"*Very well,*" the captain interrupted, handing the letter back to the stranger.

"Ah, most agreeable, Captain," the stranger said.

"But sir," said the seaman, "all the cargo has been signed off and the hatches sealed."

"Well unseal them," the captain shouted, "...and accommodate *Mister...?*"

"Y. You may call me Mr. Y," the stranger replied.

"Mr. Y," said Lord. "See that he gets whatever he needs. That is all."

"But, sir, we—"

"You'll do as I say, sailor! Or I'll relinquish you back to the docks. There're a hundred men willing to take your place on this voyage. The choice is yours," the captain commanded.

"Aye, sir. Right away, sir."

"Good man," said Lord, "and, not a word of this to anyone, sailor, do you understand? You will not utter a single word of this to anyone else in the crew. You alone will assist Mr. Y, and there's no need to update the manifest. These are captain's orders, do you understand?" Lord's tone left no room for misinterpretation.

"Aye, aye, sir."

Back in Liverpool, Ismay and his wife were packed into their motorcar, about to head to London for the evening, before their trip to New York on the *Olympic* the following afternoon. The gentle vibration of the car's engine masked the jittery nerves of Ismay, who prayed his wife couldn't feel the tremor of his hands. Lying to her about the state of their relationship was easier in the beginning, which is ironic; you'd think it'd be easier over time. The more he did it though, the harder it became. He was, by nature, a paranoid man, and he worried Florence was growing very suspicious of his routine lies.

Knock. Knock.

A servant sprinted down the steps of the manor to catch the car just as it was leaving its post. Bruce opened the door.

"What is it?" he asked the man.

"Telegraph, sir. Addressed to you, sir."

The young man handed Ismay the telegram. Ismay's eyes narrowed and his brow furrowed. Florence, taking note of his expression, asked, "Bruce, what is it?"

Immediately, he switched gears, masked his disappointment, and lied to his wife once more.

"It's nothing, darling, just business."

He took her hand in his, just to sell the moment.

"But," he continued, "we will need to make a stop on the way to the hotel this evening. It'll just take a moment. Promise."

That evening, the motorcar made its way through the busy streets. It carried them to a suburban area, packed with stately row houses; each swallowed their parcel of ground, nearly flowing into each other on both sides. The car stopped in front of one of these houses, distinguished by a bright red door.

"What are we doing here?" Florence, who'd fallen asleep on the ride, woke up as the car parked.

"I told you," Ismay said, "business."

Florence yawned, then leaned back into her nap.

"I won't be but a moment," he said, then leaned in to give his wife a quick peck on the cheek.

An ancient relic of a butler answered the door, then led Bruce into a suite of rooms near the back of the first floor.

The bedroom was dark, with the curtains drawn, blocking out nearly all of the sunlight that was left outside as afternoon had fallen into evening. The butler left him without a word, and Bruce was left standing in the doorway, unsure of where his host might be. *Was he supposed to sit? Would the butler be back? Would his host come find him?* The moment felt awkward.

"Bruce?" a gruff man's voice fizzed in the center of the room. As Ismay's eyes adjusted to the darkness, he slowly crept toward the voice. In the center of the far wall sat a large, four-poster bed, with a canopy, curtains draped at each post, concealing the resident inside.

"It's about time you got here. Come, come closer," the voice commanded.

Bruce obeyed, and as his eyes had finally adjusted, he was sorry they had. His stomach dropped at the sight. A large, burly old man, sitting naked, spread-eagle, all corners of him visibly unashamed.

"Ugh," Ismay couldn't hide his disgust. "J.P., I thought you were still in Rome."

J.P. Morgan, picking up on Ismay's discomfort, snickered to himself. He always used tactics to make those in his charge remember his position. This was little more than a power play. In moments like these, Bruce wasn't the president of the International Mercantile Marine. He wasn't the directing chair of the White Star Line. He was a puppet. Moments like these were meant to remind Ismay where he stood, to remind him of the one who held the reins.

"Rome was a bore," Morgan began, "I decided to come back early."

"I see. To get a few more days in England before you head back to the states?"

"The states?" Morgan asked.

"On *Titanic*." Bruce was confused. Morgan had booked passage on the *Titanic*'s maiden voyage months ago. He was slated to be one of the prominent passengers making the crossing. White Star had comped him the finest suite aboard, complete with its own fifty-foot private promenade. This was another improvement to *Titanic* over *Olympic*—something her more famous sister didn't have—and *Titanic* featured two such suites. J.P.'s name on the passenger list was one of the company's publicity stunts that was sure to pay off in dividends.

"Oh, that," Morgan feigned. "I'm not going."

"Not going? But I thought—"

"Listen, Bruce, I wanted to take the maiden crossing on your little ship..."

My little ship? Bruce thought to himself. *What the fuck was he talking about? He knew the importance riding on this crossing. Why would he downplay the importance of his presence aboard? This sudden change of plans may have been par for the course in his list of childish games, any other time that is, but he knew this crossing had to pay off. After all, his money and reputation were on the line here.*

"My gout's flared up, I'm afraid, and my doctor has given me strict orders to stay in bed," Morgan continued.

Just then, a woman, just as naked as this monstrosity that sat on full display, but sewn much more tightly into her youthful skin, an object much more beautiful to look at, climbed onto the bed next to Morgan and began kissing him. Morgan, as if this were all perfectly normal, routine, business as usual, continued, "You see, Bruce, I'm strictly forbidden from travel until I recover. And, Evelyn here,"

"Nadine," she said, playfully offended.

"Right, Nadine, has been assigned to take good care of me." He kissed her open-mouthed. "Isn't that right, my pet?"

"Mmmhmm. I'll take very good care of you."

The two continued kissing and snickering playfully.

"Alright, fine," Ismay interjected, asserting his discomfort and disgust at the inappropriate scene playing out before him. "This is why you called me here? To tell me that you're not sailing on *Titanic*? Is that all?"

"Oh, no," Morgan tenderly turned to Nadine. "Darling, could you give us just a minute to talk, alone? Daddy needs his privacy."

"Okay, daddy, but don't take too long," she giggled, before kissing him, then sauntering out of the room.

"Alright, Ismay, let's get down to business," Morgan's tone suddenly took a turn.

"Thank god—"

"You know how important this voyage is. *Titanic*'s maiden voyage must make headlines. Lots of them."

"Obviously, which is why I thought you were—"

"Now, how you go about them I don't know, nor do I care. That's on you. I leave this all in your capable hands."

"My hands?" Ismay asked, dejected.

"Precisely."

"I got *Titanic* to this point. She's ready to sail."

"Look at this!" Morgan threw a newspaper at Ismay, which Ismay caught. The front page featured *Titanic* in an article that read, '*Olympic*'s Sister To Set Sail For New York Next Week.' "*Olympic*'s sister! She doesn't even get her own goddamn name in the headline!"

"This is just one paper," Bruce said.

"One of many," Morgan said. "Bruce, when you approached me for the money to build these ships, I had my doubts. Your father was quite the businessman. If Thomas Ismay had asked me for the money, I wouldn't have thought twice, but you—"

"What about me?" Bruce seethed.

"Face it, Bruce. You're not half the businessman your father was. He knew it. And you know it."

"*Titanic* will be successful. Mark my words." Ismay's staccato delivery hammered each word, deliberately.

"That remains to be seen. But, like I said, that's your charge now. You'll sail on her maiden voyage and take my place," said Morgan.

"I'll what? No. No, I can't. I already—"

"You can and you will!" barked Morgan. "You have no choice in this matter, son. You're going to be on *Titanic*'s maiden voyage. End of discussion."

"Florence and I, we...I promised Florence we'd sail to New York, tomorrow. On *Olympic*. She's waiting in the car for me...I—"

"Perfect, take her along on *Titanic*. You'll have my suite. It'll be a lovely time for you both."

"J.P., I can't."

"It's settled, Bruce. *That'll be all.*"

CHAPTER 8

"**I** hope she orders me the oatmeal, and not the porridge," Margaret said, "the English do a lot of things well, but their porridge..." she gagged. As she spoke, she absentmindedly stroked the velvet curtains of the train compartment windows.

"Uh-huh," I said, my face buried in my magazine.

"You know she'll get your order right. Hot cocoa, hot cocoa, every single morning, hot cocoa. I swear, Benji, you would die before you changed your silly routines."

"Uh-huh," I said, again.

"Benji."

No response.

"*Benji!*" she demanded, taking my magazine away.

"*Birdie! Stop it,*" I cried.

"What is it, anyway?" she asked as I took it back and opened to the page I'd been reading.

"It's *The Shipbuilder*."

"The what?"

"A magazine about ships," I said sarcastically. *What do you think?*

"*I think,*" she stressed, "that my brother is *incredibly boring*, and he'll go to great lengths just to prove that point," she laughed.

"It's not boring. It's fascinating."

"Three million rivets," she read over my shoulder, "oh my god, you're right. That's so fascinating. I don't think I'll be able to sleep tonight. How'd I ever live my life without knowing—"

"Birdie, that's enough! You've proven your point," I said.

"Have I? Sometimes I swear that we can't be siblings, let alone twins," she said.

"Maybe it's just over your head," I taunted. "All this technical stuff is just over your head." I was enticing her, and, as I figured, she took the bait.

"We'll see about that. Tell me something about what you've read. Something super technical." She cocked an eyebrow and crossed her arms.

"Okay, let's see," I scanned the page. "It says here *Titanic*'s Marconi Wireless is the most powerful at sea. With a range of up to 1,200 nautical miles. What does that mean?"

"It means..." she thought for a moment, then went on, "that I'm right. My brother's incredibly boring."

"Aren't you the least bit curious about the ship we're going to be sailing back to New York on? It's the first time anyone's sailed on her, and we're on the first crossing. Don't you find that exciting?"

"The *Lusitania* was exciting. It got us to Europe in less than six days!" she exclaimed. "*Titanic*'s not that fast."

"True," I agreed, "but you threw up several times on *Lusitania*, didn't you?"

"So. It was still exciting."

"*Titanic* doesn't have to be fast. The faster the ship, the more uncomfortable the voyage. *Titanic* is much, much bigger, and much more luxurious than *Lusitania*. Sailing on her will be completely different; I promise—"

The door to our private compartment opened, and my mother's head poked in, interrupting my thought.

"Mother!" Birdie said, "did you remember to order me the oatmeal?"

"Margaret, Benji," my mother changed the conversation without answering, "I have someone I want you to meet."

In choreographed movement, my mother entered and sat on the bench seat across from us, then extended a hand to the door, welcoming our unseen guest. A mustached man gave an exaggerated bow, then slid into the compartment and joined my mother on the opposite bench.

"Hello there, you must be Margaret?" he said, gently taking my sister's hand.

"Yes, sir."

"I've got a daughter named Margaret. Light of my life. She just got married last month, but you remind me of her a great deal. I can tell we're going to get along just splendidly," the man smiled.

Birdie giggled.

"And this is Benji," my mother said, directing all attention to me.

"Benji, I've heard so much about you," he shook my hand.

"And you are?" I asked.

"Oh," the man laughed, as did my mother, the two of them laughing in unison, as if it were some sort of inside joke, some bit of fun shared between the two of them. It turned my blood cold. He continued, "where are my manners. I'm Bruce."

"This is Mr. Ismay," mother interjected, "the president of the—"

"White Star Line," I interrupted.

"At your service," Ismay nodded.

"Very pleased to meet you, Mr. Ismay," Birdie delighted.

"What are you doing here?" I asked, my tone subconsciously accusing. Something about his presence, the way he stared at my mother, the way she smiled at him; none of it felt right. None of it felt appropriate.

"I invited him, Benji," mother said.

"She was a godsend, your mother..." Ismay began, "I had to give up my compartment—"

"The Countess of Rothes!" mother blurted out.

"That's right," Ismay chuckled, taking my mother's hand. "Her party had only booked one compartment on the boat train, but they needed another. Since the train had been fully booked, I gave their party my compartment. And, had your mother not intervened, I'm afraid I'd be riding with the luggage," both of them laughed.

"Seems fair to me," I said.

"Benji!" mother chastised, "don't be rude."

Everyone seemed to notice the sharpness of my tone.

"Apologize to Mr. Ismay," she said.

"That's not necessary, Caroline," he soothed.

The fact that he addressed my mother by her first name struck me as so vulgar, so inappropriate, so—

"I'm sorry, Mr. Ismay," I said through clenched teeth.

"No harm done," he smiled, before continuing, "so, Benji, your mother tells me that you're quite the writer."

"He is," Birdie said.

"He's very talented," mother agreed.

"In fact he's going to Yale to study—"

"It's just a hobby," I cut my sister off.

"It's more than just a hobby," she tried again, "Benji, you're—"

"Business, Mr. Ismay. I'm studying business. Writing is a pastime, but it's not a stable career."

I could feel my sister glaring at me from my peripheral. The last she'd heard from me, the last time we'd talked about my studies at Yale, I'd confided in her that I was taking a full course-load of writing classes. As far as she knew, that was still the case.

"Ah, I see," Ismay smiled, "well, be that as it may, we are slated to have several rather prolific writers on this crossing, and I do think you'd benefit from networking with them. Perhaps I can introduce you."

"That's so very generous of you," my mother chimed in. "Isn't that nice of Mr. Ismay?"

"Yes," I faked a smile, "nice, but not necessary."

With that, I lifted my magazine back up and distracted myself from the scoundrel sitting across from me.

"*The Shipbuilder*, huh?" Ismay didn't seem to know when to take a hint. *Fine, I'll take him down a peg or two.*

"Benji loves to read about ships," Birdie insisted.

"Is that so?" Ismay delighted. "Have you read about *Titanic*?"

"Of course I have."

"And? What have you learned?"

This is it, I thought, *my moment to destroy him, to watch him crumple like an American dollar bill.*

"What have I learned? I've learned that *Titanic* is nothing more than the *Olympic* with a different name. You pay off the press to tout her as something revolutionary, when, in reality, she's nothing revolutionary at all."

"Benji, that's quite enough," mother shouted.

"No, it's fine," Ismay protested. "I want to hear where this goes. Keep going, Benji."

"Dimensions, the same. Navigation systems, the same. Engines, the same. Same. Same. Same," I gloated.

"Similar," Ismay waved a finger. "They are similar, but distinctly different. We've made numerous changes to *Titanic* that make her accommodations bigger, more comfortable, more luxurious."

"Such as?" I asked.

"Firmer mattresses for one," he said.

"Firmer mattresses?" mother asked.

"Precisely," Ismay smiled. "This one was all my idea. After traveling on *Olympic*, I realized that the mattresses allowed just a little too much of the ship's movement to be felt. So I proposed an upgrade to firmer mattresses."

"I'm certain we'll sleep all the better for it," mother smiled.

"Firmer mattresses? That's all?" I quipped.

"Oh, I'm just getting started, Benji, my boy. *Titanic* also has been designed with two exclusive suites, we call them the millionaire suites, each have their own fifty-foot promenade."

"Really?" my mother sounded impressed.

"One of them will be my suite for the crossing," he said.

"I'm intrigued," mother said, leaning in.

"I'd love to show you," he smiled.

"Where's Mrs. Ismay?" I interrupted their conversation.

"Excuse me?" asked Bruce.

"You said you had a daughter, Margaret, wasn't it? I just assumed that she must have a mother."

"Yes, of course," he recoiled. "Florence, and the rest of our children, are on the other train to Southampton."

"Why didn't you just go along with them?" I pressed.

"It's a train for second- and third-class passengers," he said.

"Ah, I see," I said. "So you'll send your wife and children along in steerage, but not Mr. Ismay, oh no, not the president of the line. He'd rather ride in the luggage car of first class if need be. Anything to keep away from being seen with the lesser classes."

"There's nothing wrong with the people in steerage, Benji. They're still people. Good people," my sister chastised.

"Third-class passengers," Ismay cut in, "we don't call them steerage at White Star. You're quite right, Margaret, they are fine people—"

"Just not *good enough* to be seen with *Mr. Ismay*," I said to Birdie.

"That's quite enough!" mother shouted. "Benji, what's gotten into you?"

"It's perfectly alright, Caroline," Ismay began. "Benji, I am sailing on *Titanic* as a passenger. Florence and the children are coming to see me off," he turned to my mother, "but I'll be sailing on *Titanic*, alone."

"I see," mother thought aloud.

"So," he continued, "they took the first train so that they could take their time touring the ship before it departs, while I accompany our very high-profile passengers, such as the Countess of Rothes, to ensure that their trip to *Titanic* is a smooth one. As you see, it's my job to ensure that *Titanic* is a great success. So, here I am, doing just that. Crossing the 't's' and dotting the 'i's', making sure that all is in order."

"And we're so very grateful for the fine job you're doing. I have no doubts our voyage will be all the better because of your presence here, Mr. Ismay," mother said with a flirtatious smile.

"Of course," I groaned, picking back up my magazine and pretending to read. "I don't think we'd be able to sleep a wink without the upgrade to a firmer mattress. Thank god for Mr. Ismay."

All went quiet for a moment. I could feel my mother wanting to instigate another apology. I could feel Birdie glaring at me once more. I could feel Ismay, tense, but with no recourse to offer, then, "You know, Benji," he smiled, as if beginning the conversation anew, "since you love ships, and you seem to know all there is to know about *Titanic*, I will introduce you to Mr. Andrews. He's her chief designer, and there's no one who knows the ship better. I'll wager that even you can't come up with a question that could stump him. Though I would love to see you try."

I looked up at him, glaring. That last line was a closed-ended invitation. I thought I'd cut him off at the pass, but the cheeky bastard had gotten me back. This time, I couldn't fire back.

"How very generous, Bruce," mother said. "Benji, isn't that so very kind of Mr. Ismay? He'd be delighted, Bruce. Wouldn't you, Benji?"

I threw daggers across the car at the man who smiled back at me, the sonofabitch who was now pulling my mother into his web. Whether he was a man who was bored in his own marriage or one who craved the thrill of the chase didn't matter. In that moment I vowed that Bruce Ismay would not take my mother from me, no matter how hard he tried.

"Of course," I smiled, "I'd be delighted, Mr. Ismay."

CHAPTER 9

A sullen sky hung over Southampton as the boat train made its way swiftly towards the bustling port city. The rhythmic cacophony of steel wheels grinding along in their track beds, the murmurs of conversation that vibrated between the small compartments, and the eventual release of steam pressure every now and then as the train let out its tremendous roar, a battle cry along its nearly three-hour journey, all created the sense of frantic excitement felt by each of the inhabitants of the train's pampered passengers.

As a barrage of rural landscapes, urban decay, and sprawling neighborhood streets whirled by, men, women, and their children, dressed in refinement, lauded with honorary titles to suggest an air of imagined importance, all indulged in what may've been their last breakfast on land. The boat train, in its stylish comfort and service, was operated by White Star to hint at the sort of luxury that lay ahead, as it ferried passengers from London's Waterloo Station directly to the quayside, where porters and stewards would manage the mountains of baggage and cater to the whims of their patrons, all without the slightest hint of inconvenience.

"Of course, sir." "It would be my pleasure, sir." "Right away, sir."

Such were the lies of the men and women who made up the 'soft product' of White Star. If you're in the business of selling, you must consider both your 'hard product' and your 'soft product.'

The hard product is something tangible; something that can easily be seen and touched. In this case, the *Titanic*, the boat train, even the food that was being eaten by the passengers as we chugged along to the ship; all of this is the hard product. It can easily be seen and judged.

The soft product, however, is a bit more nuanced. A bit more complicated to define. Every interaction with the crew. Every bit of small talk with a member of the company. Even the eye contact, or lack thereof, as you're being served your ten-course meals in the ship's dining rooms; all of this is your soft product. It cannot be touched, though it is felt; innately felt. It's the experience that can make or break a voyage, especially for the millionaires that might discuss their voyage with friends, family, or even the press. In many ways, the soft product is much more important than the hard product, because it's an emotional connection, a far-reaching, lingering experience, that can pay off in dividends or cause insurmountable losses.

White Star realized this and embraced the challenge by equipping their ships, especially their brightest stars, the Olympic Class, which included *Titanic*, with the best crew they had. The careful selection of crew would add to the overall luxury of the experience for their passengers—something we often overlook when we discuss the ideas of *Titanic* being luxurious. Simply put, *Titanic* wasn't just a ship full of fancy rooms and the finest food; she was an overall luxurious experience.

It would be this very thing, the careful selection of her crew, that would impact her maiden voyage in a rather critical, yet unfathomable way.

Since *Titanic* was brand new, with some growing pains, some kinks to iron out on her first crossing, the decision was made to bring on as many crew members from *Olympic* as possible. Some two hundred out of *Titanic*'s nine hundred crew members would be reassigned from *Olympic* to her nearly identical sister ship, so that the learning curve wouldn't be as steep, and thus, the transition would enhance the overall experience for the passengers as *Titanic* began her career.

About a week prior to departure, when Ismay was relegated to take the place of J.P. Morgan in his deluxe parlor suite, the *Titanic*'s captain, Edward James Smith, took this matter of seasoned crew members into consideration.

E.J., or simply Captain Smith, was a sixty-two-year-old veteran of White Star and had been given the honorary title as Commodore of the White Star Line. He'd been captain of her sister, *Olympic*, on her maiden voyage, and he knew *Olympic* inside and out. So, it made sense to place him at *Titanic*'s helm, ensuring a smooth transition. The white-haired man, with the neatly-trimmed beard and mustache, looked like the textbook picture of a salty sea-dog; yet, many would be taken aback at first hearing of his tenor, soft-spoken voice. Likewise, despite being able to bark an order, or even give the devil of a tongue-lashing to a wayward sailor if the infraction merited, Smith was remarked for his genial demeanor and his overall affinity for the pomp and circumstance that came with the territory of being the most decorated captain of the line. High-profile dinners, parties, ceremonies, any occasion that called for him to make a public appearance, he did so with delight. This led him to be very popular with his passengers, even earning him the title, 'the millionaire's captain,' as many of White Star's most elite passengers would opt to sail on ships, on particular crossings, in which Smith held charge.

With *Titanic*'s departure only days away, even with the full complement of officers and senior crew aboard and unpacked in their quarters, Smith decided to make a change. Henry Wilde, a man who'd served under Captain Smith aboard *Olympic*, would be summoned to serve aboard *Titanic* as her chief officer. This change-up would result in a trickle-down effect, changing the order and rank of *Titanic*'s senior officers, even removing one of them from the sailing altogether.

With a new chief officer aboard, serving as second in command just below the ship's captain, William Murdoch, the man who'd originally been appointed chief officer, would be demoted to first officer, while Charles Lightoller, the man who'd been slated as first officer, would now be second officer. While the demotion in rank may not've been ideal, especially to Murdoch who was excited to be serving as chief officer for the very first time in his career, especially on a brand new ship, and one with so much fanfare, the officers took the change-up in stride, and it didn't seem to affect their ability to work with each other or to embrace their new chief officer, Henry Wilde.

The changing of the guard did result in a bit of awkwardness, however, as the *Titanic*'s original second officer, David Blair, would become redundant, as Charles Lightoller had been reassigned to the role. The ship didn't need two second officers, so Blair was given orders to pack up his quarters and sail on another, less exciting, ship in the fleet. Curiously, this change would result in the strange, critical oversight I'd mentioned earlier. You see, it is the role of second officer to keep and distribute key equipment items throughout the voyage, things like binoculars. As *Titanic* sat in Southampton in the days leading up to her departure, David Blair had given a pair of binoculars to the ship's lookouts to use for the voyage from Belfast, where she'd been built, to her home port in Southampton. When Blair left the ship, he'd forgotten to return the key to the equipment locker in his cabin—the locker which contained the ship's sets of binoculars—to Charles Lightoller, the new second officer.

This meant that, while *Titanic* had ample sets of binoculars for all departments to use throughout the voyage, only one pair was accessible. The lookouts, who consisted of a crew of two men working in four-hour shifts, changing out every four hours so that a twenty-four-hour watch was maintained, were stationed high in a small platform called the crow's nest, anchored to the ship's foremast. It was the job of the lookouts to maintain a sharp watch for anything that might pose a threat to the ship, and if anything was spotted in the ship's path they could pick up a phone in the crow's nest and it would automatically ring the ship's bridge, where the officers kept their charge.

Charles Lightoller did not like the idea of the officers sailing without their own pair of binoculars, and, since most ships didn't offer binoculars to the lookouts in the crow's nest, it was decided that the lookouts didn't need their own set, and the binoculars were reassigned back to the *Titanic*'s bridge, leaving the lookouts to rely on nothing except their own eyes to spot any potential danger.

As the boat train rounded a bend, we could finally see *Titanic* for the first time. While the sky was still overcast and gloomy, sporadic rays would slice through here and there as they found the chance, and this produced a halo effect around the ship, which made her almost glow.

Even without sunlight to warm her colors, the ship was radiant. A rich red paint peaked out, just above the waterline, giving way to the ship's massive black hull. The hull of the ship gave her the sleek, soaring lines of a giant racing yacht, which would allow her to slice cleanly, effortlessly, across the Atlantic. Above the hull, with its thousands of portholes, her superstructure arose in gleaming white.

White Star made sure that the ship was touched up, and no inkling of rust could mar her perfect visage, even when the white was so susceptible to reveal it.

The three levels of superstructure made her stand out against the horizon, with large, square windows and giant open promenade decks. At the very top, lifeboats, neatly tethered in their sweeping arm davits, served almost as a joke to many, reminding them of the antiquated practices of having small boats to rescue passengers from a sinking ship. This was, after all, the twentieth century. Ships didn't sink anymore. We'd learned from those that had in the past. We'd advanced beyond that. We could design ships to be lifeboats themselves. For some, the decision to carry boats for less than half of the ship's maximum capacity was a deliberate stance to curtail their presence at all. In the modern world they were, by all accounts, obsolete.

Rising above all, prominent like the points of a crown, the ship's four monstrous funnels loomed proudly. Each funnel was wide enough that two train cars could pass side-by-side within them. There were four because the other ships had four. *Lusitania*, *Mauretania*, even the massive new German liners, all of them required four funnels. *Olympic* and *Titanic* could've been designed with three, but four looked grander. Four looked more powerful. Four was the number of the competition. So, the Olympic Class also had four. Granted, the fourth funnel wasn't a waste of space; it would be utilized so that it served a handful of purposes beyond mere aesthetics. But, whereas the first three would belch powerful billows of black smoke from the ship's massive boilers, the fourth would vent the only real burning fireplace on the ship, so it would only produce a fine string of smoke at any given time.

Each of these funnels were painted in the signature color of the line, White Star buff, a cross between brown and tan, and capped with the same black color of the hull to mask any black soot that would be discharged from the smoke as it left the chimneys.

Any other, lesser ship would've been seen in silhouette against the backdrop of the granite sky, but *Titanic* carried from within her own radiance; she refused to be ignored. From stem to stern, top to bottom, every inch of her exuded beauty, demanded attention.

"Oh my word," Birdie squealed, "look at her, she's enormous!"

"Bruce," mother said, "she's simply stunning."

"We're very pleased with her," Ismay said with delight. "Benji? Do you approve?"

I wanted to echo the sentiments of my mother and sister. I wanted to enjoy this moment as much as they were, to allow myself to unpack my emotions, to be giddy with excitement. This was the sort of thing I lived for. Technology. Architecture. A modern marvel. A thing of beauty. My affinity for writing about things that inspired me made me long to say something poetic about her tremendous size, about her graceful beauty, the way her colors warmed the otherwise dreary morning.

"It's okay," I said.

And that was that.

The port was bustling.

It was electric.

All of the planning, all of the preparation, all of the exhausting over-details, all of the last-minute changes and shuffling of the crew—all of it had led up to this moment. White Star was nearing the finish line to get their latest and greatest flagship out to sea. Not just a 'floating palace' but a luxurious workhorse that would put them back at the top of their game: champions of the transatlantic trade.

Motorcars were honking as they crept along in a showy queue, their gilt chassis catching stray rays of sunlight, hoping onlookers might take note and be dazzled, if not envious, of their expensive styling. Porters scurried with piles of bags and mountains of trunks. Finely-tailored day suits and walking canes for the gentleman, the latest in Parisian fashion for the ladies, stripes and paisley, bows and buttons, gloves, heels, and, of course, monstrous hats—although not as monstrous as the year prior since streamlined was becoming *en règle*. They'd choreograph the moments in which they'd emerge from their cars, a perfectly-timed entrance, performing for the crowd that had showed up to watch them embark. No perfect wardrobe would be complete without the right accessories, and many first-class passengers chose to complete their look with a fashionable dog. These canines somehow managed to be as regal, and sometimes arrogant, as their elite owners. Whether carried in the crook of an arm or led along on a dainty leash, their glittering noses were turned up, tails stood like regal swans, and their feet kept perfect time with the steps of their boarding party.

Further aft, still stylish, but less self-indulgent, the second-class passengers found their boarding zones. While not as expensive as the first-class accommodation, White Star catered to this upper-middle-class clientèle by offering stylish interiors, sumptuous meals, live music, even an elevator, which was unheard of for second-class on ships prior to the Olympic class. The decor in their cabins and public spaces was not only on par with first-class on many other ships at the time, many designs came directly from the first-class spaces on the previous generation of White Star ships. Likewise, their treatment would be akin to that of their elite cousins in the upper-class.

Near the second-class queues, lines of immigrants stood in winding rows, all of their worldly possessions in tow, as they made their way towards their entrance near the stern of the ship. This was third-class. While some lines still used the older vernacular of "steerage," White Star made the distinction that their ships only used the term third-class. While not as luxurious as either of the upper classes, third offered its own degree of luxury, as everything was clean and new. Many third-class passengers did not have electricity or running water in their own homes. Likewise, many of these hard-working people rarely had the luxury of more than one or two meals a day and only dined out on very special occasions. On *Titanic*, they'd have clean and comfortable conditions. Hot and cold running water, indoor toilets, and three very hearty meals every day, meals that were prepared by professional chefs. They'd also be waited upon by a staff of stewards and stewardesses that were specifically assigned to their section of the ship. Despite the excitement of traveling on the newest, largest, and most luxurious ship in the world, many of these third-class passengers were traveling with heavy hearts. Here and there they'd look back to say their goodbyes, knowing that each step led them closer to a new life in a new world, a life that would forever take them away from their native home.

There were cranes of cargo lifting and lowering, swinging to and fro, massive pallets of cargo, bags of mail, even a candy-apple-red Renault Car, all of them would be taken from the busy scene at the quay and loaded into the hungry belly of the leviathan.

"I'm afraid this is where I must leave you," Ismay said. "Florence and the children have been waiting for me. But I will leave you in the care of one of our finest."

And, with that, he summoned a porter to assist us with our bags, then Ismay politely excused himself from our party and, finally, left us alone.

We were led to a staircase that wound up several levels to where we would enter the ship on B deck, amidships. No sooner had we reached the first landing and rounded the corner to ascend the next flight of stairs, a man's eager voice rose from behind us. "Mind if I take a photograph?" We turned around and saw a young, handsome man holding a camera, waiting at the ready to take our picture.

"It's a new camera and I'm wanting to document the entire trip. Put it through its paces," the man laughed. His laugh was energetic, infectious. He was the type of person who could instantly attract anyone, to draw them in, despite their greatest efforts to resist. You couldn't resist him.

"*Of course!*" Birdie delighted, no doubt excited by the prospect of sailing on such an incredible ship, the journey of a lifetime; no doubt excited by the prospect of talking to and entertaining the whims of such a charming and charismatic young man.

"You're Americans?!" he practically squealed, "thank god! All I've seen for weeks has been drab English folk. So prim and proper. You wouldn't believe how difficult it is to get them to pose for a lousy picture."

Birdie and my mother laughed. Strangely, here in this moment, with my mother and sister casually sharing a light-hearted moment with this attractive stranger, I grew to hate him. I can't even say why, at least I didn't know why at the time. He was warm and friendly. He seemed like the type of person who could keep you rolling on the floor with laughter. He gave no red flags, no signs that you shouldn't trust him, yet, I didn't trust him. What's more, the way he looked at Margaret made my blood boil. Perhaps I was still feeling sensitive about the way my mother had been so inappropriate with Ismay on the train. Perhaps it was because I blamed Ismay, and not my mother, for the way she'd behaved. Perhaps this man, this wolf in sheep's clothing, might do the same thing to my impressionable sister. She was an hour younger than me, and, though she was mature in many ways, she was a bit too free-spirited, too liberated to act out on her impulses. This side of her had only strengthened since I'd went off to university, left her alone to her own devices. Left her unprotected. I wouldn't allow this shyster to steal her innocence. After all, I'm a man, albeit a sensible man, but I know how men can be. How they think. What they really want, even when they pretend otherwise.

"I'm sorry, sir," I cut through their laughter, "we're actually in a bit of a hurry and don't have time to pose for any photographs."

"Benji, don't be rude. I'm sorry, sir, but you'll have to excuse my brother. This trip to Europe has made him a bit wary of strangers."

"Birdie—"

"I can't say I blame you, old chap," he cut me off, shaking my hand. "The name's Miles. Miles Force, fellow American. We Americans have to stick together."

"Where do you come from, Mr. Force?" mother asked.

"New York. My father's a district attorney. So you see," he turned back to me, *"very trustworthy."*

"We're from Philadelphia," mother said. "I'm Mrs. Benjamin Sutherland-Howell, and this is my son, Benji."

"It's a pleasure," he said continuing to shake my hand. Then he turned to my sister, "and you are Miss Birdie? It is Miss, isn't it? Or is it Missus?"

"Margaret," she laughed. "Birdie is Benji's nickname for me."

"I see."

"But, yes, it is Miss."

"Delighted to make your acquaintance, Miss Margaret Sutherland-Howell." He held up his camera once more. "Now that we're no longer strangers, how about that photograph, eh? That is, of course, if Benji has no objections?"

All eyes turned on me.

"Fine. But make it quick," I rolled my eyes.

"Super!" Miles said.

We lined up against the railing of the stairs, and Miles stood back to give us a countdown.

"Three, two, one..."

Flash.

As the bulb flickered, all froze in their pose. My mother and sister smiling in delight, me scowling. The odd man out, a role I'd been playing more and more often these days. I didn't mean to come off as brutish, but these past few months had shown me parts of the world that I never knew to exist. Things that made me resent the world. Things I wish I could take back, to live in the bliss of ignorance.

"Alright," I said finally, "you have your photo. Now, we really must be going, mister—"

"Miles. No need to be so formal, Benji. We're friends now. I can tell, you and I are going to become the best of friends on this voyage."

Not a chance in hell, I thought. *The* Titanic *will sit on the ocean floor before I consider Miles Force a friend.*

frosted glass dome
canted English oak
Grand Staircase
white linoleum
wrought iron and gold leaf
overlook views
black guild star pattern

CHAPTER 10

A symphony of polished English oak, that's what I remember. The moment we stepped foot into the *Titanic*, just beyond the entry vestibule, the sight of the ship's Grand Staircase took our breath away.

The massive, sweeping staircase sat center stage and flowed from floor to ceiling, commanding full attention. Every inch pulled your eye further and further into the thoughtful design. Graceful curves. Daring detail. Every time I close my eyes I can still see it. That's the lingering impression it has left on me, and each time, it's like the first time.

Styled in the classic 'William and Mary' aesthetic, the bones of the staircase were carved of sturdy oak but glossed over in whimsical reliefs. Hand-hewn panels depicting ribbons and bows, fruit and flowers, graced the newel posts, which were crowned with ornamental pineapples, a symbol of hospitality. The top and bottom wooden handrails contained a sprawling display of wrought-iron balustrade in a somewhat Art Nouveau style, but richly adorned with occasional accents of braided rope or laurels and rosettes in polished gold leaf.

As if they were the royal court surrounding their masters, polished Doric columns held charge all around the atrium hall, capped with intricate Corinthian capitals, giving a neoclassical air. Beveled wainscoting clad every wall in the entry hall, again in English oak.

But, so as not to overwhelm the space with heavy woods and darkened tones, the floors and ceilings were gleaming in polished white. The floor was tiled in a faux white marble with the occasional accent of a black mosaic inlay, which was reminiscent of a quilt star—perhaps to lend some Americana into the motif, allowing some of the ship's richest clientele to feel a sense of home.

Overhead, white beams ran horizontally, creating a half-coffered effect, and every inch of the space between them was used to hang dozens of large light fixtures, their crystal beads hanging from a gilt crown and gathering neatly into an ornamental flourish at the tip.

Natural light also breathed life into the space as large, arch-top windows lined the room, allowing ample sunlight from the world outside.

The last note I should make about the staircase, in fact what makes it all the more impressive, is that the room I've described is only one level of the staircase. As we walked from the entryway, we noticed that where the railing met the floor, it ran parallel and connected to another level below. Walking to this parallel railing, one realized the stairwell extended up and down some six levels, each more impressive than the last.

Standing at the level railing one could see down through each level of the staircase, as well as look up to the topmost level. This overlook would become my favorite view on the entire ship. From here, you could see that, while each level of the staircase was nearly identical, each had unique attributes to make it stand out from the others. Some, like the level we were on, had bronze and brass cherub statues which held illuminated torches to provide additional lighting to the landing. Others had one central lamp that was a large showpiece in and of itself. At the top level, looking proudly down upon all levels of the staircase, a massive dome of frosted glass, adorned with the same sort of wrought-iron and gold leaf as the balustrades, tied the entire ensemble together. The dome allowed cascades of sunlight to filter down through each level of the staircase, drenching everything in its path in warmth and life.

"This is incredible," Birdie said. "Don't you think so, Mother? It reminds me of that country hotel where we spent the week in Scotland, near Loch Ness."

"Mr. Ismay has truly outdone himself," mother said. "If all of the White Star ships live up to these standards, then I'll never sail on Cunard again."

"This is only the forward staircase," I said, steering the conversation away from that of Ismay and his achievements. "There's another one at the aft end of the ship."

"This is certainly going to be a voyage to remember. I'll bet you'll have much to write about, Benji," mother said.

"Oh! *Writing!*" Birdie said, "I want to write a letter to post from the ship—"

Her words were cut short by the powerful blasts of the ship's massive whistles, ringing out that familiar warning, '*All ashore who's going ashore.*'

"That's our cue," I said. "We haven't got much time. Let's find our cabins, then head up to the deck to watch the send-off."

A steward kept post near the foot of the stairway, charged with way-finding. Mother and Birdie had adjoining cabins on our current level of B deck, so the steward directed them to the Starboard corridor amidships, and he said mine was on C deck, exactly one level below their cabins. With little time left before departure, we decided to part ways to find our cabins, with plans to reconvene at this exact spot in five minutes to head up to the promenade deck together.

Taking the next level of the staircase down, I emerged on C deck right next to the main inquiry office. There was already a crowd of passengers waiting in a queue. The chief purser and his staff were hard at work checking in valuables, upgrading cabins, and, most importantly, ensuring their passengers received their ideal seating assignments for dinner.

As I was in a hurry, I paid little attention to the circus while racing down the corridor to find my stateroom. When my parents had booked our passage they ensured that Birdie would have a cabin directly next to theirs. Mine, however, was an entire deck away. As my sister and I were days away from turning eighteen, a birthday which we'd celebrate halfway through the voyage, my parents thought that I'd finally earned the right to a little privacy, something I delighted in. The events of our European trip were still a whirl of chaos in my mind, and I needed the time and space to digest them, alone.

I opened the door to my cabin, an outboard suite, and, just like the sight of the staircase, I was awestruck by the splendid appointments of my cabin.

A long path connected my large room to the corridor, making the space feel even bigger, more removed from the hustle and bustle of the busy hallway. The design of my suite was called 'Modern Dutch.' During this period in time, the elite were taken to various aesthetic movements throughout history. They'd decorate their summer homes, their lavish mansions, their chateaus, in these period-specific styles. *Titanic*'s first-class suites were available in eleven such styles. Styles ranged from Adams to Louis XIV, Italian Renaissance to Regency, or even Old Dutch and Modern Dutch.

My room had a high wainscoting in carved oak panels, with the upper portion of the walls covered in a rich crimson wallpaper. To warm up the walls, gilded grillwork was used to trim out the edges and corners of the red. The room had plush green carpet, and soft velvet furnishings and silk upholstery. There were two brass beds, their frames coated in a bright white finish, with brass finials and adornments clinging to the frames in showy display. Rounding out the space were: red silk pillows and duvets, a large red sofa, red velvet lampshades, walnut side tables and chairs, gilt wall sconces, a red marble washbasin, and a large oak wardrobe.

There were two large portholes to provide ample views of the starboard skyline. These were outfitted with stained glass screens which could be lowered to conceal them while still allowing warm sunlight to radiate the room behind a curtain of luscious colors. Smartly, the ceiling was paneled in a decorative scheme, with painted murals which mimicked the stained glass of the windows, tying the whole room together.

I could've just as easily classified the room as 'Mission' or 'Craftsman' style, but Modern Dutch summed it up quite nicely.

"Whoa! Swanky digs, Benj!"

I whirled around at the sound of his voice. Since I'd left the door open, I hadn't heard him come in. Miles continued, "It's a helluva lot nicer than my broom closet down below. Mind if I take a picture?"

"Yes, I do."

I pushed the camera down just as he was trying to focus it.

"Did I do something wrong, Benj?"

"Please leave."

"But, I thought we were—"

"We're *not,*" I cut him off. "Not *now.* Not *ever.* Now, I've asked you once. Next time—"

"I get it," he threw up his hands in surrender. Then he slowly backed away towards the door.

"I want to hear you say it," I said, closing in on him. "You are going to stop following my family around. You're going to leave my sister alone."

He stopped.

"Wait, you think I'm after your sister?"

"Get out!" I shouted, turning him by the shoulders and throwing him into the hallway. As soon as he was outside my room, he stopped, turned back around, then, "Can I just ask one question?"

"You just did," I said, slamming the door in his face.

For a moment I stood there, heart racing, leaning against the door. *I wondered what he wanted to ask. I wondered if he'd actually heed my warning and leave us alone; some part of me seriously doubted it. I wondered if he were still out there, on the other side of the door, questioning the past few seconds of our interaction, just like I was.* Then,

Knock, knock, knock

My heart pounded even harder now.

The bastard's still out there.

"Go away!" I shouted through the door.

Silence.

I listened.

More silence. Then,

Knock, knock, knock

My blood boiled as I threw the door open. *"You sonofabitch, I told you to—"*

"Whoa, Benji," Birdie's eyes grew wide in disbelief, "is that any way to answer the door when your sister comes to visit?"

"Ugh, sorry Birdie," I recovered. "I thought you were someone else."

"Who?"

"Nevermind, we should probably go. We don't have much time."

"Oh, wow!" she pushed past me and ventured into my room. "I like your room better than mine!"

"Birdie, we need to—"

"To what, *Dad?*" she jibbed. "You know you're sounding *a lot* like him."

"Uncalled for."

"Is it? What was all of that business on the train? You were incredibly rude to Mr. Ismay."

"Rude? He was all over our mother. Don't pretend you didn't notice that."

"You know what I did notice? What I've been noticing?" she turned serious. *"You've changed, Benji."*

"You don't know what you're—"

"Something's off. Something happened in Paris."

I said nothing but lowered my gaze to the floor, unable to look her in the eye.

"What happened, Benji?"

Silence.

"I'm your sister. Hell, I'm your twin. We're a part of each other. What you feel, I feel."

She took my face in her hands and forced me to look her in the eye.

"Benji, please?"

For a moment we stared in silence. *I wanted to tell her. To tell her that she was right; something had happened in Paris. I wanted to tell her everything. I hadn't told a soul, and it was killing me.* Then,

"Birdie," I began.

"What is it?"

"I..."

Another blast of the ship's whistles jarred us back to reality.

"I think we'd better get going," I said, before she could challenge me.

With that, I took her by the hand and led her down the corridor, then up the staircase to B deck.

We found Mother waiting with a tall gentleman clad in a stylishly curled mustache.

"Benji, there you are," Mother exclaimed. Her eyes and tone said that she was thrilled to have the distraction of our arrival. "Birdie, Benji, surely you remember Mr. Gracie."

She presented the man to us in an effort to make her escape. He smiled warmly before shaking my hand and kissing Birdie's.

"My, oh my. I think the last time I saw the two of you, you were this high," he gestured to the height of his knees. His voice, robust and jolly, had that genteel air of a Southern gentleman. "Where does the time go?"

"Of course I remember you, Mr. Gracie," Birdie lied.

That was her way. My sister was very diplomatic and fancied herself a disruption to the old guard arrogance, but the refined movements, the elegant lies that spilled so easily to save face, all of the innate charms that had been instilled since childhood, they kept time within her like a tightly-wound clock.

"Your mother was just telling me that your father won't be joining us until we reach Cherbourg this evening."

"Our father had business that kept him in Paris," I said.

"So, the three of us had a two-week excursion, touring England and Scotland," mother said.

"I see," Gracie said.

Just then, Ismay walked into our conversation.

"Bruce!" mother delighted.

"Ah, I was going to introduce you all to Mr. Archibald Gracie here, but it seems you're already acquainted," said Ismay.

"I was just offering my services to Mrs. Sutherland-Howell here," Gracie began.

"Services?" Ismay asked.

"Since she's a lady traveling alone, that is to say, without her husband, I thought I'd do the gentlemanly thing and offer to escort her about. Just until her husband arrives this evening."

"Ah," Ismay said.

"And," mother began, "I was just telling him that, while I am so honored by his generous offer, it's really not necessary."

"Oh, pish posh," Gracie retorted. "It's no trouble at all. I'd be honored."

"I believe," Ismay interjected, "that what Caroline means is that she's already got an escort for the day."

"She does? Who?" Gracie asked.

All eyes fell on Ismay, who said, "Me."

Before anyone could protest—specifically me—there came that familiar, thunderous blast of the *Titanic*'s whistles as she began pushing back.

"You're going to miss the departure, children," mother said, then turned to Gracie, "would you be so kind as to escort the children to the upper decks? Mr. Ismay was just about to show me where the inquiry office is."

And, with that, mother and Ismay disappeared down the staircase.

"Well, then," Gracie took Birdie's arm in his, "shall we?"

The promenade deck was littered with clusters of animated passengers clinging to the bulwark, shouting and waving, blowing kisses to loved ones and onlookers below.

"Ah, Isidor, you old dog!" Gracie threw an arm around a distinguished, older man with white hair and a neatly-trimmed beard.

"Benji, Margaret, this is Mr. Strauss. He and his wife, Ida, own Macy's Department Store in New York."

"Pleased to meet you both," Isidor's voice was kind and warm.

"Charmed," Birdie said.

"Where's Ida?" Gracie asked.

"She's already gone back to the cabin," Isidor said.

"Not much for the fanfare, eh?" Gracie chuckled.

"When you've traveled as much as we have, sailing day doesn't have the luster it once did. In fact," Isidor gestured for us to join him at an open spot at the promenade rail, then pointed to the ship docked next to us, "the only reason she came up was to get a look at that ship right over there."

"*The New York?*" I read the nameplate aloud.

"That's right," Isidor said. "My wife, Ida, and I sailed on that ship's maiden voyage, and now, here we are on *Titanic*'s."

"Oh, how lovely," Birdie said.

"Now, the ship may not look like much, especially when you're standing aboard *Titanic*, but just over twenty years ago, that ship right there," he pointed, "was the largest, the fastest, and the last name in luxury."

"Really?" I asked in disbelief. It looked so small. So unassuming.

"Yes sir," Isidor chuckled, "it's amazing how much things have progressed in the past few decades. Now we have ships like this. In another twenty years, who knows?"

"The bottom will fall out soon enough," quipped Gracie. "Eventually there'll be a limit. Things can't just keep getting bigger and bigger. There are limits, you know."

BANG!

A loud shot rang out from the dock. Confusion followed as all eyes scanned the surroundings to try and find the culprit.

"What was that?" Birdie exclaimed.

"It sounded like gunfire," Gracie said.

"Not gunfire," I said, "look!"

Audible gasps, shouts, and chatter erupted on the promenade, as well as every deck along *Titanic*'s port side. All eyes fixed on the *New York*. The ship which had been moored next to *Titanic* had been pulled into the wake of the *Titanic*'s massive propellers, causing her mooring lines to snap, and now, she was helplessly drifting towards us.

"Oh my god!" someone screamed.

"It's gonna hit! Look!" cried another.

"Oh," Birdie covered her eyes, "I can't look."

We all braced for impact as the ship drew closer and closer, its stern so close that we could look down from the promenade and see the planks of the decks. As seconds became minutes and time stood still, my mind immediately went to Mr. Gracie's remarks about how there were limits to things. I guess he was right. *Titanic* was a marvel. She, like *Olympic*, was a renegade in their arena, but their size, while their strength, could also be their Achilles heel. Now, here we were, on our maiden voyage, and *Titanic* was poised to undergo the same fate as her sister. Perhaps it was true that these ships were just too big for 1912.

In an instant, we could feel the gentle dancing of *Titanic*'s engines stop. For a second, all was silent as we waited to see what would happen next, while the *New York* continued to drift into our path.

Then, the engines fired back up with a vengeance, in the opposite direction, creating a powerful wash to force the *New York* away from us, with only inches to spare.

Cheers and applause rang out.

"It's alright Miss Margaret, you can open those pretty little eyes *now*." Gracie put an arm around my sister.

"Well, now, Archie," Isidor exasperated, "I think you're right about one thing. There are *indeed* limits. And it would seem that we've *surpassed* them."

My Cabin C-Deck

CHAPTER II

I t wasn't much more than a few minutes after the near-collision with the *New York* that the entire ordeal seemed miles behind us, as the Southampton docks were slowly fading out of sight. Sure, there were murmurs about the slight mishap, even those who thought it might be a bad omen, especially for a ship on its maiden voyage. But, aside from the occasional huff about a slight delay in our departure time, most passengers made light of the situation, many even delighting in the fact that *Titanic*'s incredible size and power initiated the whole thing.

"Mother!" Birdie burst into the cabin, me trailing behind, "you won't believe what we just saw!"

"Darling, what's wrong? Here, come sit; catch your breath." Mother patted the spot next to her on the sofa. Birdie sat, then continued.

"We...we nearly hit something! Another ship! Didn't we, Benji?"

"We didn't nearly hit it," I poured ice water on the fire.

"We did so! Mother, I tell you, my heart was pounding the whole time."

"Where's Mr. Ismay?" I asked dryly. "Or, should I say, *Bruce?*"

Both women stopped and stared at me.

"He's not here," mother said. "I don't think I like your tone of voice, Benji. Your sister's clearly shaken up here, and you need to have a little bit of sympathy. Now, go on, Birdie, tell me what happened."

Before Birdie could begin, "He lost control," I said.

"What?" asked mother. "Who lost control?"

"That's what happens," I said, "when left unsupervised and given too much slack in the lines, things go adrift and lose all control."

Birdie looked at me, confused. But not mother. She knew exactly where I was going with this. I went on, "But, things are back under control now, as they should be. We'll have to keep a close watch to make sure that nothing so careless, so reckless, could ever happen again, eh?"

"Benjamin Sutherland-Howell!" mother stood at once.

Knock, knock, knock.

"I hope I'm not interrupting," Gracie stood at the open door.

"Not at all, Colonel," I said, "in fact, you're right on time."

My mother's gaze was unlike any I'd ever seen before. Her eyes, her smile, were always so warm and angelic; in this moment, I almost feared her, but I'd never let that show.

"Colonel Gracie, I need to run back to my cabin before lunch, but I was wondering if you'd be so kind as to escort my mother and Margaret down to the Dining Saloon?"

"As a Southern gentleman, I'd be honored," he said.

Without so much as a look back, I crossed to the door to make a quick escape.

"Uh, Benji," mother called out. I stopped but didn't look back.

"We'll finish our discussion later," she said, masking her seething rage in a glaze so sugary-sweet that only I could taste its bitterness.

Back out into the corridor, I hastily paced towards the Grand Staircase. Ismay may not've been in my mother's cabin when I arrived, but something told me he'd been there only moments prior. What's more, the fact that their cabins were mere feet from each other meant that he'd find it convenient to drop by any time, but I'd vowed to put an end to that once and for all.

As soon as I hit the floor of the staircase hall, I stopped dead in my tracks. There he was. As if tauntingly, as if knowing my intentions and thwarting my efforts. He stood there, blocking my path. It wasn't Ismay; it was the man who'd been placed squarely in the number two spot of my arch-nemesis, although, in this moment, he might've just gotten top billing.

"Oh, Benji, hello again." He coyly dropped his camera, then turned to the young man beside him. The man was also holding a camera. Miles went on, "Benji, this is Francis Brown."

"How do you do?" his cheery voice was laden with an Irish accent. He extended a hearty handshake as he went on. "Benji, is it? We're photographing the staircase. Mind posing for a picture?"

"Uh, Francis," Miles interjected, "Benji really isn't the posing sort of fellow."

"Ah, well, no harm done. We've got plenty of willing subjects," Francis chuckled. "She's a beauty though, eh?"

"The staircase?" I asked.

"The staircase, sure," Francis agreed, "but I mean, the entire ship. She's like some posh hotel. Miles and I are setting about to take as many rolls of film as we can. Got a friendly wager on who gets the most pictures before tomorrow. So far Miles is winning."

"I see," I said.

"So, you're sure I can't talk you into just one photo—"

"Francis, I already told you that Benji isn't—"

"Sure, I'll bite," I cut him off. "But just one. I am in a hurry."

Miles' eyes glinted. I'd struck a nerve, just like I wanted to. Mind you, I know that I sound like a real ass, between my vendetta with Ismay and Miles, but I had my reasons. If the past month had taught me anything, it's that the world is full of seedy, greedy individuals, individuals that'll kill you if you allow them. So, no matter the cost, you've gotta do whatever it takes to keep the upper hand.

"There we are," Francis beamed as he posed me against the rail of the staircase, the sun's jolly rays casting their warmth upon all in the space. "The lighting's perfect in here," he went on.

All the while, I never broke my gaze with Miles. I wondered what he was thinking. *Was he really as confident in that smile as he pretended to be?* Behind all of that pomp and charisma, I knew there was a scared little boy. By taunting that little boy, playing on his insecurities, I knew I could keep Miles under control.

"Three...two...one...and...keep holding that pose," Francis beamed, looking down into his camera. Finally, after a moment or two, he went on, "I think that's it, Benji. I'm much obliged."

"Of course, *anytime*," I said cheekily. One last glance at Miles, then, "Well, gentlemen, like I said before, I really am in a hurry. If you'll excuse me."

And, with that, I left them on the staircase and started once more for Ismay's cabin.

"Benji!" mother's voice rang out from behind. I stopped and turned around. Mother and Birdie stood on either side of Colonel Gracie, arms linked, mother wearing a satisfied smile on her face. She went on, "Mr. Ismay isn't in his cabin, if you're looking for him. He's already downstairs at lunch."

The tone of her voice, its threads of condescension woven so tightly that I wondered if anyone else could feel them as strongly as I could.

"Ah, I see," I said. "Well, then, I suppose we should head down to lunch ourselves."

"Of course, darling," mother smiled, knowing she was winning this round. "Shall we, Colonel?"

As we headed to lunch, we decided to forgo the use of the three available elevators and descend the staircase all the way down to D deck. We did this to see, first-hand, each level of the marvelous staircase, and also, like many of *Titanic*'s other passengers, we used it as a means to make an entrance. Being the focal point of each level, everyone was always watching the staircase, taking in its striking beauty, wondering who might happen to waltz down her stairs next. If one wanted to be seen, the staircase was the way to do it.

Upon our arrival to D deck, I noticed the massive, brass candelabra, with about twenty or so electric candles, at the base of the staircase. The Edwardian era, also affectionately referred to as 'The Gilded Age,' was a period in history, in society, where man saw himself as infallible. Armed with unprecedented technology, the sorts of things that had only been mere dreams in the decades prior, and illuminated with knowledge—something which, perhaps by design, the candelabra reminded me of as we strode past it.

The D deck landing was the largest of all landings aboard the ship. This Reception Room, which many would refer to as The Palm Court or even The Lounge, spanned the full width of the ship, more than ninety feet, and stretched all the way to the Dining Saloon. Paneled in mahogany, painted a spotless white, the richly carved walls, the ornate columns, the fine plaster mouldings on the walls and ceilings, all commanded attention. Each side of the room was lined with rows upon rows of stained glass windows, which concealed two portholes, allowing copious amounts of sunlight to rain upon the bright space. The floor was covered in a rich, crimson Axminster carpet, which felt plush underfoot and served to warm up the space. To the left and right of the staircase, the room was comfortably furnished with clusters of tables and chairs made of wicker and silk upholstery, chesterfield sofas, and handsome potted palms.

Here, the band was already set up and playing for lunch, gathered around an ornate Steinway grand piano, their precision strings and soft keys waltzing away in the gay atmosphere.

We passed lots of familiar faces as we made our way towards the Dining Saloon. The room read like a who's who of wealthy society, politicians, even members of royal families, all making polite conversation as if it were some casual party at their summer home.

The Dining Saloon was more of a continuation of the Reception Room. Carved oak double-doors with ornate grillwork screens led from either side of the Reception into the massive dining room. I say a continuation because both rooms were styled in a period known as Jacobean. Both rooms spanned the entire width of the ship. Beside the double-doors, large arch windows looked from one room into the other, so their motif was carried over to create a cohesive style. The Saloon stretched for miles and miles. The same white walls, the ornate plaster work, stained glass windows, although these were arranged in a bay window scheme, sturdy chairs of finely carved oak, clad in dark green leather and finished in brass nails gathered themselves around tables dressed in crisp white linens. The center of the room featured two handsomely-carved buffets in the same oak as the chairs, one on the forward wall and one on the aft. The forward buffet featured an inset piano. Both buffets featured turned columns, lion's heads, and reminded me of something one might see in a medieval castle.

The medieval air could also be associated to the floor, which was comprised of an ornate pattern of red, blue, and gold, which mimicked a fine Persian rug. Likewise, the plasterwork was reminiscent of curling thickets and vines, climbing up to the ceiling, where it sprouted into blooming roses. The entire room, both rooms in fact, were almost overwhelmingly illuminated with lights. Overhead, ornately carved glass bowl fixtures filled every inch that the sunlight, which poured in through the massive stained glass windows, didn't touch.

"Here we are," Gracie said, pulling out mother's chair.

Next he offered the same gesture for Birdie; I took my seat beside her. The rest of our table had quite a few empty chairs, as we were sitting at one of the larger tables built for twelve. I looked around the room. One of the most striking things was that the room had many small tables, each outfitted with chairs that weren't bolted to the floor as on other liners; these were free to move at will. The *Lusitania*, which had taken my father and I to Europe, had the typical long tables, chairs bolted to the floor, so that they could accommodate more diners.

"Ah, Mr. Stead, how lovely to see you here," mother said to the white-haired gentleman sitting across the table.

"My dear, Caroline, this ship shines even brighter with your presence aboard," he said.

"Surely you'll remember Margaret and Benji," she continued.

"Of course I do. You two have grown into fine-looking adults. Your father must be very proud. Speaking of, where is Benjamin?"

"He'll be embarking at Cherbourg this evening," mother said.

"Wonderful," he said, "glad to know I'll have someone to talk to on my way to New York."

"What'll you be doing in the states, Mr. Stead?" I asked.

"Conducting research for your next exposé?" asked Birdie.

"Heavens, no," Stead chuckled, "I've taken a break from investigative journalism."

"I'll drink to that," Gracie laughed, holding up a glass of freshly poured wine.

"I'm heading to give a lecture at Carnegie Hall. At the request of President Taft," Stead went on.

"Oh, how wonderful. A political speech?" Birdie asked. "I am so fascinated by politics."

"What do you know about politics?" I chided.

"I'm not as naive and helpless as you let on, Benji. So, Mr. Stead, what is the nature of your lecture? The women's suffrage movement?"

All of the men chuckled at the table but stopped when they realized that she was serious. Stead recovered, then went on, "Uh, no, my dear. This is a lecture on peace. A savvy young woman, such as yourself, no doubt knows that there's talks of unrest on the European front."

"War," Birdie said, with an authority that took the entire table by surprise.

"Precisely," Stead said. "So, the president wants to encourage the fine citizens of the United States that war just isn't the answer. We're in an age of enlightenment, as you well know. Extreme measures, such as war, are not only barbaric, they're antiquated."

"Well, now, Mr. Stead—" Gracie began.

"Colonel," Stead interrupted, "I know you have your strong Southern roots, and I know you pride yourself in your war stories..."

"Stories—?"

"But," Stead continued, "this is the twentieth century! We've evolved. We continue to evolve. Since the end of your Civil War, mankind has learned to harness the power of electricity. He's discovering the secrets of the body, the mind, and the universe at an alarming rate. Before you know it, he'll have a cure for any ailment that exists, and we can theoretically live forever."

"You don't really think we'll be able to live forever, do you?" Birdie asked.

"I do, indeed, dear Margaret. Perhaps not me, but you might just live for a hundred, two hundred years, or more. Long enough to see women get the right to vote," he said with a wink.

"Preposterous!" Gracie protested. "While I respect your position, Stead, I must say that I respectfully disagree with all of the above." Gracie turned the conversation to address the entire table. "As *Titanic* has shown us today, when she almost collided with another ship, there are limits to what we can do. What we should do. Those limits are in place for a reason."

"And what's the reason, Colonel?" Birdie asked, challengingly.

"Why, to protect us. Of course..."

"To protect us? Or...to control us?" Birdie asked, in a definitive tone that took the entire table by surprise.

"Mr. Ismay," mother exclaimed as Bruce walked by the table.

"Ah, Mrs. Howell, Margaret, Benji, I see you're all enjoying yourselves," Ismay said.

"Won't you join us?" mother asked. "We've got lots of open seats at our table."

"I believe they'll be taken up by dinner this evening," he said. "That is to say, I know the rest of your table will be joining us this evening at Cherbourg."

"Yes, Mother," I said, "where will Father sit if Mr. Ismay joins our table?"

"Don't be silly," mother threw those familiar daggers at me, then softened as she looked back to Ismay. "It's just for lunch. Don't fight me on this, Mr. Ismay, you don't know how persistent I can be."

"It's true, Mr. Ismay," Birdie chuckled, "she'll win."

This time I threw daggers at my sister.

Ismay smiled.

"Well then, how can I argue with that?" Bruce said, pulling out the chair next to mother. As he slid himself into position, both he and mother looked at me in a way that declared that they'd won.

"So," Bruce began, "what do you think of our little ship?"

"She's splendid!" Birdie said.

"A marvel," Gracie agreed.

"I prefer the *Lusitania*'s dining room," I said.

All eyes were on me. *Here I go again.* I didn't mean to be so obstinate, but I couldn't help myself. Something about watching my mother and Ismay wrap themselves around each other, like the plaster vines climbing the walls, swirling over my head, they were closing in tighter and tighter. I had to exercise what little firepower I had to hold my ground. To stay in this fight. Watching Ismay be made into a fool while they gazed on, or at least to watch him squirm, that was the last card I had left to play.

"Is that a fact?" Ismay asked. "And, what is it about *Lusitania* that you think is better?"

Again, their heads snapped back at me. Everyone waiting on bated breath to see how I'd retort. Waiting for me to lose yet another hand.

"It's rather obvious, isn't it?" I laughed. "The single-story, rather plain decor, and so much light that I can hardly see. I think I'm about to have a headache from all of the light."

"Is that so?" Ismay cocked an eyebrow.

"Benji," mother began.

"No, it's alright, Caroline," Ismay intercepted. "He has a point. I mean, *The Lusitania* does have a two-story dining room with a plaster dome over it..."

"And the frescoes," I said, "don't forget about the frescoes."

"Quite," Ismay quipped. "But, my dear boy, you know why she's constructed that way, don't you?"

"To be luxurious?" I asked, rather confused.

"Hardly!" he laughed. "She's built that way to make her feel bigger. If her dining room were all on one level, she'd still be a smaller room than this room you're sitting in. Lots smaller. She's built that way because she needs to be. With *Titanic*, we deliberately chose to forgo the two-story design because we didn't need it. This room is large enough to accommodate more than five-hundred and thirty people at one time. And it can do so without those long, claustrophobic tables. And you might've already noticed these chairs."

"They're not bolted to the floor," Birdie chimed in.

"Precisely, my dear Margaret," Ismay beamed. "The Olympic class liners are the first to feature a dining room with small, intimate tables, even private alcoves, with chairs that can move about freely at will. Every aspect of this room has been designed to show you just how massive *Titanic* is. When you stack the features of this room up to that of *Lusitania*, well, I think the table will agree with me that *Lusitania* just can't compare."

Quiet chatter rippled about the table. All seemed to agree with Ismay's assessment. No matter what I said in this moment, I couldn't regain my footing. Ismay had won, and he knew it. Mother had won, and she knew it.

"Now, Benji," Ismay had one more ace to play, "I promised you that I'd introduce you to Mr. Andrews," he gestured to a tall man, walking nearby, jotting notes down into a pocket journal. "Tommy!" Bruce called him over.

"Ah," the man said as he approached the table, "Mr. Ismay, good afternoon, sir."

"Thomas Andrews is the *Titanic*'s designer," Ismay directed all attention to the man that stood beside us. "Tommy, this is Benji," Ismay continued, "he seems to have quite an interest in your ship."

"Is that so, Benji?" Andrews asked.

"I'll warn ya, Tommy, he comes with lots of questions. A bit of a tough customer." Ismay turned to address the table. "As her owner, I'd like to consider myself an expert, but Tommy might just be able to give our fellow Benji a run for his money."

Everyone chuckled at Ismay's quip. Everyone except for me.

"I welcome the challenge," Tommy said. "How about this, Benji? After lunch, I'll take you on an all-access tour. Let you see areas of the ship that passengers usually don't get to see."

"Oh, Mr. Andrews," mother said, "that's so generous of you."

"Well, Benji, didn't I tell you?" Ismay smiled, still winning. "You might just have met your match going up against Tommy Andrews."

"What do you say, Benji?" Andrews asked.

"Yes, of course, Mr. Andrews."

With a simple nod and a smile to the rest of the table, Andrews retreated back to his thoughts, back to his well-worn notebook, back to his world of detailed sketches and shorthand remarks.

And we, likewise, settled back into our previous conversations. Stead talked politics and unrest on the Western Front. Gracie droned on and on about his time in the war and his self-published book. All conversation became a muffled buzz around me; all the while, mother and Ismay retreated further and further into their own little world.

And I sat there, stewing, wondering how everyone could be so oblivious. Or, perhaps more maddening, that I was the only one to care.

CHAPTER 12

Tommy Andrews' cabin was just adjacent to the aft grand staircase, on A deck. This staircase, almost identical to the forward staircase, was brilliant with light in the glow of the afternoon sun. The mammoth glass dome kept an impressive watch upon the dozens of passengers milling about or seated in the large, upholstered chairs that lined the perimeter of the landings.

Knock, knock, knock.

"Just a minute," Andrews' lilting Irish voice rang out from within his cabin.

"Ah, Benji," he threw open the door and looked at his pocket watch. Inside, I could see blueprints and papers strewn all about the cabin. Clearly, he was here to work.

"I really do appreciate this, Mr. Andrews. I know you're a busy man."

"Think nothing of it," he said, replacing his watch in its assigned pocket. "I'm just glad you caught me before we reached Cherbourg. Once we make our stop there, or worse yet, Queenstown tomorrow, I'll be tied up for the rest of the voyage."

"So, what does the designer do on a voyage?" I asked.

"Well, I'm head of a group of men called the 'guarantee group.' We're all here representing the company that built the ship."

"Harland and Wolff?" I asked.

"Precisely," Andrews smiled. "Quite simply, we're along on every maiden voyage to guarantee our ship to the company that bought it. In this case, it's White Star."

"I see," I said, "so if anything goes wrong..."

"There are always quirks," he said, "minor kinks to work out. We're along for the ride to make sure that *Titanic* sails as smooth as possible."

"Is that why you're jotting down those notes?"

"Oh, this?" he pulled the notebook out of his breast pocket.

"I noticed you were using it a lot at lunch."

"Ah, so I was," he opened the notebook and showed me a few pages.

I read them aloud, "Carpet in the Dining Saloon. Chairs on the port side, private promenade to be a darker shade of green. Too many screws in the first-class hat hooks."

"You see, Benji, it's my job to improve on each and every design. No design is perfect, no matter how hard we try. There's always room for improvements."

"So you're making notes of things you want to repair?"

"Not repair, per se, but more so improve. Not just on *Titanic*, but with the third sister, which we're currently building."

"I've read about it."

"White Star has a lot riding on the success of these ships, and it's my job to think ahead of the curve. Find ways to make each ship better than the previous. So, I took notes on *Olympic*'s maiden voyage; those improvements you'll see on *Titanic*. These notes will help me build an even better ship with the third sister."

"What are some key differences between *Olympic and Titanic?*"

"You mean *improvements*," he smiled.

"Right, improvements."

"Well, I could tell you, but I'd rather show you."

And, with that, we began our tour, starting on the aft grand staircase.

"The staircases are essentially the same," Andrews said.

"You mean on *Olympic* and *Titanic?*"

"Exactly. But with small improvements. For instance, we wanted *Titanic* to shine brighter than *Olympic*, so I played around with light. The staircase was one of the areas I did this. Both ships have the same dome, but *Olympic's* is only back-lit by sunlight. That means, at night, her dome is only lit by that center light fixture."

He pointed up to the large, two-tier light fixture that mimicked the other glass-beaded chandeliers hanging throughout the room; however this one was a show-stopper, a centerpiece. He went on.

"The domes over the staircases on *Titanic* are artificially back-lit at night, allowing the staircase to always be lit as if it were daytime. It just feels a bit more cheery. You'll have to take a look this evening after sunset. The effect really is rather remarkable."

"I can't wait," I said, looking up at the dome.

"Alright, the tour continues this way. Carry on then."

Andrews led me aft, across the upper landing, to the door to the first-class Smoking Room. He stopped just before opening the door.

"You're eighteen, right, Benji?"

"Seventeen. Why?" I asked, knowing full well that gentleman's clubs often required guests to be at least eighteen to enter.

Andrews looked around sneakily, then whispered, "Well, son, you're on a Tommy Andrews tour. And nothing's off-limits on an Andrews tour. So, if anyone asks..."

"I'm eighteen," I chuckled.

"Good lad," he said, opening the door.

The handsome room was warm and rich. Polished mahogany-paneled walls wrapped all around us. Ornate scroll-work of glittering mother-of-pearl inlay wrapped the upper perimeter. A white mullioned ceiling stretched more than ten feet overhead, playing host to polished brass chandeliers. All around the room were colorful stained-glass windows, allowing warm, colorful light to bathe the space. Large leather club chairs, wingbacks, chesterfields, and banquettes wrapped themselves around green-felt-top tables with sturdy carved legs, all ready for lowballs of scotch and bourbon, expensive cigars, and risky hands of poker. The claw feet of these tables and chairs rested atop a colorful floor of red and blue tiles, pulling from the lush palette of the stained glass display.

On the far, aft wall of the room, the stunning focal point, a large marble hearth contained the ship's only real burning fireplace.

"Plymouth Harbour," Andrews said as we drew closer to the fireplace for a merited inspection.

"The painting?" I asked, directing my gaze to the large painting that was framed above the mantle.

"By Norman Wilkinson," Andrews continued, "the *Olympic* has a similar painting by the same artist, titled *The Approach to the New World*."

He went silent for a moment, staring at the painting. We were still for so long that I wondered where he'd gone in his mind. Ultimately, the moment became a bit awkward, so to drown out the silence, I asked, "You were saying?"

"Huh?" Andrews stammered.

"*Olympic* has a similar painting by the same artist?"

"Oh, yes," he came back to the present. "The two are quite similar, in fact," he lifted a finger to the side of the painting, "if you put the two side by side, it's almost more of a continuation. That is to say, where one harbor ends, the other begins." He turned pensive once more. "You see, Benji, each ship is special to me. They're like family, but more than that, they're like a part of me." He laughed. "I suppose that sounds silly."

"No, sir. I think I know what you mean."

In that moment, I could feel what he felt. It wasn't just a sense of pride; *Titanic* was more than just a winning design. More than a flashy headline. Ships were like a religion to Andrews. To Ismay, *Titanic* was a business. To Thomas Andrews, she was a purpose.

"Sometimes," Andrews continued, "I find myself standing here, looking at the edge of the harbor, and wondering which ship I'm on. Allowing myself to be on both ships at once. Watching over them. Making sure that I make good on my design."

There was another moment of silence, though not an awkward one as before. This time, I allowed him the space to live in that ether that was his brilliant mind. Andrews smiled, the warmest, kindest smile I'd seen since...since I could remember.

"Forgive me, Benji," he finally said, "I was just..."

"On the *Olympic?*" I asked with a smile.

"Close," he said with a chuckle. "I was visiting their sister. She'll be the pride of the class."

He looked back into the painting, connecting its horizon to the third sister that was being constructed in the Belfast shipyard.

"She'll be called *Britannic*."

"*Britannic*," I echoed, testing the name on my tongue. It felt right – regal, powerful, yet somehow graceful.

"She'll be the culmination of everything we've learned," Andrews continued, his eyes still fixed on the horizon in Wilkinson's painting. "Every note I take here," he patted his breast pocket where his notebook resided, "every observation, every passenger comment – it all goes into making her perfect."

Ever so slightly, the afternoon sun dipped lower, casting longer shadows through the stained glass. The mother-of-pearl inlays caught the changing light, creating an ethereal shimmer across the walls.

"Alright, Benji, we've still got lots to see on this tour. Let's get a move on, eh?"

He made his way to the revolving door to the right of the fireplace, while I trailed obediently behind. As we left the Smoking Room, I caught one last glimpse of the painting. The ships in Plymouth Harbour seemed to float between reality and dream, much like the man leading me through his masterpiece – one foot in the present, one in his vision of what could be. In his mind, I imagined, he was already walking the decks of *Britannic*, making notes in that ever-present notebook, forever searching for perfection in every detail, every improvement, every design.

"Let's sit here, Birdie," mother said, as she sat, poised, in a wicker chair of the Reception Room.

"Should we wait for Benji?" Birdie asked.

"Nonsense. He's on his tour with Mr. Andrews," mother's gaze narrowed in on Mr. Ismay. The real reason mother had picked this particular table is that it was only a few yards away from the table where Bruce was keeping company with Captain Smith. The two men sat with cups of Turkish coffee, smoking cigarettes, blithely unaware that anyone else was in the room.

"Surely he's done by now," Birdie yawned. "It's been over an hour."

"You know that brother of yours," mother came back to the conversation at her own table. "Give him a chance to talk about something of interest, and he'll be at it for hours."

"Even still. Missing tea? Don't you think that's a bit rude?"

"Lots of men choose to miss afternoon tea, Margaret. It's your brother's choice to join us or not."

Birdie rolled her eyes at this.

"What's wrong, Birdie?"

"Nothing. I'm fine," she lied.

"Don't give me that. You and your brother have been at each other's throats all morning. I know there's something going on."

"It's just...he's changed. Benji. He's different."

"He's just going through a lot of different experiences right now. University is a different world than he's used to."

"It's not university. It's..."

"It's what?" mother asked.

"Ever since he and Father went to Paris, he's changed. He's distant. He's moody."

Mother looked away, in thought.

"Don't tell me you haven't noticed, Mother. The way he talks to you, to Mr. Ismay. It's deplorable."

"I'll admit that he seems a bit testy—"

"Testy?" Birdie laughed. "Mother, he's a boor! If I didn't know any better I'd swear it were Father who boarded with us today."

"Margaret!"

"It's true, and you know it, Mother!"

"How dare you talk about your father—"

"Come on, Mother, admit it. Father is a monster. And he's turned Benji into one too."

"That is enough!" mother snapped silently. "Margaret, you are out of control. You talk about your brother, but look at you."

"What do you mean?"

"The way you tried to spearhead the conversation at lunch today? Talking about politics like you have any inkling to comprehend what you're saying. It was most unladylike."

"You think because I'm a woman, I don't have an opinion? That I can't be informed? Mother, do you hear yourself?"

"This is a man's world, and we have to—"

"To *what?!* To smile and wink? To sit around looking pretty but acting like idiots?"

"See there? That's what I'm talking about. Margaret, you must learn to control—"

"*No.* I won't be controlled. Maybe you're fine with that, but not me. I have a mind. A voice. I want to use it. I'm tired of being used. Maybe your generation was fine with that sort of menial existence, Mother, but not mine. We crave change. We need change. You heard Mr. Stead today; we're evolving!"

"You know what I think? I think you're a spoiled, entitled brat who's been given everything but still wants more. I mean, what else do you need, Margaret? What could you possibly want that you don't already have?"

"A vote," Birdie said solemnly.

Mother swallowed hard, holding back her tongue, choosing her words carefully.

"You have so much growing up to do, child. Thank god you don't have the right to vote, because with your ignorant views of the world, you'd have no idea what to do with it."

With this last line, mother stood and left Birdie alone at the table, alone to digest those parting words.

It was nearing sunset as my tour with Andrews was coming to an end. By the conclusion he'd shown me the Veranda Cafés, which mimicked the Savoy in

London, the first-class Lounge, a lush room that mimicked the Palace at Versailles, even the accommodations of second and parts of third class; with each space, it was more and more clear to me that Andrews left no stone unturned, no detail unaccounted for. Even the crew areas were finished with the most thoughtful of touches. Like extra water fountains near the entrances to the boiler rooms—the hot bowels of the ship where firemen, stokers, slung heavy shovelfuls of coal into the *Titanic*'s massive furnaces. Apparently, on *Olympic*, Andrews had heard from a few crew members that they wished for easier access to a cold drink of water, and so, on *Titanic*, Andrews delivered.

As we walked about the ship, especially the main thoroughfare down on E deck called Scotland Road, a long corridor that ran almost the entire length of *Titanic*, it was so clear that Andrews valued the crew as much as the ship itself. This space, which served as a hallway for crew and third-class passengers, was a hive of activity. Crew members running to and fro, all by design, to keep their backstage movements out of sight from the upper classes, was an eye-opening experience. We couldn't go two steps without someone stopping us to say, "Hey Tommy!" or "Aye, Mr. Andrews!" Each one of them happy to see the man who'd been the mastermind behind *Titanic*. Each chatting with him on a first-name basis. Each willing to impart their thoughts or critiques of his design. And, most impressive, each knowing they could do so without fear.

"Wow," I said after one such encounter.

"What is it?" he asked.

"The crew. They really love you."

He chuckled at this.

"I can see why though."

"Oh?" he asked, "and why is that?"

"Because you respect them. Listen to them. Value them."

He stopped walking and looked earnestly at me.

"Of course I do, Benji. One must. You see, a ship, in itself, is a dead thing. Cold steel. Pretty furnishings. But it's not a living thing."

I considered this. He went on, "But it's the people that give her life. Without them, you're in the dark, drifting out in open waters."

"I see what you mean," I said.

He started walking again.

"And, more importantly," he continued, "in a week I'll be gone. So I rely on them to ensure things keep running smoothly when I'm no longer around."

We stopped at a door on Scotland Road, marked 'Emergency Door.'

"Know where you are, Benji?"

"No, sir. I think you've managed to get me lost," I laughed.

"Ha! Don't worry, I won't tell Mr. Ismay. We'll let that be our little secret," he said with a wink.

One quick turn of his key and the door opened. We stepped out of the crew corridor and back into first class, namely, back onto the E deck level of the grand staircase.

"Now," said Andrews, "this should look familiar. Do me a favor, Benji, look up."

As we were now on the lowest level of the staircase, I was able to look up and see, through the overlook, each level of the grand staircase, all the way up to the massive dome some six levels above us, its frosted glass still casting a cheery glow thanks to the back-lit design, courtesy of Thomas Andrews.

"Wow!" I said, nearly speechless at the incredible sight.

"Pretty great, huh?"

"I fell in love with the overlook when we boarded this morning, but I think this just might be my favorite view on the entire ship."

Andrews pulled out his watch to note the time.

"I'm afraid it's about time to conclude our tour."

"Of course," I said, "thank you, Mr. Andrews. You've been most kind."

"Call me Tommy, please," he smiled. "But I've left the last ten minutes for you. Tell me, Benji, where would you like to go? Anywhere you want. The world is your oyster."

I thought for a second, then, "The Marconi room?" I said.

"Normally passengers aren't allowed in the wireless office..." he said.

"I understand, then how about we visit the—"

"I said, normally, Benji. Don't forget, you're on a Tommy Andrews tour. And on a Tommy Andrews tour," he held up his ring of keys, "nothing is off-limits," he said with a hearty laugh.

As we reached the Boat Deck level of the staircase, an officer was standing near the top of the stairs.

"Mr. Andrews!" he called out at the sight of us.

"Lights, what is it?" he asked the officer.

"Captain's been looking for you. Wants to see you on the bridge whenever you can, sir."

Andrews' face fell for a second, then rebounded.

"Of course, Lights. Head on to the bridge and tell the captain I'll be there in just a moment."

The officer gave an affirming nod, then turned on his heels and disappeared into the corridor.

"Another time, then," I said, trying to hide my disappointment.

"Nonsense," he chuckled.

"But—"

"I told you that you'd get a tour of the wireless office, and a tour you shall get. Follow me."

He led the way to the same small corridor where the officer had disappeared only moments ago and stopped outside the door to the Marconi room. After giving a quick knock on the door, the door opened, and a young, blonde man appeared.

"Aye, Mr. Andrews," the man said.

"Hello, Bride." Andrews turned to me. "Benji, this is Harold Bride, one of our Marconi wireless operators."

"It's a pleasure, Benji," Bride said, shaking my hand.

Andrews went on, "I promised Benji that I'd give him a quick tour of the wireless office, but duty calls. I was wondering if I could leave him in your charge?"

"Of course, sir. Any friend of Tommy Andrews is a friend of ours," he gave a casual salute.

"Thank you, Bride. Well, Benji, I'll leave you in his capable hands."

"Thank you sir, for everything. Truly, it's been a pleasure."

Andrews gave a hearty wink, then left us alone in the corridor.

"So, I'm the junior operator," Bride broke the silence. "That there's Phillips, or Sparks we call him. He's the lead operator."

Bride opened the door a bit wider, revealing another young guy sitting with headphones on, tapping away feverishly on the wireless set.

"Are we bothering him?" I asked, looking at Phillips.

"Crikey, no," Bride laughed. "Can't hear a thing with that bloody headset on!"

"Is it true that *Titanic*'s wireless is the most powerful set out at sea?"

"True enough, indeed. You know much about wireless?"

"A little," I said.

"So, basically, Phillips there is tapping away messages for the passengers."

"Sending wires?"

"Uh-huh."

"Using Morse code, right?"

"Yeah. You understand Morse?"

"Very little," I shrugged, "a few letters here and there."

"Tell ya what, Benji," Bride grabbed a small stack of tear-sheets from the operators table, "here's a cypher..."

I looked down at a printed list of each letter of the alphabet, along with numbers zero through nine, each corresponding to a series of dots and dashes: Morse code. Bride went on, "Why don't you think of something you want to send, then write it out in Morse on one of these message forms; come back here and we'll even let you be the one to send it!"

"You mean, me, tap out my own message?"

"Course, free of charge. Like I said, any friend of Tommy Andrews is a friend of ours!"

Bride gave me a playful slap on the back.

"Thanks, Bride! I will."

After a quick goodbye, I walked back to the grand staircase, where I was greeted with the blowing of a bugle. The lively tune, *The Roast Beef of Old England*, alerted all passengers that dinner would be served in one hour and now was the time to begin that oh-so-cumbersome Edwardian task: dressing for dinner.

Meanwhile, on the ship's bridge, Captain Smith was in a deep discussion with Bruce Ismay.

"I know that, Captain, but she's been performing beautifully," Ismay said.

"Quite," Smith agreed.

"Mr. Ismay," Andrews approached, "I didn't expect to see you here."

"Tommy?" Ismay fumbled clumsily. "How was your tour with our young friend?"

"Refreshing. You're right, Ismay. Benji certainly understands the ship...better than some so-called experts."

Ismay picked up on the jab but paid little mind. Andrews continued, "You wanted to speak with me, Captain?"

"Yes, Tommy. I wanted to touch base with you about *Titanic*'s performance."

"So far, so good, I should say," Andrews said.

"Which is why," Ismay cut in, "I propose we increase her speed."

"Her speed? But she's not even out to sea yet. Why would we ramp up her speed before we're out of the channels?" Andrews asked.

"You're aware of the incident this afternoon?" Smith asked.

"Near incident," chided Ismay. "We never came in contact with the *New York*."

"Be that as it may," said Smith, "we are now a bit behind schedule."

"By what?" Andrews asked, looking at his watch. "Forty-five minutes or so?"

"An hour and a half," Ismay said.

"We had hoped to make it to Cherbourg before dinner," Smith agreed.

"I see. Well, gentlemen, minor setbacks do happen, especially on a maiden voyage," Andrews casually chuckled. "That's why me and my team are here. I do think it best to hold off on pushing the engines until they've got a proper head of steam."

"Precisely, Tommy. As I was telling Mr. Ismay—"

"Gentlemen!" Ismay shouted, then, after realizing the other officers on the bridge were now privy to the conversation, he dialed it back to a strong, stifled whisper, "Tommy, Captain, you both know what we've got riding on this voyage. J.P. is breathing down my neck to make headlines over this voyage. Yes, *Olympic* was a triumph, but she's hit a few snags as of late. *Titanic* is an improvement over her sister, but only marginally. We've got to find a way to spin her as the modern marvel that she is. Make people crave a voyage on her. I'm doing all I can to keep the conversations spinning in our favor, but you're going to have to meet me halfway here."

The men were silent.

Ismay went on, "Now, Captain, let's not forget the number of important people we have waiting for us in Cherbourg, including Astor. J.J. Astor exclusively books on White Star ships which sail under your charge. And you know how highly he regards punctuality. Wouldn't you hate to disappoint him?"

Smith looked up and silently gave an affirming nod.

"Good man. Now, Tommy, that's where you come in. Should you see any reason that we couldn't push the engines forward, just a little, to try and make up some of this lost time?"

Andrews looked at Smith, expecting some sort of support from his often-agreeable captain, but only saw defeat in his eyes. For a moment, Tommy thought about pushing back. After all, he knew this ship better than anyone. He knew what she could and couldn't do. Her engines were new—capable, but new. They needed time to be properly run-in. Tommy's expertise had the gravitas to shoot down this notion of speed right here and now. *He could lie. He should lie.* Put Ismay into his proper place of a passenger, nothing more.

"I see no reason why she couldn't go a bit faster," Andrews relented, opting for honesty.

"Then it's settled," Ismay beamed.

Before he could hear the captain give the order to speed up, before he could take it all back and say that he thought it better to stay the course, before giving the matter any more thought, Andrews left the bridge.

CHAPTER 13

Margaret sat in silence as the stewardess brushed her hair. Aimlessly looking into the mirror, the young stewardess, Violet, thought Margaret was looking at her reflection, contemplating her appearance. In reality, Margaret was staring right through it. Her mind, her thoughts, still swarming chaotically ever since the discussion with Mother over afternoon tea.

"Violet, do you mind?" Margaret asked, taking the brush in her own hand.

"Of course, Miss. Did I pull too much?"

"No, not at all. I'd...just...rather do it myself."

"Oh." Violet turned to the wardrobe. "In that case I'll start setting out your dress—"

"No," Margaret stopped her, "I'd rather do that myself too."

"But...the buttons?" asked the stewardess.

"I'll manage. At least let me try."

"As you wish, ma'am." Violet thought for a moment, a bit taken by her passenger's dismissive tone. "Did I do something wrong?"

Margaret stopped at this, realizing how she'd come across.

"Oh, no, not at all. I'm sorry, Violet, I know how silly this must seem to you."

"Not silly, Miss. Just not what I'm used to. Most passengers want me to fix their hair. The ladies, at least. I'm quite good at it, I assure you."

"I'm sure you are, Violet. And, believe me when I say that this has nothing to do with you."

Violet could detect a trace of sadness in Margaret's tone.

"Is everything alright, Miss?"

"Please, Violet, call me Birdie."

"Alright, then...*Birdie*. I can sense that something's troubling you. Is there anything I can do to help?"

Margaret walked over and sat on the edge of the bed, then patted the seat next to her.

"Please, come, sit."

Violet joined her.

"Violet, I know that we've only just met this afternoon, but can I ask you something?"

"Anything, Miss Birdie."

"And you'll be honest?"

Violet held up a hand as if under oath. Birdie continued, "You meet lots of people during these crossings."

"I do."

"How do you see them? What I mean to say is, how do you view them?"

"I'm afraid I don't understand, Miss Birdie."

"Just *Birdie*, please. What I mean is, are they kind to you? Do they seem genuine? Are they the kinds of people that you enjoy meeting?"

Violet thought for a moment.

"You meet all kinds," her Irish brogue cut in just a little, "just like any other corner of the world, I suppose. You have to take the good with the bad."

"And, in your experience, do the good outweigh the bad?"

"Where is all of this coming from?" Violet tilted her head.

Birdie stood and paced across the room, gathering her next thought.

"I'm not helpless, Violet," Birdie insisted, her eyes holding back tears.

"I know that, Miss—*Birdie*."

"I mean, sure, I was born into this life of privilege, and, sure, it has its merits. But I can do more than just smile and wave. I'm more than just a pretty ornament to place on your mantle."

"Of course you are."

"I have a mind, Violet. A good mind. I'm smart, I speak five languages, and I'm good at math. I stay current on politics and foreign policy—"

"Calm down, Birdie," Violet crossed to the girl and took her in her arms to stifle the fire. Birdie collapsed into the embrace. Her tears were no longer held back; she let them flow freely as she regained her speech.

"What I'm saying is, the more I come to know and understand this world, the more I realize that I'm going to have to fight tooth and nail if I want any place in it. *Any real place.*"

"Birdie, look at me," Violet lifted Birdie's gaze to match her own. "I may not know where all of this is coming from. I mean, I would give my right arm to have been given the sort of position you have in this life…" Birdie started to fade away, then Violet pulled her back, "but I *do know* what it feels like to have to fight to be *seen*. To be *heard*. I come from a large family, a family where I had to act as both father and mother to all of my siblings. And, because of that, I never really felt like I had the chance to live my own life."

"So, what did you do?" Birdie asked.

"I escaped. I went out to sea, and I've never looked back."

"Never?" asked Birdie.

"Not once. Through my career I've had my share of action and adventure. I was on the *Olympic* during its collision, but I didn't let that scare me. When they assigned me onto this ship, I accepted wholeheartedly. Some are afraid of maiden voyages, but not me. I've got nerves of steel, just like *Titanic*. So, here I am. I know that living my life, on my own terms, is worth every little sidestep that might come my way."

"I envy you, Violet. I really do."

"You have the power to do anything you want to do, Birdie."

"But that's just it, I don't. I want to go out into the world, to change the world, to have a voice; but I'm a fraud."

"Why's that?"

"Because, as my mother reminded me today, I have lived a very sheltered life. Sure, I can read about civil unrest, impoverished conditions in crowded cities, even burgeoning industries and stock market speculations, but, Violet, I've never even spoken to someone who isn't a millionaire."

"You're talking to *me*," Violet laughed.

"You know what I mean," Birdie continued. "If I want to fight for change and reform, I have to truly understand what I want to change and why it needs to be changed. I need to get out, away from all of this. Away from a world of débutante balls and polo matches and stand in a breadline. I need to talk to the common man, and woman. I need to look into their eyes, no matter how much it hurts me. I need to get a sense of their pain. To ignite the fire in me. To be honest in my efforts. So that I don't lose my fire. So that I don't...make a fool of myself."

"You're not a fool, Birdie. In fact, I think you're one of the most honorable people I've ever met."

Birdie thought for a moment, then an idea struck her.

"Violet, I need to ask a favor."

"Another one?" Violet chuckled.

"A big one," Birdie hesitated, then, "can you get me into third-class?"

"Oh, Miss Birdie—"

"Birdie."

"Birdie, right. Listen, I would if I could, but that's not allowed."

"Why not? They're just regular people."

"That they are. They're lovely people. But the classes can't mix."

"Why the hell can't they?" Birdie began pacing once again. "You know I'm getting really tired of hearing that old standby. There's nothing that puts me above them. We are all equal. We're all human beings."

"It's not my call to make, though," Violet said, "it's immigration laws. America prohibits them from coming in contact with the upper classes. Any passenger who does is required to go through a quarantine—"

"That's bullshit and you know it, Violet."

"But, Birdie—"

"Have you been down to third-class?"

"...I have, yes."

"Have you been down there *today?*"

"Yes."

"And yet you're here with me? Doesn't that prove how ridiculous this measure is?"

Violet thought about it for a moment. Birdie was right. If it were dangerous, she shouldn't be anywhere near the first-class passengers either.

"So, you see my point?" Birdie went on.

"I see your point."

"So? Can we go—"

"If I agree to get you down there," Violet insisted, "not a word can be said to anyone. It would mean my job. My *freedom*, Birdie."

"I won't tell a soul. Not a single soul."

Violet hesitated, wondering if she was really about to agree to this, then, "After dinner then. Tonight. I have a few hours to spare after dinner."

"Oh, Violet," Birdie ran and embraced her new friend. "Violet, it was fate that our paths crossed."

"I don't know about all of that," Violet said.

"I do. I'm sure of it. Just as sure as I am that you and I are going to help each other get through this voyage."

A-Deck Landing
Grand Staircase
D-Deck Landing
Reception Room
white paneled walls

CHAPTER 14

Along the picturesque chalky cliffs and Gothic abbeys that line the coast of Normandy, sits the port city of Cherbourg. The famous port, which serves anyone wishing to visit or return from Paris, is always the first port of call for the *Olympic* class liners, just as it is for many other greyhounds of the sea.

On the evening of Wednesday, April 10, 1912, the port was a scene of confusion and chaos. Here, a large number of passengers from all three classes waited anxiously, along with tons of mail and cargo, all set to board the tardy liner. In the cramped hall of the White Star Cherbourg terminal, murmurs of an incident pervaded the tense space. Details of the near-collision with the *New York* were scant, but enough to frighten a few anxious passengers. Nicholas Martin, White Star's Cherbourg representative, may've been wearing a cheery smile, but he was executing damage control on all fronts.

His nerves were rattled too, as the scene before him included a cast of not just elites, but some of the wealthiest people in society, including the richest man in America, John Jacob Astor. Astor, who was a close friend of Ismay and a stickler for punctuality, was traveling back to America after a lengthy European honeymoon with his new wife, Madeleine. John, sometimes called Jack, J.J., or even, as the press often called him, Jack-ass-Tor, was the closest thing America had to royalty.

Astor's mother had been the most influential woman in American high society, hosting parties in her splendid Fifth Avenue mansion for the infamous 'four hundred,' which was a list of those considered a part of the elite club of high society. If you wanted on the list, you had to be personally invited by Mrs. Astor, and the list only had room for four hundred people, so the only way to join the list was for someone else to leave. The family owned nearly half of Manhattan, from the slums to the grand hotels which bore their name, *The Waldorf-Astoria*.

J.J., who was forty-seven, tall and lank but still handsome, sporting a regal mustache, had recently married, or rather remarried, a young woman, Madeleine Force, who was only eighteen years old. His first wife, someone whom his mother had approved of, was a constant thorn in the side of Astor. Nineteen years and two children into their marriage, J.J. finally divorced his first wife, something he'd had to wait until his mother's passing to accomplish, and had swiftly married the young, pretty woman who'd been so different than anything he'd ever loved before.

For obvious reasons, not just the affair and eventual divorce, but Astor's decision to select such a young wife, the press had a field day with the scandal. To escape the grueling headlines, J.J. and Madeleine had an extended tour of Europe and Egypt. During their time abroad, Madeleine discovered that she'd become pregnant, thus making it crucial to extend their stay and allow the newspaper presses to cool off. Together they sat, side by side, J.J. and young Madeleine, who looked rather peaked in her fragile state, now several months along in her pregnancy. With an entourage of staff surrounding them, and Astor holding the reins of his beloved Airedale, Kitty, they certainly would've been a notable sight amongst the millionaires that sat elbow to elbow.

"Ladies and gentlemen, please," Nicholas Martin's voice rang out through the hall, "I do apologize for the delay. As you may have heard, there was a slight hiccup as *Titanic* left Southampton, but I've just received a wire from Mr. Ismay, who's sailing aboard her, that they've ramped up her speed and they should be here momentarily. So, if you'll all be so kind as to make your way to the tenders, we shall begin boarding them now."

A wave of relief washed over the restless crowd. Finally, they'd be able to leave this stuffy space and settle into the sumptuous suites awaiting their arrival. But, first, there'd be one more stop: the tenders.

The *Olympic* class liners were too large to enter the port at Cherbourg; that is to say their draught, or the amount of the ship that sat below the waterline, was too much for the shallow waters of the port. So, when designing the mammoth ships, the team also designed two small tender boats, the *Nomadic* and the *Traffic*.

Titanic and her sisters would drop anchor just outside of the shallow waters, and the small boats would bring the embarking (and sometimes debarking) passengers and mail to and from the ships. The *Traffic* carried third-class passengers and the mail that had been dropped for pick-up in France, while the *Nomadic* would take the first- and second-class passengers.

As the Astors and their staff made their way onto the *Nomadic*, they were joined by many other notable figures. There were celebrities, like the two champion tennis stars who'd played at Wimbledon, the famous movie star and model Dorothy Gibson, and the famous dressmaker Lady Lucille Duff-Gordon, along with her husband Sir Cosmo Duff-Gordon.

Lucy Duff-Gordon, who can be credited with the first-ever fashion show, was a haute couture designer who had stores in London and Paris and was in the midst of opening a location in Manhattan. Known for her use of frilly lace and bows, Lucy rose to prominence when her designs caught the attention of the Royals. As soon as word spread that Lucille's designs could be seen at the royal court, her enterprise surged. It wasn't just her progressive styles of dress that kept her name on the lips of elite ladies, but also what was underneath. In the early twentieth century, undergarments were still something that were a closely-held secret. Muted tones, understated, kept out of the limelight, Lucille dared to create lines of underwear and lingerie that commanded attention. The lacework, feathers, bows, buttons, and bright colors that she used in her clothing designs were also allowed to sit front-row center in her line of naughty undergarments, garments which were on full display in her lush, pink showrooms in Paris.

However, the majority of the who's-who on *Titanic*'s passenger list would be the 'old-money' crowd. Names like Astor, Widener, or that of Mr. Benjamin Sutherland-Howell; *my father*.

Unlike the familiar faces of the celebrities or the pampered pooches walking gracefully onto the tender, my father sulked in silence, invisible, just as he preferred. A man with a name and wealth to rival Astor, the enigma that was my father had long shied away from the cliques of society, tending to dwell in the catacombs, where he could take pride in his own misery. From the time I was a child, I'd never been able to understand the man I called my father, the man from whom half of the materials to create my being had originated. How could someone be so close to you, yet so far away? There was never a soothing word, never a warm embrace, scarcely even a touch, as though I were made of glass bones and paper skin, as though I might break if he took me off the shelf, even just one time.

When Mother and Birdie had sailed to join us in Europe, I joined them for a two-week excursion in and around London while my father stayed behind in Paris. What was he doing those two weeks, alone? I don't know. Nor do I care. My father was an acquaintance to me, nothing more.

Knock, knock, knock.

Birdie opened the door to her cabin.

"I'm almost ready," she said, turning back into the room while fixing her earring.

She walked to the dressing table and picked up her silk gloves. After sliding on the first, she clumsily fumbled with the buttons.

"Let me help," I said, strolling to her aid. She jerked her arm away from my reach. "Birdie—"

"I've got it," she said, shooting a resolute look my way.

"What's gotten into you?" I asked.

"You're one to talk, Benji," she said.

"I told you—"

"No, you didn't. You haven't told me a thing, Benji."

"It's complicated, Birdie."

"Well, then, I guess we both have our secrets, don't we?"

"Look," I gently took her by both arms, "I know I've been acting stupid lately. I apologize for that, OK? All of it."

"But you still can't tell me why?"

"Let's call a truce," I said.

"On what terms?" Birdie cocked her head.

"We start over. The last two weeks. We put it behind us and go back to the way things were before?"

"And?" Birdie insisted. "If I agree to forgive you for being such an asshole, you'll tell me?" She playfully punched my arm.

I swallowed hard, then, "I'll tell you."

"Benji—"

"Sunday, on our birthday. Consider it your birthday present from me," I laughed awkwardly, hoping to think of a way to go back on this decision.

"Deal," she stuck out her hand for a handshake.

"*Deal*," I shook it.

"Now," I continued, "let's get going before Mother sends Windbag Gracie to come and see what's taking us so long."

The Reception Room was in full sway as Birdie and I descended the stairs of the D deck grand staircase, our faces lit in the warmth of the brass candelabra.

"Over there," Birdie pointed.

"Of course," I said through clenched teeth.

The two of us strode over to the pre-dinner conversation between the pair of elegantly dressed figures, the happy couple out of some *Harper's Bazaar*.

"Mother," I leaned in with a kiss on both her cheeks, "and...Mr. Ismay. Somehow I thought you might be here."

"Benji, Mr. Ismay was just telling me that you and Mr. Andrews had a lovely time on your tour today."

"I'll bet he was—" Birdie silently dug her nails into my arm, "I mean, *yes*, we did. It was so kind of you to arrange it for me, Mr. Ismay."

All eyes fell on me, taken aback at my agreeable tone.

"Uh, it was my pleasure, Benji. Most happy to help," stammered Ismay.

"You look lovely, Mother," Birdie said.

"As do you, darling. You both do," Mother said, taking us in.

The stringed quintet finished their song, and the piano led them into their next. The cheery atmosphere of the room was palpable; an exclusive dinner party where everyone knew someone. All were friends. All belonged. All were members of the club.

"Well, then," Ismay broke the lapse in conversation, "I believe your table is ready. Shall we?" He extended an arm to escort Mother.

"Shouldn't we wait for Father?" Birdie asked.

"She's right," I said. "Aren't we near Cherbourg?"

"Indeed," Ismay said, "we've nearly made up all of the time from Southampton."

"Your father will be fine, children. You know how he is. He probably won't join us tonight anyway. He'll likely just head up to the stateroom," Mother said.

"Still, I think it's best we wait for him," Birdie said.

"Well, I'd hate to miss the first course. It's rude to waltz into dinner late," Mother sighed, looking at Ismay.

"How about this," Ismay said, "I'll escort you to dinner, and Margaret and Benji can wait for their father."

I couldn't believe he actually said it; sure, he was thinking it, but to come right out and say it.

"What a splendid idea," Mother's face lit up.

Seriously? What was happening? Was my mother openly saying this?

"Benji?" Birdie asked, fully expecting me to lose my cool again. *I should have. I should've called Ismay out for being a jackass. I should've called out my mother for her lack of tact and pedigree. I should've overreacted this one time that the situation truly merited it.*

"Sure," I said, "we'll wait."

I could feel Birdie's angry eyes on me.

"We'll see you inside, then," Mother smiled.

And, with that, both Mother and Ismay paraded themselves, arm-in-arm, into the warm glow of the dining room just beyond us.

"What just happened?" Birdie asked.

"What do you think?" I asked. "Our mother and Ismay are having an affair."

"Shhh!" Birdie scolded.

"It's true, Birdie. Anyone can see them."

"Then why didn't you say something? Do something?"

"I told you, I'm not going to get worked up anymore."

"But, Benji, everyone can see them."

"So? Let them see."

"And if Father sees?"

"Then he'll see," I said. "I can't control her, just as she can't control me, nor you. We have to live and let live. Be responsible for our own choices. No one else can live our lives for us, just as we can't live our lives for them. Understand?"

She took this in, mulled it over for a moment, then silently nodded.

I kissed her forehead.

"Where'd you get to be so wise? University?" she giggled to lighten the mood.

"I've figured a few things out on my own," I smiled.

Just then we could hear a commotion in the vestibule.

"What's that?" Birdie asked.

"We must be in Cherbourg," I said, watching the first fresh faces come aboard.

Sure enough. Outside the *Titanic*'s massive hull, the *Nomadic*'s small frame rocked on the gentle lapping of waves that had kicked up. First-class passengers began climbing the gangways that tethered the vessels together, braving the uncertain terrain, which was now cast in heavy shadow as the sun was setting. A brilliant sky of pink and peach blazed against the silhouette of the leviathan, *Titanic*, its thousands of windows and portholes all blazing from within. It looked like a giant skyscraper, lying on its side, atop the charcoal waters.

Back inside the Reception Room, Birdie and I kept watch for our father.

"Benji, look!" Birdie chirped, "it's the Astors."

John Jacob Astor emerged into the room, his canine in tow, with his frail wife, Madeleine, clinging to him for dear life.

"Poor thing," Birdie continued, "just look at her. I've heard this pregnancy is taking a toll on her health."

"Birdie, look!" I could hardly contain myself. "It's Henry Sleeper Harper!"

"Who?"

"The *publisher!*"

The Harpers Publishers, eventually *Harper Collins Publishers*, were one of the largest, most prolific publishing houses in the world. Ever since I'd first dreamt of becoming a writer, I thought that if I could just see the imprint of Harpers Publishing House on my work, then I'd know I'd made it. I could know that, despite the words of my father, I truly had what it takes to be a successful writer. In this moment, this close to the gatekeepers, I felt like I might just be able to see that dream become a reality. I would see it become a reality. I'd find my best writing, give it a thorough polishing, present it to Mr. Harper, and he'd be impressed enough to offer me a contract. *How wonderful that would feel*—to rub such a successful thing into the face of my father. To make him eat his words. To finally forge my own path and be able to escape the Howell name, forever.

"Excuse me!" a young woman's voice rang out, clear as a bell. She was summoning a steward to assist her and the older woman that had walked, or rather stumbled, in with her. The pretty young woman continued, "Thank you, sir. My mother, she isn't feeling well. Could you see that she gets to our cabin alright?"

"Yes ma'am. Of course, ma'am," the dutiful young steward replied.

"I'll be fine, Dorothy, honestly, you're making too big of a fuss over—"

"Remember the trip to Paris, Mama? You were sick as a dog. You need your rest. I'll check in on you later."

As the steward led the older woman towards the elevators, and while her daughter insisted the steward bring a hot bowl of soup to the room, Birdie yanked my coat sleeve.

"Benji, you know who that is?!" she managed to both shout and whisper at once.

"No, who?"

"Dorothy Gibson!"

"Who?"

"You know, the '*prettiest girl.*'"

I hadn't heard of 'the prettiest girl,' nor did I know her name. She and her mother were new money, obviously, but even more obvious was the fact that she did indeed live up to that name. She was 'the *prettiest girl.*'

"Mrs. Gibson!" Birdie called her over after the elevator had departed with her mother.

"Well, hello there, fellow American," laughed 'the prettiest girl.' "And whom do I have the honor of meeting?"

"I'm Margaret, but my friends call me Birdie. I'm such a fan. I've been dying to get the 'Gibson Girl' hair ever since I saw your picture in *Good Housekeeping*."

"Well, my goodness, I am flattered, Miss Birdie. It's so lovely to meet you." Then she turned to me. "And who might this handsome young man be?"

"This is my brother, Benji."

"Benjamin," I said, kissing her hand, trying my best to keep my composure, "or Benji. Either one is fine."

Dorothy laughed.

"Well, I haven't been on the *Titanic* two minutes, and I've already made two friends. Gee, Americans are so much more friendly than Europeans, don't you know?"

We all chuckled.

"Oh no," Dorothy dropped her head to keep out of sight.

"What's wrong?" I asked.

"Not that old man," she continued.

"Who?" asked Birdie.

"He was on my last crossing, and he wouldn't leave me alone," whispered Dorothy.

We both looked over to notice Colonel Gracie approaching us.

"Ah!" delighted Gracie. "I thought I noticed the 'prettiest girl' entering the party."

"Mr. Gracie," Dorothy began.

"Colonel Gracie," he corrected, "and it would appear that you might need my services yet again on this voyage."

"Oh, I would...I mean...that's so kind of you, Colonel. But I'm afraid it's not necessary. As I've already got a gentleman chaperone this voyage."

"Who?" Gracie demanded.

"Why...Benji," Dorothy beamed.

"*Benji?!*" Father's voice rang from behind, startling us all.

green leather with brass nails
Dining Saloon
white plasterwork: roses, wickets, Roman gods (Poseideon)
stained glass amber and dove grey
rust red
flooring detail: mimics a woven rug
cobalt blue
goldenrod

CHAPTER 15

"Surely not, *my son*, Benji. He doesn't have the courage to talk to pretty women," Father went on. We all turned to meet him.

"Father!" Birdie cried out, rushing into a warm embrace, albeit a bit one-sided.

"Actually, he's been the perfect gentleman," Dorothy politely scolded.

"I'm sorry, but I didn't get the chance to introduce myself on the tender over here. I'm Benjamin Sutherland-Howell." Father gently kissed Dorothy's gloved hand.

"So I've heard," she giggled, "and I'm Dorothy Gibson."

"The prettiest girl," Father wrapped his eyes tightly around her from head to toe, "so *I've heard*."

"Too many snakes in the hen house, Ben, my boy," chided Gracie to Father; he went on, "best behave yourself this crossing. You're a married man." He shook Father's hand with an iron grip.

"That makes two of us, eh, old chap?" Father laughed. The men exchanged smiles that were anything but sincere. Father went on, "Speaking of, where's your mother?"

"She's already in the Dining Saloon," said Birdie. "Shall we join her? You must be starving."

"You'd better be," Gracie laughed. "That chatterbox Stead is seated at our table, and you know how he likes to chew the fat. I do declare that every meal we take on *Titanic* might just test the tensile strength of our corsets, and I'm not talking about the food."

We all chuckled, as everyone, except Gracie, exchanged sly looks. The irony of Gracie calling anyone a chatterbox wasn't lost on anyone except for him.

"What do you say, Benjamin?" Father steered the course back to me. "Shall we head into dinner?" His eyes met mine, and a fire ignited. We each stared right through one another, bygones being anything but bygones. He wasn't asking if I was ready to head into the Dining Saloon; he was asking if he was permitted to join.

It must be noted, after Birdie's and my agreement for me to try and be more civil, despite the fact I hadn't seen my father for two weeks, despite the fact that even perfect strangers had kind words for him, I had none. So I held my tongue. I did not, nor would I, utter one syllable to acknowledge him until I felt that I could muster it without cutting him off at the knees. You'll soon see that this man, this snake oil salesman, with his charming smile, his coat of many colors, was the festering thorn in my side, the catalyst for all of my recent undoing.

"Actually," Father began, seeing the warning of my gaze, "I'm pretty exhausted and wouldn't be the best company, I'm afraid. I think I'll venture to the Smoking Room and unwind with a nightcap."

"Oh, *must you*, Father?" Birdie pleaded.

"Tell your mother I'll see her later this evening," Father kissed her cheek. "And as for Stead," Father turned to Gracie, "you tell him I have a score to settle with him at the card tables. We'll go double or nothing after dinner, if he's man enough for the stakes."

"You think you can handle both of us?" Gracie winked.

"With one hand tied behind my back," Father said, then, "if you'll excuse me, ladies, I will entrust you into the capable hands of these fine gentlemen."

As he started towards the elevators, Father turned back for one final thought. "And, Benji, don't do anything I wouldn't do. You're a man now, remember." Then came his familiar, playboy wink.

Everyone looked back to me to see my response. I gave none. More glaring silence between my father and I.

And, with that, Father was gone.

As if on cue, the strings of the orchestra sliced through the momentary silence, pulling us back into the scene of the Reception Room. The party had grown into a swell by this point, and all guests were fading in and out of the room like distant memories.

Even though the first night out at sea was always more relaxed in terms of dressing for dinner, very few seemed to be taking advantage of the friendly protocol. Men in their white bow ties and tailcoats, women in their fashionable Parisian gowns, mimicked Greek statues, from the strands of jewels woven like string into their empire hairstyles, to the diamonds embracing their swan necks, to the millions of bugle beads used to embellish their silk and satin gowns, all creating the most pleasant sounds of rustling as they glided past, all catching the light and amplifying it tenfold in the romantic space, making each of them a brilliant beacon in an endless sea of whitewashed wicker and potted palms.

With Dorothy on my arm, and Birdie on Gracie's, our party waltzed towards the starboard entrance to the Dining Saloon. I could hear the pouring of wine and fizzing of champagne, the stifled clinking of real silver against the purest of china tableware, the wafting of tulle petticoats, linen and wool, the polite hum of rehearsed conversations and the occasional chuckle, all hovered just above the gentle dancing of *Titanic*'s engines. Apparently we were back underway.

The room, while the same one we'd been in for lunch only hours ago, couldn't have looked more different. Sure, the same painted plaster walls, same tapestry floor, same green leather chairs framing linen-lined tables, but my mind went back to Tommy Andrews' remark about playing with light, and nowhere else was that more brilliantly showcased than dinner aboard *Titanic*. While light may have overwhelmed the space during the daytime, it was tamed into an elegant accessory at night. All around, small polished silver lamps with soft silk shades had been placed as the centerpieces of nearly every table. This small addition allowed the lights overhead, along with the artificial back-lighting of the stained glass windows, to be brought down to a warm, romantic glow. As such, the room no longer felt like lunch at some stuffy country club, but rather an intimate dinner party at some luxurious country estate.

By the time we four late arrivals made our way to join our table, the second course was already being served—the second out of ten exhaustive courses. Much to my surprise, even delight, Ismay was not seated at our table. Instead we found Mother and Stead engaging in conversation with a few additions that had not been in attendance for lunch. There was the infamous Countess of Rothes, cousin to the royal family, along with her cousin Gladys Cherry, and a young couple traveling home to Ontario by the names of Hudson and Bess Allison.

"Where's your father?" Mother asked me as we took our seats.

"The Smoking Room," I said.

"The Smoking Room?" she asked aloud, although her expression revealed that she hadn't meant to.

"Oh dear," said Mrs. Allison from across the table.

All eyes turned to the stunned woman, whom, like my mother, hadn't intended to voice her inner monologue aloud.

"What I meant was," she stammered, "that I was hoping I would get the chance to get acquainted with all of our tablemates this evening. Such an interesting array of people. And such a beautiful ship." She smiled, trying hard to sell this as her genuine story.

"We've got a week to get to know everyone, darling," her husband said in a calm, yet somehow disapproving way. Mr. Allison, with his soft blue eyes behind thin-framed spectacles, gave an air of gentleness, yet, perhaps by the look his wife, Bess, gave in reply, he was unintentionally overbearing, and some part of her resented him for it. No one else seemed to notice this, I don't think even Bess realized it, but I did. I felt it. She and I shared that common bond of being controlled by those we loved.

"Oh, yes. Of course," Bess said.

"But he said he'll see you later this evening, Mother," Birdie reassured.

"And he said he'll see you at the card tables this evening, Stead," chided Gracie.

"Is that so?" Stead began. "That swindler still owes me a small fortune after our crossing on the *Lusitania* last summer."

"He says he'll go double or nothing," Gracie continued.

"Well then, I guess dinner's on me tonight, ladies and gentlemen!" Stead laughed, raising a toast to the table.

Everyone chuckled.

"I might just have to join you fellas," said Gladys.

"Gladys, really," scolded the countess.

"A woman who gambles?" Bess gasped, "isn't that a little...?"

"A little what?" pressed Gladys.

"Well... *vulgar*," said Bess.

"Now, Bess, darling, that's no way to talk to—"

"She's fine, Mr. Allison," interjected Gladys. "She's just speaking her mind. Something every woman should have the right to do. I prefer the term progressive. I am a rather progressive woman, yes. Gambling, drinking, I might even smoke a cigar if the mood strikes me."

"Gladys, honestly," said the countess, embarrassed.

"She's just speaking her mind," Birdie chimed in.

All eyes turned on my sister, unsure whether it was her immaturity, ignorance, or lack of pedigree that would allow her to think it appropriate, or even permissible, to talk back to the countess in such a way. In Birdie's defense, perhaps it was her ability to know just when and how to strike. A quality that, before that very moment, I had never realized as her superpower. The collective gaze shifted back to the countess, this time to see how she'd react. Would her face flush with anger? Would she lose control? Would she pontificate a sonnet of sarcasm wrapped in a bouquet of lush floral prose, as only a royal could do?

She did none of these. She merely smiled, then began laughing.

As the awkward tension of the table demanded, we all followed suit, laughing louder and louder as though this were the funniest thing said all evening.

"Oh, my dear Margaret, you are so right. Every woman has the right to speak her mind, hasn't she?"

"She should," Birdie nodded, "but she doesn't."

"Margaret," Mother implored, "we've talked about this. This is hardly the time—"

"The right to vote, you mean?" Bess sat up, quickly finding her bearings in the conversation.

"That's right," Birdie said.

"Ah, yes," said the countess, "I've been reading about that. Sounds like your American women are putting up quite the fight."

"It's more than a fight," Birdie said, "it's a movement. First America, then the world. Soon every woman will be able to exercise their God-given right to vote."

"Hear, hear," Bess raised a glass, then lowered it quickly when she realized that all, especially her husband, gave her a look that made her second-guess her gesture.

"My dear Margaret," Gracie began, "Countess. Ladies. You know I am all for the fairer sex. You will never meet a man who is more willing to assist in any way that he can..."

"But...?" Dorothy, who'd been silent until now, sizing up her audience, shot the colonel a dangerous look.

"But, my dearest Dorothy, there is a reason that this simply cannot be."

"And, what, my dear colonel, would be that reason?" the countess asked.

"War," said Gracie.

A small eruption of whispers and murmurs swelled amongst the party. Gracie went on.

"That's right, war. It's a well-known fact that many believe a world war is inevitable before the end of this decade."

"Poppycock," said Stead.

"Now, now, W.T. I know that you have your views on peace, and believe me, I wish I shared them. But I wish you well," said Gracie.

"What do war and women having the right to vote have in common?" Birdie quipped.

"Everything," Gracie waved a finger. "You see, war is a very complex issue. It's not just fighting. It's political unrest. It's economic turmoil, yet, if played correctly, an economic windfall. It's industry. It's technology and engineering..."

"What does any of that have to do with—"

"My dear Margaret, if you'll just let me, I'll tell you," Gracie condescended. "War has the potential to make or break a nation, especially a fledgling nation like ours. Men have the mental constitution to consider all of these factors when choosing the right leaders to take us into battle. We also have the experience. We've successfully navigated democracy for generations, and we'll continue to do so. I'd say, until the threat of war is over, it's not only advisable that women sit down and keep out of the conversation, it's crucial."

CHAPTER 16

Birdie sat on the edge of her plush settee, the cobalt damask wallpaper and turned mahogany woodwork of her cabin seeming almost too loud, too opulent. Her heart hammered against her ribs to the point she imagined the ship skipping over choppy waves, but the *Titanic* was steady as ever; it was she who was fixed on a dangerous course. *Was she really going to do this?* The plan, hatched with Violet in a moment of shared confidence and frustration, had seemed bold, necessary even, in the afternoon light. Now, with the ornate sconces casting soft glows and the reality of the ship's rigid social strata pressing in, doubts gnawed at the edges of her ever-weakening resolve.

What if they were caught? What would Mother say? What would Father say? Worse, what would Benji say? The thought of his cool, disapproving gaze was almost enough to make her abandon the idea altogether. *You're in over your head, Birdie,* she could almost hear him say. But then she remembered her mother's sharp words over tea, Colonel Gracie's condescending pronouncements at dinner, her own burning desire to know, to see something beyond the gold-plated surface of her existence. *No. She wouldn't back down. She couldn't. She needed this.* Jumping ship now, no pun intended, would mean that they were all right about her. She couldn't live like that. Not anymore.

Taking a deep breath, Birdie stood. Smoothing the fine linen of her tea gown—a fashionable dress that was a few steps more casual than the opulent ensemble she'd been wearing only moments ago at dinner, something she'd chosen to help her blend in a bit better with the trappings of third class—she crossed to the door. Peeking out into the corridor, she waited until a passing couple disappeared around the corner before slipping out, closing her cabin door silently behind her. In this moment, she might as well have been Sherlock Holmes, donning a disguise, stealthily moving about the catacombs of London or Paris, risking it all for a dangerous mission that was crucial for the sake of all mankind: the assurance of another sunrise tomorrow.

The walk to Violet's cabin, located forward of the grand staircase on C deck, a cabin designated for first-class stewardesses, felt illicit. Every footstep on the linoleum tiles seemed too loud, every passing steward a potential alarm-raiser. She kept her head down, focusing on the pattern of the floor, praying she wouldn't encounter anyone she knew.

Finally she reached Violet's corridor. The first leg of her mission was accomplished without incident. The corridor, while still first class, was less ornate than the amidships corridors where the elite suites were, where the Sutherland-Howell family were hopefully fast asleep. Approaching Violet's door, she took one last look around. All was safe, so she gave a soft, hesitant knock.

The door opened a crack, and Violet's face appeared, her expression quickly shifting from professional alertness to a warm, knowing smile.

"Ah, hello again, Birdie. C'mon in," she whispered.

After one final check of the hallway, Violet closed the cabin door behind them.

Just like the corridor outside, Birdie noted the differences between Violet's cabin and hers. No rich wainscoting, no silk wallpaper, no gilt wall sconces. The room was smaller, paneled in white, and featured a single bed with an upper bunk. There was a wardrobe, dressing table, washbasin, and chair. All was perfectly nice, but simple.

"Well, what do you think?" Violet asked, noticing Birdie sizing up the room.

"It's...*nice.*"

"Nothing like the posh cabin you have, but Tommy Andrews sees to it that we're taken care of too."

"Well," Birdie laughed nervously, "are you ready to go?"

"Go *where*? High tea at *the Savoy*?" Violet chuckled.

"Excuse me?"

"Birdie, look at you. If I let you waltz down there wearing that frilly gown...they'll throw us both overboard."

"I picked the most casual gown in my trunk," Birdie sighed.

"I figured as much," Violet said, opening the small wardrobe then began rustling through hangers. "Right then. I've a spare dress. It's plain, but clean. Not precisely your style, I'd wager, but it'll do." She pulled out a simple, dark wool dress, sturdy and unadorned. "And that hair..." Violet gently began removing the pins from Birdie's intricate updo, letting the carefully arranged curls tumble down. "We need something much simpler. A low bun, perhaps. Neat, but not calling attention."

Noticing Birdie's hesitancy, Violet turned away so she could slip out of her dress. As Birdie changed, Violet went on. "No jewelry, mind. And stand up straight, but don't...glide. Walk like you've got somewhere specific to be, not like you're parading for Ascot."

"Alright, alright...I get it," Birdie said, a little annoyed.

"So, uh," Violet, her back still turned to Birdie, decided to test the sincerity of their earlier conversation, "if we're friends now, can I ask you something?"

"Sure."

"Birdie? Is that your real name?"

"Oh. No, my real name's Margaret. Birdie is just a nickname."

"Interesting. What's the story behind it?"

"When my brother and I were little, he couldn't say my name. But my mother would always tell him that he was my big brother and he had to watch out for me. Protect me. Like a mother bird watches over her young. For some reason, he took to calling me Birdie. And the name stuck."

"How sweet," Violet said.

"Yeah, he used to be."

"What do you mean?"

"I don't know. He's just...he's changed, Violet."

"*Changed*?"

"He's moody. Distant. If I didn't know any better, I'd say he was turning into our father."

"Have you tried talking to him about it?"

"I have," Birdie sighed. "He says it's all in my imagination. But it's not, Violet. I know him. There's something bothering him. Something he doesn't want to talk about."

"He will. When he's ready."

"I really hope you're right, Violet. But I just don't know."

As the mood had fallen, Violet vied for an upbeat tone to bring it back around. "Speaking of ready, are you dressed yet?"

"Yes, I just need your help with these buttons."

Violet helped Birdie fasten the plainer dress, then swiftly gathered her hair into a simple knot at the nape of her neck. Looking at Birdie's reflection in the small mirror above the washstand, Violet nodded with satisfaction. "Better. Much better."

"You don't think it's too..."

"Too what?" Violet asked.

"Too plain?" Birdie asked. "I mean, this color really washes me out."

"Nonsense, Birdie," Violet drew both of their gazes to Birdie's face reflecting in the mirror. "Even on the plainest of days, you're still the prettiest thing I ever did see."

Both of them giggled.

"Thank you, Violet. For everything."

Violet gently kissed her new friend on the forehead. The merging of their worlds was so perfectly odd, yet so perfectly perfect.

"Anything for a friend," she said, then a thought occurred to her. "One last thing, Birdie."

"What is it?"

Violet's tone became serious. "Your voice. Your accent. It screams Philadelphia society. Down there," she gestured towards the lower decks, "you'll find plenty of Irish like myself, Scandinavians, Italians...all sorts. But when you do speak to them, try for English. Not the King's English, mind you," she added with a wry smile, "just...plain English. It'll draw less attention than sounding like American royalty."

Looking at both of their reflections in the mirror, as though they were looking at two completely different people, Violet addressed the strangers, "Hello, there, lovely to meet you. My name's Violet. What's yours?"

"Birdie..." Birdie said with a patchwork tongue.

"I'm sorry, what was that?" Violet laughed.

"I said..."

"Berhdie?" Violet laughed harder, trying to imitate her friend.

"Berh, uh, uh, Berhdie," Birdie struggled to get her name out with the fresh accent, even more of a struggle as both of them couldn't stop laughing.

"Right then, *Berhdie*," Violet said, grabbing a shawl for Birdie and adjusting her own dress one final time. "Ready to see how the other half lives?"

Birdie met Violet's gaze, her earlier nervousness replaced by a renewed sense of purpose, tinged with the thrill of disguise.

"Lead the way," she said, her voice steady, still exercising a passable English inflection.

Violet grinned, opened the door cautiously, and together they slipped back out into the corridor, turning not towards the Grand Staircase, but towards the service stairs, tucked safely into linen storage closets, that led down into the heart of the ship.

Level after level they descended, passing crew all the way. Each encounter led to confused smiles, as the crew assumed Birdie was one of them, yet they couldn't quite place her face. Violet handled these moments with practiced ease, offering a quick nod or a brief, non-committal greeting that deflected further scrutiny.

The air grew warmer, thick with the smell of coal dust and boiled vegetables, mingling with the ever-present tang of saltwater. The faint, lively strains of music grew stronger, pulling them onward.

Finally, they emerged onto the main thoroughfare of the lower decks. "Scotland Road," Violet said. It was a stark contrast to the hushed, ornate hallways above. Here, rivets lined the painted steel walls, pipes ran overhead, and the pine plank floor was worn smooth by countless footsteps.

Crew members bustled past with purpose, alongside third-class passengers moving between their cabins and the public rooms. It was a hive of activity, the backstage of the grand performance *Titanic* presented to the world.

Violet led Birdie towards a wide staircase near the bow, from which spilled the full force of the music and boisterous energy they'd heard from above. "Here we are," Violet murmured, pausing at the first stair. "Remember what I said, Birdie. Plain English, walk like you belong, and try not to stare too much."

Ascending those stairs and stepping into the room was like plunging into a different ocean current. The vast space throbbed with life. Bare wooden tables and long slatted benches lined both sides of the room, many occupied by families, men talking animatedly over mugs of ale, and women chatting while keeping an eye on roving children. In the center, a space had been cleared for dancing, couples whirling with joyous abandon – and surprising skill – to the tunes of a fiddle, an accordion, and a boisterous pipe player whose foot tapped furiously in perfect timing. The air vibrated with a cacophony of languages – Irish brogues mingling with Italian, Swedish, and accents Birdie couldn't even place – and unrestrained laughter.

Violet seemed to shed her stewardess persona in an instant. Her eyes lit up, and before Birdie could fully take in the scene, a burly, smiling man with bright red hair bounded into the frame. "Aye, there's me lass!" he said, sweeping Violet out to the dance floor. She laughed, easily falling into the rhythm, becoming just another face in the joyful throng.

"Wait! What do I—? *Great*," Birdie said aloud, watching her companion go. After a moment, she turned her attention back to the room, trying to absorb it all, just as she'd planned. *This was it—the unvarnished reality she'd craved.* She saw hope and weariness etched onto faces, the easy camaraderie between strangers bound by a shared journey, the simple, uninhibited joy of a moment snatched from the hardships many had likely left behind. The hope, the joy, the fear of a new life in a brave new world. It felt more vital, more real, than the carefully curated elegance of the Palm Court.

Her gaze swept the room, catching on details – a mother patiently braiding her daughter's hair, a group of raucous young men roaring with laughter over a shared joke, the dancers spinning faster, cheeks flushed. And then she saw him.

In a corner booth, away from the main swell of the party, a man sat alone. Unlike everyone else, he wasn't drinking, talking, or even watching the dancers. He was reading a small, worn book, his focus absolute, seemingly adrift in his own quiet current amidst the boisterous tide surrounding him. He wasn't dressed poorly, but his clothes – dark trousers, a collarless shirt, a sturdy-looking jacket slung over the back of the bench – looked functional, lived-in. His dark hair curled slightly over his collar, and his face, cast partly in shadow by the overhead light, held a gravity that seemed oddly profound in this setting. It was this stillness, this quiet intensity amidst the noise, that snagged Birdie's attention. He was an island of enigma in a sea of revelry.

Drawn by a curiosity that momentarily eclipsed her self-consciousness, Birdie found herself weaving through the crowd towards his table. She hesitated a moment, suddenly aware of her plain dress and scraped-back hair, feeling like an imposter despite the disguise. Clearing her throat softly, she finally spoke. "Excuse me?"

He looked up, not slowly, but with a quick, sharp glance. His eyes – a surprisingly light grey, almost startling against his dark hair – assessed her in an instant. They held no welcome, only a cool, guarded neutrality.

"Yes?" His voice was low, resonant, with an accent she couldn't immediately place – not quite English, not quite Irish, something else.

"I...I just wondered what you were reading," she managed, instantly regretting the inanity of the question.

He didn't reply at once, his gaze flicking over her simple dress, her unadorned hair, then back to her face. It wasn't the dismissive appraisal she'd half-expected; it was more analytical, searching. He was someone who knew a thing or two about style and class, and he was judging her.

"Poetry," he said finally, his tone flat. He didn't offer a title or author. He looked back down at his book.

Birdie stood awkwardly for a moment. Clearly, the conversation was over before it had begun. But his very reticence, combined with the intense focus she'd observed, made her reluctant to retreat. *Who was this character? There was definitely more to him than met the eye. What was his story? What was he hiding?*

"Is it...*good*?" she asked, pressing slightly.

He sighed, a quiet sound almost lost in the din, and finally looked up again, closing the book over his finger to mark the page. "Why do you care?"

"I enjoy poetry," she replied honestly. "And you seemed very engrossed. It made me curious."

A faint, skeptical smile cracked his rigid face. With this, he earmarked the page, then closed the book and set it on the table so he could fold his arms and eye this peculiar creature before him. "Curiosity killed the cat, they say." He studied her again. "You don't belong down here, do you?"

"What?" Birdie stammered. "What makes you say that?"

"Your hands," he nodded towards them. "They haven't seen a day of real work. And despite the plain dress, you carry yourself...differently."

Birdie felt a flush rise. He saw through the disguise, at least partly. But she wasn't ready to give in, not yet. "Do I?"

"Oh yes, indeed. You know what they say, you can take the girl out of finishing school..."

"Does it really matter where I belong?"

"It *might*," he said cryptically. "This isn't a petting zoo for the upper class-es. People down here have real lives, real problems. They're not exhibits." His tone wasn't harsh but held a note of warning, a weariness that hinted at past encounters. He stood up, moved in close, intimately close, dangerously close, and whispered into her ear, "You're in over your head down here. You should go back upstairs." Then the corner of his mouth drew into a wicked smirk, and he retreated back to his seat and resumed his reading, like there was nothing else left to say on the matter.

His perception, his assumption that she was merely sightseeing, stung. It echoed her own fears of being a fraud. Suddenly her desperation caused her to play the card of courage, or maybe stupidity; whatever it was, it was honest.

"*Fine*. Maybe you're right that I don't belong here," she admitted, finally dropping the accent, throwing both hands down on the table, and pushing herself between him and his book. "But I'm not here to sightsee. My name is Margaret. Margaret Sutherland-Howell." She saw the flicker of surprise in his grey eyes, just as she'd hoped. "And I came down here because I'm tired of polite exhibits myself. I wanted to see something...real."

He stared at her for a long moment, the noise of the room fading into a muted buzz. The name clearly meant something, or perhaps it was the unexpected honesty. The guardedness in his expression didn't vanish, but it softened, replaced by a renewed, sharper interest.

"Margaret Sutherland-Howell," he repeated quietly, testing the name. He gestured, almost reluctantly, to the chair opposite him. "Alright, Margaret Sutherland-Howell who wants to see something real. Sit down. Tell me what's so unreal about your life upstairs that you felt the need to come down here." He closed his book, this time without marking his page, and placed it on the table. His attention, for the first time, was fully on her.

"I could tell you, but first I wanna know your name," Birdie said.

"My name? Is that important?"

"I told you mine."

"I didn't ask."

"Well, I *am*."

"*Asking*?"

"Did I stutter?"

"You American women are demanding, aren't you?"

"You haven't seen a thing yet."

"Charming."

"Your name?"

"Oliver."

"Oliver *what*?"

"Just...*Oliver*."

"You're not going to give me anything more than that?"

"The less you know about me, the better."

"What is that supposed to mean?"

"I thought we were talking about you here?"

"Well I'm talking about you now."

"Well I don't wanna talk about me."

"Why are you trying to be so mysterious?"

"Why are you trying to be so annoying?"

"Who says I'm trying?"

"*Indeed.* I'd say you're *succeeding.*"

"*Thank you.*"

"*You're welcome.*"

Their unbridled banter had become so quick, so perfectly in-sync, that they now found themselves sitting side by side on the bench, bodies touching, faces mere inches apart, the sexual tension between them palpable. His body was warm, as their breaths fought for the space between them, minimal as it was, each moving in and out as if to fill up the void. She could feel her pulse racing. Or was that her heartbeat? Was it his heartbeat? Then, just when Birdie could've sworn he was about to kiss her, her lips wishing he would, he paused, then asked, "So, uh, you said you wanted to see something?"

"I did?" she thought aloud. "I mean...yes. I did. I do."

"*What*?" he asked.

"Well," she gestured to the crowded room, "*this.*"

"A bunch of people having a good time?" he laughed. "They don't allow you to have fun upstairs?"

"Don't mock me," she rolled her eyes.

"I don't understand, Margaret. I mean, you have everything you could possibly want. People who will do anything for you. What could you possibly want that's down here?"

"You still don't get it, do you?"

"No. I really *don't*," he said.

Dejected, Birdie got up from the bench and started to walk away.

"But!" he called after her. She stopped and turned back to face him. He went on, "I want to."

As Birdie stood there, contemplating whether or not to give him a second chance, he summoned the nearby steward and asked for two pints of beer, "one for me and one for the lady," he smiled. As the steward nodded, then went off to grab their drinks, he said, "If you really want to understand us common folk, the best place to start is with a pint. Whataya say?" He gestured to the seat across from him.

With a heavy sigh, Birdie crossed back and joined him at the table.

"Fine. One drink," she said.

And so they talked. Birdie, emboldened, spoke of her frustrations, the suffocating expectations, the feeling of being an ornament. Oliver listened, interjecting occasionally with a dry, insightful comment or a question that cut deeper than she expected. He remained elusive about himself, deflecting personal questions with generalized cynicism about the world, yet she sensed a keen intelligence behind the guarded facade.

The music swelled again, and several couples nearby urged them to join the dancing. Oliver initially refused, but Birdie, caught up in the infectious energy of the room and the surprising connection she felt, persisted. Finally, with a small, self-deprecating shrug, he stood and offered her his hand.

He wasn't a polished ballroom dancer, but he moved with an innate rhythm and a surprising lightness. They joined the edge of the swirling dancers, finding their own space. Amidst the laughter, the stomping feet, and the lively music, Birdie felt a connection forged not just in conversation, but in the shared, simple joy of the moment – a moment utterly removed from the world she knew.

It felt like minutes, but it must've been hours before Violet reappeared, flushed and laughing. "Time to turn back into pumpkins, m'lady," she announced cheerfully. "Best we go before the clock strikes midnight or before someone recognizes you."

Birdie reluctantly pulled away from Oliver. "Thank you, Oliver," she said sincerely. "For the dance. And for listening."

"Don't mistake listening for agreement, Margaret," he replied, that faint, enigmatic smile touching his lips again. "The world upstairs and the world down here...they rarely mix well." It wasn't unkind, but it held the weight of experience.

The journey back up through the service corridors was filled with breathless energy. Tucked safely back in the C deck hallway, they finally let their giddy laughter spill out.

"Oh, Violet, that was...incredible!" Birdie breathed. "Thank you!"

"Told you third class knows how to have a proper time!" Violet grinned. "Though you seemed to find your own entertainment with that handsome chap."

"Oliver," Birdie said, savoring the name. "He's...complicated. But interesting. Very interesting." She recounted snippets of their conversation, his guardedness, the way he'd listened.

"Sounds like he's got secrets," Violet observed shrewdly.

"Probably," Birdie agreed, but the thought only intrigued her more. "Which is why," she added, her eyes shining with determination, "I have to see him again. Tomorrow, Violet. I'm going back."

Violet sighed dramatically, but her eyes were smiling. "You really are something else, Margaret Sutherland-Howell. Something else entirely."

Riiiiing.

The sound of the phone brought me back to the reality of the present. I stared around the dark, desolate room, lined with safe deposit boxes, now desperately reliant on the two table lamps which flanked the phone.

Riiiiing.

"Hello?" I asked, picking up the phone receiver.

"*Will*?" came the woman's voice on the other end of the line.

"Yes," I said.

"Will, it's Mabel. I just wanted to let you know that we'll be closing in ten minutes."

"Of course. I'll wrap things up in here and head out. Thank you."

As I hung up the receiver, my attention went back to the journal. *Now, what do I do with you?* I thought aloud. My head was spinning as I digested the words of *Titanic*'s first day out at sea. I was already seeing my father, my aunt, the grandparents I'd never met, through a very different lens. *I was curious to know more. Should I take the book home? Should I finish reading it tonight? I wanted to. But, no. I needed time for the words to breathe. To take root. Besides, my father kept this journal safely locked away in this room for a reason. What was the reason? Only time would tell.*

CHAPTER 17

"" Scuse me, hun," said the witch.

"Sorry," Edith said, stepping back to allow the woman to pass. Unfortunately she stepped a little too far back and could feel herself step on the foot of the person behind her.

"Hey! Watch it!" said the woman behind her.

Edith spun around to apologize.

"I am so sorry," said Edith.

"Watch where the hell you're walking," said the nun.

"Of course. Again, I'm sorry," said Edith with a smile.

"*Moron*," said the nun, as she huffed away.

Edith took another calming breath, forcing the polite smile to remain fixed. *Hollywood*, she mused, clutching her tray a little tighter. *Where else could you be accosted by a friendly witch and a foul-mouthed nun before you even had your lunch?* She finally reached the service counter, nodding her thanks as a dollop of mashed potatoes and something resembling Salisbury steak landed on her plate. The aroma of overcooked vegetables and gravy filled the air, mingling with the scent of greasepaint and hairspray.

Scanning the crowded room, Edith navigated through a sea of tables occupied by Roman centurions sharing jokes with flapper girls, cowboys deep in conversation with Egyptian handmaidens, and what looked like an entire platoon of WWI doughboys arguing over a board game. Giant feathered headdresses bobbed near dusty Stetsons, plastic swords clanked against cafeteria trays, and the general atmosphere was a unique symphony of clattering cutlery, booming stage voices, and snippets of dialogue from vastly different eras. She finally spotted a small, blessedly empty table where a faux jungle backdrop left over from some forgotten adventure film was serving as a makeshift window curtain.

She'd barely set her tray down, sinking gratefully onto the plastic chair, when two shadows fell over her table.

"Mind if we join you, doll-face?" Larry's voice oozed false charm. He didn't wait for an answer, sliding into the chair opposite her, closely followed by Geoff, who immediately started unwrapping a large sandwich.

Edith suppressed a sigh. *Just what she needed.*

"It's a free country, gentlemen. Or, at least, a free commissary."

"Attagirl," Geoff mumbled around a mouthful of rye bread. "Always liked your spunk."

"How's things, Edie?" Larry asked, leaning forward intimidatingly, ignoring his own lunch tray. "Settling in? Getting a handle on...you know. The transition?"

"I'm managing, Larry, thank you for asking," Edith replied coolly, picking at her potatoes. If she hadn't lost her appetite when it slopped off the lunch lady's spoon, she'd lost it now. She knew this wasn't just friendly lunchtime chatter.

"Good, good," Larry continued, tapping his fingers on the table. "Because, you know, Geoff and I, we've been thinking. About Ben's legacy. About keeping things running smoothly."

"About that deal with Klein over at Fox," Geoff added bluntly.

"Ah," Edith said, finally looking up, her expression carefully neutral. "I thought that might be it."

"Look, Edith," Larry dropped the fragile niceties, his voice hardening slightly. "Ben left things...complicated. You've got his contacts, his unfinished projects. That's big stuff. Too big, maybe, for someone just starting out."

"Especially," Geoff chimed in, wiping mustard from his chin, "when there's serious money on the table. That *Titanic* picture? Klein's chomping at the bit, especially if we can keep Ben's name attached. Survivor angle, you know? Box office gold!"

"Ben made his feelings about that project perfectly clear," Edith stated firmly.

"Ben was...unwell," Larry dismissed with a wave of his hand.

"Guy took his own life, for Christ's sake!"

"Christ?" Edith scoffed. "I thought you were Jewish, Larry."

"The point is, he wasn't thinking straight. This is business, Edith. A million-dollar picture. We just need you to sign over Ben's interest, let us handle the contacts, smooth things over with Klein."

"And what makes you think I'd do that?" Edith asked, meeting Larry's gaze steadily.

"Because," Geoff leaned in now, his voice low and unpleasant, "you're in over your head, sweetheart. This is the big leagues. You're a secretary, a girl Friday. What do you know about producing multimillion-dollar pictures? About dealing with sharks like Klein?"

"I've learned to deal with the two of you," she said.

"You're smart, Edie," Larry conceded patronizingly, "but you're inexperienced. You're a woman trying to play in a man's game. Sooner or later, you'll lose it all. Take the easy way out. Let us handle it. We'll even cut you in for a small piece for your trouble."

Edith felt a cold fury rise within her, but she kept her voice level. "My arrangement with Mr. Howell was outlined quite clearly in his will. I have no intention of relinquishing anything. Now, if you'll excuse me, I'd like to eat my lunch. Or am I gonna have to call the Roman guards over?"

Larry and Geoff exchanged glances, clearly frustrated by her refusal to be intimidated. "Mark my words, Edith," Larry sneered, standing up. "You'll come crawling to us eventually."

"Here, Geoff," Edith reached across the table and handed him a napkin, "ya never did get that mustard."

Both men hesitated, perhaps expecting more argument, but Edith simply retreated back to focusing on her meal. With twin expressions of disgust, they picked up their trays and swaggered away, swallowed back into the costumed chaos.

Edith let out a slow breath, the encounter leaving a bitter taste in her mouth. She stared unseeingly at her rapidly cooling Salisbury steak, the noise of the commissary fading into a dull roar. Just as she was contemplating abandoning lunch altogether, another figure slid into the seat Larry had just vacated.

"Rough crowd?"

Edith looked up, startled, and met my eyes.

"You could say that. Didn't realize the sharks swam in the commissary pool," she sighed.

I caught a fleeting glance of Larry and Geoff as they exited the scene. "Only when they're starving. Larry and Geoff giving you trouble already?"

"Let's just say they haven't wasted any time reminding me of my place," she said wryly. "What brings you slumming it down here? Thought you'd be holed up dealing with...well, everything."

"Needed a break," I admitted. "And I wanted to find you. I, uh...I found something."

I reached into my bag and carefully pulled out the thick, leather-bound journal. I placed it gently on the table between us.

Edith stared at it, her eyes clearly taking note of its age, its well-worn condition. "What is it?"

"It's...my father's," I said, my voice hushed.

"That's what was in the envelope, huh?"

"In a roundabout way, yes. He left it for me, locked away in a safe deposit box. The envelope held the key."

Edith leaned closer, intrigued. "What's inside?"

"His thoughts. His life. Things he never told anyone." I hesitated, then opened the journal carefully, scanning the open page. "He writes about...everything. His childhood, the studio, Mom..." I paused, then looked directly at Edith, my expression intense. "And he writes about the *Titanic*. His experience. What really happened, Edie. Things he never put in that newspaper story."

The very second I uttered the word '*Titanic*', Edith's eyes darted around the commissary, her entire demeanor shifting from curiosity to urgent alarm. "Will, shut the book," she hissed, leaning across the table. "Now. Put it away."

Confused, I closed the journal. "What? *Why*?"

"Did Larry and Geoff see that?" she whispered fiercely.

"Of course not. They were long gone before I sat down. *Why*? What's wrong?"

"Will," Edith's voice was low and intense, "you didn't hear what those two were just saying. They, and Klein, are desperate to make that *Titanic* movie, and they want to use your father's name – the survivor story – to sell it. If they get even a whiff that this journal exists, that it contains his real, unpublished account..." She didn't need to finish the sentence.

My eyes widened in understanding. "They'd try to take it?"

"*Try*? Will, they'd wrestle it from your hands, claim it's studio property, hire a couple henchmen to rough you up and take it...*anything*! They'd twist his words, exploit his trauma...all for box office returns. You cannot let them know about this, do you understand? Not them, not anyone at the studio. Get that journal out of here. Somewhere safe. Far away from prying eyes."

I looked down at the journal, then back at Edith, a new awareness dawning. This wasn't just my father's story; it was his legacy under threat. "Okay," I said, carefully sliding the journal back into my bag. "Okay. Where can we read it? I need to know what's in here, Edie." I reached across the table and took her hand. "And I want to share it with you."

She looked at our hands, then met my gaze.

"*Me*?"

"What do you say?"

Edith thought quickly. "How about breakfast? Tomorrow morning. *Musso & Frank*? Nice and dark in the back booth. No studio types."

"I didn't know they even served breakfast," I said.

"Exactly," she said with a wink.

"Breakfast, then. Tomorrow. *Musso's*. It's a date."

Café Parisien

The red leather booth at Musso & Frank felt like diving into another era, which seemed appropriate given the cargo I was carrying. Hollywood Boulevard buzzed outside the window, but inside, the low lights, dark wood, and scent of strong coffee mixed with stale cigarette smoke created a moody ambiance of quiet sanctuary. It felt miles away from the vibrance of the studio commissary, miles away from Larry and Geoff, miles away from the sudden, unnerving weight Edie's warning had given to my father's journal.

Edie was already there, nursing a black coffee, a file folder tucked beside her on the seat. She looked different away from the studio – softer, maybe, without the professional armor, but her eyes still held that sharp intelligence I was quickly coming to rely on.

"Morning," I said, sliding into the booth opposite her. The worn leather squeaked faintly.

"Morning, Will," she offered a small smile. "Sleep okay? Or were you up all night wondering what other skeletons might be in that book?"

"Something like that," I admitted, placing my canvas bag carefully on the seat beside me. "Mostly wondering if I was doing the right thing, bringing it out again."

"We'll be careful," she reassured me, glancing around the quiet restaurant. "No sharks. Just *us chickens* here this morning."

"Are you two ready to order?" the waitress appeared out of thin air.

"I'll stick with coffee," said Edith.

"And you?" the waitress turned to me.

"Uh...how about a hot chocolate?" I said.

Edie smiled, catching the reference. "You know what, make that *two*."

"Two hot chocolates, coming right up," the waitress said, before disappearing back into the darkness.

I took a deep breath, then reached into the bag. My fingers tingled closing around the familiar, worn leather of the journal. After Edie's timely warning yesterday, bringing it out felt dangerous, almost criminal, even here. I placed it on the table between us, its weight seeming both physical and symbolic.

Edith leaned forward slightly, her gaze fixed on the journal. "Alright, Ben, what do you want to tell us?" she whispered, as though my father himself might answer.

"He wants to say that he's glad you're here," I said, taking her hand in mine once more. She looked deep into my eyes and smiled. "We both are," I said.

"Shall we?" Edie asked.

I nodded, taking a steadying breath. Together, we were about to step back onto the decks of the Titanic, not knowing what secrets or sorrows lay waiting for us between these anxious pages. I opened the cover.

Thursday, April 11th, 1912
At Sea

The gentle, rhythmic vibration of the engines slowly pulled me from sleep. A steadiness that felt eons removed from the near chaos of yesterday's departure. Sunlight streamed through the stained-glass screens covering my portholes, painting shifting patterns of crimson and gold across the cabin's oak panels. I stretched, feeling surprisingly rested despite the whirl of events – the near collision, Father's tense arrival, the charged atmosphere at dinner.

I followed the glowing orbs of sunlight up to the ceiling when a sharp rap sounded at the door.

"Come in," I called, sitting up in my bed, expecting the usual fresh water or morning tea.

A young steward entered, impeccable in his white tunic, holding a small silver serving tray. "A note for you, Mr. Howell."

Curious, I took the folded vellum envelope. My name was elegantly looped across the front, although it wasn't addressed in my mother's hand, nor Birdie's. Breaking the simple wax seal, I unfolded the single sheet inside. The same feminine handwriting carried over to the note within, showy and confident.

Benji,

Forgive the intrusion, but last night was dreadfully dull after you and your charming sister departed. I find myself simply starving and in need of stimulating company to start the day. Might I persuade you to join me for a late breakfast? Say, nine o'clock? Meet me at the Café Parisian – I hear the espresso is simply divine.

Yours,

Dorothy G.

Dorothy Gibson. *The prettiest girl.* Despite my irritation with Father's blatant assessment of her last night, I couldn't deny a certain flutter of... interest? Intrigue? Or perhaps just the vanity of being singled out by the ship's most talked-about beauty. A private breakfast, away from the main Dining Saloon? It certainly beat navigating the political landscape of our assigned table. I scribbled a quick affirmative reply on the back of the note and handed it back to the waiting steward.

"See that Mrs. Gibson receives this promptly."

"Yes, sir. Right away, sir." He bowed slightly and retreated, leaving me to finish dressing with a newfound, unexpected spring in my step.

Meanwhile, in the vast, sunlit expanse of the First Class Dining Saloon, breakfast was indeed a more relaxed affair than the cumbersome ritual of dinner. Crisp white linens still adorned the tables, albeit lacking the romantic glow of those elegant lamps, and stewards moved with silent efficiency, but the dress code was far less stringent. Gentlemen sported tweeds and traveling suits; ladies wore simpler morning dresses or tailored skirts and blouses. The atmosphere hummed with polite conversation and the clinking of coffee cups, less a performance, more a comfortable start to the day.

At the table presided over by Caroline Sutherland-Howell, however, one occupant looked decidedly less refreshed than the others. Birdie stifled a yawn behind her napkin, her eyes feeling heavy despite the bright light pouring through the large bay windows. Last night's adventure – the descent into the vibrant, noisy world of third class, the exhilarating conversations, the dancing, the shared secret with Violet – had left her both energized and utterly exhausted. She'd barely slept, her mind buzzing with the contrasts she'd witnessed and the memory of a quiet man named Oliver reading poetry amidst the revelry.

"More coffee, Margaret darling?" Mother asked, blissfully unaware of the reason for Birdie's fatigue. Mother herself looked radiant, seemingly unperturbed by her husband's absence. He was, she'd announced briefly, still sleeping off the journey from Paris.

"Yes, please, Mother," Birdie murmured, gratefully accepting the cup.

Around the table, the morning's conversation flowed easily. Colonel Gracie recounted an exaggerated anecdote, eliciting polite chuckles. Mr. Stead engaged the Countess of Rothes in a discussion about upcoming lectures, while her cousin Gladys Cherry animatedly debated the merits of different ocean liners with Hudson Allison. Bess Allison listened quietly, occasionally adding a comment, though her gaze sometimes drifted absently towards the windows. It was all terribly civilized, terribly familiar, and, after last night, felt miles away from the raw energy Birdie had experienced below decks.

Her thoughts were interrupted by a sudden flurry of activity near the entrance. "Oh, look, here come those photography fellows again," Gladys remarked, gesturing with her fork.

Miles Force, camera held aloft, strode into the room with his characteristic, slightly brash confidence, followed by his quieter companion, Francis Brown. Brown, too, had his camera ready.

"Capturing breakfast aboard the magnificent *Titanic!*" Miles announced jovially to anyone within earshot, seemingly appointing himself the unofficial documentarian of the voyage. He snapped a picture of a nearby table laden with fruit and pastries, then turned towards their own.

"Good morning, good morning!" Miles beamed his charming smile. "Mind if we immortalize this delightful breakfast scene?"

"Not at all," the Countess replied graciously, adjusting in her seat so that her elegant profile caught the light perfectly. After years of favorable photos in the press, she clearly knew her best angles.

Francis Brown stepped forward, adjusting his lens. "Just trying to get a few more shots before Queenstown this afternoon," he explained with his pleasant Irish accent. "Have to make the most of this incredible ship while I'm aboard!" He focused his camera, ready to capture the relaxed elegance of another meal aboard the world's grandest ship.

Thanks to the mild April morning, the windows in the Café Parisian were ingratiated to remain open, allowing for a soft breeze to carry through the room from end to end. With its red runner carpet, soft green trellis walls complete with faux ivy, soft wicker furnishings, and endless natural sunlight, the effect of the room was effortless and complete. *Café Parisian, indeed.*

I tried my best to enjoy the picturesque scene, but I couldn't stop fidgeting. One, because Dorothy was late. And, two, I kept awkwardly thwarting the obvious glances of two men sitting together at a nearby table. They were distinguished gentlemen, impeccably dressed, observing the room with quiet confidence. Yet, their occasional glances my way felt specific, making my collar feel suddenly tight.

Just as I was considering signaling for my hot chocolate and making an escape, the two men rose and approached my table. The taller of the two, with a military bearing and a neatly trimmed mustache, offered a polite smile.

"Pardon the intrusion, young man," he said, his voice carrying a hint of a Southern accent, softened by years elsewhere. "But we couldn't help noticing you seem to be waiting for someone. As are we."

"I am, yes," I replied, slightly flustered by the direct approach.

"Wouldn't happen to be the charming Mrs. Gibson, would it?" asked the second man, shorter, with kind eyes behind spectacles and an artist's observant gaze.

My surprise must have shown on my face. "As a matter of fact, yes. How did you know?"

The two men exchanged an amused glance. "Small world, or perhaps a small ship," said the taller man. "She asked us to join her for breakfast as well. Seems our hostess is running behind schedule. Might we join you while we wait? Misery loves company, after all." He gestured to the empty chairs.

"Oh. Of course, please," I stammered, feeling slightly off-balance.

They settled into the chairs across the table. "Allow us to introduce ourselves," the taller man continued, extending a hand. "Major Archibald Butt, at your service. Military aide to President Taft."

I shook his hand, registering the name. A prominent figure. "Benjamin Sutherland-Howell the second," I replied. "But please, call me Benji."

"A pleasure, Benji," said the other man, offering his hand in turn. "Francis Millet. Though most call me Frank."

"The artist?" I asked, recognizing the name this time. Millet's murals and paintings were well-known.

"Among other things," Frank Millet smiled gently. "Painter, sculptor, writer… and currently wrestling with the designs for a rather significant memorial back in Washington."

"Frank is being modest," Archie interjected warmly. "He's heading up the design for the Lincoln Memorial."

"And Archie is fresh from Rome," Frank added, turning the attention back to his companion, "delivering sensitive correspondence between His Holiness and the President."

"The… *Pope?*" I asked, astonished.

"Indeed," Archie said.

I took this in. These were important men, confidantes of presidents and popes, shapers of art and architecture. What was Dorothy Gibson playing at, arranging this meeting?

"It seems," Archie mused, catching my bewildered expression, "that our mutual friend, Dorothy, may have orchestrated this little gathering. She does enjoy… connecting people."

"Especially," Frank added, his eyes twinkling behind his glasses, "when she suspects they might have something in common. She has a knack for spotting fellow '*friends of Dorothy,*' you might say."

"*Friends of Dorothy?*" I asked, the phrase unfamiliar, yet sparking a strange, undefinable resonance within me.

Frank Millet didn't answer directly. Instead, he reached across the small space between their chairs and gently, naturally, placed his hand over Archie's where it rested on the arm of the chair. Archie met the gesture with a soft, accepting smile, turning his hand slightly to clasp Frank's. The intimacy of the gesture, so quiet and unassuming yet profoundly open in the sunlit Café, struck me like a physical blow.

"People like *us,*" Frank said softly, his gaze meeting mine with understanding, not judgment. "People… like *you,* perhaps?"

Panic seized me, cold and sharp. My breath caught in my throat. *Me? Like them?* The insinuation, the gentle claim, terrified me. It touched a part of myself

I kept buried so deep, locked away behind walls of steel thicker than any on this ship. I had never allowed myself to even form the thought, let alone consider the possibility. My mind raced, searching for denial, for deflection.

"I... I don't know what you mean," I stammered, looking away, focusing intently on the pattern of the trelliswork behind them.

"Don't you?" Archie's voice was kind, devoid of pressure. "Benji, look around this ship. Look around the world. We're everywhere. Doctors, soldiers, artists, politicians, stewards, millionaires, stokers... living our lives. Sometimes quietly, sometimes... less so."

"It's not an affliction, Benji," Frank added, his hand still covering Archie's. "It's simply who we are. And finding others like oneself... it makes the world feel a little less lonely. Perhaps Dorothy sensed something in you, some shared understanding, and hoped we might... offer some perspective."

I risked looking back at them. Their expressions held no malice, no mockery. Only a calm, reassuring acceptance. They weren't accusing me; they were inviting me. Inviting me to acknowledge a truth I'd spent years denying, even to myself. The fear was still there, a lead weight in my stomach, but mixed with it now was a fragile, terrifying flicker of something else. Hope? Relief?

The silence stretched, filled only by the distant clatter of cups and the soft sea breeze. Could it be true? Could this hidden, nameless feeling I carried actually be... normal? Shared? Could I be like these distinguished, successful men?

My gaze dropped to my own hands, twisting nervously in my lap. The words felt lodged in my throat, heavy and unfamiliar. Finally, drawing a shaky breath, I looked up, meeting Frank Millet's steady, kind eyes.

"*Yes,*" I whispered, the single word barely audible, yet feeling like the loudest sound I'd ever made. "I think... I think I *am.*"

A gentle smile warmed Archie's face. Frank squeezed his hand, sweetly. There was no grand reaction, no dramatic pronouncement. Just a quiet, profound sense of understanding passing between the three of us in the sun-drenched Café Parisian, as the *Titanic* steamed steadily onward towards Ireland.

As my mind set its course for uncharted territories, strange new worlds, *Titanic* was on approach to one of her own. As she'd been constructed in Belfast, it wasn't technically her first time in Ireland, but this would be her first visit to Queenstown. The picturesque port on the Emerald Isle was always the second port of call, after Cherbourg, for the *Olympic*-class, and just about every other liner to cross the North Atlantic.

Strategically, this was an important stopover, not only a chance to deliver mail that had been picked up in England or France, or those remaining letters written by *Titanic* passengers and posted on the ship, but it was a chance to pick up a large number of Irish immigrants, eager to try their odds at fame and fortune, or even just a comfortable life, in the brave new world.

Like the previous night, the mammoth ship found herself too big to enter the shallow port, so she'd need to once again drop anchor in the deep waters, while a carefully choreographed routine of tender boats danced across the white-washed waves to meet her.

In addition to their complement of immigrants, these small boats brought a swarm of Irish artisans—their handmade wares in tow—to make a few quick bucks selling their wool sweaters, their intricate lace, to American millionaires looking for a bargain.

The air on the Promenade Deck buzzed with a different kind of energy than Southampton or Cherbourg. Less formal departure, more bustling marketplace meets final farewell. Stewards directed the flow of traffic near the entry doors where passengers would soon board or disembark via the tenders, *America* and *Ireland*, bobbing patiently below. But further along the deck, under the watchful eyes of the ship's officers, the Irish vendors had quickly set up impromptu stalls, draping sturdy railings and empty deck chairs with their colorful goods.

The rich scent of damp wool from Aran sweaters mingled with the salty air. Women with nimble fingers displayed intricate lacework – collars, shawls, handkerchiefs – their delicate patterns a stark contrast to the rugged faces of the fishermen selling sturdy caps and knitwear. The sound of bargaining, mostly good-natured, filled the air, a lively chorus of Irish brogues and American drawls.

My attention was drawn to a small crowd gathered near the aft end of the starboard promenade. In the center stood John Jacob Astor, looking every bit the American aristocrat, despite the casual tweed jacket he wore. Beside him, his young wife Madeleine looked pale and slightly overwhelmed by the commotion, leaning lightly on his arm. Astor, however, seemed engaged, examining a large, exquisitely detailed lace shawl held up by a stout, rosy-cheeked woman.

"It's the finest work, sir, finest in all of Cork," the lacemaker was saying earnestly. "Took me months, it did. Fit for a queen, or your lovely lady there." She nodded towards Madeleine, who offered a weak smile.

"It's fine work, I grant you," Astor replied, his voice calm and measured as he ran a discerning finger along the edge. "But your price is rather... ambitious, wouldn't you say? Even for a queen."

"Ah, but the quality, sir! Feel the weight of it! Pure Irish linen thread, every stitch by hand," the woman countered, though a flicker in her eyes suggested she knew the haggling dance well.

They went back and forth for several minutes, a performance of sorts, Astor pointing out supposed minor flaws, the woman extolling the virtues of her craft. Finally, a price was agreed upon – doubtless still exorbitant by Irish standards, but likely a fraction of what such a piece would cost on Fifth Avenue. Astor produced a roll of bills, peeled off several notes, and the shawl was carefully folded and handed over. He draped it gently around Madeleine's shoulders; she touched it absently, her thoughts seemingly elsewhere, but offered her husband a grateful look.

Several decks below, a different scene unfolded. A steady stream of third-class passengers, clutching worn valises and bundled possessions, were making their way from one of the tenders up the gangway, their faces a mixture of awe, apprehension, and determined hope as they stepped aboard the colossal liner that represented their passage to a new life. Stewards guided them efficiently towards the stern entrances.

Amidst this bustle, I joined Frank Millet and Archie Butt near the promenade railing, as they were waving goodbye to Francis Brown below. Father Brown, as I'd heard some call him, a Jesuit priest-in-training, had befriended Archie when they found common ground on taking audience with the Pope. With his ticket calling for him to disembark in Ireland, his once-in-a-lifetime voyage on the *Titanic* was now behind him, although he'd have countless stories and the photographs to back them up when he resumed his studies at seminary. He clapped Miles Force on the shoulder – Miles having appeared to see his shipboard friend off – before turning towards the gangway leading down to the tender.

"Got everything, Frank?" Archie called out.

"More photos than I know what to do with!" Brown grinned back up at them, patting the camera bag slung over his shoulder. "Give my regards to the President, Archie! And *Benji*," he caught my eye and gave a friendly nod, "enjoy the rest of the journey!"

He disappeared down the gangway onto the deck of the waiting tender. As the small boat prepared to cast off, laden with departing passengers, mail bags, and the now-packing-up vendors, Francis Brown raised his camera one last time. He braced himself against the tender's railing as it pulled away, framing the immense, majestic profile of the *Titanic* against the backdrop of the Irish coast. The click of his shutter felt strangely significant, capturing the last image of the great ship touching land before she turned her bow towards the vast, open Atlantic.

The ship's mighty whistles blew, signaling departure. The engines changed pitch, the steady vibration returning. Below, the tender carrying Father Brown grew smaller, just another boat heading back to the picturesque harbor. Slowly, majestically, *Titanic* began to move, leaving the Emerald Isle behind, her prow pointed west, towards the promise – and the perils – of the New World. The journey had truly begun.

Thwack. Thwack. THWACK.

The rhythmic impact of my fists against the taut leather punching bag echoed in the bright, airy gymnasium. Each blow was fueled by a confusing maelstrom of feelings leftover from breakfast – fear, disbelief, a terrifying spark of something like relief, all tangled together. Thwack. *People like us.* Thwack. *Like you, perhaps?* THWACK. *Yes.*

The word still hung in the air of my mind, fragile and monumental. Saying it aloud, even in a whisper, felt like cracking open a door I never knew existed, revealing a landscape that was both foreign and disturbingly familiar. I punched harder, grunting with the effort, trying to expel the swirling thoughts with sheer physical force. Could Father Brown see it? Could Miles? Could my own father sense this... this *difference* in me?

Sunlight streamed through the gymnasium's large windows overlooking the Boat Deck, reflecting off of the glossy white floor to illuminate the state-of-the-art equipment: the electric horse, the electric camel, stationary bicycles, weight machines, and the impressive double rowing machine that sat center stage. For a Thursday afternoon, just hours after leaving Queenstown, the space was remarkably empty. Only one other person was present – the ship's fitness instructor, overseeing the room.

He was a compact, barrel-chested man with sturdy limbs and watchful eyes, dressed in crisp flannel whites. I'd seen him observing me from across the room as I relentlessly assaulted the punching bag. Now, he ambled over, wiping his hands on a towel slung around his neck.

"Putting up quite a fight there, son," he remarked, his tone neutral but observant. His name, according to the brass plate near the entrance, was T.W. McCawley.

I paused, breathing heavily, sweat dripping down my temples. "Just... working out some kinks, Mr. McCawley."

"Indeed," he nodded, eyeing the swinging bag. "Good for the arms, that. Good for clearing the head. But if it's a real challenge you're after, something to truly test your mettle..." He gestured towards the center of the room. "Might I suggest our rowing machine? Works the back, the legs, the lungs... gives you a proper full-body workout. Nothing quite like it."

I looked over at the gleaming apparatus of polished wood and nickel-plated steel. It looked imposing, complicated. Another challenge. Maybe that's what I needed – a physical test so demanding it would leave no room for thought, no space for the terrifying implications of that conversation in the café.

"Alright," I agreed, stepping away from the punching bag.

"Excellent choice, young man," McCawley beamed, suddenly all professional enthusiasm. "Right this way. We can row together, simulate a proper race, eh?"

He took one sliding seat, gesturing for me to take the other. I settled in, gripping the smooth wooden oars. While McCawley was offering brief instructions on form, the sliding seat mechanism, the resistance settings, I could feel my mind wandering. Strangely, given this newfound freedom, I subconsciously allowed my eyes to drift to the body of the man who now sat directly across from me. The shape of his powerful chest, his narrow tapered waist. I found myself wondering how his body looked beneath the flannels. The male form was something I'd always forced out of my mind, but now, it felt exciting to consider it freely. My body tingled as he reached across and took my hand in his to relax my grip on the oars. I kept looking away to try and remain inconspicuous. So strange was the feeling, sitting side-by-side with this instructor, about to engage in simulated exertion while my mind felt like it was truly rowing for its life against a terrifying tide.

"*Ready*?" McCawley asked, gripping his own oars. "On three. One... two... three!"

We pushed off, the seats sliding back, the oars pulling against the machine's internal mechanisms. I focused on the rhythm, the burn starting almost immediately in my shoulders and thighs. McCawley kept up a steady, powerful pace beside me, offering occasional pointers. But mostly, I rowed. I rowed with a desperate intensity, pouring every ounce of confusion, fear, and fragile, nascent hope into the physical act. Each pull, each slide, was an attempt to outrun the echo of Frank Millet's gentle question, to push back against the terrifying, exhilarating possibility that Archie Butt had laid bare. Faster and faster, I rowed, the state-of-the-art machine groaning slightly under the strain, trying desperately to leave my own thoughts lost somewhere in my wake on the sunlit floor of the gymnasium, somewhere in the middle of the vast, indifferent Atlantic.

While I was trying to find solace by beating back my own demons in the gymnasium, an exhausted Birdie would find none in the restless pacing of the forward Promenade Deck. Her thoughts were consumed by the events of the previous night, circling inevitably back to the enigmatic Oliver. The thrill of their clandestine meeting, the spark of connection, the mystery surrounding him – it left her agitated, unable to settle into the quiet rhythm of an afternoon at sea.

The ship was now well clear of the Irish coast, steaming westward into the vast Atlantic. Most passengers seeking air had migrated towards the stern, hoping for final, receding glimpses of land, or perhaps simply congregating where the deck chairs were more plentiful. Here, near the bow, the decks were relatively deserted, the wind carrying a sharper, cleaner salt tang. Below her vantage point on B Deck, the forward Well Deck – an open space designated for third-class passengers – was similarly quiet, though not entirely empty.

A sturdy gate, a sign forbidding third-class passengers to pass through it, and a steep set of stairs clearly demarcated the boundary between the classes, a physical manifestation of the invisible lines she'd crossed last night. Birdie leaned against the railing, gazing down, her eyes scanning the figures below, though she knew it was illogical. What were the chances Oliver would be out here? Still, she couldn't shake the image of him, sitting alone, reading, amidst the boisterous crowd.

Just then, two young women emerged onto the Well Deck from a companionway, laughing together as they strolled towards the bow railing, their simple shawls pulled tight against the breeze. They were clearly third-class passengers – perhaps Irish girls who had just boarded in Queenstown. An idea, impulsive and perhaps foolish, sparked in Birdie's mind.

"Excuse me!" Birdie called down, her voice carrying easily in the quiet air.

The two women stopped, looking up in surprise, shielding their eyes against the afternoon sun. Seeing a first-class lady addressing them was clearly unexpected.

"Yes, Miss?" one of them called back, her accent unmistakably Irish.

"I was wondering," Birdie began, feeling suddenly awkward, "if you might know someone. I'm looking for a gentleman passenger. His name is Oliver."

The two women exchanged a puzzled glance. "Oliver, is it?" the first one asked. "And what might his family name be, Miss?"

Birdie flushed. "I... I'm afraid I don't know," she admitted, feeling incredibly naive.

The second woman giggled. "Looking for a fella and don't even know his proper name? Having a bit of fun last night, were we?"

"It wasn't like that," Birdie insisted quickly, though the women's knowing smiles made it clear that she hadn't convinced them. "He's got dark hair. Grey eyes. Quiet. Keeps to himself mostly. You've probably seen him reading, even when everyone else is singing or dancing."

Recognition dawned on the first woman's face. "Oh! You mean the writer!"

"The writer?" Birdie echoed, caught completely off guard. Oliver, a writer? It hadn't occurred to her. It somehow deepened the mystery surrounding him. "Is that what people call him?"

"Aye," said the second woman. "Always got his nose in a book or scribblin' away in a little notebook. Keeps himself apart, mostly. A bit moody, some say."

"Do you know where he might be now?" Birdie asked eagerly.

"Likely down in the General Room right below our feet, Miss," the first woman replied. "Same as usual. Reading all alone on a bench in the corner, I'd wager."

Hope surged in Birdie. "Could you possibly... would you do me a great favor? Could you go down and tell him Margaret is looking for him? Ask him if he might come up?"

The women looked hesitant, exchanging another glance. "Well now, Miss," the first one started, "it's not really our place..."

"And what's in it for us, then, eh?" the second added. "It would seem as though this might be something important for you, Miss."

Birdie didn't like the woman's tone, nor the seemingly selfish insinuation that a kind act must be bought, but her desperation made her bold. On the lapel of her walking suit, she wore a small, tasteful brooch – gold filigree set with a modest diamond chip. It wasn't one of her most expensive pieces, but it was valuable nonetheless.

Quickly unclasping it, she held it up. "Perhaps this might persuade you?"

The women's eyes widened at the sight of the glittering brooch. Diamonds, even small ones, were likely beyond their wildest dreams.

"If you fetch him for me," Birdie said clearly, "it's yours."

The hesitation vanished instantly. "Right away, Miss!" the first girl grinned, her tongue wagging.

Excited by the prospect of getting what she came for, Birdie tossed it to the women.

"We'll tell him Margaret's waiting!" said the woman who caught it.

"Thank you!" Birdie called as they scurried away, disappearing back down the companionway, giddy whispers trailing behind them.

Birdie leaned against the railing again, her heart pounding now for a different reason. Had she really just bribed two passengers with jewelry? She knew how it must've looked. But the anticipation of seeing Oliver again quickly overshadowed her concerns. She waited, scanning the companionway entrance below, expecting him to emerge at any moment.

Minutes ticked by. The two women didn't reappear. Doubts began to creep back in. Had they simply taken the brooch and run? Had Oliver refused? Or worse, had they laughed at her request as soon as they were out of sight? She pictured them showing the brooch off below decks, recounting the tale of the naive first-class girl looking for a man whose name she didn't even know. She felt foolish, exposed. Her cheeks burned with embarrassment. Maybe Benji was right. Maybe she was in over her head.

Just as she was convincing herself she'd been duped, just as she turned away from the railing, ready to retreat in humiliation, a low voice called up from the Well Deck below.

"Looking for someone, Margaret Sutherland-Howell?"

She spun back around. There, standing near the base of the dividing staircase, hands tucked into his pockets, stood Oliver. He wasn't smiling; his expression was as unreadable as ever, but his grey eyes were fixed on hers. He had come.

"I wanted to see you again," she said, crossing to the gate at the top of the stairs.

"Well, here I am. I hope you got your money's worth," he said.

"Oh, Oliver. Please, I wanted to continue our conversation from last night."

"I'm listening."

"Can't you come closer?" she asked. "I feel so stupid shouting this for the whole world to hear."

"You come closer," he said. "I'm content to stay in my world. You're the one who can't stay put."

"I can't come any closer," she said, pounding her fists on the waist-high gate. "Climb the stairs, won't you?"

"I'm not moving. If you want to talk, you'll come to me."

"What am I supposed to do, climb over this silly thing?" she asked, annoyed. Why did his being obstinate make her want him all the more?

"Just open the gate, Birdie," he said.

Birdie? she thought to herself. *I never told him that I was called Birdie.*

"But the signs—"

"It's not locked."

Sure enough, he was right. She looked at the signs. Their bold letters were warning enough to make her think twice before being defiant. Effective marketing. Apparently she wasn't the disruptor she'd imagined herself to be after all. With a deep breath, a quick look around to make sure there were no witnesses, she opened the gate and casually descended the steps to the third-class deck, as if it were all just routine.

Oliver waited for her at the bottom of the steps, that beguiling smirk both thrilling and infuriating her. She half-waited for him to praise her act of defiance, to say that he was wrong about her living by-the-book, but instead he just said, "What? No disguise?"

"Disappointed?" she rolled her eyes.

"Not at all," he said. "In fact, I rather like you this way."

"Oh yeah?"

"Yeah," he said, pausing for dramatic effect, then, "because that accent was bloody awful."

She gave him a quick punch to the arm as the pair erupted with laughter.

Oliver pulled out his cigarettes, lit one in his mouth, took a long drag, then exhaled plumes of smoke through his nostrils.

"Mind if I try?" she asked, gesturing to the cigarette.

"You smoke?" he asked skeptically.

Without a word, she took the cigarette, and after taking her own drag, blew the smoke directly into his face.

"You were saying?" she chuckled.

"You are full of surprises," he said.

"You called me Birdie."

"Yeah? It's your nickname, right?"

"Who told you that?"

"You did, last night."

"No, I didn't."

"Of course you did. How else would I know that?" he asked.

True. But she could have sworn that she intentionally never mentioned it last night. What's more, some part of her felt odd hearing him call her that.

"Speaking of secrets," she decided to change the subject, "I've discovered yours. Mr. Writer!"

"Those two women don't know what they're—"

"It all makes sense now!" Birdie delighted.

"Does it now?"

"The moodiness. The sulkiness. The strong sense of moral-superiority..."

"Well, when you put it like that..." he feigned, not quite serious, but not quite laughing.

"Oh, don't be like that," she said. "My brother's a writer, you know."

"Is that so?"

"Mmhmm."

"You come from a family of writers, do you?" he asked.

"Oh no. Just Benji."

"What about your mother?"

"My mother's a socialite. Through and through. I don't think even she knows who she truly is or what she wants out of life. She just keeps up with appearances."

"And... what about your father?"

"Father?"

"Yes. What does he do?"

"My father owns several very large steel mills. He has exclusive contracts with at least three mainline railroads. They exclusively use his steel to lay their tracks. His mills keep up with the aggressive demand. It's a win-win."

"Sounds like your father surrounds himself with some very powerful men."

"I suppose so."

As the words left her lips, Birdie felt a subtle shift in the air between them. It wasn't overt, but Oliver's easy smirk seemed to fade slightly, his grey eyes sharpening with an intensity that felt different from the challenging curiosity he'd shown before. His question about her father hadn't been idle chatter; there was a focus there, a specific weight behind the inquiry about *powerful men* that snagged her attention.

Why the sudden interest in Father's business dealings? Their conversation had meandered from playful banter about accents and writing to her family dynamics, but this felt... pointed. His tone, when he'd made the remark about her father surrounding himself with powerful men, hadn't held the same light, teasing quality as before. It was flatter, perhaps, maybe even carrying a trace of something else... cynicism? Resentment? It was hard to pinpoint, but it struck her as odd, discordant with the connection she'd felt building between them only moments ago over shared laughter and a cigarette.

She studied his face, searching for a clue in his carefully neutral expression. Who was this man, who could shift so quickly from guarded poet to challenging interrogator, who knew her nickname without being told, and who now seemed strangely interested in the sphere of influence her father commanded? The mystery surrounding him deepened, no longer just romantic or intriguing, but now tinged with a faint, unsettling edge of calculation. She shivered slightly, though the breeze hadn't strengthened.

Oliver seemed to register her sudden quietness, his expression softening again, the enigmatic mask settling back into place. He took a final drag from his cigarette and flicked it expertly over the railing into the churning sea below. The moment stretched, the comfortable silence replaced by one freighted with unspoken questions. He met her gaze, holding it for a beat longer than necessary, before giving a slight, almost invisible nod, as if acknowledging a shift only they could feel. The easy camaraderie of moments ago felt suddenly fragile, complicated by the shadows cast by her father's distant power and Oliver's opaque past.

For the first time, Birdie questioned her decision to venture out of her world and into the bewildering third class.

CHAPTER 19

The rhythmic pulse of the ship had, by now, become a familiar backdrop, a constant low hum beneath the plush carpet of my cabin. The intense physical exertion in the gymnasium had exhausted my body, but my mind, unfortunately, remained stubbornly active. I sat at the small writing table, the leather-bound journal open before me, trying to capture the whirlwind of the morning – the unnerving anticipation in the Café Parisian, the quiet revelation offered by Archie Butt and Frank Millet, the terrifying, liberating whisper of acceptance. How could a single conversation shift the foundations of my entire world?

Knock, knock, knock.

The sound startled me. I quickly closed the journal, instinctively shielding its private contents. Guests rarely called unannounced at cabins during the afternoon lull.

"Who is it?" I called out, keeping my voice even, trying to mask the lingering turmoil.

"Benji? It's Dorothy. Dorothy Gibson." Her voice, though muffled by the heavy oak door, was unmistakable, carrying a note of hesitant worry.

Dorothy? Now? After abandoning me – or rather, *us* – at breakfast? I walked cautiously to the door, my hand hovering over the latch. What could she possibly want?

Steeling myself, I opened the door. She stood there in the corridor, looking genuinely apologetic, her usual bright confidence dimmed ever so slightly. Even her fashionable afternoon dress seemed less vibrant than her usual attire.

"Oh, Benji," she began immediately, her eyes searching mine, "do you hate me?"

The question disarmed me. I had wanted to be angry, furious even, at her blatant matchmaking, at being put in such an exposed, unexpected position. But the encounter she'd orchestrated... it had changed something fundamental.

"Hate you?" I echoed, stepping back to allow her entry. "No, Dorothy. I don't hate you."

She stepped inside, glancing around my suite with perhaps less enthusiasm than she might have otherwise shown. "May I?" she asked, gesturing towards the settee. I nodded, closing the door behind her.

She perched on the edge of the seat, tugging at the fabric of her skirt nervously. "I owe you an apology, Benji. For this morning. It was terribly presumptuous of me, arranging things like that without... well, without asking."

I sat in the armchair opposite her. "I admit, I was... surprised. And perhaps a little annoyed that you left me waiting."

"I know, it was dreadful of me," she rushed on. "But Archie and Frank are such dear men, truly pillars, you know? And I just had this feeling... when I met you yesterday, talking with you and your sister... there was just *something*. I thought you might enjoy their company, find some common ground perhaps. I hoped... well, I hoped you might find them as reassuring as I do." She looked up at me hopefully, then her face fell slightly. "But it was meddling. I shouldn't have interfered. If I caused you any embarrassment—"

I held up a hand, stopping her apology. "Dorothy," I began, searching for the right words. "Like I said, I wanted to be angry. I wanted to hate you for putting me on the spot, for... for *assuming*." The memory of the panic that had seized me in the café briefly resurfaced. "But," I took a breath, the next words feeling both strange and freeing on my tongue, "I can't. Because... you were right."

Her eyes widened slightly. "Right?"

"Meeting Archie and Frank... talking with them... it was..." I hesitated, the lifetime of suppression making vulnerability feel like shedding skin. "It helped me, Dorothy. More than you can know. You inadvertently gave me the courage to... to finally come to terms with some things. Things I've wrestled with my entire life." I looked away, unable to hold her gaze as I admitted this truth aloud for only the second time.

A soft silence fell between us. When I looked back, Dorothy's expression was one of gentle understanding, devoid of shock or pity.

"Oh, Benji," she said softly, reaching out to briefly touch my hand. "I'm so glad. Truly."

We sat in comfortable silence for another moment, the shared, unspoken understanding creating a new kind of intimacy between us. Finally, the question that had been nagging at the back of my mind surfaced.

"Dorothy," I asked, meeting her eyes directly now. "There's something I have to... how? How did you *know*? I never said anything. Not to you, not to anyone."

She smiled, a knowing, gentle expression. "No, you didn't say anything," she agreed. "But sometimes, my dear Benji, it's everything someone *doesn't* say that speaks the loudest."

"I don't understand."

"Darling," she leaned forward, her voice understanding and kind, "I grew up in and around the theatre. My mother, bless her, I fancy that she's always lived out her dreams through me. So, you see, I've spent my life surrounded by actors, artists, writers, musicians... creative, sensitive souls. You learn to see things. A certain reserve, a way of holding oneself apart even in a crowd, a flicker in the eye when certain topics arise... nuances. Things you perhaps don't even realize you're projecting." She shrugged delicately. "I recognized things I've seen over the years. I simply... put two and two together. Hoped I wasn't wrong."

I absorbed her words. It wasn't magic, wasn't mind-reading. It was observation, intuition, honed by experience in a world perhaps more understanding, or at least more observant, of such things than my own rigidly defined upbringing. It was strangely comforting.

"Thank you, Dorothy," I said, and this time, the gratitude was entirely sincere. "For seeing it. And for... well, for the introduction."

She beamed, her usual sparkle returning. "Any time, darling. Absolutely any time."

The strains of the string quintet drifted softly through the elegant Reception Room, providing a soothing backdrop to the gentle clinking of teacups and murmured conversations. Sunlight, now angled lower in the sky, still poured through the tall, stained-glass windows, warming the white-paneled walls and highlighting the plush crimson of the Axminster carpet. Afternoon tea was in full swing, a cherished ritual of civilized leisure aboard the *Titanic*.

At a wicker table nestled amongst potted palms, Birdie sat with Mother, the Countess of Rothes, and her cousin, Gladys Cherry. Dainty sandwiches, scones with clotted cream and jam, and an array of delicate pastries adorned the tiered stand between them. While the Countess recounted an amusing anecdote about a recent charity bazaar, Birdie found her own attention drifting. Across the room, near the grand piano, sat Bruce Ismay and Captain Smith, engrossed in what appeared to be a serious discussion at their small table. Yet, more than once, Birdie intercepted a fleeting glance that passed between Mr. Ismay and her mother. Mother would meet his gaze for just a fraction of a second, a subtle softening around her eyes, before turning back to the conversation at their table with perhaps just a touch more animation. It was discreet, yet Birdie saw it, a silent conversation happening just beneath the surface of polite society. Clearly, despite the fact that Father was now aboard, Mother and Ismay were continuing their liaison.

Gladys laughed at the Countess's story, then turned to Birdie. "You're very quiet this afternoon, Margaret. Still contemplating world peace after Mr. Stead's lecture at lunch?" she teased gently.

Birdie smiled, deciding to lean into the reputation she seemed to be acquiring. "Not peace, precisely," she began, setting down her teacup. "But I was reading an article Mr. Stead recommended about the proposed income tax in America. It's rather fascinating, don't you think?"

The shift in topic drew a surprised look from Mother, but the Countess leaned forward with interest. "Ah, yes. Income tax. A subject causing considerable consternation on both sides of the Atlantic, I assure you," she sighed, delicately selecting a cucumber sandwich. "It puts a rather dreadful strain on things."

"A strain, Countess?" Birdie asked, genuinely curious. "How so?"

"My dear girl," the Countess lowered her voice slightly, though her tone remained poised. "Much of the aristocracy, the 'old guard' as some call it, relies on income from land, from investments passed down through generations. Fortunes built over centuries. This new notion of taxing income directly... well, it changes the landscape entirely. It's not like the fortunes being made overnight in steel or railroads or..." she paused delicately, no doubt thinking of Father and his businesses, "...*other industries*. Our sort of wealth isn't designed for constant liquidation to pay yearly taxes. It forces one to seek... alternative investments."

"Alternative investments?" Birdie prompted.

The Countess gave a wry smile. "Indeed. In fact, that's part of my own business in the States. After visiting family, I'm traveling on to California. Pasadena, specifically."

"Pasadena?" Mother inquired politely. "How lovely. For pleasure?"

"Partly," the Countess admitted. "But primarily to view some orange groves. Apparently, citrus farming is proving quite profitable, a reliable source of taxable income to... supplement the traditional estates, you see. One must adapt to the times, mustn't one? Especially with the middle classes becoming so..." she searched for the word, "...prosperous." The unspoken concern about the shifting balance of wealth and power hung in the air.

"Speaking of adapting," Gladys interjected, perhaps sensing the slightly heavy turn, "where is your husband keeping himself, Caroline? I hope he's not avoiding our stimulating company?"

Mother placed a hand delicately to her chest, adopting an expression of concern. "Oh, the poor dear," she sighed, just loudly enough for Mr. Ismay, who happened to glance over at that precise moment, to potentially overhear. "Benjamin hasn't been feeling at all the thing since we left France. Terribly seasick, I'm afraid. He's barely left the cabin. Prefers to suffer in silence, you know how men can be."

Birdie nearly choked on her tea. *Seasick?* Her father? The man who'd crossed the Atlantic countless times without a hint of malaise? She caught the Countess's eye, saw a flicker of something – skepticism? Polite disbelief? – before it was masked by sympathetic concern. Birdie quickly looked down at her plate, avoiding Mother's gaze, the fabricated excuse hanging awkwardly amongst the delicate aroma of Earl Grey and petit fours. The intricate dance of appearances, it seemed, continued unabated.

Dinner, Thursday Evening

Feeling lighter than I had in years, yet paradoxically burdened by the weight of newfound self-knowledge, I left my cabin as the bugle sounded its cheerful call to dinner. Dorothy had insisted I escort her, a request I now accepted not with apprehension, but with a quiet sense of gratitude for her unlikely allyship.

Walking down the corridor towards her cabin, I nearly collided with Miles Force, heading briskly in the opposite direction. We stopped short, face to face for a split second. His usual confident swagger seemed slightly restrained, his eyes holding a question, or perhaps just surprise at seeing me. I felt an urge to say something – an apology for my earlier hostility? An acknowledgment? – but the moment was too brief, too public. Before I could form a word, he gave a sharp nod and continued on his way, leaving an awkward silence in his wake. Some barriers, it seemed, were harder to cross than others.

Shaking off the encounter, I reached Dorothy's room and knocked. The door swung open almost immediately, revealing Dorothy, radiant in an evening gown of shimmering sea-foam green silk that brought out the dazzling sparkle of her eyes.

"Benji, darling! Right on time," she beamed.

Standing beside her was the older woman I'd seen her with upon boarding – her mother, Pauline. Mrs. Gibson looked considerably improved from her reportedly peaked state, her posture upright, her eyes bright and assessing, though lacking Dorothy's effervescent charm.

"Mother, this is the gallant Mr. Benjamin Sutherland-Howell I told you about. Benji, my mother, Pauline Gibson."

"A pleasure to meet you properly, Mrs. Gibson," I said, offering a polite bow. "I trust you're feeling more yourself this evening?"

"Much better, thank you, Benji," Pauline replied, her voice carrying a certain theatrical projection. "Nothing a bit of rest and the sea air couldn't cure. Dorothy tells me you've kindly offered to escort her to dinner?"

"He has, Mama," Dorothy confirmed, looping her arm through mine. "But now that you're joining us, perhaps Benji wouldn't mind escorting two lovely ladies? It's Mama's first time venturing out of the cabin for dinner, you see."

"It would be my honor, unless you've made prior arrangements with Colonel Gracie?" I joked.

"Oh, you naughty thing," Pauline laughed.

"Didn't I tell you, Mother? Benji is quite the charmer."

"Well, then, shall we?" I asked, extending an elbow for each of them. Two Gibson ladies were certainly better than navigating the Dining Saloon alone.

Together, the three of us made our way towards the Reception Room.

Heads turned as Dorothy, a recognized starlet, made her entrance flanked by her mother and myself. The Reception Room buzzed with pre-dinner energy, the ever-present quintet playing a lush waltz, champagne glasses clinking.

As we neared the Dining Saloon entrance, Pauline suddenly stopped, her face lighting up. "Harry! Renee! Fancy seeing you here!"

A well-dressed couple turned towards us. The man was sharp-featured, with intelligent eyes and the unmistakable air of someone important; the woman beside him elegant and poised.

"Pauline, my dear!" the man exclaimed warmly. "We heard you were aboard! How are you? We heard you were feeling a bit under the weather."

"Rumors of my demise have been vastly overrated, thank you, Harry," Pauline lightheartedly quipped. "You know my Dorothy, of course." She practically pushed Dorothy forward. "And this charming young man is Mr. Sutherland-Howell."

"Pleased to meet you," I said, shaking Harry's hand.

Pauline turned to me. "Harry and Renee Harris are the finest theatre producers in all of New York."

"You're too kind," said Harry. "Well, it's been a pleasure, but—"

Pauline stopped the fleeting couple, barely able to contain her excitement. "Harry, darling, I must tell you, Dorothy is simply primed for her return to Broadway. We're heading to New York specifically to meet with producers – that is, of course, unless you might have a project that would suit her talents?"

The famed Broadway producer exchanged a brief, knowing glance with his wife, Renee. "Is that so, my dear Dorothy?" he asked halfheartedly, his smile polite but noncommittal. "I will certainly keep you in mind if anything crosses my—"

"Do you sing?" Renee cut him off.

"Does she sing?" scoffed Pauline. "Like a nightingale, this one."

"I can hold a note or two," Dorothy blushed.

Just then Harry's eye caught John Jacob Astor in the dining room. "Renee, J.J.'s been waiting on us. You know how he hates to be kept waiting."

"Of course, dear," Renee added gracefully, subtly steering them away. "Perhaps we can chat more later in the voyage. Enjoy your dinner, Pauline, Mr. Sutherland-Howell." They offered polite nods and continued towards the Saloon doors.

Dorothy watched them go, then turned to her mother with a comical look of exasperation. "Subtle, Mama. Really subtle." She turned to me, rolling her eyes playfully. "I forgot to mention, Benji – this isn't just my mother, she's also my manager. Comes with the territory."

I chuckled, appreciating her candor. Together, we finally reached our familiar table. Mother and Birdie were already seated, along with the Countess, Colonel Gracie, Mr. Stead, and the Allisons.

"Ah, Benji, Dorothy, welcome," Mother greeted us, though her eyes flickered briefly towards Pauline with polite curiosity.

"Good evening. Mother, everyone, may I present Mrs. Pauline Gibson, mother of our dear Dorothy Gibson."

Pauline gave a gentle bow. The men stood as she took her seat, relishing her moment as the center of attention, then the rest of us took our seats.

"So glad you could join us, Mrs. Gibson," the Countess offered graciously.

"We've gained one, but we're still down two," remarked Gracie.

"Yes, where is that husband of yours tonight, Caroline?" Stead asked, looking across the table at his empty chair. "Still under the weather?"

"I'm afraid so," Mother replied smoothly, picking up her water glass. "The poor dear remains indisposed."

"On that same note, Gladys sends her apologies," the Countess added, addressing the table. "She was invited to join a small party in the À La Carte Restaurant this evening and felt she simply couldn't refuse."

"Speaking of invitations," this time it was Gracie who addressed the table, "I would like to begin by apologizing for my behavior these past few meals we've shared. I'm afraid this old hound only knows how to hunt, so when the conversation of war is put on my plate, I tend to devour it whole."

The party exchanged glances, somewhat confused by the analogy, but seeming to understand his point. Gracie went on, "but, I must say, Miss Margaret here, you did put up quite a fight."

"A fight, Gracie? I'd say she held her own next to the likes of you," chuckled Stead. The table agreed with smiles and laughter.

"Um, yes. I suppose," Gracie said, awkwardly clearing his throat. "In fact, you'll remember my friend Isidor Strauss? Who joined us for the departure yesterday."

"Of course," said Birdie.

"He and his wife are the owners of Macy's Department Store, in New York," I said to the table. The table reacted with impressed chatter.

"Quite," Gracie went on, "he and his wife Ida were so impressed with my stories of your candor, they wanted me to invite you to their cabin for afternoon tea tomorrow."

"How lovely," said Mother.

"What do you say, Margaret?" Gracie smiled.

"I would love to, that is, if it's alright with you, Mother?"

"Tell the Strausses she'd be delighted to join them," Mother said to Gracie.

After Dinner, Thursday Evening

Dinner concluded, and the various parties dispersed. Mother and Birdie had retired early, pleading fatigue from the day's activities. Pauline Gibson, despite her recovery, decided a quiet evening was still in order and accompanied them. Gracie, along with Stead, had convinced the teetotaler Mr. Allison to join them in the masculine sanctuary of the Smoking Room for cards and cigars, while his wife ventured to their suite to kiss their children goodnight. This left Dorothy and me somewhat adrift in the still-lively Reception Room.

The orchestra took up their residency around the grand piano. Being the professionals that they were, perhaps reading the mood of the room, they opted for some livelier fare now, weaving upbeat melodies through the chatter and laughter. Several couples took to the small, cleared space near the piano, attempting waltzes or two-steps. Dorothy, never one to sit idle when there was music, was quickly swept into the mix, laughing freely as she navigated the steps with various partners. I watched her from the relative quiet of a wicker sofa, a glass of untouched brandy beside me. As her feet left the floor, heels clicking mid-air, she practically floated; but then, that was her way. There was an effortless joy about her, a complete lack of inhibition. She moved as if no one was watching, or perhaps as if she didn't care if they were – simply existing, brightly and authentically, in the moment. Oh, how I longed to share just one ounce of her vigor. Her unabashed lust for life. To shed the suffocating weight of expectation and fear, to show my true colors without a second thought.

After a particularly energetic tune, Dorothy collapsed onto the sofa beside me, fanning herself with her hand, her cheeks flushed and her eyes sparkling.

"Goodness! These shipboard romances move fast!" she giggled. "That last fellow nearly spun me clear off my feet! Oh, dear. Forgive me, Benji. I hope I didn't make you jealous!" she said with a laugh.

"How dare you," I paused for dramatic effect, "I had my eye on him first!"

Dorothy burst out laughing, just as I'd hoped she would.

I laughed along with her, her infectious energy momentarily dispelling my own introspective mood.

"Oh, Benji. It's so good to hear you laugh. I feel like I'm meeting you for the first time."

"That makes two of us," I agreed.

"Now, how about a dance?" she pointed to the party across the room.

"I'm afraid I could never keep up with you," I smiled. "You certainly seem to be enjoying yourself."

"Immensely! Isn't that what these crossings are for? I mean, why just cross the ocean, when you can have a week-long party instead?" As she was speaking, the subjects of our earlier encounter, Harry and Renee Harris, approached our sofa.

"Dorothy, my dear," Harry began, his producer's eye appraising her flushed, happy state. "We were just discussing you."

"Oh, dear," Dorothy laughed nervously. "Nothing too scandalous, I hope?"

"Quite the contrary," Renee Harris interjected, her expression more serious, more focused than it had been earlier. "Harry and I were talking about a new production we're planning for the autumn season back in New York. A musical comedy."

"How exciting!" Dorothy replied politely.

"Indeed," Renee continued, her gaze intent. "And there's a particular role... the lead, actually... that requires a certain spark, a vivacity... someone who can command the stage with charm." She paused, letting the implication hang.

"Listening to your mother praise your talents," Harry cut in, "and seeing you now... Renee hasn't stopped talking about it, Dorothy. She thinks you might be perfect for it."

"Truly? A lead role?"

"It's a demanding part," Harry cautioned, though there was a genuine interest in his tone now. "Requires strong comedic timing, stage presence, and... well, it is a musical."

"Which will be no problem, so long as you can indeed sing," said Renee.

"Like a nightingale, according to Mama," Dorothy quipped, regaining her composure, though a spark of professional ambition now lit her eyes.

"Quite," chided Harry. "But producers cannot cast *solely* based on the word of mothers."

"Would you, perhaps," Renee asked, leaning in slightly, "be willing to indulge us? A rather impromptu audition? We have some sheet music for one of the key numbers right here." She produced a folded score from Harry's inside jacket pocket.

Dorothy didn't hesitate. "Absolutely," she said, her voice clear and determined.

"Splendid!" Harry rubbed his hands together. "Now, where can we find a piano and a bit of quiet...?" His eyes scanned the busy Reception Room.

"These folks love money," Dorothy said, "maybe if you throw a dollar in the elevator, send it up, you'll clear out the whole room!"

Everyone laughed.

"See? That's the charm I was talking about, darling," Renee said to her husband.

"The Dining Saloon?" I suggested. "It should be empty by now, no one but the stewards clearing up."

"Excellent idea, Benji!" Harry agreed.

Our small party made its way back towards the doors to the Dining Saloon. As I'd predicted, the vast room was dim, most overhead lights extinguished. Stewards moved quietly amongst the tables, clearing linens and resetting silver for breakfast, their movements creating a soft, clinking counterpoint to the distant murmur from the Reception Room.

Leading the way, Harry approached the forward buffet where the inset piano resided. A steward, polishing cutlery nearby, looked up a bit begrudgingly. "Beg pardon, sir, but the Saloon is closed for the evening."

"Just need the use of the piano for a moment, my good man," Harry said smoothly. "A quick rehearsal. You won't even know we're here."

The steward was curt, no longer feeling the need to maintain his polished demeanor now that his dinner duties were over. "Well, sir, we're trying to clear up…"

Harry discreetly palmed a folded bill and pressed it into the steward's hand. "For your trouble. Five minutes, that's all."

The steward's reluctance vanished. "Very good, sir. As you wish." He nodded and moved discreetly towards the kitchens.

Against the backdrop of his retreating footsteps and the annoyed glances of a few other stewards eager to finish their shifts, Renee settled herself at the piano bench, flexing her fingers over the keys.

Dorothy took center stage in the relative emptiness of the vast Saloon, looking surprisingly composed as Renee handed her the sheet music. Harry and I found chairs at nearby tables to watch.

Dorothy scanned the music for a moment, humming the melody softly under her breath. Then, she took a deep breath and began to sing, her voice clear and pure in the quiet room, needing no instrumental introduction for the first few lines:

Another Day. Another Night. Another's come and gone. Another who felt so right. But the heart goes on…

Her voice was lovely, technically proficient, but more than that, filled with genuine emotion. Renee came in softly on the piano then, the melody simple but poignant, supporting Dorothy's clear soprano.

I tell myself, the heart goes on… The twinge of pain, that comes with love. Guess I've got the taste, 'cause I can't get enough… Because you've come, and then you've gone. And the more I've lost, the more I want.

As Dorothy poured her voice into the hopeful, pleading lines, something caught my eye from the shadowed periphery near the Saloon entrance. A figure, half-hidden. My breath hitched. The figure stepped slightly forward, into a stray shaft of dimmed light filtering from the Reception Room. Miles.

He wasn't looking at Dorothy. His gaze was fixed directly on me, unwavering, holding an expression I couldn't quite decipher – vulnerability? Recognition? Shared understanding? It felt as if the lyrics weren't just resonating with me, but with him too, bridging the space between us.

What now? What now, my love? If this is me and you, if this is us? Do you stay? Do you run? Know that I'll fight for you, cause I'm not giving up...

Dorothy continued singing, her voice filling the cavernous room, seemingly unaware of the silent drama unfolding before her. Just before she reached the final lines, Miles moved. He pushed away from the door frame and walked timidly, hesitantly, across the empty floor towards my table. My heart fluttered against my insides. I froze as Miles casually pulled out the empty chair right next to mine and sat down.

Neither of us spoke. Neither of us looked at the other. Our eyes remained fixed somewhere ahead, lost in the music, lost in the implications of the lyrics, lost in the magnetic pull that seemed to exist between us.

As Dorothy sang the final line, *"On us..."* Renee let the last chord hang softly in the air. I felt a tentative pressure against my hand where it rested on the table. I looked down. His hand was covering mine. I didn't pull away. We sat there, hands clasped in the dim light of the deserted Dining Saloon, the echo of the song settling around us like a fragile truth.

Finally, ever since the moment we met, I was exactly where I wanted to be, holding the hand of the man who took my breath away.

CHAPTER 20

The heavy leather cover slammed shut with a thud that felt final, definitive.

I stared down at the book resting between our long-ago-finished hot chocolates, a sudden, violent storm brewing behind my eyes. Rage warred with a nauseating sense of betrayal.

My thoughts raced, incoherent, colliding like panicked birds trapped in a cage. My own heartbeat blasting, a frantic drum inside my chest, loud enough to pulse in my throat, deafening in my ears.

His hand was covering mine... The words echoed, Benji's words, my father's words, describing a moment that twisted everything I thought I knew into a grotesque caricature.

"Will?" Edie's voice was soft, questioning, but it felt miles away.

Something snapped. Control vanished.

I shoved myself out of the red leather booth, the worn material peeling back like a Band-Aid.

"Air. I need air," I said, racing for the door, stumbling slightly. I ignored the startled glances of the waitress and the few other lunch patrons who'd appeared in the last hour. Unable to slow my mind, my body, I was propelled by a force I couldn't name or control.

"Will!" Edie shouted, bolting after me.

Outside, the bright California sun and the cacophony of Hollywood Boulevard hit me like a physical blow. Cars honked, their sounds merging with the distant drone of a plane sailing overhead. I kept running, dodging pedestrians, pushing blindly down the sidewalk, trying to outrun the images searing themselves into my brain, trying to catch a breath that wouldn't come.

"William Sutherland-Howell!"

Edie's voice sliced through the noise, sharp and commanding. The gravity of my full name, rarely used, stopped me dead in my tracks. My chest heaved, ragged breaths tearing through me, but I couldn't turn. Couldn't face her. Couldn't face the pity or confusion I knew I'd see in her eyes. *Was I crying?* I didn't know. Didn't even know if I wanted to. *What was this feeling?* This hollowed-out, burning nausea?

"Will," she said again, her voice softening as she reached me, placing a gentle, understanding hand on my back. The warmth of it felt alien against the frantic energy vibrating through me. Her mind must've been racing too, for the right words to say. She'd seen everything I had.

I shook my head, still staring blindly ahead at the blur of traffic.

"A lie," I choked out, the word tasting like ash. "My entire life... my father... it was all a lie." The anger surged again, hot and raw.

"Will, that's not fair..."

"Did he...? All those years... telling Mom how much he loved her... was he cheating on her? With men?" The question hung there, ugly and accusatory, poisoning the air between us.

"Will, listen to me," Edie urged, her grip firming slightly. "We don't know the whole story yet. That's why he left you the journal. There's a reason he wanted you to read it, to understand. Come back inside. We can read it together."

"No," I whispered, shaking my head more violently. "No more secrets, Edie. I can't... my head... my heart... I feel like they're going to explode."

The image from the journal – his hand covering Miles' – flashed again, visceral and sickening.

"I just... *can't.*"

Those familiar nineteen steps leading to the second floor of my parents' Sunset Boulevard mansion felt like climbing a mountain. Each footfall a droning echo across the cavernous foyer, amplifying the oppressive silence of the house. My charge? A welfare check on my mother. The recent developments, combined with a mental image of my frail mother unable to leave her bed, left me yearning to perform the one trick I thought I could still manage: lifting my mother's spirits.

As I reached the landing, one of the doors to my parents' suite opened quietly. Gil emerged, closing it with practiced silence behind him, his posture momentarily collapsing, following a weary battle.

"Gil?" I asked quietly. "How is she?"

"Finally asleep, Master Will," he replied, his voice a low murmur. "Exhausted herself, I think. Best we let her rest."

"Yeah," I agreed, running a hand through my already messy hair. "Good."

Gil's perceptive gaze lingered on me. He'd always seen more than he let on, this quiet man who was more of a father to me than the man whose secrets were currently tearing me apart. "And how are you holding up, son?"

The question hung there. I could give the easy answer, the expected one. But looking into Gil's steady eyes, I knew I didn't have to. "Do you want the truth, Gil? Or do you just want the answer that's going to make you feel better?"

A faint, knowing sadness came over his features. "You've never had to mince words with me, Master Will."

"I know that, old man," I managed, a rough affection breaking through the turmoil. My shoulders felt tight, coiled springs of tension.

Gil nodded slowly. "Come downstairs. Let me fix you a nightcap."

"It's three-thirty," I said, looking at my watch.

"Indeed, son. One nightcap, then it's off to bed for you. *Doctor's orders.*"

The gleaming, industrial-sized kitchen felt strangely sterile under the harsh overhead lights. Gil placed a heavy crystal tumbler filled with amber liquid – whiskey, neat – on the island in front of me. He poured a smaller measure for himself and took the stool beside mine.

He raised his glass. "To Ben," he said quietly, his voice carrying a weight of history. "A great man."

"So the history books will say," I sighed.

I subconsciously clinked my glass against his, the sound sharp in the quiet room, but I couldn't bring myself to drink. I just stared into the swirling liquid, the image of my father – the stranger, the liar – superimposed over it.

Gil took a slow sip, then set his glass down, his gaze steady on me. "Alright, Will. Out with it. What is it that's been eating at you?"

I took a shaky breath. "My whole life... I thought I wanted to know him. *Really* know him, you know? The man behind the movies, behind the silence." I finally looked at Gil. "Now... the more I learn... the more I wish I could just... go back. Erase it."

Gil was silent for a long moment, studying my face. Then, softly, he asked, "You mean... about his 'secret'?"

The word, spoken so calmly, so matter-of-factly, jolted me. My head snapped up. "You... you knew?"

Gil nodded slowly, his expression filled with a deep, quiet sorrow. "I knew Ben for a very long time, Will. Longer than anyone, perhaps. There wasn't much he could hide from these old eyes, even when he tried."

"Did... did my mother know?" The question felt treacherous, heavy with implication.

"Good heavens, no," Gil said firmly, shaking his head. "Your mother... Adelaide loved your father with her whole heart. And he, her. Knowing... that particular truth... would have shattered her. Ben would never have allowed that."

He leaned closer, his voice earnest. "Will, I understand this is... a lot to digest. More than anyone should have to bear, perhaps. But I need you to listen to me." He paused, ensuring he had my full attention. "Despite what you might be thinking, despite how things might look through the lens of this secret... Ben was never unfaithful to your mother. He loved her, Will. Deeply. And in his own complicated, broken way... nothing ever changed that."

The California sun, already climbing high, felt warm on my face as I walked towards the garage the next morning.

Gil's 'doctor's orders' last night – a decent pour of whiskey and an order to get some actual sleep – had worked surprisingly well. The raging storm in my mind had subsided, leaving behind a landscape that was bruised but navigable. *I have a good doctor*, I thought with a smile.

Gil had appeared as I came downstairs, keys already in hand, insisting he drive me wherever I was headed. "Let the old man take care of you, Master Will," he'd said, his eyes conveying concern. But I shook my head. Despite Gil's gentle protest, despite the lingering exhaustion, this was a trip I had to make alone. Some things you just have to face head-on, behind your own steering wheel.

The familiar drive to the studio lot felt different today. Different than it ever had. Less burdened by anger, more weighted with a complex sorrow and a dawning, reluctant understanding. Dad's journal, while safely tucked in the backseat of the car, couldn't hide its anticipation. It had more to tell me, and finally, I was ready to listen. But I wouldn't be listening alone.

When I pulled up to the administration building, Edie was already waiting outside, bathed in the early afternoon light, looking sharp and composed, a welcome anchor in the choppy sea of the past few days.

She climbed into the passenger seat, bringing the scent of coffee and something subtly floral into the car's leather interior. She buckled her seatbelt, then glanced over at me with a playful glint in her eye.

"Well, aren't we fancy today?" she teased. "Taking the lady out? Wouldn't you prefer the commissary? It'd be a much cheaper date, you know."

Her lightheartedness was exactly what I needed. I felt the tension in my shoulders ease. I put the car in gear but didn't pull away just yet, turning to face her fully.

"So, this is a date then?" I asked, letting a smile spread across my face. "Good. I'm glad we don't have to tap-dance around the obvious anymore."

Edie's smile widened, a blush creeping up her neck. Before she could respond, before the moment could break, I leaned across the console. She met me halfway, her lips soft and hesitant at first, then pressing more firmly against mine. It wasn't frantic or desperate like my flight from Musso's yesterday; it was quiet, searching, a connection forged in the midst of chaos. It felt... *right. Grounding.*

When we finally pulled apart, both slightly breathless, I rested my forehead against hers for a beat. "Edie," I began softly, pulling back enough to meet her clear gaze. "About yesterday... bolting like that... I need to apologize."

She started to shake her head, "Will, it's not necessary, I understand—"

"No, let me," I insisted gently. "I'm sorry. For running out. For dumping all that... intensity on you. And I'm sorry if anything I said came off as insensitive." I took a breath, gathering my thoughts, needing her to understand the shift Gil's quiet wisdom had brought. "Despite what I might have said yesterday, in the heat of the moment... learning what I learned..." I paused, the memory still raw. "I can appreciate the struggle now. The stress my father must have been under, living his life in secret like that."

I looked directly into her eyes, wanting her to see the sincerity, the change wrought by a night of reflection and Gil's reassurance. "I'm certain now... the man I'm slowly learning to call my father... he wasn't a cheater. I believe he loved my mother, deeply. And I think he did everything he could, in his own way, to show her that love."

CHAPTER 21

The cheerful clatter of cups and saucers seemed unnaturally loud in the bright morning air of the Café Parisian. Sunlight poured through the inviting bank of open windows, warming the familiar trellis-work walls and the wicker tables. It should have felt relaxing, this charming replica of a sidewalk café perched high above the Atlantic, but my stomach churned with a nervous energy that had nothing to do with the gentle sway of the ship.

I checked my pocket watch for the third time in five minutes. Nine-fifteen. He was late. *Or maybe he wasn't coming at all.*

Sending that note via the steward this morning had felt like leaping off a cliff. *Meet me for breakfast? Café Parisian, nine o'clock? Had it been too forward? Too presumptuous?* After last night... after sitting there in the dim Dining Saloon, his hand covering mine, the air thick with unspoken words and the romantic echo of Dorothy's song... we hadn't spoken further. He'd simply squeezed my hand once, met my eyes for a fleeting, intense moment, and then vanished back into the thinning crowd of the Reception Room, leaving me breathless and utterly confused.

What did it mean? Where did we go from here? Could we even talk about it? The thought of trying to navigate such a conversation in this open, airy café, with stewards gliding past and other passengers potentially within earshot, tightened the knot in my stomach further. Perhaps he wouldn't come precisely because he knew we couldn't talk freely here. Perhaps last night was just... a moment. A silly one-off fueled by music and dim lighting.

Just as I was convincing myself I'd been a fool, just as I was about to signal the waiter for my usual hot cocoa and retreat back to the safety of my cabin, I saw him.

Miles paused at the entrance, framed against the bright backdrop of the sky and sea beyond. He scanned the café, his usual easy confidence seemingly shaken by a similar flicker of uncertainty. He looked impossibly handsome, effortlessly stylish even in his casual morning attire. Then his eyes found mine.

The world seemed to stop for a heartbeat. A slow, hesitant smile touched his lips, mirrored, I realized with a jolt, by my own. He started towards my table, the crimson runner pulling him right to me.

My breath caught. *He came.*

He slid into the wicker chair opposite me, the easy grace of his movements belying the nervous energy I sensed beneath the surface. We simply looked at each other for a moment, the unspoken questions hanging heavy in the sunlit air.

"Morning," he finally said, his voice a little huskier than usual.

"Morning," I managed, my own voice tight.

The waiter, noticing Miles' arrival, materialized beside our table with practiced efficiency. "Good morning, gentlemen. Are you ready to order?" his French accent completing the atmospheric effect.

"Yes," I said quickly, desperate for the distraction. "I'll have a hot cocoa, please."

Miles let out a soft, playful scoff. "Benji, honestly. Your American is showing."

"What do you mean?" I asked, confused.

"Hot cocoa? We're sitting in the Café Parisian. When in Paris..." he gave the waiter a charming grin. "Espresso is mandatory, wouldn't you agree?"

The waiter smiled playfully. "Oh, mais oui, monsieur."

"I've... I've never had espresso," I admitted, feeling a blush rise.

Miles' gaze met mine again, holding it. That playful glint was back in his eyes, but deeper now, carrying the weight of last night. "Well then," he said softly, deliberately, "perhaps it's time you tried something new?"

The double meaning hung there, unmistakable. Trying espresso. Trying... this. Whatever this was. I swallowed hard, the knot in my stomach tightening, but this time, it wasn't entirely from fear.

"Yes," I said, meeting his gaze steadily. "Yes, I think I am." I turned to the waiter. "Two espressos, please. And perhaps... perhaps we could share a chocolate croissant?"

"Perfect," Miles said with a wink.

"Excellent choice, messieurs," said the waiter, before fading back into the muted chatter of the Café.

"How'd you sleep?" Miles asked once the coast was clear.

"I didn't," I said.

He smiled. "I had a feeling."

For a moment we sat in silence. Unsure of who should speak first. Unsure of what there was to say. Finally, Miles spoke up, "I told you I wasn't after your sister."

We both laughed.

"I'm glad," I said.

"And why's that?"

"Because she's too good for you," I joked.

"Oh! He's got jokes, ladies and gentlemen. Benjamin Sutherland-Howell—"

"The second!" I playfully interjected.

"The second, of course! But, to be fair, you don't even know anything about me, Benji, so how can you judge?"

"So? Tell me," I said.

"What do you want to know?" he asked.

"Everything," I began, "how old are you? What's your middle name? Favorite—"

"Whoa, Benji, calm down," he playfully threw up a hand. "There's no need to rush this, alright?" He stood and casually moved his chair next to mine, then sat back down. "I'm not going anywhere, OK?" In the privacy of the corner, where no one could see, he quietly took my hand once again, all of the same sparks from last night returning as he did. The feeling of his touch was electric. The warmth of his hand wrapped around mine. The strength of his fingers, wrapping mine tightly enough to feel his pulse running through them. I suddenly felt a million different emotions. But, mostly, I wanted to kiss him. Some part of me, some fleeting wave of confidence which I'd never felt before, made it seem alright to act on these impulses. But, before I could do so, he went on. "Let's just enjoy each moment as it comes, alright? Live for the moment, Benji. Don't make them come to you. They'll come. You just have to accept them as they do."

The waiter focused back into frame, tearing our gaze away from each other, and back to the reality of breakfast, back to the crowded Café, where we'd been sitting all alone, our own little world, only a second ago.

"Alright, we have two espressos." He sat each in front of us. "And one chocolate croissant."

We thanked him, and he was gone once more. Again, we were all alone in the crowded room, focused only on each other.

"Are you ready for this?" he asked, holding up the tiny cup.

I took mine, mimicking his exaggerated elbow, extending my pinky finger in an ever-so pretentious manner. "Like this?" I mocked.

"Perfect," he laughed. "Three, two, one."

We each took a sip, slurping the bitter black froth. Then sat the cups back on their saucers. I did all I could to hide my disgust at the horrid drink.

"So?"

"It's... good," I lied.

"You'll learn to like it," he said with a wink.

I picked back up the cup, poised to attempt the next sip, but waiting for him. "To trying something new."

He picked up his cup. "To trying something new."

CHAPTER 22

The door to the Strauss suite on C deck opened into a world of quiet, established luxury. Birdie stepped inside, momentarily awestruck. Rich, dark mahogany paneled the walls, catching the afternoon light, its warmth amplified by intricate gold leaf flourishes that traced elegant patterns around the raised panels, doorways, and ceiling cornice. Plush velvet armchairs and sofas were arranged invitingly, but the undeniable centerpiece was a large, ornately carved Regent-style fireplace dominating one wall – clearly electric, a modern marvel disguised as old-world grandeur, yet radiating a convincing, welcoming glow.

"Ah, Miss Sutherland-Howell, Margaret, come in, come in!" Isidor Strauss greeted her warmly, rising from an armchair where he'd been reading a newspaper. His smile was genuine, his eyes kind behind his spectacles. "Ida, my dear, our young guest of honor has arrived."

Ida Strauss turned from adjusting a bouquet of flowers on the room's central table. She was a sturdy woman, her bearing poised and dignified, but with a warmth in her smile that mirrored her husband's. "Margaret, welcome. We're so pleased you could join us."

"Thank you for inviting me, Mrs. Strauss, Mr. Strauss," Birdie replied, feeling slightly intimidated yet honored by the summons. "Your suite is simply magnificent."

"Nonsense, just comfortable," Ida waved a dismissive hand, though her eyes twinkled. "Isidor insists on bringing half the house with us whenever we travel."

"Only the necessary comforts, my love," Isidor chuckled, patting his wife's hand affectionately as she sat beside him. "Unlike some people, I don't believe in darning my own socks when perfectly good new ones can be purchased."

"And waste perfectly good wool? Never," Ida retorted playfully. "Besides, someone has to be mindful of our indulgences, especially when one of us can't seem to stop indulging in items that aren't on the ship's kosher menu."

"My dear, it was merely a lobster salad, a minor transgression!" Isidor protested with mock horror, placing a hand over his heart.

Birdie smiled, observing their easy rapport. There was an undeniable, deep bond between them, a comfortable intimacy built over decades, yet kept fresh with affectionate teasing. It was a stark contrast to the strained politeness or outright distance she often witnessed, even in her own family.

Just then, a knock sounded at the parlor door. A steward announced the arrival of more guests. First came the Countess of Rothes, elegant as always, accompanied this time not by Gladys, but by a strikingly pale yet composed Madeleine Astor. Moments later, another woman entered – vibrant, middle-aged, with an air of robust confidence and eyes that seemed to miss nothing.

"Margaret Brown, from Denver," Ida Strauss introduced her after greeting the others. "An absolute force of nature. Mrs. Brown has done tireless work for women's rights and labor reform back in Colorado."

"Just call me Maggie, dear," Mrs. Brown said with a hearty smile, shaking Birdie's hand firmly. "Heard from the Countess here you're quite the firebrand yourself, young lady. Glad to meet you."

As the ladies settled with their tea, Ida Strauss explained her reason for the impromptu gathering. "Colonel Gracie has been keeping us up to speed on your dinner conversations, Margaret," she began, addressing Birdie directly. "About a woman's place, about the suffrage movement. It resonated with me. Anytime I hear of a woman speaking her mind, striving for something more, especially one as young as yourself, I feel inspired. I knew I simply had to invite you for tea."

She gestured around the room. "And I thought, who better to join us than these remarkable ladies? Women of influence, women of conviction. Madeleine, dear, navigating your new life with such grace under scrutiny; Countess, your tireless charity work; Maggie, your activism... We are all women navigating a changing world, are we not? A world where our voices are starting, finally, to be heard."

Encouraged by the supportive atmosphere, so different from the dismissive or argumentative tones she usually encountered when voicing her opinions, Birdie found herself speaking freely. She shared her frustrations with the limitations placed upon her sex, her belief in education and equality, her hopes for a future where women could contribute fully to society, not just adorn it.

The other women listened intently, nodding, interjecting with echoes of agreement. The Countess spoke of the subtle ways women of means could influence politics through philanthropy and social connections. Maggie Brown shared rousing stories of organizing miners' wives and lobbying politicians in Denver. Even Madeleine Astor, usually so quiet, murmured her assent.

"It's all well and good to believe these things," Birdie admitted after a pause, a vulnerability creeping into her voice. "But sometimes… sometimes I feel like such a fraud. I talk about wanting change, but I live this life of privilege. I haven't earned the right to speak for those less fortunate. And I worry… what if I try and fail? What if I'm not strong enough, or smart enough? This… imposter syndrome, I suppose you'd call it."

A knowing silence fell for a moment, the shared experience of self-doubt familiar to women of any station. It was Madeleine Astor who broke it, her voice soft but surprisingly firm.

"My dear Margaret," she began, setting her teacup down carefully. "If anyone understands the fear of 'what ifs,' perhaps it is myself." She gave a small, self-deprecating smile. "Marrying John… well, it invited opinions from the entire world, none of them particularly kind. This pregnancy…" she instinctively touched her stomach, "… under such circumstances… it has not been easy. There were days I felt terrified, utterly overwhelmed by the judgment, by the uncertainty, by the feeling that I was unequal to the task society – and perhaps even my own heart – had set for me."

She looked directly at Birdie, her youthful eyes holding an unexpected depth. "But what I have learned is that pushing through that fear, facing those 'what ifs' head-on, is precisely what makes us stronger. Every setback, every unkind word, every moment of doubt I overcame, taught me something about my own resolve. Marrying John terrified me," she admitted quietly, "and sometimes, living this life still does. But I wouldn't trade the learning, the strength I've found. I'd do it all again."

She leaned forward slightly, her voice gaining intensity. "Sometimes life presents us with opportunities that shed light on our biggest fears and insecurities," Madeleine said, her gaze seeming to encompass not just Birdie, but perhaps her own reflection. "But it is a necessary evil, because if the choice were easy, we couldn't appreciate the satisfaction we feel when we come out on the other side, triumphant. Sometimes," she concluded, a faint smile returning, "we just have to close our eyes and say, 'to hell with it,' and just jump."

Birdie absorbed Madeleine's words, feeling their resonance deep within her. *To hell with it, and just jump.* The phrase echoed in her mind, colliding with the image of Oliver's challenging grey eyes, the memory of stepping over the threshold onto the third-class deck, the confusing mix of thrill and unease his presence evoked. Madeleine was talking about marriage, about societal expectations, but her words spoke directly to Birdie's own internal conflict – the fear of pursuing this connection with Oliver, of venturing further down a path that defied every rule she'd ever known, yet felt undeniably, compellingly real. Could she find the courage to simply… jump?

While Birdie forged meaningful connections and uplifting conversation in the Strauss suite one deck above, a different sort of afternoon tea unfolded in the main Reception Room below.

Mother presided over a smaller, more intimate gathering, flanked by the lively Gladys Cherry and a noticeably more relaxed Bess Allison. With the Countess occupied upstairs and Mr. Allison presumably enjoying a cigar with the other gentlemen, the atmosphere at their wicker table felt considerably less formal, buzzing with that sort of excitement that stems from unsupervised freedom.

"Honestly, Caroline, Bess," Gladys leaned in, lowering her voice though her eyes danced with amusement, "you simply must try the À La Carte Restaurant before we dock. Last night was divine!" She proceeded to recount her dinner engagement from the previous evening, painting a picture of the exclusive, Ritz-like dining room – its rose-colored ambiance, the haute cuisine, and, of course, the clientele.

"Everyone who's anyone holds court there, it seems," Gladys continued. "The Astors, naturally. And Sir Cosmo and Lady Duff-Gordon – Lucille, you know, the designer? – holding forth at a corner table, positively dripping in silks and attitude." She took a delicate sip of tea. "Some go to be seen, of course, flashing their jewels and ordering the most expensive champagne. Pure theatre. But others..." she paused for effect, "... others clearly choose it for the privacy. Tucked away in those little alcoves, hoping to avoid prying eyes and idle gossip."

"Oh?" Bess Allison prompted, clearly intrigued now that her husband's steadying presence wasn't felt. "Like whom?"

"Well..." Gladys scanned the room discreetly, then nodded towards a nearby table where two gentlemen sat in quiet conversation. "Ladies, don't look now, but that fellow facing us? Algernon Barkworth. He was in there last night with his... companion."

Mother and Bess subtly angled their heads. Mr. Barkworth, a distinguished-looking man of middle age, was indeed recognizable from the passenger list – English gentry, involved in local politics back home. He seemed oblivious to their attention, focused entirely on the man seated opposite him, whose back was currently turned to the ladies' table.

"Barkworth," Gladys went on, her voice a pointed whisper. "Charming enough, quite wealthy, Justice of the Peace, I believe. But the rumor mill simply loves to churn about him."

"Oh, now, Gladys," Mother interjected, though her lips twitched with amusement. "Must we?"

"How so?" Bess leaned in eagerly, ignoring Mother's mild protest.

"Never married, you see," Gladys explained. "Lives alone on his estate... well, alone except for his gardener." She delivered the last word with significant emphasis.

"Gladys, really—" Mother started, but Bess cut her off with a delighted giggle.

"His gardener? Oh my!" Bess stifled her laughter behind her hand. "I suppose the grounds aren't the only thing he's tending!"

All three women dissolved into laughter, momentarily forgetting their decorum. The shared joke, the slightly scandalous implication, felt liberating in the polite confines of the Reception Room.

"Do you think that is the gardener with him now?" Mother asked, joining the game, her eyes sparkling.

"Hard to say with his back to us," Gladys admitted, squinting playfully. "But that's definitely the same chap he was with last night. Inseparable, they were. Very devoted to their... conversation."

Bess and Gladys continued to chuckle, imagining the supposed affair. Just then, Mr. Barkworth and his companion signaled a steward, preparing to leave. As the two men stood and turned towards the Grand Staircase to exit, the ladies finally got a clear view of the second man.

Gladys and Bess exchanged another knowing, amused glance, their earlier speculations seemingly confirmed in their minds by the companion's appearance or demeanor.

Mother, however, went utterly still. The laughter died on her lips, her teacup frozen halfway to its saucer. Her eyes fixed on the face of Barkworth's companion, a man she instantly recognized. A wave of something unreadable – shock? Fear? Recognition? – washed over her features, draining the color from her cheeks. She said nothing, her breath caught in her throat, as the two men, entirely unaware of the scrutiny they'd just endured or the silent bomb their appearance had detonated at a nearby table, disappeared from the Reception Room.

The rhythm of life at sea had settled in. Queenstown was a memory, the last sight of land swallowed by the endless blue horizon. Now, there was only the vast expanse of the Atlantic, the steady thrum of the engines beneath our feet, and the endless sky above. The general conversation amongst everyone had become our speed. How much distance would we travel each day, now that we had nothing ahead of us but miles of ocean.

After the intensity of the morning – the espresso, the shared croissant, the unspoken acknowledgments – Miles and I found ourselves strolling along the sun-drenched Boat Deck, a comfortable silence initially stretching between us. The polite, surface-level conversations of the past day or so felt insufficient now. We had crossed some invisible line, admitted some fragile truth, and the air felt charged with the potential of genuine connection.

I wanted to know more, everything, about this man who had appeared so unexpectedly and shifted my world on its axis. Steeling my nerves, I decided to start simply.

"So," I began, trying to sound casual as we leaned against the railing, watching the whitecaps crest and fall below. "We skipped the formalities this morning. How old are you, Miles?"

He turned, a familiar playful glint in his eye. "Careful, Benji, asking a gentle-man his age?" He grinned. "Thirty-seven."

"Thirty-seven?" The number genuinely surprised me. I would have guessed late twenties at most. "Forgive me, but... you don't look it."

He chuckled, a warm, easy sound. "Thank you, I think. Comes from refusing to grow up properly, I suspect. Most people peg me for younger." He paused, then tilted his head. "And you? Let me guess... twenty-two?"

Twenty-two? If only. Suddenly self-conscious of my mere seventeen years – nearly eighteen, but still – especially after learning his age, I heard myself lie before I could stop it. "Twenty-one," I said, hoping it sounded convincing.

"Ah, twenty-one," he repeated thoughtfully. "Old enough to know better, young enough not to care." He smiled again. "And Benjamin Sutherland-Howell the Second... quite the mouthful. Very formal. Very... formidable."

"It's my father's name," I shrugged, feeling the familiar weight of it.

"Of course it is," Miles said, his tone softening slightly. He seemed to under-stand more than he let on. "Well, Mr. Formidable the Second, since we're sharing state secrets like age, what about your full name?"

"My full name?" he asked, feigning surprise. "You sure you can handle it?"

"Try me," I challenged.

"Alright then," he took a mock-serious breath. "Miles Hyacinth Force."

I stared at him, then burst out laughing despite myself. "Hyacinth? Really? Isn't that... isn't that a girl's name?"

"Now who's being rude?" Miles retorted, though he was smiling. "And for your information, it's a perfectly respectable name. Greek mythology, you know."

"*Still...*"

"It was my mother's doing," he explained, his expression turning more earnest. "It's her favorite flower. Reminds her of home." He looked out at the sea for a moment. "She grew up near Naples. Hyacinths grow wild there, she says, but they struggle in New York. She gave me the name so... so whenever she says it, she's taken back there. And," he looked back at me, a surprising vulnerability in his eyes, "whenever she looks at *me*, her son, she feels like she's *home*, even far away."

His explanation silenced my teasing instantly. It was unexpectedly sentimental, deeply personal. "That's... actually quite beautiful, Miles."

He shrugged, slightly embarrassed now. "Well, it's *still* a *ridiculous middle name*," he laughed.

Then I considered his last name. "*Force... Force...* I know I've heard that name." That's when it clicked. "*Wait*. Madeleine Astor... her maiden name was *Force!*"

Miles nodded. "My cousin."

"Your *cousin?*" I laughed again, this time in disbelief. "Madeleine Astor is your cousin? Of course! Now it all makes sense." I shook my head. "And you wanted to act like my family name was pretentious! You're related to the richest man in America!"

"Only by marriage," Miles clarified quickly, perhaps defensively. "And believe me, the Astors move in circles far removed from my own usual haunts."

The conversation shifted then, naturally, towards the future waiting for us on the other side of this voyage. "So, what does Miles Hyacinth Force do when he's not charmingly dodging questions about his age or connections?" I asked.

His smile faded slightly. "What I do," he emphasized, "is prepare to become a very bored, very underpaid clerk in my father's law firm."

"A law clerk?" The image didn't fit the man beside me at all.

"Afraid so," he sighed. "What I want to do... is take photographs." His eyes lit up with genuine passion now. "Maybe even work in moving pictures someday. Have you seen them, Benji? The flickers? It's magic! Capturing life, movement... telling stories without words. I took this trip, bought this camera," he patted the leather case hanging from his shoulder, "to really learn, to practice, to see if I could actually do it."

"Why can't you?"

"Because," his enthusiasm deflated again, "according to my father, taking pictures is a hobby, not a career. Law is respectable. Law is secure. Photography is for... well, not for a Force, apparently." He kicked lightly at the railing. "This trip was my last taste of freedom. He gave me an ultimatum before I left – come home ready to start at the firm, or be cut off entirely. My mother... she understands. She wants me to follow my passion. But Father..." he trailed off.

"I know the feeling," I said.

Miles looked at me, sensing the shift. "Your father?"

I nodded. "He doesn't approve of my ambitions either. Wants me in business. Steel, railroads, banking... something solid."

"And what do you want to do?"

"To write," I admitted. "Stories, maybe even plays. But Father thinks it's frivolous, unstable. I had to pretend I was studying business at Yale, just to appease him. Took mostly writing courses behind his back."

"Did he find out?"

"Something happened," I said, the memory rising like bile, stinging my throat. "An incident... last semester. It ruined everything. He knows now." I looked away, the shame and anger still raw. "I'm... I'm not ready to talk about it yet."

Miles didn't press. He just stood beside me in silence for a long moment, a comforting, non-judgmental presence. He allowed me the space to just breathe, to let the shadow of that unspoken event pass over me without demanding explanation. It was a profound relief.

Finally, he broke the silence, his voice suddenly alight with a new idea. "You know what?" he exclaimed, turning to face me fully, his earlier passion reignited. "This is fate!"

"Fate?"

"Yes! Think about it! You're a writer, hiding from a disapproving father. I'm a photographer – a budding cinematographer! – hiding from a disapproving father." He grinned, the idea clearly taking shape in his mind. "Forget law firms and steel mills! We should do it ourselves!"

"Do what?" I asked, bewildered by his sudden energy.

"Start our own moving picture studio!" he declared, his eyes shining. "Seriously, Benji! You write the stories – real stories, brilliant stories! And I'll film them! We'll make our own magic, tell the tales we want to tell! Forget our fathers, forget their expectations! We'll build our own world!"

The idea was outlandish, impossible, a ridiculous fantasy born of shipboard dreams and shared frustration. Yet... the thought of it, the sheer audacity, sparked something within me. A flicker of defiant joy. Him behind the camera, me with the pen... creating something new together.

A giddy laugh escaped me, mirrored instantly by Miles. Whether we were serious or not hardly mattered. For now, standing there on the deck of the Titanic, somewhere in the vast, unbridled ocean, we were allowing ourselves the freedom to dream, to imagine a different future, to simply live in the possibility of the moment. Together.

The heavy velvet curtains in the B deck suite were drawn tight against the setting sun, plunging the cabin into premature twilight.

Mother moved through the dimness towards her dressing table, the ritual of preparing for dinner usually a welcome distraction, a familiar performance. Tonight, however, her movements felt stiff, mechanical. In the darkened room, she could hear the occasional rustle of sheets – Father lay in bed, claiming the lingering effects of seasickness still rendered him incapable of making a public appearance.

An excuse she no longer believed.

She sat, staring at her reflection without really seeing it, picking up a long silk evening glove. Her fingers fumbled with the tiny pearl buttons at the wrist, usually a simple task, but tonight they felt impossibly small, resistant. A wave of frustration, fueled by the afternoon's unsettling revelation and years of swallowed discontent, suddenly surged through her. With a choked cry, she ripped the glove off, tossing it violently onto the dressing table, scattering silver-backed brushes and crystal perfume bottles.

"Caroline? What is it? What's wrong?" Father's voice came from behind, thicker than usual. He sat up on the bed, pulling his dressing gown tighter, his face wrought with weary concern.

The sight of him, playing the invalid while she wrestled with the fragments of their life, snapped the last thread of her control. The storm brewing within her finally broke.

"Where have you been, Benjamin?" she demanded, spinning around to face him, her voice trembling with suppressed fury.

"What are you talking about? I've been right here. Feeling dreadful, as you well know."

"Have you?" she challenged, her voice dripping sarcasm. "Because it's funny, Gladys Cherry mentioned seeing you hale and hearty in the À La Carte Restaurant last night. Enjoying a rather intimate dinner, apparently. With... *another man.*"

Father's face paled slightly, but he attempted a dismissive scoff. "Gladys? Really, Caroline, I've never met her, so how would she even know what I—"

"I saw you myself," she cut him off, standing now, her hands clenched. "This afternoon. In the Reception Room. Having tea with the same gentleman that Gladys saw you with in the restaurant last night. Does the name *Algernon Barksworth* ring a bell, Benjamin? Because he's got *quite* the reputation!"

Father fell silent, his bluff called, no denial readily available. Mother stared at him, the years of doubt, suspicion, and lonely transatlantic crossings coalescing into a bitter certainty.

"It's happening *again*, isn't it, Benjamin?" Her voice broke, thick with pain. "Just like *before*. I'm... I'm no longer good enough for you? Is that it?"

"Caroline, that's not—"

"Perhaps it never stopped."

He started, reaching a hand towards her.

"Don't!" she recoiled as if struck. "Don't touch me. Don't insult me with more lies." Her voice hardened, fueled by a sudden, icy resolve. "All those trips you took. To Europe, to 'see doctors,' to 'rest your nerves,' to work on your 'health.' It was all just an excuse, wasn't it? An excuse to..." The word lodged in her throat, too ugly, too painful to speak aloud. "... To pursue your... *interests.*"

He tried again, "My dear, *please*, listen. Your fears are unfounded, I assure you—"

"Save your words, Benjamin," she interrupted, her voice flat, devoid of its earlier heat, replaced now by a chilling finality. "It's over. *I'm done.* Done trying, done pretending, done waiting for a man who clearly doesn't want the life we built. A life he never would've had without my family's money!"

She walked towards the suite door, grabbing a wrap from a nearby chair. "You are free," she said, not looking back at him. "Do whatever you wish, be with whomever you wish. But you will leave me and the children alone for the remainder of this voyage. I'll move into Birdie's room tonight. I don't want to see you or hear from you again until we dock." She paused at the door, her hand on the latch. "And when we arrive in New York, I am taking Margaret and Benji, and we will be going our separate ways. Permanently."

Without waiting for his response, she pulled the door open and stepped out into the corridor, closing it firmly behind her, shutting out the man, the marriage, the life she could no longer hold together. She leaned against the cool wood for a moment, trembling, taking deep breaths to collect herself before anyone saw her distress. Then, fueled by a desperate, reckless impulse, she turned and walked swiftly towards the forward staircase, towards Ismay's suite.

She knocked, her knuckles rapping harder than intended. Bruce Ismay opened the door himself, surprise evident on his face at her unannounced arrival. His eyes quickly registered the tear tracks on her cheeks, the tremor in her hands.

"Caroline? Is everything alright?"

She met his gaze directly, lifting her chin, forcing a semblance of composure. "Mr. Ismay... *Bruce,*" she corrected herself, her voice steadier now, sharpened with a defiant edge. "You mentioned... a *private* promenade?" She gave a fragile smile. "I find myself in sudden need of some fresh air. I'd like to see it now, if you're still willing to show me."

Wordlessly, sensing the turbulent emotions beneath her request, Ismay stepped aside, allowing her into the opulent parlor suite. She walked past him, heading directly towards the doors she presumed led outside. He followed, closing the suite door quietly behind them. She pushed open the door to the private deck. The rush of wind was immediate, stronger here in this sizable, yet sheltered, space. It whipped strands of hair across her face and billowed the fabric of her wrap as the ship sliced powerfully through the darkening waves, the increased speed tangible.

She stood at the open mouth of the window, arms wrapped about herself tightly, drinking in the bracing air, the sudden surge of rebellious freedom. She had done it. Said the words she'd held back for years. Behind her, Ismay closed the distance between them, his presence warm, solid. His arms came around her waist from behind, pulling her back gently against his chest. He lowered his head, his lips brushing the sensitive nape of her neck. For a lingering moment, she allowed herself to lean into the embrace, to relish the intoxicating energy of his closeness, the forbidden thrill of it.

"I thought you'd never come," Ismay whispered, his breath warm against her skin.

"Up until a moment ago," she replied, her voice barely audible above the wind, "neither did I."

The momentum built, the unspoken invitation hanging heavy in the air. Ismay began to graze her neck with the soft pulp of his lips, his playful mustache sending shivers down her spine. The sensation, undeniably desired only moments ago in her anger and hurt, now jarred her back to a colder reality. The implications, the risks, the potential for swapping one form of betrayal for another – it hit her with sudden clarity.

"Wait!" She stiffened, pulling away slightly within his embrace.

"What?" Ismay murmured, his voice thick with wanting.

"I can't," she exhaled, turning slightly to look back at him, her eyes filled with turmoil. "*We*... we *can't*."

His arms loosened, allowing her to step back out of his world, confusion replacing the desire in his expression. "But, Caroline... I thought..."

"I know," she said, regret flooding her voice. "And I'm sorry, Bruce. Truly. I thought so too, just now. But... we both have so much to lose. Our families, our reputations... it's too much."

They stood there, inches apart, the whistling wind seeming to carve a sudden chasm between them. Ismay looked at her, his expression shifting to one of understanding, perhaps, mixed with disappointment. Letting her walk away now, he seemed to convey without words, was the last thing he wanted. But he remained silent.

"I won't bother you anymore, Bruce," she said quietly, stepping fully out of his reach.

"*Caroline—*" he began, taking a step towards her.

"Bruce, please," she interrupted firmly. "I'm asking you... leave me alone."

He stopped, respecting her boundary, though his eyes followed her intently. With a final, fleeting look back at him, she turned and walked back through the suite, leaving Ismay standing alone on his private promenade, the wind whipping around him as the Titanic sped onward into the night.

CHAPTER 23

Dinner in the Saloon that evening felt different, though on the surface, little had changed. The same opulent room, the same starched linens, the same quiet efficiency of the stewards navigating between tables. Our usual party was assembled – Mother, Birdie, the Countess, Gladys, Gracie, Stead, the Allisons, Pauline and Dorothy Gibson – everyone, that is, except Father. His empty chair at the head of the table felt less like an absence and more like a statement.

The conversation flowed around me, polite, predictable, yet underneath it all, I sensed a subtle discord, an awareness perhaps shared only by myself. Mr. Stead, oblivious, provided the first awkward note.

"Caroline, my dear," he announced jovially, gesturing towards the vacant seat with his wine glass, "I must confess, I specifically requested a seat at Benjamin Sutherland-Howell's table for this voyage! Aside from a few hands of poker in the Smoking Room, it's almost like he's avoiding me. If the man doesn't make an appearance soon, I shall be forced to demand a partial refund from Mr. Ismay!"

Polite laughter rippled around the table. Everyone chuckled, except Mother. She offered a tight, strained smile that didn't quite reach her eyes. "I assure you, W.T.," she replied, her voice smooth but lacking its usual warmth, "no one is more disappointed by Benjamin's indisposition than I am."

It was then I noticed it definitively – the shift in her. Mother still radiated her effortless beauty, perfectly composed, yet something vital, some inner light, had dimmed. It was almost imperceptible, a subtle drawing-in around the eyes, a tension in her posture beneath the elegant gown. But I felt it. The easy grace seemed overlaid now with a brittle fragility. *Had the strain of maintaining the facade finally begun to crack it?*

My thoughts, however, were inevitably drawn across the vast dining room. Miles was seated several tables away, laughing easily with his own dinner companions. I found myself stealing glances, catching his eye once or twice, sharing a fleeting, private smile that sent a jolt through me. The urge to invite him over, to bridge the distance, was strong, especially now that Father's absence was a confirmed fixture. But Mother's reaction to Stead's harmless joke gave me pause. Best not to introduce any further complications tonight.

As the fish course was being cleared, I saw a steward approach our table and discreetly hand Birdie a small, folded note. She slipped it beneath the tablecloth, unfolding it in her lap. A slow smile spread across her face as she read, her eyes lighting up with a secret excitement. She quickly refolded the note and tucked it away. A message from her stewardess friend, Violet, confirming their plans for another clandestine adventure later tonight. Birdie looked lost in thought for the rest of the meal, likely already planning what she'd say to her mysterious third-class "writer."

The usual migration occurred after the final course, the gentlemen largely peeling off towards the allure of the Smoking Room, while most of the ladies congregated for coffee and liqueurs in the Reception Room. The orchestra played softly, conversations hummed, the atmosphere thick with perfume and cigar smoke drifting in from adjacent spaces.

I saw Mother draw Birdie aside near the entrance to the Grand Staircase. Their conversation was quiet, but I caught snippets.

"... poor Father still feeling dreadful..." Mother was saying, her voice conveying practiced sympathy. "... needs his rest, complete quiet... I thought it best, darling, if I moved into your adjoining room for the rest of the voyage. Just until he's feeling more himself."

Birdie's face fell, her earlier secret smile vanishing instantly. I could almost see her mind racing, her plans for sneaking below decks with Violet evaporating. But years of training in polite society took over. "Of course, Mother," she replied, forcing brightness into her tone. "Whatever you think is best. It's no bother at all."

"Such a good daughter," Mother patted her cheek. "Why don't we head up now? You can help me move a few essentials over." And with that, Mother led a visibly crestfallen Birdie towards the staircase, her own plans foiled.

Seeing my chance, I scanned the room for Miles. He was sitting alone on one of the plush settees near the windows, nursing a drink and smoking a cigarette, observing the room with a detached amusement. I walked over, my heart rate picking up slightly.

"Room for one more?" I asked, gesturing to the empty space beside him.

He looked up, a welcoming smile instantly lighting his face. "Benji. Was wondering where you'd got to. Pull up some settee."

I sat down, the proximity closer than our walk on deck earlier, the scent of his cigarette familiar now. We chatted easily for a few minutes about the dinner, the other passengers, the sheer scale of the ship. The conversation felt comfortable, easy, yet I felt the unspoken questions lingering from our earlier walk.

"Getting a bit stuffy in here," Miles remarked after stubbing out his cigarette. "Fancy relocating? We could try our luck crashing the Smoking Room?"

My stomach tightened. The Smoking Room, with its exclusive, masculine atmosphere, felt intimidating. And technically... "I'm not sure I'm quite old enough for that crowd," I admitted, trying to sound casual, hoping my lie about being twenty-one wouldn't unravel. "Perhaps just a walk on deck? Get some air?"

"Suits me," Miles agreed easily, standing up and offering me a hand. "Lead the way."

We stepped out onto the Boat Deck. The night air was cold, crisp, carrying the immense emptiness of the open ocean. Above, the sky was a velvet canvas strewn with impossibly bright stars, more than I'd ever seen on land. The only light came from the warm glow spilling from the ship's windows and the faint illumination of the deck lamps, leaving the railings and the lifeboats shrouded in deep shadow. We instinctively huddled closer together as we strolled towards the bow, the shared warmth a welcome shield against the chill wind.

We walked in silence for a while, simply absorbing the vastness, the quiet power of the ship moving through the darkness.

"So," Miles said finally, his voice quiet beside me. "You never did tell me."

"Tell you what?"

"Why you were so determined to bite my head off when we first met," he glanced at me, a gentle curiosity in his eyes. "On the gangway stairs? In your cabin? I thought you were going to throw me overboard."

I stopped walking, leaning against the cold railing, looking out at the dark water. This was it. The opening I hadn't known how to create myself. He deserved an explanation. And maybe, just maybe, I needed to finally say it aloud to someone other than myself.

Taking a deep, cold breath, I turned to face him in the starlight. "It wasn't about you, Miles," I began, my voice a mere scratch against the wind. "Not really. It was about... it was because of what happened in Paris." I paused, realizing that wasn't quite the beginning. "No, that's not right. Paris was the consequence, not the cause. Now, to understand what happened before Paris, the reason I was even in Paris, I guess you'd first need to understand how I got there in the first place. So, I guess our story begins last semester, at Yale."

Miles leaned back against the railing beside me, listening patiently, giving me the space to find the words.

"Going to Yale... it felt like my first real taste of freedom," I began, the memory still holding a bittersweet edge. "Finally away from home, away from the constant, watchful eye of my father. Away from his expectations. I thought I could finally take courses that actually interested me, explore my passion for writing, maybe even figure out who I really was, without judgment."

"I remember moving into the fraternity house – the same one Father had belonged to, naturally, and his father before him. Legacy demanded it. And that's where I first saw him." I didn't need to say his name; the memory was vivid enough. "He was magnetic. One of those fellows who just... fills a room the moment he enters. Handsome, charming, effortlessly confident. Everyone wanted to be around him. I won't lie, I envied him. Envied that ease, that charisma he possessed, whatever it was that made him seem so special, so untouchable."

"To my complete surprise," I continued, shaking my head slightly at the recollection, "out of all the freshmen pledging the house, many far more outgoing or athletic than myself, he seemed to single me out. He took a liking to me, sought out my company. Me – quiet, studious, always lost in a book. I couldn't understand it, but I didn't question it. I relished the attention, honestly. It boosted my confidence. I figured, foolishly perhaps, that maybe some of that effortless charm might rub off on me if I stayed close enough. So, I did. Stuck to him like glue."

I paused, gathering myself for the next part. "Then came Hell Week. The hazing rituals to prove we were worthy of joining the fraternity. One night, the upperclassmen dared us – charged us – with breaking into the Dean's office after midnight. Utterly idiotic, but... you know how it is. Peer pressure, wanting to belong."

"We actually managed to jimmy a window and get inside," I recounted, the memory still sharp with adrenaline. "But no sooner were we in, than we heard footsteps, keys rattling. Security. We scattered like rats. He and I ended up running off together, ducking behind hedges, hearts pounding, laughing breathlessly at the thrill of the near-miss, the shared danger."

"We ended up on the main commons, hidden in the shadows beneath the old elms. The adrenaline faded, the laughter died down. And then... he just looked at me. Really looked at me. The moonlight caught his eyes... And then... he kissed me."

I stopped, the memory hitting me with unexpected force even now. Miles remained silent beside me, his gaze fixed on the dark horizon, allowing me to continue at my own pace.

"I was... stunned," I finally went on. "Taken completely by surprise. But... not entirely unwilling, if I'm being honest with myself now. It was confusing. When he pulled back, I just managed to ask, 'What was that?'"

"His whole demeanor shifted instantly," I remembered, the change still jarring. "The confidence vanished, replaced by sheer panic. Fear. He grabbed my arm, his voice a harsh whisper. 'You'd better keep your mouth shut about this, Howell,' he threatened. 'Never tell a soul.' And then he just... ran off. Left me standing there alone under the moon, my head spinning."

"The days and weeks after that were... awful," I continued, my voice low. "I couldn't stop thinking about it – the kiss, his reaction, what it all meant. Did I enjoy it? Did it mean... what Frank and Archie suggested yesterday morning? Meanwhile, he became paranoid. Every time I saw him, he'd throw these suspicious, almost accusatory glances my way, like he expected me to expose him at any moment."

"I guess it was about two weeks later, I was summoned to the Dean's Office. My first thought was the break-in, that someone had identified us. My blood ran cold. When I walked in, my father was sitting there, across from Dean Whitmore. That seemed to confirm my fear."

"The Dean asked me to sit down. His tone was grave. 'Benjamin,' he said, 'some very serious accusations have been made against you.'"

"My father immediately jumped in, defending me before I even knew what the accusation was. 'Whit,' he said – of course, I thought, they're no doubt fellow alums, probably were in the same fraternity – 'this is absurd. My son would never... It's hearsay, baseless slander. There's no proof Benji is guilty of anything!'"

"Guilty of *what*?" I finally managed to ask.

"The Dean looked uncomfortable, exchanged a glance with my father. He empathized, he said, but he had to consider the school's reputation, the interests of the alumni, the potential scandal." My father then turned to me, his face grim, his eyes hard. And he asked me, point-blank, 'Benjamin. Did you kiss another male student?'"

The world tilted. "I was blindsided," I told Miles, shaking my head at the memory. "The break-in was forgotten. He – the boy who kissed me – had clearly panicked. Fearing I might say something, he'd gone to the Dean first, twisted the story, painted me as the aggressor to save his own skin."

"Suddenly, the entire tone of the room shifted. It wasn't about truth anymore; it was about damage control. Protecting the fraternity, protecting the university's image. The Dean said, given the accusation, true or not, the potential for rumor was too damaging. He spoke about the prestigious alumni, the endowment... He said he'd have no choice but to expel me."

"I tried to protest, to claim my innocence, explain what really happened, but it was like shouting into a void. My father didn't even ask for my side of the story. He just... negotiated."

"He asked Dean Whitmore for one semester. He'd pull me out of Yale immediately, let the 'heat' die down, let the rumor fade. Then, perhaps, we could revisit the matter next year. The Dean reluctantly agreed. But they made one thing crystal clear." I looked at Miles, the bitterness rising again. "If anyone asked – my mother, Birdie, anyone – the official story was that I'd been placed on academic probation due to poor grades. That I needed a semester off to 'refocus my studies.'"

I turned back to the ocean, the lie feeling colder, sharper than the night air. "A lie," I finished quietly. "To protect everyone but me. A lie that felt infinitely more shameful, more damaging, than the confusing truth of that kiss ever could have."

I paused, the cold air biting at my cheeks, the memory of that imposed lie still feeling like a fresh wound. Miles waited patiently beside me, his silence a steady presence in the vast darkness.

"So," I finally continued, my voice rough, "the official story was 'academic probation.' The unofficial result was exile. Father decided a change of scenery was required – perhaps to ensure I didn't 'relapse' into academic failure, or more likely, to get me far away from Yale before any real whispers started. A week later, I was in Paris."

The transition was jarring, abrupt. One moment, I was reeling from the betrayal in the Dean's office, the next, I was adrift in the chaotic, intoxicating, and ultimately hollow heart of Paris. We barely spoke, Father and I, during that first week. We coexisted in a suffocating silence, each word unsaid a heavier blow than any argument. We both knew the truth, and we both hated each other for it.

He tried to immerse me in Parisian culture – museums, operas, endless dinners – but it all felt like a facade. Then came the night he took me to the Moulin Rouge. The real Paris, perhaps, or at least the one he wanted me to see. The air was thick with cheap perfume, cigar smoke, and desperation disguised as gaiety. Tawdry dancers kicked listlessly on stage while wealthy men leered from the shadows, using the voyeuristic spectacle as permission to shed their own inhibitions. Father encouraged me to drink the Absinthe, that bitter, licorice-laced 'green fairy' famed for blurring the edges of reality. And blur it did. The sting of the drink, the cacophony of the room, the sheer weight of my unspoken shame... I drank to forget, to escape, to let my own rigid rules dissolve, hoping, perhaps, to simply float away on the tide of forced revelry.

The next thing I truly remember is the smell. Overpowering. Rotting teeth mingling with stale sweat, the cloying sweetness of cheap rosewater failing to mask the underlying decay of unwashed skin in the muggy heat of a small, unventilated room somewhere above the glittering chaos. She didn't have a name, not one she offered anyway. Perhaps she'd forgotten it herself, lost within the persona she sold nightly to men like my father, men seeking a different kind of oblivion.

She was all aggression, her painted smile a grotesque mask. "Kiss me," she demanded, her French accent thick but somehow still haughty, despite her circumstances. I tried. God, I tried. But the rancid stench of her breath turned my stomach. The room swam – the Absinthe butterfly flapping its restless wings, warping the peeling wallpaper at the seams. I recoiled.

"If I have to do all the work, it's gonna cost you extra, love," she grumbled, grabbing at my shirt.

"Come on, Benjamin, goddammit!" Father's voice roared from the shadows. He'd been sitting in a plush armchair in the corner, watching. Observing. Judging.

"I... I can't, Father," I choked out, nausea rising. "I really can't."

In an instant, he was beside the bed, his face contorted with rage. He grabbed the back of my head, forcefully shoving my face towards hers. "Like this, you nitwit!" he seethed, his grip like iron.

Panic flared. I flailed, pushing against him, against her, shouting for him to stop. My fist connected blindly, a lucky punch landing somewhere on his face. He swore, shrinking back for a crucial second.

In that fragile moment, I scrambled off the bed, yanking open the door, bolting down the narrow hall, down the creaking stairs, bursting out onto the bustling street below, still alive with late-night revelers.

"Get that ass of yours back in here, now!" Father's voice pursued me, closer than I expected. He caught me easily, his hand clamping down on my arm like a vice, spinning me around to face him under the flickering gaslight.

"Benjamin," his eyes blazed, pinning me in place. "This is not a game, son." Then, his expression shifted, the anger replaced by something harder, colder. "Look, I don't want to do this either, but you've left me no choice."

"I didn't do anything—"

"Benji," he cut me off, the use of my nickname startling, a sudden, manipulative attempt at connection. "This world is not fair. You know that. Whether you did, or you didn't, that doesn't matter now. What matters is what people think. And if they think you're..." He couldn't say the word, the label he feared as much as I did. "... Then you are. It's as simple, and as brutal, as that."

"But how is this," I gestured desperately back towards the building, "going to help? No one will know about this!"

"You'll know," he said, and his face softened then, in a way I'd never seen, a flicker of something that looked almost like shared pain, almost genuine. "Men like you... like... me..." The admission hung there, stunning me into silence. Him? My father? "... We have to work harder than others in this life, Benji. We have to do things we don't want to do. Be people we'd rather not be. Prove things we shouldn't have to prove. But that's just the way it is."

My mind reeled. People like him? Was this monstrous act some twisted form of kinship? Some horrifying lesson passed from one generation to the next?

"This is what men are supposed to do, Benji," he insisted, his voice low, urgent.

"But I don't want to," I whispered, the thought of going back into that room making me physically ill. "I don't even think I can." A knot twisted in my stomach.

"Use that rage, Benji," he leaned closer, his eyes intense. "All that unfairness, all that shame they piled on you, all that bottled-up rage... let it out." He pointed back towards the dimly lit window above us. "She's waiting. Let's go back up there, together. And we'll both take out our rage."

Numb. That's the only word for it. A thick fog enveloped my thoughts, my movements. My judgment ceased to exist. It felt as if I were watching someone else, a marionette bearing my likeness, moving through a scene not of my choosing. I wasn't really there. He – that other Benji – was the one who allowed Father to lead him back up the stairs, back into that horrid, cloying room. He was the one who took one side of her compliant, indifferent body, while his father took the other. Each man performing a grotesque parody of desire, trying desperately to prove something – to each other, to themselves, to the ghosts of judgment that haunted them both – proving they were real men. Proving that despite the impulses they would forever have to suppress, they could still do what men were apparently born, and required, to do. To her, it was a business transaction. To me, it was my innocence.

And afterwards, in the suffocating silence, he looked across the disheveled bed, into his father's eyes – eyes that held not pride, nor disgust, nor even relief, but only a shared, hollow acknowledgment of the necessary, ugly act they had committed together. And they both knew.

The swell of ocean waves brought me back to the Boat Deck of Titanic. An angry surge had kicked up below us, perhaps echoing the flutters of anxiety that were coursing through me—being spilled out in the maiden retelling of this tragic event. My eyes, icy with their manifest of tears, made my cheeks quiver in their exposure to the salty chill of the Atlantic breeze.

I looked over at Miles, who'd been listening with an intentional silence. Not once did he interrupt. Not once did I feel that he desired me to hold back, to mince words. Not once did I. It felt incredible to get this out, the poison drawn from the wound, at least as much as it can be to admit the horrible sins of this past Spring.

"Benji," he finally said, so tenderly, so softly.

I merely looked at him in reply, afraid to say anything more for fear that I might shatter this fragile moment of honesty, this unexpected sanctuary.

"May I... hug you?"

The question suspended itself in the cold night air, simple, direct, yet holding immense weight. A hug? After everything I'd just confessed? The ugliness, the shame, the horror of it all? I hadn't expected judgment, perhaps, not from Miles, but I hadn't expected... this. This simple offer of comfort. I couldn't find my voice, couldn't trust it not to break, so I just nodded, a single, jerky movement.

He stepped closer, closing the small space between us, and wrapped his arms around me. It wasn't tentative or awkward; it was firm, solid, encompassing. I instinctively leaned into the embrace, burying my face against the rough wool of his jacket, shielding myself from the wind, from the memories, from everything. The solid warmth of him, the steady beat of his heart against my ear, felt like the only anchor in a world that had just been ripped apart and terrifyingly reassembled.

For a long moment, we just stood there, locked together against the vast, indifferent ocean and the star-strewn sky. The tears I hadn't realized I was holding back finally came, hot and silent, soaking into his coat. He didn't say anything, didn't offer platitudes or try to fix it. He just held me, letting the storm break, his steady presence a quiet testament to understanding, to acceptance.

Finally, my breathing evened out, the shivers subsiding. He loosened his hold slightly, allowing me to pull back, though his hands remained resting gently on my arms. I couldn't quite meet his eyes, feeling exposed, raw.

"Thank you," my voice cracked.

"*Thank you*, Benji," Miles replied softly, his gaze filled with an empathy that didn't feel like pity. "For trusting me." He gave my arm a gentle squeeze before letting go completely. "No one," he added, his voice firm now, quiet but intense, "should ever have to go through something like that. Especially not alone." He took my chin, with a gentle hand, and raised my face to meet his. "You're not alone, Benji. Not anymore."

We stood there for another moment, the shared weight of my story settling between us, somehow lighter now that it wasn't mine alone to carry. The wind whipped around us, but the chill felt less biting now, tempered by the unexpected warmth of connection, of being truly seen, perhaps for the very first time.

CHAPTER 24

Violet stood behind Birdie, expertly twisting her hair into a simple but elegant daytime style, suitable for breakfast. The cabin, usually Birdie's private escape, felt subtly altered by the presence of our mother's belongings – a half-unpacked valise open on one chair, an extra dressing gown draped over the settee where Mother herself now sat, staring blankly towards the window, seemingly lost in a world miles away from the gentle sway of the ship.

"Do you think Mr. Stead will truly ask for a refund, Mother?" Birdie asked lightly, trying to break the heavy silence that had settled in the room since she'd woken. "His joke last night seemed to fall rather flat with you."

There was no response. Mother continued her vacant stare, her teacup resting untouched on the table beside her.

"Mother?" Birdie tried again, louder this time, catching Violet's eye in the mirror with a questioning glance.

Mother started, blinking as if roused from a deep sleep. "Hmm? What was that, darling?" She attempted a bright smile, but it faltered, not quite masking the shadows beneath her eyes. Clearly she hadn't slept well, if at all. "Forgive me, my mind was elsewhere."

"I was just asking about Mr. Stead's joke last night," Birdie repeated patiently.

"Oh. Yes. Rather silly, wasn't it?" Mother replied vaguely, her gaze already drifting back towards the window.

Something was definitely wrong. Birdie had seen Mother put out before, certainly, or stressed before a social event, but this was different. This was a profound distraction, an inward turning that felt heavy, unsettling. Even Violet, usually adept at maintaining professional discretion, seemed to sense the unusual tension, her movements becoming quieter, more tentative as she finished pinning Birdie's hair.

All at once, Mother seemed to gather herself, standing abruptly. "Well," she announced, forcing that air of brightness back into her voice. "I really must... attend to something before breakfast. You just run along when you're ready, darling. I shall see you downstairs shortly." She patted Birdie's shoulder distractedly and swept out of the room before Birdie could inquire further, leaving a palpable sense of unease in her wake.

As the door clicked shut, Birdie sighed, slumping slightly at her vanity table. Violet met her gaze in the mirror again, her expression sympathetic.

"Everything alright, Birdie?" Violet asked softly, tidying away the hairpins.

"I don't know," Birdie confessed. "She's been like this since she moved her things in last night. Quiet. Distant. Like she's here, but not really here."

"Perhaps she truly is worried about your father's seasickness?" Violet suggested gently.

Birdie scoffed lightly. "Father? Seasick? Not likely. He's got sea legs older than I am." She hesitated, then lowered her voice. "Speaking of last night... Violet, I'm so sorry I didn't meet you."

"I wondered what happened," Violet admitted. "Waited for a bit down near Scotland Road, but figured something must have come up."

Birdie sighed dramatically. "Mother. She announced – right after dinner, mind you – that Father was so terribly ill he needed absolute quiet, and therefore she was moving in here." She gestured around the now-shared cabin. "Completely ruined our plans. But, how could I say no?"

"Ah," Violet nodded in understanding. "Well, that explains her mood, perhaps? Upset about being displaced?"

"Maybe," Birdie conceded, though she didn't sound convinced. "But it feels like more than that. Did you see her just now? It's like... like she's seen a ghost."

Violet frowned slightly, considering. "She did seem... preoccupied. Hopefully, a good breakfast will lift her spirits." She gave Birdie's shoulder a reassuring pat. "And yours too. Pity about last night, but there's always tonight, eh?"

Birdie managed a small smile, the thought of seeing Oliver again momentarily pushing aside her concern for her mother. "Oh, Violet, yes, please," she said, standing up and smoothing her morning dress. "I'll find a way to go back with you."

Mother closed the door to Birdie's cabin behind her, the brief interaction leaving her resolve hardened, not softened. She walked the few steps back to the main suite she had occupied with Benjamin up until last night. Taking a steadying breath, she pushed the door open and stepped inside.

The heavy curtains were still drawn, casting the room in a gloomy twilight that smelled faintly of stale cigars and perhaps brandy from the night before. Father stirred in the large bed as the latch clicked, pushing himself up against the pillows, blinking against the intrusion. He looked rumpled, weary, whether from feigned illness or actual lack of sleep, she couldn't tell. Nor, she realized with a chilling clarity, did she particularly care anymore.

He opened his mouth to speak, to question her return, but she cut him off before a sound could emerge, her voice low and steady—final.

"I was awake all night, Benjamin," she stated flatly, standing near the foot of the bed, refusing to come closer. "Thinking. And I've decided what must be done."

He watched her, wary now, sensing the shift in her demeanor, the absence of the tearful vulnerability from last night.

"For the sake of the children," she continued, her voice gaining strength, fueled by a cold, hard certainty. "For Margaret and Benji. We *will* find a way to make this... work. At least for now." She saw confusion flicker in his eyes, maybe even a glimmer of hope, and swiftly crushed it. "We can determine the precise terms of our arrangement once we are home. But for the remainder of this voyage, appearances will be maintained. You will cease this *pathetic* charade of seasickness. You will attend *all* meals. You will make polite conversation. You will act the part of a devoted husband and father."

She paused, letting the commands sink in. "We are committed to the Wideners' dinner party tomorrow evening, and you will be there, by my side. Furthermore," she added, a new thought crystallizing, "Monday is Margaret and Benji's eighteenth birthday. I had planned to surprise them by celebrating it Sunday night, but as we're already committed to the Wideners' party, I've decided we will celebrate it tonight, at dinner. Properly. As a family. I expect you to present a cheerful front and have their gift ready. A gift that shows me that you're serious about this family."

Benjamin stared at her, his expression unreadable. He seemed to weigh her words, the implications, the undeniable shift in power, but remained silent, offering no argument, no protest. Perhaps he recognized the finality in her tone.

Seeing his silence as acquiescence, if not agreement, Mother took a step closer, her voice dropping again, laced now with the bitterness of years of ignored warnings and stifled pride.

"My father told me what you were, you know," she said quietly, the words sharp as shards of glass. "'Benjamin Howell,' he said, 'is a two-bit conman with an award-winning smile. He's after our money, Caroline, nothing more.' I should have listened to him then. But I didn't."

She took another step. "I should have listened to all the catty rumors, too. All the whispers about Benjamin Sutherland-Howell spending more time with his business partners than with his wife and children. All the speculation about what kind of 'business' he was really conducting with them." She let the implication hang in the stale air. "But I didn't listen. I defended you. I maintained the facade."

Her eyes locked onto his. "Well, now it's my turn to play the upper hand, Benjamin. Let's be clear. Without my family's money to broker your deals, to fund your ambitions, you'd likely be lying in a gutter somewhere. And believe me, a part of me wishes you were. But," her voice softened subtly, her motivation laid bare, "if that were the case, I wouldn't have my children. Those two beautiful children who have grown into adults far too quickly. Children who will likely leave us soon enough if they sense this... rot at the core of our family."

Her resolve hardened again. "But God as my witness, Benjamin, I refuse to let that happen. Not without a fight. I will not lose my children because of your failings. So, if pretending this marriage still functions is what it takes to keep them close, to give them one last semblance of normalcy before their lives truly begin, then so be it. That is what we will do."

She turned towards the door, her back straight, her head held high. "Now, get up. Wash the stench of cigars and brandy off of you. And shave that face. You look appalling." She paused with her hand on the doorknob. "I'll see you downstairs at breakfast."

And with that, she left the room, closing the door with quiet finality, leaving Father alone in the dim, silent suite to contemplate the new terms of their fractured existence.

The Café Parisian was quickly becoming our sanctuary. By Saturday morning, meeting there felt like an established routine, a silent agreement forged in the wake of shared vulnerability and genuine connection.

Sunlight once again streamed through the open windows, the cheerful trellis-work and wicker furniture a familiar, comforting sight. Today felt different, lighter. We had agreed, unspoken, to spend the day together, exploring the ship, simply existing in this bubble outside of our ordinary lives. Not rushing things, not forcing things. Living in the moment.

Miles arrived shortly after I did, sliding into the seat opposite me with an easy smile that seemed less guarded than yesterday. He placed his camera carefully on the table beside him. I, in turn, had my leather-bound journal resting on my lap, ready to capture thoughts or observations as they came. We were two chroniclers, preparing to document the day in our own distinct ways.

The waiter approached, recognizing us now. "Messieurs? The usual?"

Miles grinned at me. "Two espressos?" he prompted gently.

I sighed inwardly but nodded at the waiter, managing a smile. "Yes, please. Two espressos. And perhaps another chocolate croissant?" Might as well lean into the routine fully, even if the coffee remained an acquired taste I had yet to acquire.

As the waiter departed, I looked across at Miles, the events of last night still feeling both incredibly raw and profoundly relieving. "Miles," I began, my voice softer than usual, "about last night... on deck..."

He met my gaze, his expression open, patient.

"Thank you," I continued, the words simple but carrying immense weight. "For listening. For... everything. For letting me flush that wound. Get all of the poison out." I hesitated, searching for the right phrase. "It felt... well, it showed me what having a true companion should feel like."

Miles reached across the table then, briefly covering my hand with his own, his touch warm and reassuring. "Benji," he corrected gently, his eyes holding mine, "this is what having a true companion is."

His simple affirmation resonated deeply, settling something within me. It wasn't just a hypothetical feeling; it was real, happening now, here, between us. The shared understanding, the acceptance without judgment – it was unlike anything I had ever known.

The waiter returned with our espressos and the pastry. We raised the small cups. "What should we toast?" Miles asked. "Good health? Good fortune?"

"To companionship," I said quietly.

"To companionship," he echoed, his smile genuine.

I took a sip of the espresso. It was still strong, still bitter, but perhaps... perhaps not quite as horrid as yesterday. Or maybe everything just tasted different today. We broke the croissant, the conversation flowing easily now, lighter, filled with plans for the day – exploring the ship, Miles taking photographs, me perhaps finding inspiration for my journal – two companions ready to face the day, together.

While Miles and I were navigating the complex notes of espresso and unspoken feelings in the Café Parisian, breakfast in the main Dining Saloon was a more bustling affair. At the Sutherland-Howell table, Birdie found herself surprisingly energized, perhaps fueled by the sleep she got last night by staying in, or simply the intellectual sparring that her wits enjoyed. Either way, her senses were sharp this morning, and she was firing on all cylinders.

"...and to my earlier point, Colonel Gracie, that women in ancient Egypt could own land and manage businesses," Birdie argued, leaning forward slightly, "it demonstrates a societal respect for female capability that seems to have diminished rather than grown in subsequent millennia. Wouldn't you agree?"

Colonel Gracie chuckled, dabbing his lips with his napkin. "Capability, perhaps, my dear Margaret, but not political authority. They couldn't vote, could they?" he countered playfully, clearly enjoying the debate.

"And yet," Mr. Stead interjected before Birdie could respond, always ready for historical discourse, "one might argue that the Egyptians achieved stability for centuries longer than the Greeks or Romans who followed, despite their patriarchal voting structures."

"Precisely!" Birdie declared, pointing a finger for emphasis. "Those esteemed civilizations, run entirely by men making all the crucial decisions, eventually collapsed anyway, didn't they?"

A ripple of appreciative chuckles went around the table, even from Mrs. Allison, who seemed more animated this morning, little by little coming into her own, even when her husband gave her a wary eye. The Countess smiled encouragingly at Birdie, encouraging her to keep up the good fight. Only Mother seemed distracted, offering polite but fleeting attention to the conversation.

Just as Gracie was formulating a rebuttal, a sudden hush fell over their immediate section of the dining room. All conversation at their table ceased. Birdie looked up to see Father standing awkwardly beside the table, looking freshly shaven, impeccably dressed, and attempting a smile that didn't quite penetrate the surface of his face.

"Good morning, all," Father announced, his voice trying for its usual confident charm but falling slightly flat. "Hope I'm not too late? Mind if I join you?"

"Benjamin!" Mr. Stead exclaimed, breaking the momentary stunned silence. "We thought you'd abandoned us entirely! I was just about to demand Mr. Ismay refund my passage, having specifically requested your table!"

More polite laughter, though strained this time. "Forgive me, W.T.," Father replied smoothly, taking the empty seat beside Mother that a steward quickly pulled out. "Just needed an extra day to find my sea legs." As he sat, his gaze met Mother's across the table. It was brief, almost undetectable, but Birdie saw the flicker of understanding pass between them – a silent acknowledgment, a confirmation of terms agreed upon in private. Mother inclined her head slightly, accepting his presence with practiced grace, though the subtle dimness Birdie had noticed earlier remained.

Gladys, who stared rather peculiarly at the sight of my father, looked awkwardly at my mother. *What was that look? Was it pity?* Mother wondered. A few tables away, Ismay leaned his chair back to note the recent addition to our table. His movement caught Mother's eye, but the second her impulse allowed her to look at him, she quickly snapped her head back, as though she'd never seen him.

The table conversation slowly resumed its rhythm, though Father remained mostly quiet, focusing on his breakfast. Mr. Stead, however, turned his attention back to Birdie.

"Margaret, my dear, your points this morning are exceptionally well-argued," he said approvingly. "It gives an old journalist hope for the next generation." He leaned forward slightly. "Tell me, have you made use of the ship's library yet? It's remarkably well-stocked for a vessel at sea."

"I haven't had the chance, Mr. Stead," Birdie admitted.

"Well, perhaps after breakfast, you might join me in the Lounge? I intend to do a bit of reading myself – research for that speech I mentioned. You could perhaps find some texts to further bolster your arguments for... your worthy cause." He smiled kindly. "We could assist each other."

"Oh, I'd be delighted!" Birdie's eyes lit up at the prospect.

"Splendid idea, Stead!" Colonel Gracie boomed, overhearing them. "Count me in! Happy to offer my assistance as well. Always good to understand the opposing viewpoint, eh?"

Birdie forced a gracious smile, trying not to let her dismay show. Mr. Stead merely offered the Colonel a polite nod, while Birdie caught the Countess and Mrs. Allison exchanging barely concealed, sly smirks across the table. Gracie's offer of "assistance" was entirely unnecessary, but refusing it would be impolite. It seemed her research session would have an uninvited, opinionated chaperone.

"I'll join too," said Father. All heads turned to face him, making him feel slightly awkward sitting in the limelight. "Perhaps you'll both benefit from an impartial point of view."

"Splendid idea," Mother said, taking Father's hand. "I'm excited to see where this goes."

Leaving the bright airiness of the Café Parisian behind, a shared sense of purpose seemed to propel us forward. The day stretched before us, an uncharted territory much like the ocean surrounding us. Miles, camera slung over his shoulder, had a mischievous glint in his eye. I clutched my journal, ready to record whatever adventures unfolded.

Instead of heading towards the familiar passenger decks, Miles steered me towards a less-trafficked corridor, eventually stopping before a heavy steel door marked plainly with stark, black letters: CREW ONLY. NO PASSENGERS BEYOND THIS POINT.

I hesitated. "Miles, are you sure about this? What if someone sees us?"

He grinned, already pushing the door open a crack and peering down the utilitarian passageway beyond. "Oh my gosh, I'm so sorry. I didn't see that sign, sir. We'll be on our way, then," Miles mocked, practicing the phony, apologetic tone he'd apparently use if we were caught. He looked back at me. "You worry too much, Benj. I promise you, it's not a big deal to break the rules every now and then. Live in the moment, remember?" he said with that now-familiar, infectious wink.

"Live in the moment," I agreed, though my heart had become a restless canary, fluttering about the prison bars of my ribcage. The thrill of breaking the rules, especially with Miles, was undeniably potent.

He pulled me through the doorway into a world starkly different from the passenger areas. Spartan whitewashed steel walls, exposed pipes overhead, the steady thrum of machinery vibrating through the floor. We moved quickly, our footsteps echoing slightly, Miles occasionally pulling me into an alcove or behind a stack of supplies as uniformed crew members bustled past, thankfully too preoccupied with their duties to pay much attention to two out-of-place young men.

"I told you..." Miles whispered conspiratorially as we hurried along, "I have something I want to show you. Something incredible. You're going to love it, Benj."

His certainty, his excitement, was contagious, overriding my nervousness. Where on earth was he taking me?

Finally, after navigating a maze of corridors and descending a steep metal ladder, we arrived at another heavy door. Miles wrestled it open with ease, as if he'd done it all before, revealing a vast, dimly lit space – one of the forward cargo holds. The air was cool, smelling of dust, wood shavings, and something faintly mechanical, perhaps mechanical grease? Giant crates were stacked high, secured with ropes, alongside countless bundles, sacks of mail, and various pieces of luggage too large for the cabins. Light filtered down in dusty shafts from openings high above.

My eyes immediately landed on the most incongruous object in the room: a gleaming, candy-apple red Renault motorcar, lashed securely near the center of the hold. It looked impossibly sleek and luxurious amidst the drab functionality of the cargo space.

"Wow," I breathed. "This is the one I saw them loading in Southampton. The crane lowered it right down into the ship."

"Isn't she a beauty?" Miles agreed, already pulling out his camera. "Quick, stand next to it."

We took turns snapping quick photographs – me awkwardly posing by the gleaming fender, Miles leaning casually against the bonnet with his signature confident grin. The absurdity of having our picture taken with a French automobile deep in the bowels of an ocean liner wasn't lost on me.

"Alright," Miles said, capping his lens. "As lovely as she is, that's not what I brought you down here to see."

He led me further into the hold, towards a large, sturdy-looking wooden crate tucked away between stacks of other cargo. I noticed immediately that several nails had been carefully pried loose along one edge, suggesting recent entry. Miles glanced around, ensuring we were still alone, then turned back to me, his eyes wide with excitement.

"Are you ready to see this?" he whispered dramatically. "The real reason I risked life and limb – and your reputation as a law-abiding citizen – to bring you down here?"

My curiosity was piqued beyond measure. I nodded eagerly.

With another theatrical flourish, Miles carefully lifted the loosened lid of the crate. Inside, nestled amongst layers of protective raffia packing material, was a large object carefully wrapped in a plain linen bag.

"You wanna do the honors?" Miles asked, gesturing for me to reach in.

My fingers trembled slightly as I reached into the crate and lifted the linen-wrapped object. It was heavy, substantial. Carefully, I untied the drawstring of the bag and slid the contents free.

My breath caught. It was a book, yes, but unlike any book I had ever seen or imagined. Heavy, leather-bound, perhaps Morocco leather dyed a deep peacock blue or green, it was dazzlingly inlaid with intricate gold tooling and an astonishing array of jewels. Hundreds, perhaps thousands, of them – glittering diamonds, deep green emeralds, fiery rubies, luminous pearls, rich amber, turquoise, amethyst – all meticulously set into elaborate patterns across the cover. It was overwhelmingly lavish, breathtakingly opulent.

"Oh my word," I whispered, aghast. "It... it can't be. I thought it was only a legend. I didn't know it actually existed."

"The Great Omar," Miles confirmed quietly beside me, his voice filled with reverence. "The jeweled binding of the Rubáiyát of Omar Khayyám. One of a kind. Priceless."

"How on earth did you find it?" I asked.

"Well, to be honest, I was looking for the mummy they say is buried somewhere down here." We both laughed. He went on, "Knowing you're a writer and all," he looked at me earnestly, "seeing this... I instantly thought of you. Thought you might want to see it too. A masterpiece of bookbinding, holding a masterpiece of poetry. There's only one in the whole world, Benj. And I wanted you to see it. To hold it."

I was overwhelmed. Speechless. The sheer artistry, the value, the legend made real... but more than that, the fact that Miles, upon discovering this incredible treasure, had thought of me. That he had risked getting caught simply to share this moment, this discovery, with me because he knew it would resonate with my passion for words, for books.

"Miles... I..." I struggled for words.

"Pictures first," he grinned, breaking the spell slightly, camera already back in hand.

We carefully lifted the magnificent book, taking photos of each other holding it, photos of the cover's intricate details, documenting this secret encounter with a piece of legendary artistry hidden deep within the Titanic.

"Now, give me one like you're really excited, Benj. It's the Rubáiyát for crying out loud," he said with a laugh.

I smiled bigger than I could ever remember smiling in my life. Here I was, laughing, delighting with the man who wanted to show me that he cared about me, unconditionally. It wasn't because of anything I could do for him. I didn't have to be anything that I wasn't. He did this all, he chose me, simply because I was me. No one else. And, what's more, I was living in the moment, finally living.

As we carefully placed the book back in its linen bag and nestled it amongst the raffia, I felt overcome by the moment – the shared secret, the thrill of discovery, the sheer, unexpected kindness and consideration Miles had shown me. Setting the crate lid back in place, I turned to face him in the dim light of the cargo hold. The air crackled with the energy that had been building between us since breakfast, since last night.

Caught up in a wave of gratitude, adrenaline, and the undeniable pull I felt towards him, I acted purely on impulse. I stepped forward, reached up, tangled my fingers in the hair at the nape of his neck, and pulled his face down to mine. I kissed him.

It wasn't hesitant or questioning like the kiss under the elms at Yale. This was unbridled, passionate, a release of all the angst, fear, hope, and confusion that had been bottling up inside me. It was the frantic energy from the punching bag channeled into something entirely different. It was the acknowledgment whispered to Archie and Frank made real. It was the companionship toasted over espresso, sealed here in the dusty silence of the cargo hold, surrounded by crates and secrets. For a moment that stretched out, timeless, there was only the press of his lips against mine, the shared breath, the dizzying confirmation of something undeniable blossoming between us amidst the hidden treasures of the deep.

Diana of Versailles
Carrara marble
Lounge
Inspired by Versailles
green velvet

CHAPTER 25

Following breakfast, Birdie's slightly expanded research group made its way towards the First Class Lounge. Father trailed slightly behind Birdie, with Mother bringing up the rear, her composure impeccable but still carrying that faint, underlying fragility.

Entering the Lounge always felt like stepping into the Palace of Versailles—albeit smaller, even if only slightly so. The room was magnificent – vast, high-ceilinged, paneled in exquisitely carved English oak reminiscent of the famous French palace, though stained a lighter, warmer tone. Plush armchairs and sofas upholstered in green velvet were arranged in intimate groupings around small tables, inviting quiet conversation or contemplation. Sunlight streamed through the enormous arched windows overlooking the Promenade Deck, illuminating the intricate carvings and the room's centerpiece – a massive, grand marble fireplace, complete with a cheery glowing electric insert. Opposite to it, dominating the aft wall, stood an equally impressive bookcase filled with leather-bound volumes, anchoring itself to the center of the room.

Mr. Stead and Colonel Gracie were already seated at a large table near the bookcase, papers spread before them. Gracie appeared to be meticulously polishing his spectacles, while Stead scribbled furiously on a sheet of Titanic stationery.

"Ah, there you are!" Stead looked up as we approached. "Find yourselves seats. I'm just finishing a rather urgent letter." He touched down his pen once more, dashed off a signature with a flourish, and folded the paper swiftly.

He sealed the letter in an envelope, addressed it simply, then flagged down a passing steward. "My good man," Stead instructed, handing over the letter, "see this gets posted with the outgoing mail. Destination: New Amsterdam."

The steward, seemingly familiar with this request, gave a knowing bow. "Right away, Mr. Stead. To New Amsterdam it is." He tucked the letter into his pouch and departed.

"Mr. Stead," Birdie pointed towards the entrance, "there's a letter drop box right by the door, for passengers' mail."

Stead chuckled heartily. "Indeed there is, my dear Margaret. But 'posting to New Amsterdam' is a bit of an old shipboard tradition of mine. An inside joke with the postal clerks, you might say. Ensures it gets special handling." He winked, though the logic seemed rather dubious.

As everyone settled into chairs around the table or pulled volumes from the nearby bookcase, Mother's focus still hadn't joined her party. Her gaze had fixed on a group of ladies seated across the expansive room, near the fireplace. Eleanor Widener sat among them, holding court over what looked like seating charts spread across her table.

"If you'll excuse me for just a moment," Mother murmured politely to our group, her eyes still locked across the room. "There's someone I simply must have a quick word with." She rose gracefully and glided across the lounge towards Mrs. Widener's table.

Eleanor Widener looked up as Mother approached, her face breaking into a warm smile. "Caroline, darling! We were just trying to solve the puzzle of tomorrow night's seating chart. Come, give us your opinion." She gestured to an empty chair beside her.

"Thank you, Nora, but I can't stay," Mother demurred, leaning in slightly, her voice low and confidential. "Actually, that's what I wanted to speak to you about." She paused, choosing her words carefully. "Could you possibly do me an enormous favor?"

"Of course, dear, anything," Eleanor replied readily, though she looked intrigued.

"The dinner party," Mother continued, her gaze steady but carrying an undercurrent of strain. "Mr. Ismay... would it be terribly difficult if... if perhaps he wasn't invited?"

Eleanor's perfectly plucked eyebrows rose in surprise. "Bruce Ismay? Not invited? But Caroline, he's already accepted! Days ago. George would never hear of uninviting the head of the line!"

A flicker of dismay crossed Mother's face, quickly masked. "No, no, of course not. How silly of me. Please, disregard that." She took a breath. "Then, perhaps... another smaller favor? Regarding the seating?"

"Naturally. What is it?"

"Could you possibly ensure," Mother's voice dropped further, almost pleading, "that Mr. Ismay is not seated anywhere near Benjamin or me. Another table altogether." She hesitated. "In fact, Nora, if you could place him as far away from us as protocol allows, I would be eternally grateful."

Eleanor Widener stared at her friend, confusion warring with concern. She knew Mother well enough to recognize genuine distress beneath the polite request. She also knew better than to pry into the intricate, often unspoken dramas of her social circle. "Is something the matter, Caroline?" she asked gently, already suspecting she wouldn't get a straight answer.

"It would simply be... *easier*," Mother replied vaguely, offering a small, tight smile that fell short of being genuine. "Less complicated for everyone involved."

Understanding dawned in Eleanor's eyes – not understanding the specifics, but understanding the need. She placed a reassuring hand on Mother's arm. "Say no more, my dear. Consider it done. I'll rearrange things immediately. He'll be seated at the overflow table, clear across the room. Will that suffice?"

Relief washed over Mother's face, softening her features. "Oh, Nora, thank you. Truly. You're a lifesaver."

Mother placed a grateful hand on Mrs. Widener's arm, offered a brief smile to the other ladies, and turned back towards her own table, her composure seemingly restored, though perhaps a touch paler than before.

She rejoined the study group just as Father had opened a thick tome on political history and Birdie was scanning the shelves for works on ancient civilizations. "Sorry for the delay," Mother said smoothly, taking her seat. "Just confirming details for the Wideners' dinner party tomorrow night."

We emerged from the dim functionality of Scotland Road, back through the doorway marked 'Emergency Door', blinking as our eyes adjusted to the familiar elegance of the lowest landing of the Grand Staircase. The air here felt different – warmer, scented faintly with polish and perhaps the distant aroma of baking from the galleys further aft. The transition felt like surfacing, leaving the secret depths of the cargo hold and our shared discovery behind, though the electric charge of that kiss still tingled on my lips and fingertips, among other parts of me.

"You're sure your family won't mind my joining your table for dinner tonight?" Miles asked.

"Not at all. My father's never there, his chair's been gathering dust every meal. They'll love you," I said, pausing for dramatic effect, "I mean, who wouldn't?" I gave him a wink, with a newfound confidence that impressed both of us.

"Alright then, I'll dress to impress," he chuckled.

Miles looked around, taking in the fine oak paneling and polished brass of the E deck landing. "Back among the civilized, eh?" he murmured, though his smile held the shared secret of our recent transgression.

"Wait," I said, stopping him before he started up the stairs. "Before you take another step... look up." I gestured straight up, to the cutout of the stairwell.

He followed my gaze, tipping his head back. From here, the lowest level accessible to passengers, the full majesty of the staircase unfolded above us – deck upon deck spiraling upwards, the intricate wrought-iron balustrades, the gold leaf accents catching the light, drawing the eye relentlessly towards the magnificent glass dome six levels above. Even filtered down this far, the light from the dome gave the entire space a soaring, cathedral-like quality. A hallowed, sacred space. It truly was my favorite view on the entire ship.

"Wow," Miles breathed, genuinely impressed. He instinctively raised his camera, framing the shot. "Incredible perspective." He took the picture just as a uniformed steward approached as he descended from D Deck.

"Excuse me, sir," he addressed Miles directly. "Mr. Force?"

"Yes?" Miles lowered his camera, looking surprised.

"A wireless message for you, sir. Just arrived. I was headed to your cabin, but as luck would have it I saw you gents down here." The steward presented a small envelope on a silver tray.

"Oh. Thank you," Miles took the envelope, his expression clouding slightly with apprehension. The steward gave a polite nod and departed as silently as he'd arrived.

Miles turned the envelope over in his hands for a moment before sliding a finger under the seal and extracting the Marconigram flimsy. I watched his face as he read, saw the easy smile fade, replaced by a familiar tightness around his jaw, the deflation of the hopeful energy we'd shared just moments before. The reality of the world beyond this ship, it seemed, had found him even here.

He folded the paper slowly, tucking it into his pocket without comment, but the carefree mood had vanished. The weight of his father's expectations, the looming reality of the law firm, settled back onto his shoulders.

"Bad news?" I asked gently, already guessing the answer.

He sighed, leaning back against the base of the staircase. "Just Father," he said, trying for lightness but failing. "Confirming arrangements. Apparently, my desk at the firm is already waiting, polished and ready for my immediate post upon arrival in New York. No time to waste starting my illustrious career as a glorified paper-pusher." His voice was laced with a bitterness that mirrored my own feelings about Father's plans for me.

The reminder of the futures waiting for us – futures neither of us wanted – dampened the moment. The giddy fantasy of our own film studio suddenly felt impossibly distant, childish even.

"Hey," I said, stepping closer, longing to restore the connection, the hope, we'd felt in the cargo hold. "Don't let him ruin this. We still have days left." I offered him a tentative smile. "To live in the moment, remember?"

"To live in the moment," he agreed with a soft smile.

"Now," I climbed a few steps, put on my game face, then, confidently, spun back to face him. "All we need is to come up with a plan."

He looked at me skeptically. "What kind of plan, Benji? One that involves running away to join the circus?"

"Our studio," I insisted, lowering my voice conspiratorially. "We just need investors, Miles. People with vision. People with money who aren't afraid to take a chance on something new, something exciting like moving pictures."

He snorted softly. "And where exactly do you plan on finding these mythical investors between here and New York Harbor?"

"They're right here," I said eagerly. "On this ship. Think about it! Millionaires, industrialists... people looking for the next big thing." My mind raced, latching onto an idea I'd had earlier. "Mr. Harper, for instance! Henry Sleeper Harper, the publisher. He's aboard."

"The publisher?" Miles looked intrigued.

"Yes! Imagine," I continued, the idea gaining momentum, "if I could just get him to read some of my writing. A story, a play... If he liked it, offered an advance... It could be seed money, Miles! Enough to get started. Enough for us to make our escape. To run away together, pursue our dream!"

For a moment, the spark returned to Miles's eyes. The shared dream, however improbable, flickered back to life. He pushed away from the staircase, caught up in the possibility. "Harper... yes, I know the name. But Benji," his practical side resurfaced, "how on earth do you plan to get someone like Henry Harper, head of one of the biggest publishing houses in the world, to even glance at your work, let alone meet with you?"

I allowed myself a small, confident smile, remembering the connections, however strained, that had offered to arrange that very thing. "Don't worry about that," I said, meeting his hopeful gaze. "I know someone who can make it happen."

As gay strings swam between the alcoves of the Reception Room, J. Bruce Ismay sat nursing a cup of tea, though the delicate china felt like it might crack in his restless grip. His nerves fuming like the roll of tobacco—belching smoke—between the vise of his fingers. Opposite him, Captain Smith sipped his own tea, his weathered face calm, betraying none of the pressure Ismay felt churning within him. The gentle sounds of polite conversation seemed miles away.

Ismay carefully unfolded the Marconigram he'd received that morning, smoothing it flat on the small table between them. The stark typed words seemed to leap off the page:

> UTMOST IMPORTANCE TITAN-
> IC MAKES HEADLINES THIS VOY-
> AGE STOP ENSURE SUCCESSFUL
> CROSSING REFLECTS WELL ON
> LINE STOP NO EXCUSES ACCEPT-
> ED STOP MORGAN.

He slid the paper across to the Captain. Smith picked it up, read it slowly, his expression unchanging, then placed it back down.

"JP certainly doesn't mince words, does he?" Smith remarked quietly, his voice maintaining its usual soft tenor.

"He holds me responsible, Captain," Ismay said, unable to keep the edge of anxiety from his voice. "For the cost of these ships, for the Olympic's recent troubles... he needs a resounding success with Titanic. Not just a smooth crossing, but a headline-grabbing one."

"She's performing beautifully, Mr. Ismay," Smith reassured him calmly. "Smooth as silk. We've had remarkably clear weather, and she handles like a dream."

"Yes, yes, she's a fine ship, testament to Andrews and his men," Ismay conceded impatiently, taking a frantic drag on his cigarette. "And her performance improves daily. I've been looking at the logs. Her daily runs are already exceeding Olympic's on her maiden voyage for the same days."

"Indeed," Smith nodded. "A credit to her design."

"But that's not enough, Captain!" Ismay leaned forward, lowering his voice. "No one prints headlines about beating a sister ship by a few nautical miles! It's insignificant! We need something substantial. Something that screams speed, power, triumph!"

Smith sighed softly. "Mr. Ismay, we've discussed this..."

"I've been doing the calculations," Ismay pressed on, ignoring the Captain's weary tone. "The last few boilers – the ones in boiler room number one – they haven't been lit yet, correct?"

"Standard procedure for running-in new engines, sir," Smith confirmed. "We bring them up to speed gradually. You know this."

"Exactly! But if we were to light them now... give her the full head of steam she's capable of...?" Ismay let the question linger, his eyes fixed on Smith. "I estimate we could increase our speed significantly. Enough, perhaps, to arrive in New York Tuesday night, instead of Wednesday morning." He leaned back slightly, playing his trump card. "Imagine the headlines, Captain! 'Titanic Shatters Maiden Voyage Record!' Arriving nearly a full day ahead of schedule! That's the kind of success Morgan expects. That will silence the critics."

Smith frowned, swirling the tea in his cup. "The engines are new, Mr. Ismay. I'm still hesitant to push them to their absolute limit until they've had more time."

"Tommy Andrews himself assured me before Queenstown that the ship was proving more than ready for anything we asked of her," Ismay countered, perhaps stretching Andrews's cautious assessment slightly. "He said she could handle it."

Smith hesitated, then reached into his own pocket, extracting several folded wireless slips. He laid them on the table beside Morgan's demanding message.

"And what about these, sir? Ice warnings. Several received just today. Mesaba, Baltic, Amerika... all reporting field ice, growlers, large bergs directly in our path as we approach the Grand Banks."

Ismay glanced dismissively at the warnings. "Ice is always a possibility this time of year, Captain. Nothing unusual."

"Perhaps not," Smith conceded gravely. "But the number of reports, the specific locations noted... it gives me pause. Pushing for maximum speed as we head into known ice fields..." He shook his head slowly. "My inclination is to maintain our current speed, perhaps even reduce it slightly tonight as a precaution, until we are well clear."

Ismay felt a surge of frustration. Caution wouldn't get headlines. Caution wouldn't appease JP Morgan. He leaned forward again, his voice taking on a persuasive tone. "Captain, we have the finest officers on the Atlantic watching our course. Two lookouts in the crow's nest, alert for any hazard, are they not?" He didn't wait for an answer. "And at the helm? The most experienced, most respected commander in the White Star Line. Commodore Smith." He allowed himself a flattering smile. "A man completing a long and distinguished career with this final, historic crossing. What better way to cap that career than by guiding this magnificent vessel to a triumphant, record-setting arrival in New York? Think of the acclaim, Captain. For the ship... and for her commander."

Smith looked down at the ice warnings, then across at Ismay, whose gaze was unwavering, expectant. The Captain's shoulders slumped slightly. The weight of expectation – from the owner, from the public, perhaps even from his own legacy – seemed to settle upon him. He picked up the ice warnings, folding them slowly.

"Very well, Mr. Ismay," he said quietly, his voice resigned. "Inform the Chief Engineer. We'll light the remaining boilers after dinner tonight."

A surge of triumph coursed through Ismay, quickly masked by a nod of sober agreement. "Excellent, Captain. A wise decision."

Just as Smith gathered the wireless slips, a steward approached their table, holding a familiar silver salver. "Excuse me, Mr. Ismay. A note for you, sir."

Ismay took the folded note, recognizing the handwriting on the envelope with a flicker of surprise. He opened it quickly. It was from young Benjamin

Sutherland-Howell, politely requesting that Ismay make good on his earlier offer to arrange an introduction with Mr. Henry Sleeper Harper.

Ismay beamed inwardly. *Perfect.* An opportunity to ingratiate himself with Benji, and by extension, perhaps smooth things over with the suddenly frosty Caroline Sutherland-Howell after her baffling behavior last night. *Yes, things were finally lining up quite nicely.* He tucked the note away, already calculating the best way to leverage this small favor.

frosted glass dome

overlook, looking up

CHAPTER 26

Descending the Grand Staircase towards the D deck Reception Room for dinner that evening, I felt a lightness I hadn't experienced... well, possibly ever. The day spent with Miles – the shared secrets, the passionate moment in the cargo hold, the burgeoning dream of a shared future, the simple comfort of companionship – had fundamentally shifted something within me. *Tonight*, I thought, *tonight I would introduce him properly.* Bring him to our table. Make him a part of my world, at least this shipboard version of it. Upon receiving Ismay's response that he would be honored to introduce Mr. Harper, I decided that Miles *could be there, should be there, would be there.* Every step of the way, moving forward, we were moving as one. Living in the moment—together...

My optimistic thoughts came to a screeching halt as I reached the landing. There, standing near the entrance to the Dining Saloon, amongst our usual party – Mother, Birdie, the Countess, Gladys, Gracie, Stead, Dorothy and her mother, the Allisons – stood my father. Not sequestered in the cabin under the guise of illness, but dressed for dinner, looking freshly shaven and impeccably attired, a polite, if slightly stiff, smile fixed on his face.

My stomach plummeted. I had already promised Miles my father's chair tonight. *How was I going to remedy this one?*

"Benji, darling!" Mother spotted me, her smile radiant, almost unnervingly bright. She glided over, Birdie close behind, equally beaming. "Look who's decided to grace us with his presence! Father is feeling much improved!"

"Considerably," Father added, stepping forward. "Amazing what a day's rest can do." His eyes met mine briefly, carrying the weight of Mother's ultimatum from that morning.

"And," Birdie chimed in, her earlier disappointment seemingly forgotten, re-placed by genuine excitement, "Mother and Father have decided, since they'll be at the Wideners' party tomorrow night, that we'll celebrate our birthday tonight! Isn't it wonderful?"

"Wonderful," I echoed numbly, glancing past them, searching the crowded Reception Room for Miles, wondering how I could possibly signal the change of plans. Before I could formulate a thought, let alone excuse myself, Mother was linking her arm through mine.

"Come along, darling, let's not dawdle. Our table is waiting, and tonight is all about you and Margaret!"

I was swept along with the group into the glittering expanse of the Dining Saloon. Stewards led us to our usual table, where places had been rearranged slightly, placing Birdie and myself as the head of the table – the designated guests of honor. As everyone took their seats amidst polite chatter, my eyes scanned the room frantically.

There he was. Miles, looking devastatingly handsome in his dinner jacket, was just entering the Saloon. He caught my eye, a hopeful, expectant smile on his face as he started towards our table. My heart sank. I could only offer him a helpless, apologetic shake of my head, gesturing subtly towards my father now firmly installed in the seat beside me. Understanding dawned instantly in Miles's eyes, quickly followed by a flicker of disappointment, masked by a polite nod. He veered off course, intercepted by a steward who led him towards his own table across the room. I watched him go, a pang of longing and regret tightening my chest.

Champagne was poured almost immediately. Once everyone had a glass, Mother raised hers. "To Margaret and Benjamin," she announced, her voice clear and bright. "On the eve of their eighteenth birthday. May your futures be filled with health, happiness, and all the success you deserve."

"Hear, hear!" echoed around the table. We all sipped.

Then, Mother turned expectantly to Father. "Benjamin, dear?"

Father cleared his throat, rising slightly in his seat. He looked first at Birdie, then at me, his expression carefully composed. "Your mother and I," he began, his voice practiced, smooth, "could not be prouder of the young adults you have both become. Intelligent, capable...," he glanced towards Birdie, "... spirited...," then towards me, "... determined. This is a brave, new, modern world dawning, and we have no doubt that you will both find your places in it, perhaps even change it for the better."

I listened, a cynical part of me marveling at the performance. Was this the same man who had dismissed my passions, who had stood by while my future was negotiated away? Birdie, beside me, seemed to hang on every word, her face glowing with pleasure. Having missed the confrontation between our parents, perhaps this apparent reconciliation felt genuine to her, a return to the normalcy she craved. A lie that she was buying, hook, line, and sinker—all because she wanted it to be true.

"As your mother mentioned," Father continued, reaching into his inner jacket pocket, "since we will be otherwise engaged tomorrow evening, we wanted to give you your birthday gifts tonight." He produced two identical, crisp white envelopes, handing one to Birdie and one to me. "Go on, open them."

A buzz of anticipation went around the table. Birdie tore hers open eagerly. I followed suit more slowly, a strange sense of detachment settling over me. Inside was a single sheet of heavy vellum, bearing the letterhead of Father's primary holding company.

"Read it aloud, darlings," Mother prompted gently, addressing not just my sister and me but the entire table.

Birdie went first, her voice filled with excitement. "'My Dearest Margaret,'" she read, "'On the occasion of your eighteenth birthday, marking your formal entrance into adulthood, it is time for you to begin forging your own path. To provide you with the means to do so, your mother and I have today established a trust in your name, funded in the amount of one million dollars, for you to utilize as you see fit in staking your claim in the world. May you use it wisely. With deepest affection, Father.'"

A collective gasp went around the table. One million dollars. It was a staggering sum, even by the standards of our fellow passengers. Birdie looked utterly stunned, tears welling in her eyes.

"My turn, I suppose," I said quietly, unfolding my own letter. The words were identical. "'My Dearest Benjamin... one million dollars... With deepest affection, Father.'" I finished reading, the words feeling distant, unreal.

"Oh, Benjamin! Caroline! How incredibly generous!" the Countess exclaimed. Murmurs of awe and congratulation filled the air. Birdie was speechless, clutching her letter, tears of joy now streaming down her face.

I forced a smile, mimicking overwhelmed gratitude. "Father, Mother... I... I don't know what to say. Thank you." But inside, the gift felt... complicated. Weighted. Was it an apology? An attempt to buy forgiveness? Or simply another transaction, a way to launch us into the world and absolve himself of further responsibility? The million dollars felt less like freedom and more like a gilded cage, another expectation to live up to, or fail beneath. Across the room, I risked a glance at Miles. He wasn't looking my way. He was staring down at his own plate, seemingly lost in thought, a world away.

The formal dinner concluded, but the evening's energy merely shifted venues, flowing from the Dining Saloon back into the adjacent Reception Room. The orchestra struck up another waltz, couples returned to the dance floor, and the hum of conversation rose again, fueled by coffee, liqueurs, and champagne.

I found myself chatting with Dorothy near one of the potted palms, ostensibly discussing the various passenger types but mostly just enjoying her easy company. She was excitedly talking about the burgeoning moving picture industry, a topic that, after my conversation with Miles earlier, held a newfound fascination.

"They're all heading west, you know," she said surreptitiously, leaning closer. "To California. Land is cheap, the weather's reliable year-round for filming... it's becoming quite the hub. A sound investment, I'd wager, for someone with capital." She gave me a pointed look, clearly implying the news from dinner. Then her voice dropped slightly. "And California... especially places like Los Angeles...

they're different, Benji. More open-minded than the East Coast establishment, less concerned with old family names and rigid traditions." She smiled knowingly. "Sunshine, fresh air, a place where people can reinvent themselves... I suspect someone like you would thrive there."

Her words, hinting at an understanding deeper than just business prospects, resonated with me. Before I could respond, however, my attention was caught by movement near the Grand Staircase, someone passing the voluminous candelabra, momentarily interrupting its light. Miles. He was ascending the stairs, alone, his expression thoughtful, perhaps distant after witnessing the family celebration from afar. An uninvited guest.

"Dorothy, forgive me," I interrupted politely, "but there's someone I need to catch."

"Go," she waved me off with an understanding smile. "Don't keep him waiting."

I hurried across the room, reaching the base of the staircase just as Miles reached the landing. "Miles! *Wait.*"

He stopped, turning on the step, looking down at me.

"I'm sorry," I said quickly, feeling flustered. "About dinner. *About...* my father being there. I mean... everything happened so fast... the birthday surprise..."

He offered a small, reassuring smile, though the earlier disappointment lingered in his eyes. "It's alright, Benji. I understand. Family occasion." He gestured vaguely back towards the crowded room. "Can we talk? Somewhere... *quieter?*"

"Yes," I agreed immediately, relieved. "The deck?"

He nodded.

Together we climbed the stairs, bypassing the bustling upper decks and heading straight out onto the now familiar territory of the windswept Boat Deck. The starry sky, the cold air, the rhythmic sound of the waves rushing past the hull – it felt like our space now, a refuge from the social complexities below.

We walked in silence for a few moments, finding a relatively sheltered spot near the officers' quarters. The night air colder than it had been thus far.

"So," Miles began, his tone carefully neutral, "quite the birthday surprise."

I nodded, the weight of the gift settling heavily again. "You could say that." I took a breath, then plunged ahead. "They gave us... my parents gave Birdie and me... a million dollars each."

Miles stopped walking, staring at me in stunned silence for a beat. Then his face broke into a wide, incredulous grin. "A million dollars? Benji, that's... that's incredible!" His eyes lit up with the same fervent excitement I'd seen earlier when he spoke of the film studio. "Don't you see? This changes everything! Our studio! Your writing advance, seed money... this is it! This is the answer! We can actually do it!"

His enthusiasm was infectious, yet I couldn't quite meet it. My own feelings remained tangled, complex. Seeing my lack of shared excitement, Miles's grin faltered, replaced by a look of dawning realization and swift apology.

"Oh, god, Benji, I'm sorry," he said quickly, running a hand through his hair. "That was presumptuous of me. Forgive me. It's... it's your money, of course. Your gift. I shouldn't have just assumed... shouldn't have jumped to..." He trailed off, looking embarrassed.

"No, Miles, it's not that," I reassured him quickly, touching his arm. "Honestly? If it were just about the money, I'd give you every last cent tomorrow to start our studio, to chase that dream." *I meant it.* The money itself, the number, felt abstract, unreal compared to the possibility of the future we'd imagined together.

"Then what is it?" he asked, searching my face in the dim light.

"It's..." I struggled to articulate the knot of unease in my stomach. "It's where it comes from. Who it comes from. It feels like... strings, Miles. Like another way for my father to control things, even when he's pretending to grant freedom. As long as his money is involved, am I ever really free of him? Of his expectations? Or am I just playing a part in a different production he's financing?"

Miles leaned back against the railing beside me, staring out at the dark water, processing my words. After a long silence, he nodded slowly. "I understand," he said quietly. That simple phrase, imbued with the shared knowledge of overbearing fathers and unwanted futures, spoke volumes. He did understand.

"So," he asked after another pause, his voice gentle, "what are you going to do?"

I looked out at the vast, dark ocean stretching endlessly before us. "Honestly, Miles?" I sighed, the cold air catching the words. "I haven't the faintest idea. I've got a lot to think about between here and New York." The million dollars, meant as a key to unlock the future, suddenly felt like another heavy lock I needed to somehow pick.

"Well, how about this. Don't make any decisions tonight," Miles smiled gently, his hand briefly squeezing mine before letting go as another couple strolled past further down the deck. "Get some sleep, clear your head. We can talk about it more over breakfast tomorrow. Deal?"

The suggestion of their established routine, their sanctuary at the Café Parisian, felt immediately comforting. "The usual spot?" I asked, a small smile returning to my own face.

"The usual," he confirmed, his eyes meeting mine in the starlight, holding a promise of companionship for the morning to come.

CHAPTER 27

S leep offered little respite Saturday night. My mind, restless and churning with the day's revelations – Miles, the Rubáiyát, the million dollars, my parents' fractured truce – refused to quiet. So, I found myself awake before dawn on Sunday, the ship gliding smoothly through calm, starlit waters.

Most of the morning passed in a blur. At Mother's request, our entire family, the new and improved Sutherland-Howells, would keep up the charade by attending breakfast together. Even though I was meeting Miles in the Café at nine, I made a brief appearance in the Dining Saloon, just to sip a hot cocoa, and appease my mother in our staged family portrait. Unlike most mornings, perhaps due to the fact that following Sunday breakfast the Saloon would be used for the weekly religious service, the orchestra was on hand, and decided to play relaxed tunes to gently wake the drowsy royalty before them.

The crunching of toast, muffled by marmalade and jam, the pouring of coffee and stirring of cream, and of course the gentle swell of strings, music from the nearby orchestra, all reminding me why I'd grown accustomed to the quiet ambiance of the Café. Beautiful women and handsome men, dressed in their Sunday morning finery, reclining into those green leather chairs and carefully choreographing every moment as they ate their breakfast. Dainty fingers, silent sips through sturdy pursed lips, carefully muted chuckles and conversations, all the result of the airs of pedigree.

"Go on, Benji, take another sip," she said.

Across the table Mother looked stunning, so regal she might've been a post-card—hair piled perfectly atop her subtly painted features. She gave an encouraging smile. "Are you enjoying your breakfast, darling?"

"Yes," I said. Refusing to engage in more than polite small-talk. Afraid any unintended conversation might keep me here a minute longer than was absolutely necessary. All the while, Father, still sitting awkwardly at the head of the table, tried his best to pretend that he chose to be a part of this. That he was happy in his role. The charming host. The happy husband. The doting father. I couldn't believe that I was the only one who could see through this entire parody. But, perhaps I was the only one who wanted to.

By mid-morning, most of the ship's first-class passengers had remained in the Dining Saloon for the Divine Service, presided over by Captain Smith himself. Seeking refuge from both piety and the potential for awkward social encounters, I retreated to the grand, echoing quiet of the nearly deserted First Class Lounge. With a borrowed book from the impressive library shelves, I settled into a plush velvet armchair near the bookcase, hoping to lose myself in someone else's words for a while. The immense room, usually humming with conversation, felt almost reverent in its emptiness. Like it had been reserved just for me and my thoughts.

I'd been reading for perhaps half an hour, the only sounds the rustle of my turning pages and the distant, muffled strains of a hymn filtering up from below decks, when footsteps approached my quiet nest.

"Glad to see I'm not the only sinner avoiding chapel this morning," a dry, amused voice remarked.

I looked up, startled, into the sharp, mustached face of one of the wealthiest men in the world. "Mr. Astor," I said, surprised, automatically starting to rise.

"J.J., please, son," he waved me back down. "No need for formalities. We're just two sinners, playing hooky together." He gestured to the chair opposite mine. "Mind if I join you?"

"Not at all, sir. J.J.," I corrected myself quickly, feeling flustered. *What could John Jacob Astor possibly want with me?*

He settled into the chair, crossing his legs elegantly. "It seems to me, Benji," he began, his eyes holding a shrewd but not unkind glimmer, "that we might have a mutual friend."

My mind immediately went to the whirlwind of introductions over the past few days. "Oh?"

"Young Mr. Force," Astor clarified. "Miles. Energetic young man. Rather taken with you, I gather."

I felt a flush creep up my neck, unsure how much Miles might have said. "Miles is... a good friend," I managed.

"Indeed," Astor nodded slowly. "He also mentioned, quite enthusiastically I might add, something about a rather ambitious business venture you two have been discussing. Moving pictures, wasn't it? Something about starting your own studio?"

My embarrassment deepened. Discussing our fledgling, half-baked dream with J.J. Astor felt absurd. "It's... just an idea, sir. I'm not sure it's the sort of serious investment you'd typically be interested in," I mumbled, already picturing his polite dismissal of such a childish, speculative endeavor.

"I wouldn't be so sure about that, Benji," Astor said thoughtfully. He stood, walked over to the massive bookcase that dominated the wall, and scanned the leather-bound spines for a moment. "Ah, here we are," he murmured, pulling out a thick volume. He returned to the table and placed the book before me.

Curious, I looked at the cover. The title was embossed in gold: A Journey in Other Worlds: A Romance of the Future. "What's this?" I asked.

Astor opened the book, flipping through the pages until he reached the title page, then pointed. "Ever read this one, Benji?"

I read the indicated line aloud. "'By John Jacob Astor.'" I looked up at him, stunned. "You? You wrote this? You're a writer?" Disbelief warred with a surge of unexpected kinship.

He let out a short, self-deprecating laugh. "Well, 'writer' might be stretching it, according to the critics. I'm afraid it wasn't exactly a best-seller." He tapped the cover. "In fact, the only reason this esteemed library likely carries a copy is because I sail White Star Line ships almost exclusively. Probably Ismay's idea of an inside joke, keeping it stocked."

He turned serious then, leaning forward slightly. "The point is, Benji, this book," he tapped the cover once more, "was my passion project. Something I had to write, whether anyone else cared or not. If I had listened to the advice of everyone around me – stick to business, J.J., don't waste your time on fanciful stories – I never would have published it."

"But I thought you said it wasn't successful," I reminded him gently.

"Commercially? Not in the slightest," he chuckled again. "But I don't regret writing it. Not for one second. You know why?" He met my gaze intently. "Because seeing my name in print, holding this book in my hands, knowing I created something from nothing... that was the success. That was the dream realized. Even if it didn't make anyone happy but me, that alone was enough."

I absorbed his words, stunned by the unexpected encouragement, the shared understanding from such an unlikely source. He saw the passion for creation, not just the balance sheet.

"So," I asked, a tentative, teasing note entering my voice, testing the waters, "does this mean you'd actually like to hear our pitch for this... fanciful moving picture idea?"

Astor smiled, a genuine, crinkling smile this time. "I tell you what," he said, glancing at his pocket watch. "I generally take my Airedale, Kitty, for a jaunt around the deck every afternoon after tea. Bring your pitch then. We'll walk and talk. Sound good?"

"I'd be honored, sir. Mr. Astor. Sir," I stammered, overwhelmed, reaching out to shake the hand he offered.

"J.J.," he corrected firmly, returning the handshake. He rose from his chair. "And Benji," he added, pointing to the book still lying open on the table between us. "Keep it. Consider it an early birthday present." He gave me a playful wink. "And maybe, if you read it, you won't find your own ideas quite so silly after all."

And with that, the wealthiest man in America turned and left the lounge, leaving me alone with his unexpected gift, his surprising encouragement, and a renewed sense of possibility flickering brightly against the odds.

I sat there for a long moment after J.J. left, his gifted book resting heavy on the table beside my journal. A Journey in Other Worlds. A publisher, a millionaire, encouraging me to pursue my dreams, however fanciful. The encounter felt surreal, hopeful. *Perhaps, just perhaps, things could work out.* I picked back up my own book, the one that had been getting me through the morning, settling back into the quiet solitude of the Lounge, ready to lose myself in its pages.

I'd barely finished a paragraph when another presence registered beside my chair, casting a long shadow over the page. An unwanted specter of memories barely put to rest.

"Reading as always," the familiar voice stated, coolly observant.

I didn't have to look up to know it was Father. I kept my eyes fixed on the text, refusing to acknowledge him.

He walked around the table, peering over my shoulder at the book. "Ah," he read aloud, "Peter Pan. 'The boy who refused to grow up.' How fitting." His tone held its usual edge of condescending amusement.

That was enough. I snapped the book shut, the sound sharp in the quiet room. Placing it firmly on the table, I crossed my arms and finally looked up at him. "What do you want, Father?"

He raised an eyebrow, feigning surprise at my directness. "Ah, the direct approach. Maybe you are growing up after all." His expression softened then, shifting into one of careful sincerity – a look I recognized as one of his tools. "Benji, look," he began, pulling up a nearby chair without invitation, "I know you have... strong feelings... about me right now. About recent events. But I need you to understand, son. Everything I've ever done, everything I do, has been to help you. To prepare you for the world."

I remained silent, unmoved. His justifications rang hollow after the events in Paris, after the lifetime of dismissal.

He sighed, apparently realizing his attempt at paternal warmth wasn't landing. He placed his leather briefcase on the table with a soft thud, carelessly, or perhaps intentionally, covering my journal. "I came up here to give you the second half of your birthday present, Benjamin."

He opened the briefcase and produced two small, embossed cards. Tickets. He slid them across the table towards me. One was for an appointment at the ship's Turkish Bath complex, the other for the Swimming Pool. Both were timed for later that morning.

"What am I supposed to do with these?" I asked, bewildered.

"Those appointments," Father explained, leaning forward, "just happen to coincide precisely with the times Mr. Henry Sleeper Harper has booked the very same facilities."

My head snapped up. Harper. The publisher. The man whom I was determined to meet before we reached New York. *Was this Father's attempt at an olive branch? Or something else?*

"Mr. Ismay has already arranged for me to discuss my... ideas... my work with Mr. Harper tomorrow afternoon," I stated, perhaps intentionally revealing Ismay's intervention, to make my father uncomfortable. To sting his pride. Unsure if he even knew about Mother's history with the man. Unsure if he'd even care.

Father waved a dismissive hand. "An afternoon walk? Charming, but inadequate." He leaned closer, his voice taking on the didactic tone he used for business lessons. "Benji, listen to me. You don't understand how these things truly work. Real deals, real connections – they aren't forged over polite tea or coffee, or even during a brisk walk on deck. They're made on the golf course, in the club lounge, in the sauna." He tapped the ticket for the Turkish Bath. "You get a man out of the boardroom, away from the formalities, into a place where he can relax, let his guard down... you make a genuine human connection... that's where you make progress. Men don't ultimately do business with mere businessmen, Benji. They do business with men they like, men they trust, men they'd want to grab a drink with. Men they'd invite along on a weekend hunt."

He paused, letting the words sink in. "If you want a real chance with Harper, a chance for him to see you and not just some kid with a manuscript, you have to seize opportunities like this. Create an 'accidental' encounter. Build rapport before you pitch." He leaned back, a familiar glint in his eye. "Don't wait for tomorrow, Benji. Live in the moment. Take advantage."

The phrase – *live in the moment* – echoed Miles's words from yesterday, but used here, by my father, it felt manipulative, strategic. Yet... his logic, however cynical, resonated. He knew this world, knew how these men operated. Despite my profound distrust, his advice felt uncomfortably pragmatic.

"Alright," I conceded slowly. "Perhaps meeting him informally first... it might make sense."

"Good," Father nodded, satisfied. Then his expression turned serious once more. "But, Benji, part of being a smart operator, part of being successful in any field, is knowing when an avenue is closed. Knowing when to walk away."

"What do you mean?" I asked.

"Harper knows his business," Father stated flatly. "The man's name is publishing. If you get the chance to show him your work, and he tells you... frankly... that writing isn't your forte, that this particular story is a dead end... you have to be willing to accept that judgment. Thank him for his time and walk away. Don't waste your energy, or his, flogging a dead horse. Don't keep heading down a dead-end road just because you want it to lead somewhere."

His words landed like cold stones. Pragmatic, yes. But also a convenient way to potentially validate his own dismissal of my writing ambitions. Still... the core advice felt sound, however self-serving his motives might be. "I understand," I said quietly.

"Good man," Father clapped his hands together decisively, standing up. "Then we'll go now."

"Now?" I glanced at my watch. It was nearing breakfast, our appointments weren't for another hour or so. And more importantly... "But I... I'm supposed to meet someone—" *Miles*, I thought to myself. Our plans for the day.

"Benji," Father cut me off, his tone allowing for no argument. "I just explained this. You have to seize the moment. Opportunity knocks, you answer. Now is the time to prepare, to think about what you're going to say, before we head down. Harper needs to be impressed by you, I can help you to be ready. Are you coming, or are you going to let this chance slip away?"

I hesitated, torn. Miles. Our day together. Our plans. But then... Harper. An actual chance, however orchestrated by my father, to get my work seen, to potentially gain an advance. If Mr. Harper did like my writing... if he did offer a contract... that money wouldn't have Father's strings attached. That could be the seed money. That could be our escape, Miles's and mine. Our studio, funded independently. It was a long shot, a gamble, relying on the very man whose judgment I dreaded, the proverbial deal with the devil, yet... it was a chance. *A win-win, perhaps?*

The internal calculation, the rationalization, happened in seconds. "Alright," I said, standing up, grabbing Astor's book but leaving my journal behind. "Let's go."

CHAPTER 28

M iles Force sat alone in the usual corner of the Café Parisian, hiding behind the table—now unspokenly held for us by the waiters—doing little to soothe his growing unease. He glanced at his watch for what felt like the tenth time. Nearly ten. Benji was almost an hour late for their established breakfast meeting, their planned day together dissolving with each passing minute. Where could he be? Had something happened? Or had the intense connection forged over the past two days, culminating in that breathless kiss in the cargo hold, perhaps scared Benji off? Miles tried to push the thought away, focusing instead on the half-empty espresso cup before him. The chocolate croissant that he'd been waiting to cut in half and share—which had now grown stone cold in the chilly air of the Café. He scanned the entrance again, but there was still no sign of Benji.

Meanwhile, on the Bridge

High above the passenger decks, the atmosphere on the sheltered bridge was one of quiet, professional routine, though the underlying thrum of the engines felt subtly more powerful today. Captain Smith stood near the forward windows, gazing out at the endless expanse of calm, sunlit ocean, the morning's Divine Service now concluded. Thomas Andrews, _Titanic's_ meticulous designer, joined him, holding a rolled-up schematic.

"A fine service this morning, Captain," Andrews remarked quietly. "Well attended."

"Indeed, Mr. Andrews," Smith replied, turning with a polite nod. "Good for morale. Helps pass the time on these long crossings."

Just then, the door from the officers' corridor opened, and Junior Wireless Operator Harold Bride stepped onto the bridge, holding a decoded Marconigram slip. "Message for you, Captain. Just received."

Smith took the slip. "Thank you, Bride." The young operator nodded and retreated back to his post. Smith scanned the message quickly. "Ah. From the *Caronia*. Reporting icebergs, growlers, and field ice ahead." He handed the slip casually to Andrews.

"First one today," Smith remarked, almost conversationally, as Andrews read the coordinates.

"So, we're nearing the ice then?" Andrews asked, his brow furrowing slightly as he looked up from the warning.

"Aye," Smith confirmed, taking the slip back and placing it with a few others already tucked into a holder near the chart table. "Likely have a few more reports like this before the day is out. Standard for this time of year, this far north."

Andrews nodded slowly, then hesitated. "I have noticed, Captain... we seem to be making excellent speed this morning."

"She's running splendidly," Smith agreed, a hint of pride in his voice. "After dinner last night, as discussed with Mr. Ismay, I gave the order to light the remaining boilers in number one room. Decided it was time to test her properly before we reach New York."

Andrews looked thoughtful, choosing his words carefully. "Is that... standard procedure, Captain? Given the warnings? Pushing her to full capability while approaching reported ice fields?"

Smith chuckled lightly, clapping Andrews reassuringly on the shoulder. "Don't you worry yourself, Mr. Andrews. This ship is magnificent. Responsive. If any danger should present itself," he waved a confident hand towards the clear horizon, "we'll spot it and jump out of its way long before it becomes a threat. But, rest assured, Tommy, I've changed our course to follow the Southern route. We should be too far south to even see a berg."

At that moment, Second Officer Lightoller stepped onto the bridge from the wing. "Excuse me, Captain. Just confirming the time for this morning's lifeboat drill?"

Captain Smith glanced out the bridge windows again, seemingly considering. "How's that wind holding up, Mr. Lightoller?"

"Still going strong, sir," the officer confirmed. "Bit of a chop picking up out there."

Smith stroked his white beard thoughtfully. "Hmm. Don't want passengers getting chilled standing about on deck during a muster." He made a decision. "Cancel the drill for today, Mr. Lightoller. We can reschedule for tomorrow morning, perhaps, if the weather improves. No need to rush things on a Sunday."

"Aye, aye, Captain. Cancel the drill," the officer acknowledged, making a note before returning to his station.

Thomas Andrews watched the exchange, a flicker of something unreadable—concern? acceptance?—in his eyes before he turned back to his schematics. On the bridge of the *Titanic*, as she raced westward at over twenty-one knots, routine, confidence, and the promise of a swift passage held sway over caution and canceled drills.

Sunday, April 14, 1912 Approx. 11:00 AM The Turkish Baths

Father led the way down the corridors, past the entrance to the racquetball court and swimming pool, towards the exotic allure of the Turkish Bath complex. Stepping inside felt like entering another world entirely, something conjured from the mysterious pages of *Arabian Nights*. Intricate, glazed tiles in vibrant blues, greens, and golds covered the walls in Moorish patterns. Carved doorways were crowned with elaborate gilded cornices. Teak tables and long, crimson reclining beds lined the glossy walls of the cooling room, and the gentle splash of water echoed from a marble drinking fountain carved into the shape of a lion's head. The air was warm, humid, scented with something vaguely like eucalyptus. It was staggeringly lush, designed to transport its occupants a million miles away from the cold realities of the North Atlantic.

After changing into the provided wraps in a small cubicle, Father guided me towards the hottest room—the sauna, essentially. The heat hit us like a wall, nearly two hundred degrees, shimmering in the air. Through the steam, I could see a lone figure reclining on the tiled benches—Henry Sleeper Harper, a towel draped around his neck, his face flushed from the heat but relaxed.

"Henry, my good man!" Father called out jovially, apparently unbothered by the intense heat or the informality of the setting. "Hope we're not intruding."

Harper looked up, blinking sweat from his eyes, then broke into a friendly grin. "Benjamin, you old dog! Not at all, not at all! Just sweating out last night's indulgences. Come in, come in!"

We settled onto the bench opposite him, the heat immediately prickling my skin. I felt ridiculously exposed, both physically and metaphorically.

"Henry," Father continued smoothly, "I don't believe you've properly met my son, Benjamin Jr. Benji, this is Mr. Henry Sleeper Harper."

"A pleasure, sir," I managed, offering a hand which Harper shook warmly.

"The pleasure's mine, son," Harper replied, his eyes sharp and intelligent despite the relaxing setting. "Your father speaks highly of you. Tells me you have aspirations towards the literary world yourself?"

"I... yes, sir. I enjoy writing," I admitted, feeling my cheeks flush under the heat.

"He's being modest, Henry," Father interjected, taking charge of the conversation. "Benji's quite talented. Shows real promise. Been honing his craft at Yale," he added, conveniently omitting the 'academic probation'. "Stories, plays... quite the imagination."

"Is that so?" Harper looked at me with genuine interest. "Always keen to discover new voices. What sort of things do you write, Benji?"

The conversation flowed surprisingly easily. We talked about literature, about plays, about the burgeoning world of storytelling. Father, to my astonishment, was actually complimentary about my supposed talents, weaving anecdotes—somewhat embellished—that painted me as a dedicated wordsmith. "An undiscovered, goddamn prodigy," as Father put it. Harper listened intently, asking insightful questions. The mood was light, agreeable; for a moment, I almost forgot my deep-seated wariness of my father, caught up in this unexpected connection, this validation from the Henry Harper. Even Father seemed genuine, playing the proud parent convincingly.

"Well, Benji," Harper said finally, "you've certainly piqued my interest. Do you happen to have anything with you? A sample of your work I might glance at?"

My heart leaped. *This was it!* The opportunity I'd only dreamed of. "Yes! Absolutely, sir!" I exclaimed, perhaps too eagerly. "I have my journal... well, not with me, obviously," I gestured at my skimpy wrap. "But I can fetch it! It has several story drafts. I'll go retrieve it right now! I can meet you both later, perhaps at the pool?"

"Excellent," Harper smiled. "I look forward to it."

Excusing myself quickly, high on adrenaline and hope, I practically ran back through the cooling room, changed hastily, and made my way back up towards the First Class Lounge as fast as decorum allowed.

Bursting into the grand room, I scanned the table where I'd been sitting earlier. Empty. My journal wasn't there. Panic began to set in.

I flagged down a passing steward. "Excuse me, did anyone happen to turn in a leather-bound journal? Left on that table," I pointed, "a couple of hours ago?"

The steward looked thoughtful. "No, sir. Nothing of that description handed in. Are you quite sure you left it here?"

My blood ran cold. If not here... then where? Frantic now, I turned and bolted from the Lounge, heading for my cabin on C deck, praying I had simply forgotten bringing it back earlier. I rounded the corner to my corridor and stopped dead.

Miles was standing there, waiting right outside my door, his arms crossed, his expression a tight mask of hurt and confusion.

"Miles," I breathed, momentarily forgetting the journal in the shock of seeing him there, looking so upset.

"Where have you been, Benji?" he asked, his voice low, tight. "I waited. At the café. For hours."

"Miles, I..." My mind scrambled, torn between his hurt and my own panic about the journal. I pushed past him, fumbling with my cabin key, needing to check inside now. The door burst open and I ran inside, Miles close behind me.

"Where were you, Benji? I think I deserve that much."

"The Turkish Bath," I said as if an afterthought, while digging feverishly through my bag.

"The Turkish Bath? *Why*?" Miles asked.

"Look, I can't talk right now, I'm in a hurry." I began searching the desk, the bed, the settee. No journal.

"*A hurry*?" Miles followed me into the room, his voice rising slightly. "You stand me up for our entire day together, vanish without a word after breakfast, and now you're 'in a *hurry*'?"

"It's important!" I snapped, turning to face him, my own frustration and panic boiling over. "I'm meeting with Mr. Harper! The publisher! Father set it up, it's happening right now! This could be my chance, Miles! Our chance!" I added desperately, hoping that might appease him.

"Your father set it up?" Miles repeated, his eyes narrowing with suspicion. "The same father you were just telling me last night uses every opportunity to control you? The same father whose money felt like a cage? That sounds like a fantastic opportunity, Benji. Really healthy."

"You don't understand!" I shot back, stung by his sarcasm, by his lack of support when I needed it most. "This is it! My shot! I'm finally doing something, fighting for the future I want!" My voice rose, defensive, maybe even cruel. "One of us has to be the grown-up here, Miles! Make the hard choices! Even if it means doing things we don't want to do! We can't all spend years traipsing across Europe, squandering away our trust funds until there's nothing left."

The hurt in Miles's eyes deepened, hardening into anger. "Stop," he said quietly, dangerously. "Just stop and think about what you're saying, Benji. What you're doing."

"I am thinking!" I shot back, throwing his own words back at him, twisting them. "I'm living in the moment! Seizing the opportunity! Isn't that what you told me to do?" I scoffed bitterly. "Or does that advice only apply when it's convenient for you? When I'm doing exactly what you want?"

The accusation landed like a physical blow. Miles stared at me for a long second, his face pale, his jaw clenched. Then, something seemed to break within him. "Fine," he said, his voice flat, cold. "If this is what you want, Benji. If this is the 'moment' you choose to live in... then I won't stand in your way."

He turned sharply to leave. As he reached the door, he paused, looking back at me one last time, his eyes filled with a chilling clarity, a profound disappointment.

"Your father must be so incredibly proud of you right now," he said, each word precise, deliberate, finding its mark. "You've *finally* become the man he *always* wanted you to be."

And then he was gone, leaving me standing alone in the cabin, the echo of his words ringing in the silence, the missing journal suddenly the least of my worries.

The click of the cabin door closing echoed in the sudden silence, amplifying the hollowness Miles's final words had left behind. "...the man he always wanted you to be." The accusation stung, sharp and true in a way that made me want to curl up, to disappear. He was right, wasn't he? I had twisted his own words, prioritized ambition—or perhaps just Father's approval disguised as ambition—over connection, over him.

But the opportunity... Harper... it felt too real, too close to let slip away now because of wounded feelings or complicated truths. Anger, sharp and defensive, surged, replacing the hurt. Miles didn't understand the pressure, the stakes. He didn't understand what it took to navigate my father's world. This was living in the moment, wasn't it? Seizing the chance, however compromised?

Driven by that desperate need to prove something—to Miles, to Father, maybe most of all to myself—I couldn't afford to dwell on the argument. The meeting with Harper was happening now. I pushed Miles's parting words away, locking them down with the other unwanted feelings. Action was required.

My journal was gone—a problem for later. But Harper needed something to read. I grabbed several sheets of the heavy cream *Titanic* stationery from the writing desk, the embossed White Star Line flag mocking my frantic state. Pen in hand, I forced myself to write. Inspiration felt miles away, my mind a frantic battlefield, hardly limber enough to showcase the best of my craft. Yet, I pushed words onto the page—fragments of an old story, a half-formed scene, anything that might seem presentable, coherent. I filled three pages, the script perhaps less elegant than usual, fueled more by adrenaline than art.

Despite the fire in my belly, the relentless drive compelling me to chase this dream, to throw caution to the wind, something inside—a still, small voice, perhaps the echo of Miles's concern, or maybe just my own conscience—gave me pause. Was this right? Was this me, or was it the role Father had cast me in? I shoved the doubt down along with everything else. There wasn't time. I stuffed the pages in my pocket and bolted for the Swimming Pool several decks below.

Pushing through the doors, the warm, humid air, thick and heavy, enveloped me. The pool itself gleamed under the electric lights, its turquoise water inviting, though only a few hardy souls were taking advantage. And there they were. Father and Mr. Harper, leisurely treading water near one end, engaged in easy conversation, their laughter echoing slightly off the tiled floor.

They both looked up as I approached the edge of the pool.

"Ah, Benji!" Harper called out cheerfully. "We were beginning to wonder if you'd gotten lost in this monster of a ship! Find what you were looking for? Got that portfolio?"

"Just a small sample of my work, sir," I replied, trying to sound confident, holding up the folded stationery pages. "But I hope it's enough to give you a sense of my style." My heart pounded. This felt incredibly unprofessional, handing over hastily scribbled pages poolside.

"No need to be modest, son," Father interjected smoothly from the water. "Henry knows talent when he sees it."

"Well, I look forward to reading it," Harper said agreeably. "Tell you what, leave the pages in my changing stall—number four, I believe. I'll have a look as soon as I finish a few more laps." He pushed off the wall, resuming a steady crawl through the water.

Father swam to the ladder and pulled himself out of the pool, grabbing a thick towel. He walked over to where I stood, drying himself off vigorously. He lowered his voice, sidling up next to me.

"*Well*?" I asked quietly, unsure of the protocol now. "Now *what*?"

Father draped the towel around his neck, a satisfied glint in his eye. "And now..." he murmured, his voice barely audible above the splashing, "...we wait." He clapped me lightly on the shoulder. "The trap has been set, Benjamin. Now we just have to be patient, see if the bear takes the bait."

The hunting analogy felt unsettlingly apt. Before I could dwell on it, Father's demeanor shifted back to jovial, his voice resuming a normal volume. "Right then! Enough business for one afternoon. Your mother sent word down—she's headed up for a walk on the Promenade Deck. Since the pair of us seem to have missed lunch entirely due to our various shenanigans," he winked, looping me into his 'informal business' narrative, "perhaps we'd better make an appearance before she decides to hang us both out to dry."

His tone was light, playful, utterly out of character, yet fitting the relaxed role he'd adopted since breakfast. Join Mother on deck. Maintain appearances. Act the part. I nodded, still feeling off-kilter from the encounter with Miles, the missing journal, the pressure of Harper potentially reading my frantic scribbles. But the path, it seemed, was set. "Alright," I agreed. "*Let's go.*"

CHAPTER 29

The rhythmic tick of the bridge clock seemed unusually loud in the quiet concentration of the steering room. Outside the large windows, the afternoon sun was slowly slipping toward the western horizon, the warmth of the day leaving the ship in a looming chasm of arctic chill. Smith surveyed the sea before him, balancing a saucer and teacup to warm his hands, while quietly chatting with First Officer Murdoch.

The door from the officers' corridor opened, and J. Bruce Ismay entered, his expression questioning. "You wanted to see me, Captain?" he asked, stepping onto the bridge.

"Yes, Mr. Ismay," Smith replied, his tone neutral. He turned to Murdoch. "Carry on, Mr. Murdoch. Thank you." The First Officer gave a crisp nod and moved towards the forward windows, affording the Captain and the Managing Director a measure of privacy.

Smith picked up a Marconigram slip from the chart table and quietly handed it to Ismay. Ismay unfolded it, read the contents quickly, his brow furrowing slightly before smoothing again into practiced nonchalance.

"Another ice warning, Captain?" he inquired, folding the paper neatly.

"Indeed," Smith confirmed, watching Ismay closely. "From the *Baltic*. They're reporting large quantities of field ice. Received about fifteen minutes ago."

"Hardly surprising. Ice warnings aren't uncommon in April crossing these latitudes, Captain," Ismay remarked dismissively, tucking the message casually into his evening jacket pocket as if it were a theatre ticket stub.

A muscle twitched in Smith's jaw. "It's the fifth such warning today, Mr. Ismay," he stated, his voice low but firm.

Ismay met the Captain's gaze, a hint of impatience entering his own. "Just what are you getting at, Captain?"

"You and I both know what I'm getting at, Mr. Ismay," Smith countered, his voice still quiet but hardening. The easy deference from their discussion yesterday afternoon was gone.

"Have you seen any ice today, Captain?" Ismay challenged. "Have any of your lookouts reported so much as a growler?"

"I have not," Smith admitted reluctantly.

"And these ships," Ismay gestured vaguely towards the table where the other warnings lay, "the *Caronia*, the *Noordam*, even the *Baltic*... have any of them been directly on our current track? Or anywhere near our present position?"

The Captain sighed, conceding the point. "Not precisely, sir. Their reported positions were some hours away from our own projected track."

"Then it would seem to me, dear Captain," Ismay pressed, his tone smoothly reasonable, "that we might be worrying prematurely, are we not? Reacting to phantoms when we should be focusing on our progress?" He paused, letting the implication hang. "If it were up to me, purely as an observer, mind you, I would think it prudent to keep covering ground efficiently while we have this clear weather and calm sea. Time enough to slow down if, and when, we are actually in the presence of ice. Wouldn't you agree... Captain?"

Smith started to speak, perhaps to reiterate his earlier concerns about the new engines or the sheer number of warnings, but Ismay cut him off smoothly, feigning deference once more.

"...Of course, what do I know?" he smiled thinly. "I'm just a passenger. You are the commander. I know you'll leave it entirely up to your own expert judgment to decide which is the best, and safest, course of action to take."

The carefully chosen words, the polite tone—it was anything but deference. It was pressure, skillfully applied. Ismay was making it clear that he expected speed to be maintained until danger was imminent and unavoidable.

The tense silence stretched between them, broken only by the ticking clock and the low hum of the ship. Just as Smith opened his mouth again, the door opened once more and Harold Bride, the junior wireless operator, stepped quickly onto the bridge, another message slip in hand.

"Apologies for the interruption, Captain," Bride said, handing the slip directly to Smith. "Another ice warning, sir. From the steamer *Amerika*; they note extensive field ice."

"Thank you, Bride," Smith said tersely, his eyes never leaving Ismay's face as he took the message. The young operator nodded and quickly withdrew.

Captain Smith didn't bother handing this latest warning to Ismay. He simply held it up slightly, his gaze locking with the Managing Director's, his voice flat, heavy with unspoken meaning.

"The sixth one today, Mr. Ismay."

Sunday Afternoon, The Promenade Deck

The Atlantic stretched out, vast and impossibly blue under the clear Sunday afternoon sky. A brisk wind whipped across the open Promenade Deck, pulling at scarves, skirts, and, of course, hats, but many passengers were still out strolling, enjoying the sunshine and the crisp sea air after lunch. Among them were Mother and Birdie, walking arm-in-arm near the railing, their pace leisurely.

After a few moments of comfortable silence, punctuated only by the cries of distant gulls that still followed the ship and the rhythmic rush of water against the hull, Mother gently squeezed Birdie's arm.

"Margaret, darling," she began, her voice softer than usual, lacking the forced brightness of the morning. "I wanted to let you know... I'll be moving my things back into the main suite before dinner tonight."

Birdie looked over, surprised. "Oh? Is Father feeling better then?"

"Considerably," Mother replied, though a flicker of something unreadable crossed her face. "He seems quite recovered. And," she added, meeting Birdie's gaze, "I must apologize if I've seemed... tense, these past few days. Distracted. I haven't been the best company, I know."

"Not at all, Mother," Birdie replied quickly, resorting to practiced politeness, though she knew perfectly well her mother had been distant. "I hadn't noticed a thing."

Mother stopped walking, turning to face her daughter fully, a look of surprising vulnerability in her eyes. "Margaret," she said quietly, her usual social mask slipping away. "I need to be honest with you. Watching you lately... especially at the breakfast table this morning, holding your own with Mr. Stead and the Colonel... I admire you. Greatly."

Birdie stared, taken aback by the unexpected sincerity.

"I'll admit," Mother continued, her voice trembling slightly, "my initial reaction... my hesitation about your... your zeal, your strong opinions... it wasn't entirely about propriety." She looked down at her gloved hands for a moment before meeting Birdie's eyes again. "Part of it, I realize now, was fear. Fear of losing you."

"Losing me?" Birdie asked, confused.

Mother sighed, a deep, weary sound. "You and Benji... you're becoming adults. Independent thinkers, ready to forge your own paths. And it's wonderful, truly. But..." She hesitated. "It's likely no great secret to you, darling, that my marriage to your father has been... challenging. An ongoing battle, often fought in silence, but one I know you children have felt the tremors of."

Birdie nodded silently, acknowledging the unspoken truth that had always hung between them.

"My relationship with you and Benji," Mother confessed, her voice thick with emotion, "has often felt like the only real, true semblance of family I possessed. And the thought of you both growing up, finding your own lives, spreading your wings... it left me facing the prospect of being left truly alone. Alone in a marriage that offers little comfort, little companionship." She looked out at the ocean. "So, any... sharpness... these past few weeks, any resistance to your growing independence... it stemmed from that fear. Selfish, I know. But terrifying nonetheless."

Birdie felt a wave of empathy wash over her, seeing her mother not just as the poised socialite, but as a woman grappling with her own loneliness and uncertainty. She reached out, taking both of her mother's hands.

"Oh, Mother," Birdie said softly. "Just because I want to spread my wings doesn't mean I intend to fly away from you. Yes, I want to fight for change, I want to have a voice, I want to build my own life... but I have no desire to leave you behind." She squeezed her mother's hands. "I want you there with me. Cheering me on, advising me, arguing with me even... where do you think I got that relentless spirit? I got it from you!" Both laughed, then Birdie went on, "I want nothing more than to have my mother championing me, every step of the way."

Tears welled in Mother's eyes—not tears of sadness this time, but relief, gratitude. She pulled Birdie into a tight embrace, holding her close for a long moment, the wind whipping around them.

"Oh, Margaret," Mother whispered, pulling back slightly to look into her daughter's eyes. "You have no idea how much that means to me." She stroked Birdie's cheek, a genuine, radiant smile finally breaking through. "I am so incredibly proud of the woman you are becoming. Your maturity, your strength... your spirit." She chuckled, a hint of her old fire returning, mixed with newfound admiration. "I'm certain the world will be a better place because of that restless spirit of yours." She paused, giving Birdie a pointed wink, her voice dropping to a raw, surprisingly coarse whisper, "And because you, my darling girl, clearly don't take shit from anyone."

Father and I emerged from the ship's interior onto the wide expanse of the Promenade Deck, the bright afternoon sun almost blinding against the fresh white paint. We found Mother and Birdie, standing near the bulwark, watching the endless roll of the deep blue waves. The bracing wind whipped color into their cheeks.

"Mother! Birdie!" I called out, hurrying towards them, the excitement of the morning's meeting still buzzing through me. "You won't believe it!"

They both turned, surprised by my sudden enthusiasm. "What is it, darling?" Mother asked, her smile cautious but welcoming.

"Mr. Harper!" I announced, perhaps a bit too loudly. "Father arranged for me to meet him—well, 'accidentally' meet him—in the Turkish Baths and the pool! He seemed genuinely interested in my writing! He's going to read some pages I gave him!"

Mother's face lit up, this time with what looked like genuine pleasure, tinged perhaps with surprise at Father's actions. She looked towards him as he joined us. "Benjamin? Is this true? You helped Benji arrange this?"

"It is," he confirmed, placing a proprietary hand on my shoulder. "I realized... well, I realized our Benji truly does possess a talent for the written word. Even I have to admit that." He gave me a look that was equal parts pride and warning. "And if my son is determined to pursue a precarious career like writing, over join-ing the family business," he continued, addressing Mother now, "then the least I can do is ensure he has the best possible chance to succeed. When I asked your father for your hand all those years ago, Caroline, I vowed I would protect and uphold the Sutherland-Howell name, ensure its continued prominence. This," he gestured towards me, "is simply me making good on that promise. Giving our son the best possible shot."

Mother seemed genuinely moved by this explanation, her eyes softening as she looked at Father. Perhaps she saw it as a sign of his commitment to the truce they'd forged yesterday morning. "Oh, Benjamin," she murmured. "Thank you."

We found a cluster of empty deck chairs nearby, settling into them to enjoy the afternoon sun, the dangerous undercurrents momentarily smoothed over by this display of family unity. For a while, we simply sat, watching the ocean glide past. Each of us weighing over in our minds the events of the voyage thus far. The highs, the lows. The things which had seemed impossible to us only days ago, now looming on the horizon. I guess that's the magic of the sea. Anything can happen.

The fragile peace was soon interrupted. A familiar figure approached along the deck—Bruce Ismay, looking dapper in a blue tailored suit, a confident air about him. He stopped before our little group, his eyes immediately finding Mother's before turning to Father.

"Forgive the intrusion," Ismay began smoothly, extending a hand towards my father. "I'm sorry but I don't believe we've been introduced. Bruce Ismay."

Father stood, shaking Ismay's hand politely but with a certain reserve. "Mr. Ismay. A pleasure."

"Ah, the famous Benjamin Sutherland-Howell," Ismay continued, his gaze flicking pointedly towards Mother, then back to Father, a knowing smirk playing on his lips, "whom I've heard so much about." He lingered on the last words, leaving no doubt about his implication, referencing conversations likely held only with Mother. "So very much."

Mother shifted uncomfortably in her chair, her earlier ease evaporating under Ismay's targeted charm. Birdie, perhaps sensing the tension, the implication, tried her best to throw Ismay's ship off-course.

"Mr. Ismay," she asked, "is it true what people are saying? That *Titanic* is going to arrive in New York on Tuesday night?"

Ismay turned his attention to Birdie, his expression becoming playful. "Sharp ears, my dear Margaret! Well, I shouldn't officially say, but between us..." he lowered his voice slightly, "...let's just say Captain Smith and I are confident she can show her older sister a thing or two about punctuality. We may indeed surprise everyone with an early arrival. Break *Olympic's* time by nearly a full day, perhaps." He beamed, clearly relishing the prospect.

"But what about the passengers?" I asked, thinking practically. "People have onward travel booked, hotel arrangements for Wednesday..."

Ismay waved a dismissive hand. "Minor details, Benji. Easily managed. Any passenger wishing to remain aboard Tuesday night will be welcome to do so, disembarking at their leisure Wednesday morning after breakfast. Think of the press, my boy! The headlines! It's precisely the sort of triumphant debut this magnificent ship deserves. Proving she's far superior to her sister." He shot me a sly look. "Far better than just firmer mattresses, wouldn't you agree?"

Most seemed caught up in Ismay's enthusiasm for a record crossing. Except Mother.

"But Mr. Ismay," she interjected, her voice quiet but firm, cutting through the excitement. "Aren't we moving rather... fast?"

All eyes turned to her. "Too fast, Caroline?" Ismay asked, his smile tightening.

"I only mean," she continued, choosing her words carefully, "that I understood there was some... ice... reported in the vicinity."

"Ice? Yes. Ice warnings are quite common for April on the North Atlantic, as I told the Captain."

"Yet you're not slowing down?" Mother asked. "It seems rather reckless to me." Her words implicated more than just speed; she was questioning Ismay's motives for being in this conversation, so close to danger.

Ismay chuckled lightly, reaching into his pocket. "I want to show you something." He produced the crumpled Marconigram slip—the *Baltic* warning he'd pocketed earlier. "This is the sixth ice warning we've received just today."

"The sixth?" I pressed.

"But you know what?" Ismay's eyes were still glued to my mother's. "We're not slowing down. No, sir. We're ramping up speed."

"Mr. Ismay," Father spoke up, his tone cautious but firm, siding unexpectedly with Mother. "I'm all for seeing this ship perform well. I've even wagered a few dollars on her daily run totals myself. But Caroline has a point. Pushing for maximum speed into an area with multiple ice warnings does seem a bit—"

"Reckless?" Ismay cut him off, his smile gone now, replaced by a steely determination. He addressed Father but his intense gaze settled back on Mother, the words clearly carrying a double meaning aimed directly at her. "My dear Benjamin," he said coolly, "what seems reckless to one cautious soul... is called progress by another." His eyes were challenging my mother. "When I see something I want, Caroline, I go after it. Full speed ahead..." He paused, letting the words hang heavy with implication. "...fates be damned."

"...so, essentially," I concluded, feeling slightly breathless after laying out the admittedly half-formed but passionate idea for a moving picture studio that Miles and I had dreamt up, "that's the pitch. Using my writing, his eye for photography... telling real stories, maybe." I braced myself for the polite dismissal, the gentle letdown from the man who controlled empires. Or at least half of Manhattan.

J.J. Astor continued strolling at a measured pace, his beloved, Kitty, trotting happily beside him on her lead, occasionally sniffing at a deck chair leg. Astor was silent for a long moment, gazing out at the horizon, seemingly digesting everything I'd just poured out.

"Well, Benji," he said finally, turning his thoughtful gaze towards me, "it certainly sounds like an ambitious project."

There it was. The polite lead-in to the rejection. "I understand, sir," I began quickly, trying to preempt the inevitable. "It's probably not the sort of stable venture you typically invest in, perhaps a bit too speculative, too..."

"I'm in," Astor cut in smoothly, stopping his walk.

I blinked, thrown off balance. "Wait. You... you are? Really? Just like that?"

"Just like that," J.J. confirmed with a small, decisive smile. He seemed to enjoy the element of surprise. "Of course," he added pragmatically, "we'll need to go over the specifics—projections, potential costs, your actual plan beyond youthful enthusiasm. But the core idea? Moving pictures? Telling stories? Yes. Consider me interested. Consider me... your first investor."

My head spun. Delight, disbelief, sheer shock warred within me. J.J. Astor? Investing in our dream? Just like that? Overwhelmed, I bent down instinctively to scratch Kitty behind the ears. The Airedale responded immediately, showering my face with enthusiastic, wet licks, her tail wagging furiously.

I laughed, pulling back slightly. "Well, someone's excited."

"Any pictures starring an excitable pooch?" Astor chuckled, watching the interaction.

"She does have that star quality," I laughed. "J.J., if you don't mind my asking, what convinced you? I mean, I know it wasn't my unpolished pitch."

"Kitty likes you. That's what convinced me."

I looked up, puzzled. "Your dog?"

"Absolutely," Astor stated matter-of-factly. "'The more I learn about people, the more I like my dog.' Know who said that?"

"No," I admitted, slightly embarrassed by my ignorance.

"Mark Twain," Astor said. "And he was right. Dogs are amazing judges of character, Benji. They operate purely on instinct. And you know what? Humans have those same instincts."

"Really?" I asked, intrigued.

"Certainly," he said. "We just choose not to follow them. We're burdened, you see, with intellect, with reason, with societal rules that tell us how we should feel, what we should think. So we question our gut feelings. That very gift evolution gave us—the one that tells us to run when something feels wrong, to trust when someone feels right—we choose to question it, ignore it, or worse," he paused, his gaze becoming more intense, "convince ourselves we never felt it at all."

His words resonated deeply, stirring echoes of my own recent struggles, my denial, the confusing kiss at Yale, the confrontation with Father, the undeniable pull towards Miles.

"You know that still, small voice inside you, Benji?" Astor continued, his voice quieter now, more personal. "The one that sometimes whispers, 'Hey, this isn't right!' or maybe, just maybe, 'This is right, go for it'?"

"Mmhmm," I murmured, nodding.

"You've got to learn to listen to that voice," he advised earnestly. "You're becoming a man now—eighteen tomorrow, isn't it? You're entering a world that's often designed to make you doubt that voice, to tell you that logic and appearance and what other people think are more important. A world that tells you to fight tooth and nail to make that inner voice shut up, especially if it tells you something inconvenient or unconventional."

He stopped walking again, placing a hand briefly on my shoulder, his expression serious. "Listen to me, son. The day you stop listening to that voice, the day you let fear or societal pressure silence it completely, is the day you stop truly living. It's the day you start letting them—your father, society, whoever—control who you really are." He held my gaze. "Never stop listening to that voice, Benji. Trust it. Understand?"

I stood there on the deck, the wind whipping around us, absorbing the unexpected weight of his words. John Jacob Astor, titan of industry, was telling me not about finance or power, but about instinct, about listening to the quiet truths within. Coming from him, the advice felt strangely profound, another piece of the puzzle clicking into place, another nudge towards embracing the frightening, exhilarating path that seemed to be opening before me.

CHAPTER 30

My meeting with J.J. Astor had run longer than anticipated, filled with unexpected advice and dizzying possibilities. By the time I returned to my cabin, the first bugle call for dinner was already echoing through the corridors. I rushed through my preparations, acutely aware that with Mother and Father attending the Wideners' exclusive dinner party in the À La Carte Restaurant tonight, the role of escorting Birdie fell solely to me.

I scrubbed my hands vigorously at the washbasin, trying to remove the lingering scent of Astor's Airedale, Kitty – hardly appropriate for the formal Dining Saloon. As I fumbled with the stiff studs of my dress shirt, my mind raced, oscillating between the heady potential of Astor's investment and the looming question of Harper's verdict. Had he read the pages yet? What would he think?

A sharp knock sounded at the door, startling me. "Just a moment!" I called out, hastily shrugging on my dinner jacket. Assuming it was Birdie, impatient as always, I didn't bother asking who it was. "Come in, the door's open!"

But it wasn't Birdie who stepped inside. It was Henry Sleeper Harper, impeccably dressed in his evening attire, looking every bit the publishing magnate.

My heart leaped into my throat. "Mr. Harper! Sir," I stammered, surprised by the unexpected visit. "Please, come in."

"Thank you, Benji," he said, stepping just inside the doorway, his expression pleasant but difficult to read. "Forgive the intrusion, I know you must be preparing for dinner, but I was on my way down myself and wanted to stop by personally."

"Of course, sir, anytime," I replied, my nerves fraying. This was it.

He clasped his hands behind his back, rocking slightly on his heels, drawing out the moment with an almost theatrical pause that felt excruciating. "I read the pages you left for me this afternoon," he said finally.

I held my breath, waiting.

"Well-written, certainly," he continued thoughtfully. "Clean prose. A good command of language." He paused again. The silence stretched.

"And?" I prompted, unable to bear the suspense any longer. "Your thoughts, sir?"

Mr. Harper sighed softly, his gaze meeting mine with what seemed like genuine, if slightly paternalistic, regret. "Benji," he began gently, "you're a bright young man. Intelligent, clearly well-educated. And your father is right, you do have imagination." He hesitated. "But...perhaps writing, as a profession...perhaps it simply isn't your strongest suit?"

The words landed like a physical blow, knocking the air from my lungs. Not your strongest suit. It was a polite, cushioned dismissal, but a dismissal nonetheless. All the hope, the validation I'd felt after talking with him in the baths, the dreams fueled by Astor's encouragement – it all seemed to crumble in an instant.

"Oh," was all I could manage, the sound small, hollow.

"I'm sorry, son," Harper continued, his tone sympathetic now. "It takes more than imagination and good grammar, you see. It requires a certain...innate storytelling ability, a unique voice. And while your writing is competent, I just don't..." He trailed off, perhaps realizing further explanation was unnecessary, even cruel. "There's no shame in it, Benji. Many intelligent people excel in other fields. Business, perhaps? Like your father?"

The mention of Father felt like salt in the wound. I forced a smile, a feeble show of politeness, desperate to hide the crushing weight of disappointment, the hot sting of embarrassment behind my eyes. "Thank you for your honesty, Mr. Harper. I appreciate you taking the time."

"Of course," he nodded, seemingly relieved to have the awkward task completed. "Well, I mustn't keep you. Enjoy your dinner." And with another polite nod, he turned and left, leaving me standing alone in the sudden, suffocating silence of the cabin.

I walked numbly to the mirror above the dressing table, staring at my own reflection. The hopeful young man who had practically run back from the pool earlier was gone, replaced by someone pale, shaken, his eyes shadowed with doubt. Maybe writing isn't for him. Harper's words echoed in my mind, merging with Father's warning from yesterday afternoon: "...if he tells you that it's a dead end...you have to be willing to accept that. To walk away. Don't keep heading down a dead-end road."

Was Father right? Was Harper right? Was this entire dream, this core part of who I thought I was, just a foolish, dead-end road? Should I accept it, walk away, become the businessman Father wanted, the man Miles now thought I was becoming? The weight of their combined judgment felt crushing, definitive.

But then, another voice surfaced, quieter, less certain, but persistent. J.J. Astor's voice. "...seeing my name in print is a dream realized...even if it doesn't make anyone happy except for me, that alone is enough." And his final advice: "Never stop listening to that voice, Benji. Trust it."

My own voice. That still, small voice inside that had always whispered stories, that found solace and truth in crafting sentences, that felt more me when I was writing than at any other time. Could Harper, could even my father, truly know better than that voice? Harper had read three hastily scribbled pages, written under duress while my mind was elsewhere. Was that truly enough to judge a lifetime's ambition? Something about the finality of his verdict, the neat dismissal, didn't feel entirely right. It felt...too easy. Too convenient, *perhaps*, for my father's narrative.

I looked at my reflection again. The disappointment was still there, etched onto my features. But beneath it, a tiny ember of defiance began to glow. Harper's opinion was just that – an opinion. Astor, a published author himself, had encouraged me. Miles had believed in our shared dream. And that inner voice...it wasn't ready to be silenced. Not yet.

Taking another deep breath, I straightened my tie, squared my shoulders. I would go to dinner. I would escort my sister. I would face the evening, face myself, face the uncertainty. What it all meant, what path I would ultimately take, I didn't know. But I wouldn't let one man's opinion, however esteemed, extinguish the possibility. I would keep listening. And, most-important to me in this moment, I would make things right with Miles.

And with that newfound, fragile resolve, I left the cabin to find my sister.

Sunday Evening, April 14th, 1912
The À La Carte Restaurant

Entering the À La Carte Restaurant on the Titanic felt like being admitted to an exclusive Parisian salon. The ambiance was deliberately intimate, a stark contrast to the grand scale of the main Dining Saloon. Softly glowing, rose-colored lamp shades cast a warm light upon tables draped in fine linen, set with sparkling crystal and gleaming silver under the watchful eye of the maître d'. Walnut paneling in delicate Louis XVI style adorned the walls, and the air hung thick with the almost overwhelmingly sweet perfume of hundreds upon hundreds of American Beauty roses, arranged in lavish bouquets on every available surface. Tonight, the room buzzed with the quiet confidence of the ship's most elite passengers, gathered for George and Eleanor Widener's much-anticipated dinner party honoring Captain Smith.

Mother allowed herself a small, internal sigh of relief as she was shown to her seat at the main table. Eleanor, true to her word, had worked her magic. Bruce Ismay was nowhere near. Instead, she found herself seated beside a stout, powerfully built man whose military bearing was softened by a surprisingly sunny disposition and a twinkle in his eye—Major Archibald Butt, President Taft's aide, whom she'd met never before, but felt an instant connection to. His conversation was light, witty, and blessedly free of undercurrents, allowing her to maintain the necessary facade of relaxed enjoyment. She exchanged pleasantries with the other guests nearby – the Thayers, the Carters, her hosts George and Eleanor Widener – playing her part impeccably. Benjamin, seated further down the table beside Mrs. Thayer, seemed to be holding up his end of their bargain as well, engaging in polite, if somewhat reserved, conversation. *Maybe*, she thought to herself, *this is going to work out after all.*

As the sumptuous courses progressed – caviar, consommé Olga, poached salmon – the conversation flowed easily, dominated by talk of business, politics, and upcoming New York social events. Finally, as dessert plates were cleared and champagne glasses refilled, George Widener rose, tapping his glass gently for attention.

"Friends," he began warmly, "if I may have your attention for just a moment. It gives me great pleasure, on behalf of Eleanor and myself, to host this small gathering tonight in honor of a man who requires no introduction, a commander whose skill and experience fill us all with the utmost confidence – our esteemed Captain, Edward Smith."

A murmur of polite applause went around the table. Captain Smith inclined his head graciously.

"To Captain Smith!" Widener declared, raising his glass.

"To the Captain!" echoed the guests.

Just as everyone was about to sip, a confident voice cut through the room from near the entrance, where he must have been lingering, observing. "If I may add a word!"

All heads turned. Bruce Ismay strode forward, positioning himself near the head of the table beside Captain Smith, effortlessly commanding the room's attention. Mother felt her stomach tighten, her earlier relief evaporating. So much for keeping him across the room. He clearly felt his position warranted inclusion in the main toast.

Ismay beamed, raising his own glass. "George, thank you for those kind words. I merely wanted to echo your sentiments and add my own personal tribute." His gaze swept the table, pausing when it met Mother's, before settling warmly on the Captain. "Commodore Smith represents the very best of the White Star Line. More than just the 'Millionaires' Captain,' as he's fondly known," Ismay chuckled, "he embodies the leadership qualities we value above all: steadfastness, experience, and," he paused, his eyes briefly finding Mother's again across the table, "an unwavering commitment to putting the greater good – the success and reputation of the Line, the swift and comfortable passage of our patrons – ahead of all other considerations."

The words, ostensibly praise for the Captain, landed differently for my Mother. The greater good ahead of all. Was that Ismay's justification for dismissing the ice warnings? For pushing the ship faster and faster through the darkening, freezing waters? For what? To impress her? That barbaric notion that women love a man who lives dangerously? For prioritizing headlines and profits over caution? The hypocrisy, wrapped in a silken toast, felt suffocating. She forced herself to maintain a polite smile, mirroring the others who raised their glasses once more, unaware of the chilling subtext only she seemed to fully grasp.

Sunday Evening Dinner,
Continued

While Mother and Father performed their roles at the Wideners' gala in the À La Carte Restaurant, our own dinner in the main Saloon felt unusually subdued. With so many prominent passengers attending the party upstairs, the vast room seemed sparsely populated tonight, the distance between occupied tables more noticeable, the usual buzz of conversation somewhat muted.

Our table, however, had gained a small, unexpected guest. Taking advantage perhaps of the less crowded room Bess Allison had allowed her young daughter, Loraine, to join them. The little girl, barely two years old, sat perched remarkably straight in a dining chair, her bright eyes taking everything in with solemn curiosity, looking like a miniature adult trained for formal occasions since birth. Her presence lent a certain sweetness to the table, with everyone – Birdie, Gracie, Stead, even a quiet Mr. Allison – delighting in her occasional, often surprisingly poignant, remarks.

I tried to participate, to enjoy the relative calm after the emotional upheavals of the afternoon, but my gaze kept drifting across the room to where Miles sat alone at a small table, staring disconsolately at his plate. Our earlier argument, his final cutting words, hung heavy between us. We exchanged glances several times – unhappy, longing, accusatory – before quickly looking away again, the distance across the grand Saloon feeling like a vast chasm.

Our quiet meal was interrupted by the arrival of Thomas Andrews, notepad in hand as always, making his customary rounds after dinner. He stopped beside our table with a warm smile. "Good evening, all. Enjoying your meal?" His eyes immediately fell upon the smallest diner. "Well now," he said kindly, "I didn't realize we had such a distinguished young lady gracing us with her presence this evening."

Bess Allison flushed slightly. "Mr. Andrews, forgive us. I know children aren't typically permitted," she apologized quickly, "but with the room being rather deserted this evening..."

"I love dessert!" Loraine chirped brightly, overhearing the end of her mother's sentence.

Everyone chuckled, and Mr. Andrews' smile widened. He knelt beside Loraine's chair. "It's no trouble at all, Mrs. Allison. A pleasure, in fact." He addressed the little girl directly. "I have a daughter back home in Belfast who's just about your age, I'd wager."

"I'm two!" Loraine announced proudly, holding up three fingers.

More laughter followed. "Two!" Andrews confirmed gently. "A very important age. Well now, Miss Loraine Allison, what do you think of our big ship, hmm?"

Loraine looked around the grand Saloon thoughtfully, everyone at the table leaning in slightly, curious to hear her childish assessment. After a moment, she stated with conviction, "There's no playroom."

Andrews blinked, momentarily surprised. Her mother jumped in to explain, "We sailed over on the Mauretania, Mr. Andrews. She quite enjoyed the children's playroom they have aboard."

"And so she should have!" Andrews agreed readily. "A fine feature on the Cunarders."

"But there's not one on Titanic," Loraine reminded him firmly.

"You know what, Miss Loraine?" Andrews' expression turned thoughtful. "You are absolutely right." An idea seemed to strike him. He straightened up, pulled his familiar notepad and pencil from his breast pocket, and flipped to a fresh page. "What do you think we should do about that?" he asked Loraine seriously. "Send a wire? Tell the newspapers about this egregious oversight?" He winked at the adults, then scribbled quickly in his book.

After a moment, he tore out the page. "There," he said, holding it out. "Can you read that, Loraine? Or would you like me to read it for you?"

"You read it," she commanded solemnly.

Andrews cleared his throat dramatically. "'Sunday, April 14th, 1912,'" he read aloud. "'Note for Britannic design: Add dedicated children's playroom. Essential amenity.'" He folded the note carefully. "You see, ladies and gentlemen," he addressed the table, "it is my job, as chief designer for Harland and Wolff, to accompany our newest ships on their maiden voyage, looking for any improvements we might make on future vessels. We are currently building Titanic's third sister, the Britannic."

He held up his notebook. "This book is filled with notes – bigger closets here, more lights there, maybe repositioning a serving pantry. Small things, mostly. I have been scratching my head trying to think of a truly significant improvement, something Olympic and Titanic lack that would make Britannic stand out." He smiled warmly down at Loraine. "And now I know. The children, perhaps our most important passengers, have been overlooked. So, I say, no more! Britannic will have a playroom, a space just for them. And it will be entirely thanks," he bowed slightly towards the girl's chair, "to the invaluable consultation provided by Miss Loraine Allison."

"Hear, hear!" Mr. Stead raised his water glass in a toast. "To Miss Loraine Allison, *Ship Designer*!"

Everyone at the table, even the usually-reserved Mr. Allison, raised their glasses with amused smiles.

"I shall wire my office with the design change recommendation immediately after dinner," Andrews assured Loraine seriously. "How does that sound?"

"Alright," she replied simply, eliciting another round of gentle laughter.

"Here's your receipt, to make sure I make good on that promise," he handed her the folded piece of paper from his notebook.

Andrews stood, offered another polite bow to the table, and especially to Loraine, then moved off towards his own table. Bess Allison caught his eye as he passed, silently mouthing, "Thank you," a grateful smile on her face. The brief, charming interaction provided a welcome moment of warmth, though it did little to bridge the cold distance I felt growing between myself and Miles across the now-emptying room.

Sunday Evening,
À La Carte Restaurant

Dinner at the Wideners' table had finally wound down. The elaborate courses had been cleared, replaced now by delicate cups of coffee, snifters of brandy, and the low murmur of satisfied conversation. The air remained thick with the sweet scent of roses and the lingering smell of sugared-glaze desserts.

Mother found herself engaged in an unexpectedly deep conversation with her dinner partner, Major Archibald Butt. While others around the table discussed politics or society gossip, she and the Major had somehow ventured into the less-charted territory of the supernatural, finding a surprising alignment in their views on the possibility of an afterlife, of connections beyond the tangible world.

"It's just so rare," she confided, swirling the amber liquid in her brandy glass, "to find someone willing to discuss such matters seriously. Most people dismiss it out of hand, or worse, tell you that you're crazy."

Both laughed.

"People are afraid of what they don't understand," Archie suggested, his gaze thoughtful. "Or perhaps they simply haven't allowed themselves to consider the possibilities."

"Exactly," Mother agreed, feeling a sense of camaraderie with this kind-eyed, articulate man. As she spoke, she noticed his hands were restless beneath the table, twisting his linen napkin into knots in his lap. "Archie," she asked gently, leaning forward slightly, "forgive me for noticing, but you seem...rather tense this evening? Is everything alright?"

He started slightly, apparently unaware his anxiety was showing. He forced a smile. "Just the usual pressures, Caroline. Nothing to concern yourself with."

"Are you sure?" she pressed softly. "You seem...burdened."

He hesitated, then sighed, the polished military aide facade cracking slightly. "It's the return voyage," he admitted quietly. "Knowing what awaits me back in Washington." He saw her questioning look and elaborated. "As you may know, I serve President Taft. But I was also extremely close to his predecessor, Mr. Roosevelt." He paused, rubbing his temples briefly. "With them both now vying for the Republican nomination, both expecting...demanding...my loyalty...well." He shook his head. "Being caught between two such powerful men, both dear friends and confidantes...the strain became unbearable. This trip to Europe, visiting the Pope...it was meant as an escape. A chance to clear my head before facing the inevitable political storm back home. Now that the voyage is nearing its end..." He nervously twisted the napkin again. "...I confess, I'm dreading facing the music. Returning to that reality."

Mother listened with genuine empathy. "Oh, Archie, that sounds incredibly stressful. Have you spoken to anyone about it? A doctor, perhaps?"

He waved a dismissive hand. "Doctors aren't terribly helpful in matters of political anxiety or nervous strain, I'm afraid."

"Nonsense, Archie," she countered firmly but kindly. "That's simply not true." She leaned closer, lowering her voice. "My husband...Benjamin has suffered from similar fits for years. Overwhelming stress, anxiety that can be quite debilitating." (She carefully omitted the likely source of his stress.) "He's seen some of the finest specialists in Europe. They taught him several rather effective exercises – breathing techniques, mental focusing methods – to help combat these emotional triggers when they arise." She smiled encouragingly. "They work wonderfully, Archie, truly they do, if one actually practices them."

Archie looked intrigued, a flicker of hope in his eyes. "Really? Do you think. ..would you perhaps be willing to teach me some of them?"

Mother considered for a moment, then her face lit up. "You know what? I have a brilliant idea," she declared. "Why don't you join us for breakfast tomorrow morning? Our usual table in the main Saloon. We can continue our discussion then, and yes," she smiled warmly, "I would be delighted to show you the exercises."

He looked immensely grateful. "Caroline, I couldn't impose..."

"Nonsense. It's settled." She felt a surprising sense of purpose, of connection. "It feels strange," she mused aloud, "how quickly one can feel comfortable with someone. As if we've known each other for years, yet we only just met."

"I feel the same," Archie admitted sincerely.

"You know," Caroline added thoughtfully, studying his earnest expression, his underlying sensitivity beneath the military polish, "I think I know why."

"Oh?" said Archie. "Why is that?"

"You remind me so much of someone," Mother smiled fondly.

"Who?" Archie smiled.

"My son. Benji."

Archie's expression flickered almost imperceptibly. Benji. The intense young man from the Café Parisian, the one Dorothy Gibson had clearly orchestrated for him and Frank Millet to meet. He instantly recalled the boy's quiet intelligence, his vulnerability, the sense of something deep and perhaps troubled beneath the surface. It would seem Dorothy wasn't the only one making connections. He thought it best, however, not to reveal their prior meeting to her just yet. Let her have this connection untainted for now.

"Is that so?" Archie replied smoothly, offering a warm smile. "Well, I take that as a high compliment indeed, Caroline."

CHAPTER 31

Dinner concluded with the usual polite sliding of chairs and murmurs of thanks to the stewards. The sparse crowd began to thin further, most drifting towards the Reception Room next door where the orchestra was already tuning up for the post-dinner concert and socializing. The night owls, Gracie and Stead, excused themselves to the Smoking Room, leaving Birdie and me alone amidst the clearing tables.

Birdie subtly scanned the double doors leading from the Reception Room. After a moment, her eyes softly flickered, as Violet appeared. Birdie gave a tiny, affirming nod in that direction, then turned back to me, gathering her wrap.

"Well, Benji," she announced, sounding convincingly tired, "I think I shall call it an early night. All that excitement this afternoon..." She leaned down and gave me a quick kiss on the forehead. "Don't stay up too late."

"Shall I walk you up?" I asked.

"No need," she smiled, already turning away. "We're practically adults now, aren't we? Or we will be after midnight, anyway." And with a final wink, she was gone.

I remained at the table, swirling the dregs of water in my glass, the events of the day crashing over me again. Harper's rejection. Astor's unexpected encouragement. My father's manipulations. The fight with Miles... his final, wounding words. Where did I go from here? What did any of it mean?

"Figured I might find you still brooding over here."

I looked up, startled. Miles stood beside the table, his earlier anger replaced by a guarded, almost hesitant expression. He slid into the chair Birdie had just vacated, right next to mine.

I managed a weak, apologetic smile. "Waiting for the other shoe to drop, I suppose."

He studied me for a moment. "What? No insults? No punches thrown my way?" He attempted a half-smile, though his eyes remained serious. "I'm not exactly sure what to make of you sometimes, Benji Sutherland-Howell the Second."

"Miles, I know," I began, needing to apologize, to explain. "About today..."

"I've got something for you," he cut me off gently, reaching into the inner pocket of his dinner jacket. He placed a familiar object on the white linen between us. My journal.

My breath caught. "Where... How did you...?"

Miles leaned closer, lowering his voice. "Your father took it, Benji. From the Lounge this morning. I told you today when I went to your cabin," he added, a hint of justification entering his tone, "something just didn't feel right about that whole meeting setup by your father. So, I left your cabin and went down to the Turkish Baths, by myself. Kept out of sight. Overheard your father talking to Mr. Harper near the changing stalls."

He paused, looking uncomfortable, clearly unsure how much to say. "Benji... your father... he told Harper exactly what to say to you. Gave him the gist—competent, good grammar, but no 'unique voice,' writing 'isn't your forte.' Said Harper owed him a favor." Miles shook his head slightly. "I'm sure Harper never even read them. Your father just told him to 'handle it'." He looked me straight in the eye. "He wanted Harper to crush your dream, Benji. He set the whole thing up."

I stared at him, then down at the journal, Miles's words confirming the sickening suspicion that had begun to form after Harper left my cabin. Now, it was all so obvious.

"I'm sorry, Benj," Miles said quietly, placing his hand over mine on the table. "I truly am."

A strange sense of calm washed over me, snuffing out every ounce of that earlier turmoil. I could see it for what it was, now—finally, clarity.

"I'm not," I said, surprising myself. "Well, not sorry to know the truth." I looked down at my journal, then back at Miles, covering his hand with my free one. "This just proves what I've suspected all along. What that *still, small* voice," I squeezed his hand, recalling Astor's words, "has been shouting at me all day."

"What's that?" Miles asked softly.

"That," I met his gaze, the connection between us reigniting, clear and undeniable, "*this*," I nodded towards our joined hands, "is what's *right*. Not Father's plans, not Harper's cheap lies. *This*."

We shared a moment, without words, but all peace was made between us. I looked down at the journal. "You know," I said, looking back up at Miles, "thank you for this. I needed it. The *truth*, that is." I slid the journal back to him. "But, I don't need *this* anymore."

He looked at me, confused. "I don't understand. You're not giving up on your writing?"

"Of course not," I said. "But this journal," I tapped the cover, "represents all that I thought I wanted... up until now."

"And, *now*?" Miles smiled.

"A brand new chapter. Written on a fresh page. I don't know what'll happen, and that's the beauty of it all. The story will write itself, I just have to step back and watch, as I learn to live in the moment. *With you*," I said.

He took my hand. "That sounds perfect," he said. "But," he slid the journal back into his pocket, "I think I'll hold onto this for you, just in case you change your mind."

I smiled at him. I had never been so certain of anything before. Miles was the dream that I never knew I had wanted, but now that I'd experienced him, I didn't want anyone to wake me up.

Just then, the music from the orchestra in the Reception Room swelled, filtering more clearly into the now nearly empty Dining Saloon. A familiar, hauntingly beautiful melody began—the *Barcarolle*. Miles's eyes lit up. He stood abruptly, pulling me gently to my feet.

"Come with me," he whispered.

He led me not towards the crowded Reception Room, but into the darkened vestibule just off the Reception Room, partially hidden behind the orchestra's setup. Here, shielded from view, the music enveloped us. Miles turned to face me, the strains of the slow, romantic waltz swirling around us. He gave a formal bow.

"May I have this dance, Mr. Sutherland-Howell?" he asked.

My heart leapt. It *soared*. I glanced around instinctively—no one. But even if the entire ship had been watching, in that moment, I wouldn't have cared. "I would love to," I smiled.

He took my hand, placed his other gently on my waist, and drew me into the slow, graceful steps of the waltz. We moved together in the dim, secluded space, our bodies finding an easy rhythm. His hand was warm against mine, his other firm against my back, guiding me effortlessly. Every time Miles stepped back, I stepped in, a delicate push and pull, the simple choreography feeling more intimate, more exciting than any touch I'd ever known.

In my mind's eye, the empty vestibule transformed into a vast, glittering ballroom. We were the only couple dancing, bathed in a spotlight, all other onlookers frozen, watching in awe as we created the kind of magic usually reserved for fairy tales, for history books. I drank in every moment, every intoxicating drop; never wanting this to end. *No, not yet,* I cursed the slowing tempo of the strings as the beautiful melody hinted at its end, wishing this moment, this feeling, could last forever. My heartbeat raced, my body aching with a confusing mix of tenderness and desire for the man holding me close.

As the final, lingering note of the *Barcarolle* evaporated into silence, we stood motionless for a beat, breathless, still holding each other.

"Let's go for a walk," Miles whispered, his lips close enough to graze my ear.

Sunday Evening Third Class General Room

While I was dancing dangerously close to the gaze of so many familiar faces in that secluded vestibule, Birdie was doing much the same miles away, deep in the heart of third class. The faces surrounding her weren't familiar, perhaps, nor was the music a lush, orchestral waltz. Instead, she found herself caught up in a boisterous Irish chorus, the driving rhythm of fiddles and pipes was infectious, her hand linked arm-in-arm with an endless parade of laughing strangers.

But they didn't feel like strangers down here, not really. Not like the carefully curated acquaintances above. Down here, the stiff pretense of high society, the constant calculation and judgment, was absent; down here it was the butt of jokes, not a daily practice. Birdie reveled in the perfect chaos. The carefree, unvarnished atmosphere felt more liberating than she could have ever imagined. Tonight, unlike her previous visits, she wasn't just observing; she was participating, letting her hair down, throwing caution to the wind with perfect, reckless abandon.

As the lively song ended, the accordion drawing its breath before diving into the next, Birdie glanced towards that familiar, wide staircase leading into the room. There he was. Her enigmatic prince, Oliver, reaching the summit, pausing to watch the scene playing out before him. That dangerous allure, those handsome risky features catching the contrast of the bare electric lights. At the sight of him, she'd forgotten how to breathe.

Deciding she could sit the next one out, she excused herself from the circle and made her way through the crowd towards Oliver's usual corner table. He watched her approach, his expression unreadable as always, a half-empty glass of ale resting on the table before him. She slid onto the chair opposite him, needing a moment to catch her breath from the dancing. He pushed the glass towards her wordlessly.

"I didn't know if you were going to come back," Oliver stated quietly, his grey eyes studying her face.

"I didn't know if I was going to either," Birdie admitted honestly, taking a grateful sip of the bitter ale.

"So I scared you off then, did I?" A faint smirk played on his lips. "Or was it just this world? Too rough around the edges compared to your cotton-candy clouds above?"

"I don't scare that easily, Oliver," Birdie retorted, meeting his gaze evenly.

"Oh no?" His smirk widened slightly. "Then what was it?"

She hesitated, then, bluntly, "I don't like liars."

His expression didn't change, but his eyes sharpened. "Who says I've lied to you, Margaret?"

"Don't patronize me," she snapped, leaning forward slightly. "I come from a family of liars, Oliver. An entire world built on them. No one says what they're really thinking. Everyone speaks in riddles. They've gotten so good at it," she added bitterly, thinking of her parents' performance at dinner, "that I think even they forget they're doing it most of the time."

Oliver's gaze was piercing now, those steel-grey eyes trying to look right through her, but unwilling to let her into them. "But not you?" he countered softly, dangerously. "Not the girl who comes down here in disguise, peddling that phony accent," he nodded pointedly, "trying to convince everyone, maybe even herself, that she can just make herself belong wherever she pleases?"

His words struck a nerve; there was truth in them, and she knew it. She thought about the plain dress Violet had lent her, the accent she'd attempted. He went on, his voice gaining a cynical edge.

"Birdie, listen," he said, using the nickname again, though this time it felt less intimate, more like a tool, "I'll admit, you've got brains. You've got spunk. And maybe your heart's in a better place than most up there." He paused, his gaze hardening slightly. "Hell, compared to me, you're practically a saint. But don't fool yourself. We're all victims of circumstance, shaped by the world we're born into. It's easy for you to stand on high moral ground, preaching about honesty, when you've never had to pull yourself up from the muck, never had to make impossible choices just to survive. Maybe," his voice dripped with sudden bitterness, "you just long to fix the world to make yourself feel better about all that privilege you never had to earn."

His words, though aimed at her, felt like a self-inflicted blow. He wasn't just talking about her; Birdie could sense it now. He was talking about himself. Projecting his own struggles, his own compromises, onto her.

"What did you do, Oliver?" her voice was low, direct.

His eyes flared defensively for just a second before the mask snapped back into place. But it was too late; she'd seen it. She was flexing that superpower of knowing just when to strike.

"You don't belong down here either, do you?" Birdie observed softly, leaning across the table. "You think you sized me up completely that first night, playing the mysterious working-class intellectual. But I've noticed a thing or two myself.

Your hands, like mine, haven't seen much real labor. Your vocabulary... too re-fined. Your cynicism... too... educated." She paused, letting her observations land. "You're not from this world any more than I am. Maybe somewhere closer to mine."

She saw the flicker of shock, the denial waging war with the recognition in his eyes. Before he could respond, before he could flex his defenses again, Birdie slid from her chair, gliding onto the bench beside him, closing the distance between them until their faces were mere inches apart. The warmth of his breath grazed her cheek, sharp, passionate bursts syncing with her own shallow, rapid breathing.

"You're running from something, Oliver," she whispered, holding his intense gaze. "What is it?"

For an instant, she saw raw, unbridled turmoil in his eyes—anger, pain, maybe even fear—quickly followed by something else, something powerful and over-whelming. And then, shattering the tension, shattering the questions, shattering everything, he kissed her. Hard. It wasn't gentle or tentative; it was a sudden, almost violent claiming, a desperate silencing of words with action. And Birdie, caught completely off guard yet somehow expecting it, kissed him back, matching his intensity with her own surge of confused, reckless, undeniable desire.

Sunday Evening The Boat Deck

We practically burst through the doors leading out onto the Boat Deck. Whether it was Miles pulling me by the hand, or me, him, I can't remember. I just remember the need to make our escape.

The arctic chill of the night air hit us instantly, a welcome shock against our heated skin. The deck was deserted here, bathed only in the distant glow of the deck lamps and the impossibly bright starlight overhead. The wind cut deeper now, colder than it had been even an hour ago, carrying the scent of pure, freezing ocean. We leaned against the railing, catching our breath, the silence punctuated only by the wind's whistle through the rigging and the steady rush of the ship cleaving through the black water.

"Howl! Howl!" Miles turned his gaze to the open sky, beating his chest, a cross between man and wolf. A dangerous prospect indeed.

"What are you doing?" I laughed, looking around to see if we'd caught anyone's attention, though the deck was indeed deserted.

Miles just turned and looked at me. His smile glittering in the dazzling backdrop of stars. The heat between us had reached a fever-pitch, not even remotely dampened by the cold. I felt an overwhelming sense of erotic wanting, a physical ache so intense, so specific, it was unlike anything I'd ever allowed myself to feel before. Parts of my body becoming rigid, with me unable to contain them. It was terrifying, exhilarating. I could sense it radiating from Miles too, in the way he watched me, the tension in his stance, the slight tremble in his hand as it rested near mine on the railing.

"Tell me what you're thinking, Benji," he whispered, his voice husky.

The directness of the question flustered me. My mind raced, filled with a thousand conflicting thoughts—desire, fear, the echo of his lips, the shadow of my father, the ghost of Paris. "I... I don't know," I stammered, the answer feeling inadequate, dishonest.

"You don't know?" Miles raised an eyebrow, a soft, knowing smile playing on his lips. "Really?" He wasn't pushing, just gently challenging my deflection.

I looked down, knowing my eyes would say everything my words didn't want to. "I can tell you what I'm feeling..." I reached out hesitantly, took his hand, and pressed it firmly against my chest, over my rapidly beating heart. He could feel the uncontrollable rhythm, the unbridled blaze stirring inside me.

His smile softened into tenderness. "*Nervous*?" he whispered gently.

"Terrified," I admitted, the word weaving itself into the blustery wind.

Without saying a thing, Miles took my other hand, and placed it flat against his own dinner jacket, mirroring my gesture. Beneath my palm, I could feel the strong, rapid thudding of his own heart, just as frantic as mine.

"I guess we both are," I breathed, looking up into his eyes.

The shared admission, the mutual vulnerability, floating in the air between us. The next thing I knew, he leaned in, his hand sliding from my chest to cup my jaw, tilting my face up to his. He kissed me again, and this time it was even more passionate than in the cargo hold—deeper, more searching, fueled by the intimacy of the dance, the honesty of our fears. His mouth opened, coaxing mine to follow, his tongue waiting for mine to venture out, to explore this forbidden space of each other. It felt wanted, desperately wanted, a confirmation of everything unspoken between us.

But even as I kissed him back, feeling myself diving head-first into the moment, the ghosts stirred. The memory of Father's rage, the smell of that horrid room in Paris, the feeling of being forced, controlled... it flashed through my mind, a chilling counterpoint to the warmth of Miles's lips. The gentle caress of his tongue, which was now grazing mine. Reality struck, cold and sharp as the night air.

I pulled away abruptly, gasping for breath, my heart pounding now with panic instead of passion. "We can't!" I insisted, stepping back, putting distance between us. "Not here! Not out here where anyone could see us!" The fear of discovery, of judgment, of repeating the past in any way, shape, or form, overwhelmed the desire.

Miles looked taken aback, hurt flickering in his eyes before being replaced by concern. "Okay," he said softly, holding his hands up slightly in a goodwill gesture. "Okay, Benji." He took a breath. "We could... go to my cabin," he suggested reasonably. "No one would see us there. We could even... just... talk."

His cabin. Privacy. The thought was both incredibly tempting and utterly terrifying. To be alone with him, with these feelings... "I... I can't," I whispered, shaking my head, unable to accommodate his eyes again.

Miles sighed, a quiet sound of disappointment, not anger. Not the reaction I would have expected from Father, or the boy at Yale. But, then again, Miles wasn't like any other man I'd ever been close to. "It's not," I rushed to explain, needing him to understand, "it's not that I don't want to, Miles. Believe me, I do. I'm just..." I struggled for the words. "...not ready yet. Not for... that."

"Benj, it's alright." He stepped closer again, but slowly this time, gently taking my hand, his touch steady and reassuring. He didn't try to pull me closer, just held my hand firmly in his. "Do I want to be with you? You know I do." His voice was low, sincere. "I want that more than anything right now. But," he squeezed my hand gently, "I would never ask you to do something you didn't want to. I would never push you. Not until you're completely ready."

He paused, his gaze incredibly soft, understanding dawning in his eyes as if he finally grasped the true root of my fear. "I'm not your father, Benji," he said quietly, but with firm conviction. "This isn't... Paris."

The explicit acknowledgment, the gentle naming of the source of my deepest fear, combined with his unwavering reassurance, felt like a lifeline thrown in this stormy sea.

"Whenever you're ready," Miles continued softly, still holding my hand, "whether it's tonight, tomorrow, or weeks from now... I'll be here." He gave my hand one last squeeze before letting it go. "Waiting for you."

Sunday Evening, April 14, 1912 Approx. 9:50 PM The Bridge

Tonight the bridge was an oasis of dim light and quiet professionalism against the immense, freezing darkness outside. The reverently hushed conversations and the faint hum of the telegraph indicators were the only sounds breaking the quiet concentration. Captain Smith stood near Second Officer Charles Lightoller, who was nearing the end of his watch, both men gazing through the large windows into the impenetrable, moonless night.

"Remarkable calm out there tonight, Lightoller," Captain Smith commented, his voice a low murmur. "Hardly a breath of wind."

"Indeed, sir," Lightoller agreed. "Like a mill pond. Flattest I've seen it on the Atlantic run in quite some time."

The regimented footfalls of an officer's shoes trailed in from the outside deck. The shoes carried First Officer William Murdoch into the room, arriving a few minutes early to relieve Lightoller for the 10:00 PM watch. He joined the two men near the windows.

"Evening, Captain. Mr. Lightoller," Murdoch greeted them quietly.

"Mr. Murdoch," Smith acknowledged with a nod. "We were just remarking on the sea. Like glass tonight."

"Aye, sir. Extraordinarily calm," Murdoch agreed, his own experienced eyes scanning the dark horizon. He frowned slightly. "Makes spotting the growlers difficult, though. No swell breaking against them."

"My thoughts exactly," Lightoller concurred. "Especially with no moon to help us. They'll be practically invisible."

"Any further ice reports since dinner, Mr. Lightoller?" Murdoch asked, preparing to take over the watch.

"Just the one relayed from the *Californian* around dinnertime, sir," Lightoller confirmed. "Reported ice some fifty miles or so north of our projected track now. Seemed quite concerned."

Captain Smith nodded gravely. He turned to face both senior officers. "Right then. Maintain course and speed, Mr. Murdoch. But keep a sharp lookout. Instruct the crow's nest to be particularly vigilant for icebergs, growlers, and field ice." He paused, emphasizing his next words. "Reduce speed immediately if you are in the slightest doubt, if there's the slightest hint of danger or haziness."

"Aye, aye, Captain," Murdoch replied crisply, understanding the weight of the command. Maintain speed, yes, but caution was paramount.

"The slightest hint, Mr. Murdoch," Smith reinforced, commanding the First Officer's gaze directly. His confidence from the afternoon discussions with Ismay seemed tempered now by the late hour and the accumulated warnings. "Wake me if you see anything, or if you have any concerns whatsoever."

"Understood, sir," Murdoch affirmed.

Satisfied, Captain Smith gave a final nod. "Very good. I'll turn in, then. Goodnight, gentlemen."

"Goodnight, Captain," Lightoller and Murdoch replied in unison.

Captain Smith turned and left the bridge, heading towards his cabin just aft, leaving First Officer Murdoch in command of the world's largest liner as she raced silently at over twenty-two knots through the freezing, flat-calm, and dangerously deceptive waters of the North Atlantic night.

Sleep was impossible. I knew that much. Back in my cabin, hidden in darkness, the events of the evening replayed relentlessly. Every thought, no matter how abstract, how distant, always came back to him. Miles.

I lay in bed, the portholes fully open, allowing the sharp chill to swirl around the room, yet doing little to cool the heat building within me. I thought about the dance in the vestibule, the feel of his hand on my waist, the pressure of his lips against mine on the boat deck. Allowing myself, perhaps for the first time ever, to fully explore these feelings, this overwhelming sense of erotic longing, I let my hand slide beneath the thin cotton of my shirt. My fingertips traced patterns across my skin, gently swirling the sensitive peaks of my nipples, feeling the blood rush, the skin tighten in response.

Passion, unfamiliar yet insisting, pulled my reach further, exploring uncharted regions that were craving the soft graze of my fingertips. Goosebumps chased up my back, down my arms, the fine hairs standing on end as my hand slid beneath the waistband of my pajama pants. I closed my eyes, imagining it wasn't my own touch, but Miles's—his warm hand exploring my body, his lips working in tandem to cover more ground, the shared breath between us, the spark of electricity. My own breath quickened, rising and falling in low waves that matched the distant surge thrown up by the propellers outside. My body yearned for more, arching instinctively towards that imagined touch. My fingers glided over miles of skin, delving into its crevices, climbing its mountains, the building pressure, the swelling intensity, the raging fluids working their way towards a release, an electric jolt of pure ecstasy...

Knock. Knock. Knock.

The sound shattered the carnal moment, sharp and intrusive against my cabin door. My eyes snapped open, my heart still racing, but for an entirely different reason now. I froze, scrambling to pull myself back from the brink, struggling to regain composure, my breath still ragged.

"Just a minute!" I called out, my voice fighting against my breath. I swung my legs out of bed, hastily pulling on my dressing gown, tying the belt tightly as I walked gingerly towards the door.

"Benji, darling? It's me." Mother's voice beckoning from the sleeping corridor. *Strange*, I thought, *she'd be asleep in Birdie's room.*

Taking a steadying breath, I opened the door. She stood there, bathed in the dim hallway light, but radiating an energy completely different from the strained politeness of the afternoon or the fragile tension of the morning. She looked... happy. Genuinely, incandescently happy. Her eyes sparkled, her smile was warm, real.

"Mother? Is everything alright?" I asked, stepping back to let her in.

"More than alright, darling," she practically beamed, gliding into the room, bringing a sense of lightness with her. "Better than it has been in years." She perched on the edge of my settee, looking utterly vibrant. "Oh, Benji, the party was lovely, but you'll never guess who I spent the most delightful evening conversing with!"

"Mr. Ismay?" I asked, turning on the table lamp.

"Heavens, no," she waved a dismissive hand, though the name didn't seem to cause the same reaction it might have yesterday. Her expression softened then, becoming earnest. "But, first, darling," she began, reaching out to take my hand, "I wanted to apologize. For my behavior lately. I know I've been... difficult. Tense." She sighed. "I've been dealing with so many things, Benji, fears I haven't been willing to face. About your father, about myself, about you and Birdie growing up..."

Her honesty, her vulnerability, took me by surprise.

"But," she continued, her eyes shining with newfound clarity, "I realized something tonight. Watching you children navigate this world with such spirit, such conviction... especially Margaret... it made me see. I can't control what life throws my way, can't control your father, can't stop you both from becoming the incredible adults you already are. But I can control how I choose to see it, how I choose to handle it." She squeezed my hand. "The future I want is the future I create, starting today."

She looked at me intently. "Thank you, Benji. You and Birdie both. For being strong enough to stay true to yourselves, even when... well, even when I haven't made it easy. You've both inspired me."

"Well," I began, "if we're apologizing—" Mother put a finger to my lips to stop me. "Bygones, my Benji. Bygones," she winked.

After we took a moment, allowing our unspoken words to finish what we each had to say, I recalled our earlier conversation. "So? You met someone at dinner?"

"Oh! Yes! A Major Archibald Butt. President Taft's aide! Utterly charming, intelligent, suave, sensitive... we talked for ages! About everything under the sun." Her enthusiasm was infectious. "There's something about his eyes, his manner. I told him that he reminds me so much of someone."

"Who?"

"Why, you, Benji," her smile warmed even more as she drew the comparison.

"*Me*?"

"Oh, Benji, you simply must meet him. You two would hit it off beautifully, I just know it!"

Apparently, Dorothy wasn't the only one who could see right through me. Something that I hadn't even seen myself. Was I letting down my guard? Showing my true colors? Or was Mother simply allowing herself to see what she had always known was there?

She paused, her gaze searching mine. "Benji... we've always had a special bond, haven't we? I can feel... I sense there's something on your mind. Something you want to tell me?"

Her words, her openness, her complete acceptance radiating from her in that moment... it created a safe harbor I hadn't known existed. The truth about Miles, the confession I'd barely dared to even consider myself until days ago, rose to my lips. *Could I? Here? Now?* Feeling liberated by her honesty, by my own recent steps out of the shadows, I was finally about to do it.

"Mother," I began, my voice thick with emotion, "there is something I want to tell you."

"Anything, darling," she replied instantly, her eyes so wanting, her smile so safe, so reassuring. "You know you can tell me anything."

I knew, in that instant, that she meant it. That I could tell her, and she would be my champion, my ally, no matter what. As I opened my mouth, Miles's name was right there, on the very tip of my tongue... but, suddenly, it felt wrong. Rushed. I couldn't tell her about the man I was falling in love with, couldn't share that timid, evolving joy, until I had properly told him how I felt first.

"Breakfast," I smoothly deflected, the idea forming as I spoke. "Tomorrow morning. Can you... can you and your new friend, Major Butt, meet me for breakfast? In the Café Parisian?" A smile touched my lips. "Their espresso is apparently to die for."

Instead of just telling her, I would show her. I would let her meet Miles herself—not just the joking American from boarding, the social charmer with the camera attached to his arm, but the deep, caring man who rounded out my weaknesses, and me, his. I would let her see the connection, the happiness. I knew, somehow, that she would love Miles, just as I was beginning to. And more than anything, I wanted her to see us happy, truly happy, as I knew she ultimately wanted me to be.

Her answering smile was radiant, completely unsuspecting of the true nature of the invitation. "Why, Benji, how thoughtful! I'd be delighted! And I'm sure Archie would be too. A birthday breakfast in the Café Parisian. It's a date!"

She stood, leaned down, and kissed me goodnight on the forehead. "Get some sleep, darling. You look tired." She practically waltzed out of the room, leaving me sitting there in the dim lamplight, the turmoil replaced by a profound sense of hope.

I couldn't remember the last time I'd seen her so genuinely happy. And perhaps, just perhaps, I'd never been happier either. Because for the first time in my seventeen, moments away from eighteen, years, I felt truly seen. I had found love, astonishingly, unexpectedly. And now, even more astonishingly, in my mother, I knew, without a doubt, I had found an ally. The future suddenly felt less like a terrifying void and more like an open door.

CHAPTER 32

The small wireless cabin aboard the Leyland liner SS *Californian* felt cramped, buzzing faintly with the stored energy of the Marconi apparatus. The small, discreet liner, which had set sail about a week before *Titanic*, still devoid of passengers, still carrying her complements of blankets and sweaters, with the last-minute addition of the ominous Mr. Y, had been making a rather conservative crossing, and now found herself only miles ahead of *Titanic's* aggressive charge.

Outside, the night was preternaturally black and freezing, the ship motionless, engines stopped. Captain Stanley Lord ducked his head as he entered the wireless shack, his expression grim. The ship's wireless operator, Cyril Evans, looked up from his logbook.

"Just wanted to let you know officially, Sparks," Captain Lord stated gruffly, "we're stopped for the night. Surrounded by pack ice. Can't proceed safely until daylight."

Evans nodded. He'd heard the engines stop and felt the unnatural stillness that had fallen over the ship nearly half an hour ago.

"Are there any other vessels in our vicinity?" Lord asked, peering out the small porthole into the impenetrable darkness.

Evans adjusted his headset, listening intently to the faint crackle and Morse chatter filling the ether. "There's that big liner, sir. The one I mentioned earlier. *Titanic*. Her spark is getting much louder now. Can't be more than ten or twenty miles off, I'd reckon, coming up behind us."

"Right," Lord nodded decisively. "Get hold of her, Evans. Advise them we are stopped and surrounded by ice. Tell them to relay the danger to their commander immediately."

"Aye, aye, Captain," Evans replied, already turning to his transmitter key. Captain Lord gave a curt nod and exited the cabin, leaving Evans alone with the task of warning the rapidly approaching giant.

Simultaneously, Marconi Room RMS *Titanic*

A few miles away, the atmosphere inside the state-of-the-art Marconi 'Silence' cabin aboard the *Titanic* was anything but calm. Senior Wireless Operator Jack Phillips sat hunched over the powerful transmitter, his fingers flying across the Morse key, sweat beading on his forehead despite the cooling fans. Scrawled Marconigram forms lay in precarious stacks around him—hundreds of messages from wealthy passengers eager to broadcast greetings, stock trades, dinner arrangements, and trivial gossip across the Atlantic via the newly reachable station at Cape Race, Newfoundland.

The ship's wireless set had malfunctioned for several hours earlier in the day, creating a frustrating and immense backlog just as they came within direct range of the North American coast. Phillips felt the pressure intensely—pressure from the passengers paying handsomely for the service, and pressure from the Marconi Company itself, which paid the operators based partly on message revenue.

Harold Bride, the junior operator, appeared in the doorway connecting the operating room to their small sleeping quarters, rubbing sleep from his eyes, still dressed in his pajamas. He watched his senior colleague work, the rhythmic, high-pitched dit-dah-dit filling the small space.

"Still hard at it then, Phillips?" Bride asked, noting the frantic pace and the formidable pile of outgoing messages still waiting.

"Only thing moving faster than *Titanic* tonight is me," Phillips quipped without looking up, his focus absolute. He had the volume on his headset turned up high, straining to clearly distinguish the relatively weak signal from the distant Cape Race towers amidst the general static.

Bride surveyed the stacks of unsent messages. "Good Lord, you've still got all these? They keep coming, do they?"

"Like locusts," Phillips grumbled, as two more messages dropped from the pneumatic tubes, which carried passenger messages up from the purser's office. Phillips rolled his eyes and nodded towards the new messages which had just fallen into the outgoing basket. "See what I mean?"

"Want some help then?" Bride offered, yawning. "You've been at it for hours. Let me have a go. You take a break, Jack."

"Aren't you supposed to be getting your beauty sleep before your watch?" Phillips retorted, though without malice.

"So you're saying you don't want my help then?" Bride teased.

"Hold on now, I didn't say that," Phillips managed a brief laugh, finally pausing his transmission for a second.

"Alright, alright. I'll get dressed properly and take over," Bride said, turning back towards the sleeping quarters.

Just as Bride turned, an incredibly loud, crackling burst of Morse code blasted through Phillips's headset, so strong that even Bride could hear the sharp buzz from across the small room.

"Bloody hell!" Phillips ripped the headset off, wincing and rubbing his ears. "Fucking idiot!"

"What on earth was that?" Bride asked, startled by the volume and Phillips's reaction.

"That steam bucket, *Californian*," Phillips grumbled, turning down the volume knob before cautiously replacing the headset. "Her spark's so loud she can't be more than twenty miles off, maybe closer." He listened for a second, his expression turning to one of annoyance. "Ugh," he sighed, "still going on about ice. Says," he translated the incoming Morse, "'Say, old man, we are stopped and surrounded by ice.'"

"Lovely," Bride commented dryly, rolling his eyes. Just what they needed while trying to work weak, long-distance signals.

Phillips, his patience frayed, his focus entirely on clearing the backlog of paid messages to Cape Race before its signal faded further, didn't even acknowledge the content of the warning. He slammed his own key down, transmitting with sharp, angry bursts, saying the words aloud for Bride's benefit as he sent them:

"KEEP OUT! SHUT UP! I'M WORKING CAPE RACE!"

He released the key and listened intently for a second, headset pressed tight against his ears. The ether where the *Californian's* loud signal had been was now silent.

"Think he got the message?" Bride asked, half-amused, half-appalled.

Phillips listened a moment longer. "Well," he said with a grim chuckle, turning back to his log and the pile of passenger messages, "I'll take his silence to mean that he did." He resumed tapping out a society woman's dinner plans to her friend in New York; the vital warning from the ship stopped in the ice just miles ahead unheard, unheeded, and unreported to the bridge. Bride sighed and went back to get changed, ready to relieve his exhausted senior partner.

Late Sunday Night, Continued Miles's Cabin, D Deck

Miles's words, "Waiting for you," echoed in my mind as I stood outside his cabin door on the quieter D deck corridor. The walk down from my cabin, only a deck above, felt both impossibly long and instantaneous. Every rational thought screamed at me to turn around, to return to my own cabin, to retreat into solitude and safety. But the memory of his touch, his understanding, the profound relief of being seen... it pulled me forward, stronger than the fear. This wasn't Paris. This wasn't Father. This was Miles. This was... freedom.

My knuckles hovered before the painted wood, trembling slightly. It was late, maybe eleven, midnight perhaps. What if he was asleep? What if he hadn't meant... But Astor's words returned: *Never stop listening to that voice.* My inner voice, hesitant but clear, urged me forward. I knocked softly, barely a whisper against the grain.

Silence for a beat, then his voice from within, low and quiet. "Come in."

I pushed the door open. The cabin was utterly dark; the curtains weren't drawn, but the moonless night offered little, save the gentle beam that sliced into the single, open porthole across the room, spilling onto the floor. Shadows pooled in the corners, rendering the small space intimate, mysterious. Even with the soft light spilling in from the corridor, I couldn't see him.

"Close the door," Miles's voice commanded softly from the darkness.

I hesitated for only a second, then pushed the door shut, the latch behind me clicking softly, decisively. I was closing myself inside this private world, forsaking the judgment, the rules, the watchful eyes of the ship beyond. In the absolute darkness, my pulse surged, pounding with the thrilling, dangerous possibility of the unknown, of finally embracing the desires this room seemed to represent.

"I didn't think you'd ever come," Miles said. The soft, glowing ember of a cigarette flared briefly as he inhaled, pinpointing his location—sitting on the edge of his bed in the far corner.

"I couldn't sleep," I replied, my voice barely a whisper, still standing near the door, letting my eyes adjust.

"You want to talk?" he asked, the ember dipping as he spoke. He stubbed it out, plunging the room back into near-total blackness, then I saw his silhouette stand, taking shape as he moved slowly towards the faint circle of muted starlight.

There, stepping into that pooling glow, his form becoming clearer—dressed only in his pajama trousers, his bare chest sculpted by shadow and icy stars. He looked impossibly beautiful, vulnerable, real. In that moment, he was Michelangelo's *David*, and I, a breathless spectator, reveling in his beauty. The sculpted marble of his skin, the fine veins Roman roads, carrying my thoughts, my desires, to every inch of his perfect body. Longing to reach out and touch him, just to see if he was indeed real.

"No," I managed, the single word thick with unspoken meaning. Talking wasn't what I needed now.

He took another step closer, stopping only inches away. "Then why are you here, Benji?" he asked softly, though his eyes, even in the dimness, held the answer.

The unbridled blaze returned, that restless, fluttering canary trapped behind my ribs. Words failed me. "Miles..." I began, but the name was enough.

Action took over where language fell silent. I closed the final distance between us, my hands finding his bare shoulders, pulling him towards me. He met me willingly, his arms encircling my waist, pulling me tight against him as our lips met. The kiss was different again—not the tentative exploration of the cargo hold, nor the passion tinged with fear on the boat deck. This was a kiss of arrival, of acceptance, deep and consuming, blotting out everything but the sensation of him, the reality of this moment.

Hands slid over skin, first touching tentatively, then grabbing, sampling what was unseen, holding its weight in our hands, wrapping around each other's warmth as if drowning men clinging to a raft. Clothes became obstacles, shed hastily in the darkness, discarded onto the floor without thought. The bottoms of his feet grazing the tops of mine. The feeling of his strong legs wrapping securely around mine. Skin against skin, the shock of contact now electric, igniting nerve endings I never knew existed. Exploring each other's naked bodies felt like mapping new continents by touch alone—the curve of a shoulder blade, the dip of a waist, the surprising softness of hair against a hard chest. It was discovery, exhilarating and profound.

"Is this alright?" Miles breathed against my ear, his voice a vapor, pulling back just enough to check, even now, even amidst the rising tide.

His consideration, his care, shattered any final remnants of the Parisian ghosts. Before another word could be said, fueled by a surge of trust and desperate need, I guided him gently down until his knees touched the floor, pulling his head towards me, reclaiming agency, taking control of the moment in a way I never could before.

There were no words then, only sensation, shared breath, the overwhelming intensity of mutual pleasure freely given, freely taken. Moments of pure ecstasy, sharp and bright against the darkness, where fear dissolved into feeling, where shame was replaced by the simple, undeniable truth of being wanted, accepted, safe in his presence.

His skin became my skin. Until I couldn't tell where I ended, and he began. When I touched myself, I touched him. We were two halves finally made whole, adrift together on a dark ocean, finding our own world in the confines of that small, starlit cabin.

Sunday Night, Late Third Class Corridor & Cabin

The lingering intensity of Oliver's kiss left Birdie breathless, the boisterous energy of the General Room fading into a muted background roar. The ale she'd consumed, combined with the adrenaline of the confrontation and the unexpected passion, made her feel unsteady, exhilarated, and profoundly confused all at once.

Oliver took her hand, his touch sending another jolt through her system, and began leading her away from the crowded room, down one of the narrow, dimly lit corridors lined with third-class cabin doors.

They stumbled slightly as they walked, suppressed giggles escaping them both, the earlier tension seemingly forgotten, replaced by a tipsy, magnetic pull. They didn't so much walk as they did dance their way down the corridor, Oliver humming a line from one of the Irish tunes they'd heard earlier. Birdie was boldly leaning into him more than was necessary.

He stopped before one of the identical doors, fumbling slightly in his pocket for a key. Before inserting it into the lock, he paused, turning to face her fully in the scattered hallway light. His expression was serious now, the earlier intensity returning, but softened with something else—concern, perhaps?

"Margaret," he said quietly, using her proper name, his gaze searching hers. "Are you sure? About this? Is this what you want?" He gestured towards the cabin door. "There's still time to turn back. No judgment." He was giving her an out, a clear opportunity to walk away from whatever waited behind that door.

Birdie looked into those complex grey eyes. Her mind screamed caution—the mystery surrounding him, his earlier evasiveness, the sheer recklessness of it all. But her heart, fueled by intrigue, defiance, and the undeniable spark between them, urged her forward. Instead of answering with words, she reached up, tangled her fingers in his dark hair just as she'd imagined doing earlier, and pulled his face down to hers, kissing him with a fierce, assertive passion.

When they finally broke apart, both slightly breathless again, Oliver let out a shaky laugh. "Right then," he murmured. "I'll take that as a yes." He turned back to the door, finally managing to get the key into the lock.

He pushed the door open into a tiny cabin. Birdie blinked, her eyes adjusting to the dim light filtering from the single bulb overhead. It was minuscule—she was quite certain she had seen larger broom closets on the upper decks. Two narrow bunks were built against one wall, though only the bottom one looked occupied, piled high with blankets. A small, battered trunk sat at the foot of the bed. On the opposite wall was a simple washstand, a tiny fold-down table, and a single stool. What caught her eye immediately, however, was the clutter on the bottom bunk—not just blankets, but a portable typewriter surrounded by a chaotic stack of loose papers and notebooks.

Oliver grimaced slightly at the state of the room. "Apologies for the mess," he muttered, clearly not having expected company. "My... office." He moved towards the bed to clear the typewriter and papers, intent on moving them to the unoccupied top bunk.

"Here, let me help you," Birdie offered, stepping further into the small space, still slightly unsteady from the ale and that lingering kiss.

"No, I've got it, really—" Oliver protested, but it was too late. As Birdie reached to gather an armful of loose papers, her slightly tipsy coordination failed her, and the stack fumbled through her grasp, scattering across the narrow floor space.

"Darn it! Sorry!" Birdie exclaimed, bending down immediately to retrieve the mess.

"Don't worry, I'll get that!" Oliver insisted, kneeling beside her, clearly wanting to gather the papers himself. But Birdie had already scooped up several sheets, her eyes subconsciously scanning the topmost one as she straightened up.

Her brow furrowed in confusion. "This is... a letter of credit," she read aloud slowly, recognizing the bank letterhead. "Payable to... W.T. Stead?" She looked up at Oliver, bewildered. "Mr. Stead? The journalist at our dinner table? How do you have this? Did you... did you steal it?"

Oliver snatched the paper from her hand, his expression instantly guarded. "No, of course not! It's nothing, Margaret. Just some papers I was holding for someone." He began hastily gathering the rest of the scattered sheets, trying to shield them from her view.

"But..." Birdie's gaze fell on another piece of paper near her foot—a familiar-looking envelope, identical to the one Mr. Stead had given the steward in the Lounge yesterday. Clearly visible on the front, addressed in Stead's distinctive hand, were the words: "To New Amsterdam."

Her mind flashed back instantly—Stead's insistence on posting it that way, his dismissal of the letter box, his comment about it being an "inside joke." It wasn't a joke. It was code. And Oliver had the envelope.

"It's an inside joke, Birdie," Oliver said quickly, perhaps too quickly, snatching the envelope as well.

The use of her nickname, combined with the evidence before her, struck Birdie with sudden, sickening clarity. "You work for him," she stated flatly, the pieces clicking into place.

"What? Who?" Oliver feigned ignorance, stuffing the papers haphazardly back onto the top bunk.

"Mr. Stead!" Birdie insisted, her voice rising, the earlier warmth between them evaporating, replaced by cold suspicion. "You're working with him, aren't you? On what? Some sort of story? But... why?"

Oliver avoided her gaze, busying himself with straightening the blankets on the lower bunk. "C'mon, Birdie. Let's not talk about this now. I think maybe we should call it a night. You're tired, you've had a bit to drink—"

"No, I'm not!" Birdie's passion flared, no longer fueled by desire, but by anger and betrayal. She stepped towards him, blocking his attempt to deflect. "I told you I hate liars, Oliver! And my name! I never told you my name was Birdie! Who told you? Was it him? Did Stead tell you who I was?"

Oliver finally stopped fussing with the blankets, turning slowly to face her, his expression resigned, cornered. He hesitated, then let out a long breath. "Yes," he admitted quietly. "Yes, I've been working with Stead. I used to work for him at the *Pall Mall Gazette* back in London. He brought me onto this project."

"What project?" Birdie demanded, dread coiling in her stomach. "What kind of exposé is he working on now?"

Oliver looked deeply uncomfortable, running a hand through his hair. Finally, reluctantly, he met her gaze. "It's about... perceptions. About homosexuality in modern society. The hidden lives." He swallowed hard. "I was supposed to... observe. Gather material about how it manifests, how people cope, down here among the lower classes. While Stead," he added bitterly, "monitored the elites upstairs."

Birdie felt sick. An exposé? On such a private, dangerous topic? Then a horrifying thought struck her. "And me?" she whispered. "Why did you and Stead discuss me? Why did he tell you my nickname?"

Oliver couldn't meet her eyes now. "He... Stead traveled on *Titanic* specifically hoping to gather material about your father," he mumbled. "There have been... rumors... for years. About his affairs. With men. Stead thought sitting at his table, being in close proximity..." He trailed off. "But your father wasn't showing. Confined to his cabin. Stead was getting frustrated, told me the voyage might be a wash for his purposes." Oliver finally looked up, his eyes pleading for understanding. "And then... then I met you. That first night. You told me your name was Margaret Sutherland-Howell. Suddenly, Stead had a connection. An 'in'. Someone who could potentially provide... information."

The implication hit Birdie with the force of a physical blow. "So," she whispered, her voice trembling with fury and hurt, "this whole time? Everything? Talking to me, dancing with me, letting me think..." She couldn't finish the sentence. "...You were just using me? To spy on my father?" The realization felt like ice water pouring through her veins. This wasn't the 'real world' she'd craved; it was darker, more twisted, more treacherous than anything she could have imagined.

"It started like that, Margaret, yes," Oliver admitted wretchedly. "Just gathering information. I mean... I was just doing my job. But look!" He fumbled for one of the letters amongst the pile on the top bunk. "This just came yesterday! From Stead! Read it! He's asking me why I haven't reported back, why I'm not getting him anything useful!" He held it out to her desperately. "I haven't given him anything, Margaret! Not about you, not about your father. Because after I met you... after talking with you... I couldn't. It changed."

But Birdie recoiled from the offered letter as if it were poison. His confession, his pathetic attempt at justification, meant nothing. "I tried to push you away, but you wouldn't listen to me, Birdie!"

"Do not call me Birdie," she seethed, her voice low and dangerous, tears of anger finally spilling over. "Birdie is for my family. For my friends." Her gaze swept over him with utter contempt. "You," she spat the word, "are nothing to me."

And with that, she turned, yanked the cabin door open, and fled into the corridor, slamming the door shut behind her, leaving Oliver standing alone amidst the scattered papers and the ruins of their brief, deceptive connection.

CHAPTER 33

High above the liner's forward deck, suspended in the freezing darkness, Frederick Fleet stamped his feet, pulling his watch cap lower over his ears. The wind cut like a razor at this height, howling past the small enclosed platform of the crow's nest, bringing tears to his eyes and making observation almost impossible. Beside him, Reginald Lee hunched deeper into his greatcoat, squinting into the blackness ahead.

"Bloody freezing," Lee muttered, his breath pluming white. "Should've issued rum rations tonight."

"Should've issued binoculars," Fleet grumbled back, rubbing his stinging eyes. "Couldn't scrounge up another pair of bloody glasses for the lookouts, oh no."

"We had 'em coming from Belfast," Lee reminded him, his voice muffled by his collar.

"Yeah, but where are they now?" Fleet shot back bitterly.

"Told you. Mr. Lightoller wanted 'em back for the bridge before we left Southampton. Said the officers needed them more than we did."

"Bloody hell," Fleet spat into the wind. "We're the eyes of the ship, mate! What good are eyes that can't bloody see?"

Lee shrugged, peering uselessly into the void. "Calm down, Fred. You and I both know a pair of glasses wouldn't help you see the end of the forecastle tonight. Not with your eyes tearing up in this bloody chill, and not a scrap of moonlight to see by."

"Aye, and no moon makes the bergs harder to spot," Fleet agreed grimly. "No waves breaking at the base neither, not on a sea like this."

"Well," Lee sniffed, rubbing his nose, "it's a good thing you can smell ice then, ain't it?"

Fleet bristled slightly. "Ha! Laugh all you want, Reggie. I've heard you mock me before."

"Now, is that just a joke, Fleet, or do you actually believe that load of bollocks?"

"It's true," Fleet insisted stubbornly, sniffing the frigid air again. "There's a scent to it. A particular coldness." He fell silent, straining his eyes, trying to penetrate the star-dusted blackness ahead.

The Bridge

On the enclosed bridge, First Officer Murdoch stood near the helmsman, Quartermaster Hichens, while Sixth Officer Moody paced slowly near the chart table. The atmosphere was quiet, the rhythmic tick of the ship's master clock marking time as the *Titanic* raced onward at over twenty-two knots. Outside the windows, the sea was an expanse of flat, black glass reflecting the impossibly bright stars, merging seamlessly with the sky. There was no horizon.

Moody picked up the bridge binoculars, raising them to his eyes and scanning the darkness ahead.

"See anything with those, Mr. Moody?" Murdoch asked quietly, his own eyes fixed on their path.

Moody lowered the binoculars with a short, humourless laugh. "Not a bloody thing, sir. Might as well be looking into a pot of ink." He handed the glasses to Murdoch, who took a turn sweeping the invisible horizon. Moody shivered slightly, despite the warmth of the bridge. "No moon. No horizon line. It's like we're sailing straight into a void."

Murdoch lowered the binoculars, his expression thoughtful, perhaps slightly concerned, but raising no undue alarm. The warnings were noted, the lookouts alerted, the ship steady under his command.

Crow's Nest, Approx. 11:39 PM

"Anything, Fred?" Lee asked, his teeth chattering slightly.

Fleet didn't answer immediately. He leaned forward, pressing his face closer to the forward edge of the nest, his tearing eyes straining, desperately trying to make sense of a subtle disturbance in the seamless blackness ahead. A patch of darkness that seemed... darker. Larger. Closer than the stars.

His heart leaped into his throat. It wasn't a wave. It wasn't a shadow. It was mass. Dead ahead.

CLANG! CLANG! CLANG!

Fleet yanked the lanyard for the warning bell above his head three times—the urgent signal for danger directly ahead. Simultaneously, he grabbed the bridge telephone receiver, which instantly connected him with the bridge.

The Bridge

The jarring clang of the crow's nest bell cut through the quiet routine of the bridge. Both Murdoch and Moody snapped to attention, their eyes instantly fixed on the telephone indicator. It rang sharply.

Moody snatched the receiver. "Yes? What do you see?"

Fleet's voice came down the line, strained, urgent: "Iceberg, right ahead!"

"Thank you," Moody replied automatically, hanging up the receiver and turning instantly to Murdoch, relaying the message clearly, urgently:

"Iceberg, right ahead, sir!"

11:40 PM

Time seemed to fracture. Murdoch reacted instantaneously, instinctively.

"Hard-a-starboard!" he roared to Quartermaster Hichens at the wheel, the command that would turn the ship's bow to port, away from the obstacle.

"Hard-a-starboard, sir!" Hichens repeated, spinning the wheel rapidly, the indicator showing the rudder angle changing.

Simultaneously, Murdoch sprang to the engine order telegraphs, slamming the handles first to "Stop," then immediately pulling them further down to "Full Astern," the bells clanging in the engine room far below, ordering a reversal of the mighty propellers in a desperate bid to slow the liner's immense forward momentum.

On the bridge wings, in the crow's nest high above, officers and lookouts held their breath, eyes riveted on the scene unfolding in agonizing slow motion. The great ship began to respond, her bow starting a slow, ponderous swing to port. But the dark mass loomed impossibly large now, dead ahead, silent, monstrous, glittering faintly under the starlight.

Closer. Closer. The turn agonizingly slow. The silence on the bridge absolute, save for the frantic ticking of the clock and the pounding of hearts. Would she clear it? Inches. Feet. The shadow of the berg towered over the starboard bow. Closer...

Late Sunday Night, April 14, 1912 Miles's Cabin & Corridors

We lay tangled together in the narrow bed, wrapped in each other's arms, the darkness a comforting shroud. The earlier frantic energy now subsided, leaving behind a profound sense of peace, of rightness.

I gently stroked Miles's hair, his forehead lying in the crook of my arm, my fingertips tracing the almost invisible miles of warm skin exposed above the blankets, acutely aware of his steady breathing against my chest. Outside, the arctic wind still howled past the open porthole, but inside, there was only warmth.

"What are you thinking, now?" Miles's voice was a muffled murmur against my shoulder.

We both chuckled softly, the question echoing his earlier one on deck, but the context felt entirely different now. "I was thinking," I began honestly, my voice low, "that I could get used to this."

"Me too," Miles agreed, shifting slightly to look up at me, his eyes luminous even in the dim starlight filtering through the porthole.

"No," I clarified, needing him to understand the depth of the feeling. "I mean... this. This feeling. Being here, with you. This is what I want. Forever. I never want to leave this moment. Right here. Right now. This is what it's supposed to feel like."

"It doesn't have to end, Benj," Miles said softly, his gaze serious now.

"And," I continued, emboldened, "I was also thinking... tomorrow..."

"Mmhmm?" he prompted gently.

"Breakfast. I'd like you to meet my mother. Properly this time."

Miles leaned up slightly on one elbow, searching my face in the faint light, probably checking if I was joking, or not. "Your mother?"

"I'm being serious," I chuckled, touching his cheek. "I invited her and Major Butt to join us at the Café Parisian. I want her to meet you. Really meet you." A sudden certainty filled me. "She's going to love you, Miles."

"What makes you so sure?" he asked, a hint of teasing returning to his voice.

"Because I love you," the words slipped out, simple, true, and utterly terrifying in their finality. Yet, saying them felt like unlocking the last restraint. "I mean it, Miles. All my life, I've felt like I was living in someone else's skin. Doing things not for me, but for everyone else around me. Playing a role. One I didn't like. But then I met you." I smiled. "This crazy, carefree, infuriating breath of fresh air who somehow barged in and taught me what it actually means to live in the moment. To be... me."

Miles was smiling now, a wide, radiant smile, but he didn't say anything immediately.

"Okay," I laughed softly, "now you have to tell me what you're thinking, because I definitely can't read your mind."

Instead of answering, he sat up and climbed out of bed, walking to the writing table across the room. By now, our eyes had adjusted to the faint starlight. I saw him unfold a familiar Marconigram form and grab a pencil. I watched his every movement, delighting in the casual intimacy of seeing his naked form simply moving across the cabin in the cold light, doing something as mundane as writing a message. All the while thinking, *this is for me. It doesn't have to end.* After scribbling quickly, he tore the sheet from the pad, folded it, and walked back to the bed, handing it to me.

"Happy Birthday, Benj," he whispered.

Confused, I sat up, holding the paper towards the faint light from the porthole, which seemed strangely brighter now, less muted than before. My eyes strained to read the pencil marks.

"It's a wire," Miles explained softly beside me. "To my father."

I focused on the words:

FATHER STOP PLANS CHANGED
STOP WILL NOT BE JOINING FIRM
STOP MOVING TO CALIFORNIA
TO PURSUE FILM OPPORTUNITY
STOP BENJI IS COMING WITH ME
STOP WILL EXPLAIN LATER STOP
MILES.

My breath caught. He'd already done it. Made the leap. For us. "Miles..."

Reality, however, intruded. "But the money..." I started, thinking of my father's gift, Astor's offer. "I don't want to accept my father's money now. Not after learning the truth."

"Then don't," Miles said simply. "We don't need it."

"But Astor hasn't actually committed yet, and Harper..."

"Forget about Astor," Miles interrupted gently but firmly. "Forget Harper. Forget your father." He sat back down on the edge of the bed beside me. "Benji, listen. We're two smart, talented, capable guys, right? We know what we bring to the table." He took my hands in his. "Fear. That's the only thing that's really been holding us back. Fear of failure, fear of judgment, fear of our fathers." His eyes bored into mine. "But I say... fuck fear."

We both laughed then, a release of tension, of absurdity, of pure, defiant joy.

"Say it, Benji," Miles urged, grinning.

"Fuck fear," I whispered, the words feeling foreign but powerful.

"Louder," he laughed.

"Fuck fear!" I giggled, feeling lighter than air.

"See?" Miles squeezed my hands. "We don't have to be afraid anymore. We don't know if we'll even see tomorrow, Benj. We can't keep holding ourselves back, worrying about 'what-ifs'." He pulled me closer, crawling back under the covers, wrapping his arms around me again. "And even if everything else goes wrong," he murmured against my hair, "if the studio plan fails, if every publisher hates your writing, if Astor changes his mind... I'll still have you. And you'll still have me." He held me tighter. "And that means we'll never have to give up this."

We lay there for another few moments, lost in the quiet intimacy, the profound sense of peace, listening only to the sound of the wind howling past the open porthole and the steady beat of each other's hearts.

Then, cutting through the night, sharp and urgent, carried on the wind: CLANG! CLANG! CLANG!

The sound was jarring, alien. "What was that?" I asked, shooting bolt upright in bed, instantly alert.

"I don't know," Miles said, sitting up beside me, equally confused, listening intently.

I swung my legs out of bed, pulling on my trousers, needing to see. I stumbled towards the porthole, peering out into the blackness. Just as I reached it, I felt it—not a crash, but a subtle, jarring shudder that ran through the very deck beneath my bare feet. A low, grinding vibration pulsed through the ship's structure. And then, drifting slowly, silently past the open porthole, an immense shape of impossible blackness against the starlit sky, blotting out the stars themselves. Casting the room in total darkness. Then it was gone, leaving only the freezing wind and the now-still deck.

"Something's happened," I breathed, turning back to Miles, already pulling on my shirt.

"We should go check it out," Miles agreed instantly, scrambling out of bed and reaching for his own clothes.

"I have to go check on Mother and Birdie first," I said quickly, my mind racing. "They're probably terrified out of their wits."

"Right. Go," Miles nodded, pulling on his trousers. He grabbed the folded Marconigram from the bedside table where I'd dropped it. "Here," he thrust it into my hand. "Can you stop by the Inquiry Office on your way up? Try and send this? If something has happened, I want to get this out before there's a crazy line of people trying to send out their Marconis."

"Of course," I said, taking the message. I turned back just as he finished buttoning his shirt, met his worried eyes, and acted on pure impulse again, leaning in for a quick, firm kiss. "I love you."

"I love you too," Miles replied, managing a quick, playful smile despite the nervous tension. "Now go! Hurry! Before there's a line!"

"Alright!" I called back, already yanking open the cabin door and dashing out into the now eerily quiet D deck corridor.

I took the Grand Staircase upwards, my footsteps echoing. As I reached the C deck landing, I saw them—a small cluster of people, mostly men in dressing gowns, already gathered outside the Purser's Inquiry Office window, likely asking the same questions I had, or, as Miles predicted, trying to send urgent wires. Checking on valuables, demanding refunds for this sudden inconvenience.

I looked down at the folded message in my hand, then at the growing queue. No time for this. I knew where the messages really went out. I spotted a blank message card and pencil on the counter, quickly scribbled my own brief, urgent wire:

BROWN BROS AND CO STOP
DENY ALL FUNDS INTO TRUST
STOP PLEASE REMIT ANY FUTURE
FUNDS STOP BENJI SUTH HOW-
ELL.

Without skipping a beat I turned and sprinted up the next two flights of the Grand Staircase, towards the Boat Deck and the Marconi room.

Reaching the familiar door, I knocked sharply. It opened almost immediately, revealing Harold Bride, looking surprised to see me, especially at this hour.

"Bride," I said breathlessly, "I don't know if you remember me—"

"Tommy Andrews' friend," he interrupted with a nod of recognition, his expression serious now, clearly aware something was amiss. "Of course. What is it?"

"Look," I glanced nervously down the empty corridor, "I know things are likely about to get very busy up here, but I have two messages." I held out the slips—Miles's defiant declaration to his father, my own hasty refusal of my inheritance. "They need to get out. It's urgent."

Bride started to reach for them automatically, his operator's instinct kicking in. But I hesitated, pulling them back slightly. The contents felt suddenly, intensely private, too revealing to just hand over impersonally. I looked him in the eye, relying on the flicker of connection I'd felt when we met before.

"Uh, Bride," I lowered my voice, "these messages... they're kind of... delicate. If you know what I mean."

His eyes flickered down to the names and brief text visible on the slips, then back up to my face. Understanding dawned quickly. He glanced over his shoulder towards the inner operating room, where Phillips was still working frantically, then turned back to me, his expression discreet, professional, but kind.

"I see," he said quietly. "Don't worry, lad." He took the two slips from my hand. "I understand. I'll see to it that these go out. *Personally*." He stressed the last word just enough, a quiet promise passing between us.

"Thank you, Bride," I breathed, immensely relieved. "Truly."

He gave me a quick, reassuring nod, then slipped back inside, closing the door firmly, leaving me alone once more in the hushed, expectant silence of the upper deck corridor.

Sunday Night Just After Impact The Bridge

The faint, grinding shudder that vibrated through the mighty liner's frame sent an immediate jolt of adrenaline through the hallowed bridge. First Officer Murdoch, who'd stepped out onto the starboard bridge wing moments before impact, hoping against hope they might clear the towering mountain of ice, now rushed back inside, his face grim, pale under the dim navigation lights.

Sixth Officer Moody looked up from the chart table, startled by the tremor and Murdoch's abrupt return.

"Note the time, Mr. Moody," Murdoch commanded sharply, his voice tight but controlled. "Enter it into the log."

"Aye, sir," Moody replied instantly, reaching for the logbook and pen. 11:40 PM.

Just as Moody began to write, the door to the captain's quarters burst open and Captain Smith rushed onto the bridge, his uniform jacket hastily pulled on over his nightclothes, his expression alarmed.

"Mr. Murdoch! What was that? We've struck something?" Smith demanded, his voice urgent.

"An iceberg, sir," Murdoch reported immediately, facing his commander squarely. "Dead ahead. I hard-a-starboarded and reversed the engines, tried to port around it, but she was too close under the helm... I'm afraid she hit it along the starboard side, sir. A glancing blow, but..." He didn't need to finish. The vibration told its own story.

"Close the watertight doors!" Smith ordered instinctively, turning towards Moody.

"Watertight doors are already closed, sir," Murdoch confirmed quickly, indicating the lever on the bridge that activated the system. "I actioned it the moment we struck."

The Captain nodded curtly, his mind already processing the next steps. He strode quickly out onto the starboard wing which Murdoch had just vacated, peering down into the darkness along the massive flank of the ship, searching for any visible signs of damage left behind by the collision. Murdoch followed close behind, waiting for orders. Below, the inky water rushed past, offering no immediate clues in the darkness.

"Find the carpenter," Smith ordered, his voice sharp against the sudden, unnerving silence now that the engines' powerful thrum had ceased. "Get him down below to sound the ship immediately. Check all forward compartments."

"Aye, sir," Murdoch replied instantly, already turning on his heel to relay the command.

"And hurry, man!" the Captain called after him urgently.

Murdoch disappeared back inside, leaving Smith alone for a moment on the wing, staring down at the flat, black, freezing ocean. The *Titanic*, the unsinkable marvel, sat idle now, her forward momentum bled away by the reversed engines, drifting silently under the indifferent stars. The great heart of the ship was quiet, cradled by an ocean that was, moment by moment, beginning its inexorable claim, swallowing her whole as she drifted precariously off course in the icy darkness.

CHAPTER 34

While Captain Smith stood frozen for a moment on the starboard bridge wing, peering into the ominous darkness, the immediate consequences of the glancing blow were unfolding violently several decks below.

In the vast, dimly lit forward cargo hold No. 1, the icy seawater surged through the compromised starboard plates not as a leak, but as a torrent. The initial impact had buckled the steel, shearing rivets, and opening seams below the waterline. Now, the Atlantic poured in with ferocious speed, swirling around the stacked crates and bundled cargo. Water, dark and freezing, rose rapidly, lifting lighter wooden crates off the deck plates, sending bundles of parcels and luggage bobbing like corks. The gleaming red Renault motorcar, lashed securely mid-hold, was suddenly surrounded by rising water, its vibrant paint job a bizarre splash of color in the murky chaos. The large, nondescript wooden crate containing the priceless, jeweled *Rubáiyát* shifted in the surge, bumping gently against the car's shiny fender before floating carelessly free across the room.

Further aft, in Boiler Room No. 6, the scene was one of controlled, urgent chaos. The grinding shudder of the impact had been felt intensely here, deep in the ship's bowels. Almost immediately, icy water began to gush in from a breach low on the starboard side, swirling around the stoker's ankles, rising with alarming speed over the floor plates. Following emergency protocols drilled into them, the stokers and trimmers scrambled. Furnace doors were slammed shut, dampers closed to starve the fires of air. Above the hiss and splash of the invading water, a deafening roar erupted as engineers opened the main steam valves, venting the immense pressure from the boilers directly up the funnels far above. With the engines stopped abruptly by Murdoch's order from the bridge, this was crucial to prevent the boilers from exploding as the cold seawater inevitably reached their scorching surfaces. The roar of escaping steam would soon become a defining sound of the night, audible across the decks. Soon, the same scene began to play out in Boiler Room No. 5 next door, as water seemingly found its way past the supposedly watertight bulkhead.

Meanwhile, summoned urgently by First Officer Murdoch, the ship's Carpenter, John Hutchinson, joined a grim-faced Thomas Andrews near the forepeak hatchway. Armed with sounding rods and flashlights, they began their rapid descent into the affected areas, needing to assess the damage firsthand for the Captain.

Their initial findings in the forepeak tank confirmed significant intake. Moving aft, hold No. 1 was flooding rapidly. Hold No. 2, the same. Hold No. 3—water poured in, rising fast. Each compartment breached brought a deeper line of worry to Andrews's usually composed face. He knew the ship's design intimately; he knew her safety margins. She could float with any two compartments flooded. She could even survive the unprecedented breaching of the first four compartments.

They pushed aft, wading now through ankle-, then knee-deep water sloshing along the crew passageways on the lower decks. Reaching Boiler Room No. 6, the scene confirmed their worst fears. Water cascaded in, the stokers already retreating to higher levels as the sea rose towards the furnaces amidst the deafening roar of vented steam. Five compartments breached.

Andrews exchanged a grim look with Hutchinson. They pressed on towards Boiler Room No. 5. There too, water was entering, slower than in No. 6, but undeniably present. The watertight door between 5 and 6 was closed, but the damage had clearly extended past it, at least below the waterline. The sixth compartment.

Andrews stopped, leaning against a damp steel bulkhead, the implications hitting him with the force of mathematical certainty. Five compartments flooding rapidly, the sixth already taking on water. No ship, not even this one, his masterpiece, could survive such damage. The calculations were brutal, simple, and undeniable. He looked at Hutchinson, seeing the same dawning horror reflected in the Carpenter's eyes.

"Sweet Mother Mary," Hutchinson whispered, making the sign of the cross.

Andrews pushed himself upright, his mind racing, calculating the time they had left.

"I've got to send word to the Captain," Andrews stated, his voice strained but resolute. Without another word, he turned and began pushing his way back through the rising water, back towards the stairways leading up to the passenger decks, up towards the bridge, carrying the ship's death sentence with him.

Early Monday Morning, April 15, 1912 Outside Birdie's Cabin

Leaving Bride and the humming quiet of the Marconi office behind, I raced back down the Grand Staircase, my earlier hope replaced by a gnawing anxiety. The ship felt unnervingly still now, the powerful thrum of the engines silenced, replaced by an anticipating hush occasionally broken by opening doors and questioning voices in the corridors. That's what struck me the most, the silence, allowing me to hear everything and nothing at the same time.

I hurried along B deck towards my parents' cabin. Before I even reached the door, it opened, and Birdie peered out, her face pale, her eyes wide. Seeing me, she pulled me quickly inside.

The cabin was brightly lit. Mother stood near the settee, fully dressed now beneath her dressing gown, while Father, also surprisingly present and mostly dressed, paced near the window. They had clearly all been awakened by the jolt or the subsequent silence.

"Benji, darling, there you are!" Mother rushed towards me, pulling me into a tight, relieved hug. "Thank heavens! We felt a shudder... Did you feel it? Do you know what's happened?"

"Something," I confirmed, pulling back slightly. "I think we hit something. Ice, maybe? I saw... well, I saw something enormous drift past the porthole just after the bells rang. A huge black mass. But it was too dark to be certain."

Father stopped pacing. "Ice? In these latitudes? Unlikely." His tone was dismissive, attempting normalcy, but I saw the flicker of concern in his eyes.

"Well," Mother attempted a shaky laugh, trying to lighten the tense atmosphere, "I told you children I wanted your eighteenth birthday to start with a bang, but this is rather ridiculous, isn't it?" She managed a watery smile. "Happy Birthday, my darlings."

Father turned towards us then, his expression softening momentarily. "Yes. Happy Birthday, Margaret, Benji." He cleared his throat. "Your mother and I... we promise we'll make this up to you both once we reach New York."

The sentiment, however forced, felt strangely poignant amidst the growing uncertainty. Before either Birdie or I could respond, a firm knock sounded at the cabin door.

Father opened it to reveal one of the bedroom stewards standing in the corridor, his face polite but serious.

"Beg pardon for the intrusion, Mr. Sutherland-Howell, Madam," the steward addressed my parents formally. "Captain's orders. All passengers are requested to dress warmly, put on their life jackets, and proceed to the First Class Lounge on A Deck."

Life jackets? The words hung heavy in the air.

"Is there any real danger, steward?" Father asked, his tone laced with impatience, as if this were merely an inconvenient drill interrupting his night. "Surely just a minor precaution?"

"Just a precaution, sir, yes," the steward affirmed smoothly, though his eyes weren't as certain. "But the Captain does request everyone report to the Lounge promptly. And please, sir, madam, ensure you put on your life jackets before leaving the cabin. Further instructions will be given there."

He gave a slight bow and moved on down the corridor, presumably to deliver the same message to other cabins. We stood there for a moment in stunned silence, the steward's final instruction—put on your life jackets—echoing louder than any reassurance. The vague sense of unease had suddenly solidified into something cold, sharp, and terrifyingly real.

Early Monday Morning, Continued Grand Staircase & The Bridge

As stewards began gently but firmly rousing passengers from their beds, a suite door further forward on B deck burst open, ejecting a pair of occupied carpet slippers. Frantically, the slippers carried their owner—J. Bruce Ismay, clad hastily in pajamas and a heavy robe pulled on over them—down the corridor and towards the Grand Staircase. His face was a mask of anxiety, his mind racing. What was that shudder that had awoken him from his sleep? Why had the engines stopped? He climbed the stairs with determined speed, needing answers, bound for the bridge.

Rounding the landing onto A deck, he nearly collided with Thomas Andrews, who was hurrying upwards, clutching a roll of deck plans under his arm, his face pale and grim.

"Mr. Andrews!" Ismay called out sharply, his voice a low hiss, drawing close so nearby passengers emerging from their cabins wouldn't overhear. "What in God's name is going on with this ship of yours? Don't tell me she's thrown another propeller blade like the *Olympic*!"

Andrews stopped, turning to face the Managing Director, his expression resolute despite the gravity of the situation. "She's not my ship, Mr. Ismay," he stated firmly, meeting Ismay's accusatory gaze. "She is yours. And I only wish I could tell you that a propeller blade was all she required." He held up the rolled plans. "Now, if you'll excuse me, I must deliver some urgent news to our Captain."

Andrews turned to continue his ascent, but Ismay, his anxiety spiking at Andrews's grim tone, fell into step beside him without invitation. "I'm coming with you."

They reached the bridge together moments later. The atmosphere had shifted entirely from the quiet routine of half an hour prior. Captain Smith stood near the helm, flanked by Chief Officer Wilde and First Officer Murdoch, rapidly issuing orders to Second Officer Lightoller and Fifth Officer Lowe, who had also been summoned along with others just stirred from sleep.

"...go ahead and uncover the boats," Smith was saying, his voice calm but carrying undeniable urgency. "Swing them all out. Check the plugs are in. Send word down to the Chief Steward—have the bakers send up bread and water supplies for provisioning. We need to be ready for anything, gentlemen."

"Aye, Captain," the officers acknowledged, dispersing quickly to carry out the commands.

"Captain," Andrews stepped forward as the officers moved away, Ismay hovering just behind him. "Might I have a word, sir? In private?"

Smith looked at Andrews, then at Ismay, his expression unreadable. "Mr. Wilde, Mr. Murdoch, join us," he commanded quietly, gesturing towards the relative privacy of the chart room just off the main bridge.

Inside the small room, Andrews quickly unrolled a large profile schematic of the *Titanic* across the chart table, the stark diagram outlining her hull and watertight bulkheads. Ismay and the officers crowded around as Andrews pointed with a pencil, his voice low and urgent.

"Captain, I've just completed a rapid inspection below, along with Mr. Boxhall here," Andrews began, indicating the Fourth Officer who nodded grimly in confirmation. "The damage is... extensive." He traced a line along the ship's forward starboard side. "Forepeak, holds one, two, and three are flooding rapidly. Boiler room six is taking water fast, and," his voice dropped further, "water is already entering boiler room five."

"Six compartments," Smith breathed, his face paling slightly as he grasped the implication.

"This is terribly inconvenient, Mr. Andrews," Ismay interjected, his mind still focused on schedules and appearances. "How long will repairs take? What does this mean for our arrival time?" His words seemed to hang, absurdly trivial, ignored by the others focused on the grim reality before them.

Andrews didn't even glance at Ismay. "It means," he continued, addressing Smith directly, "that the first five compartments are breached well below the waterline. With number six also damaged... water is already beginning to spill over the top of the bulkhead between boiler rooms six and five." He used the pencil to illustrate the progressive flooding on the diagram. "Once five fills... it will spill over into four. And so on. Her design cannot withstand this."

"What about the pumps, Mr. Andrews?" Smith asked, grasping at straws. "Can they keep pace?"

Andrews shook his head slowly, his eyes filled with regret. "They might hold it off for a time, Captain. Buy us minutes. But they cannot stop the inevitable."

"The inevitable?" Smith repeated soberly, though his eyes showed he already knew the answer.

Andrews met his Captain's gaze directly, delivering the fatal diagnosis. "There is no saving her, sir," he said, his voice thick with emotion but unwavering. "No matter what we do now. This ship... is going to sink."

"But..." Ismay stammered, finally grasping the horrifying reality, his face draining of color. "She... she can't! She's... unsinkable!"

A flicker of bitter irony crossed Andrews's face. "Only if you believed the headlines, Mr. Ismay," he retorted quietly. "I assure you, tomorrow's headlines will tell a very different story."

Captain Smith seemed to absorb the terrible news, his shoulders slumping for just a second before squaring again with command authority. "How long would you say we have, Mr. Andrews?"

"I'd give her an hour. If the pumps and bulkheads stand up to the fight, maybe two. Not much more."

Smith turned to Murdoch. "How many aboard tonight, Mr. Murdoch? Passengers and crew?"

"Approximately two thousand, two hundred souls, sir," Murdoch replied grimly.

Smith nodded slowly, then turned his gaze fully onto Ismay, his eyes cold now, devoid of any earlier deference. "Did you hear that, Mr. Ismay?" he asked quietly, the question laden with accusation. "Two thousand, two hundred souls." He paused, letting the number hang in the air, then added with deliberate, chilling weight, "That's approximately how much you paid for those headlines."

Without waiting for a response, Captain Smith turned abruptly and strode out of the chart room, back onto the main bridge to oversee the preparations. Wilde and Murdoch followed immediately behind him, their faces grim. Ismay stood frozen for a moment, stunned into silence, staring down at the deck plans, before slowly looking up to meet the steady, sorrowful gaze of Thomas Andrews, the man who had designed the magnificent ship that was now, irrefutably, doomed.

CHAPTER 35

Inside the small, humming Marconi cabin high on the Boat Deck, Harold Bride sat hunched over the transmitter key, the headphones clamped over his ears. He'd taken over the watch a bit early, hoping to give his exhausted senior partner, Jack Phillips, a chance for some much-needed rest before his own official shift began. He also hoped, discreetly, to slip young Benji Howell's "delicate" messages into the outgoing queue without Phillips noticing their unusual nature amidst the backlog.

Phillips poked his head around the doorway to their adjoining sleeping quarters, stifling a yawn, still in his shirtsleeves, "Everything under control, Bride? Not letting those society ladies overwhelm you?"

"Smooth sailing, Jack," Bride replied with a grin, tapping out the end of a passenger's message. "Got it all handled. Now, get back in there and get your beauty rest before your bunk gets cold."

Phillips chuckled wearily. "Alright, alright, I'm going..."

"Good," Bride added playfully under his breath as Phillips disappeared back into the sleeping quarters, "...God knows you need it."

"I heard that!" Phillips's laugh echoed faintly from the other room.

"Goodnight!" Bride called back, smiling to himself as he reached for the next message flimsy.

Just then, the cabin door opened abruptly, startling him. Captain Smith stood framed in the doorway, his face sober, his eyes holding a depth of seriousness Bride had never seen before. Both wireless operators instinctively jumped to attention, Bride half-rising from his chair, Phillips reappearing instantly from the sleeping quarters, pulling on his uniform jacket.

"Captain, sir," Phillips addressed him formally.

"Gentlemen," Smith's voice was low, deliberate, devoid of any pleasantries. "Duty calls." He stepped fully into the small cabin, holding out a sheet of navigating bridge notepaper towards Phillips. His hand trembled slightly, but noticeably. "We require immediate assistance."

Phillips took the paper, his eyes scanning the hastily scribbled coordinates. Bride leaned closer, reading over his shoulder.

"Send out the call for assistance," Smith commanded, his voice strained but clear. "Tell them we've struck an iceberg. We're going down by the head. These are our coordinates, as best calculated. Make sure you transmit them accurately."

The words lingered, heavy, unbelievable. Going down? Both young operators stared at the Captain, then at each other, shock rendering them momentarily speechless. This had to be some sort of drill, some mistake. But the look in the Captain's eyes, the tremor in his hand, the stark finality in his voice – it was terrifyingly real.

Smith seemed thrown off slightly by their stunned silence, their palpable unease. "That's all," he said curtly, perhaps needing to escape the suffocating confines of the small room and the weight of the message he'd just delivered. He turned and left as abruptly as he'd arrived, closing the door behind him.

Silence descended again, broken only by the faint hum of the Marconi equipment. Phillips stared down at the coordinates in his hand, then slowly looked up at Bride, his face pale beneath his customary operator's pallor.

"Bloody hell," Phillips sighed. Then, snapping into action, professional instinct overriding personal shock, he gestured sharply towards the operator's chair. "Get up, Bride. Let me take it."

Harold Bride relinquished the seat immediately, stepping back as the senior operator slid into place, flexing his fingers over the Morse key, preparing to send the most important message of his life – the call for help, the CQD, echoing out from the doomed liner into the freezing, indifferent night.

Early Monday Morning, April 15th, 1912
The First Class Lounge

We joined the stream of passengers heading towards the A Deck Lounge, all dressed somewhat haphazardly in warm coats over evening wear or nightclothes, the bulky cork-and-canvas life jackets making movement awkward. The room, usually a picture of serene elegance, was now crowded, buzzing with nervous energy, confusion, and forced attempts at nonchalance. Stewards moved through the throng, offering blankets or reassurances that felt increasingly thin.

I spotted our usual dinner companions – the Countess and Gladys Cherry huddled together near the fireplace, Colonel Gracie holding court with a small group nearby, trying to maintain spirits with loud pronouncements, and Mr. Stead, remarkably, already seated at a small table with a book, as if this were just another quiet evening at sea.

Mother guided us towards an empty settee and chairs. As we settled, my eyes scanned the anxious crowd until I found him. Miles stood near the aft entrance, looking lost, clearly searching for me. Our eyes met across the room, relief washing over his face. Excusing myself quickly from my family, I intercepted him before he could be swept away by the tide of confused passengers.

"Miles," I breathed, reaching him. "Thank God."

"Benji," his relief mirrored mine. "What's happening? Is it serious?"

"I don't know," I admitted honestly. "But they told us to put on life jackets and come up here." I took his hand. "Come on. Stay with us."

I led him back to where my family was gathered. Mother looked up as we approached, her gaze flickering over our joined hands before settling on Miles's face with polite recognition from boarding. Birdie, too, seemed to register him with faint surprise. Father merely raised an eyebrow.

"Mother, Father, Birdie," I began, keeping my voice steady, "this is my friend, Miles Force. You met briefly when we boarded in Southampton."

"Mr. Force, yes, of course, the fellow American," Mother said graciously, extending a hand. "So lovely to see you again, though perhaps under less...chaotic circumstances."

"Likewise, Mrs. Sutherland-Howell," Miles replied smoothly, shaking her hand, then nodding politely to Father and Birdie.

"Miles and I reconnected over dinner in the Saloon tonight," I explained quickly, offering a partial truth. "Became fast friends." I risked a quick, sly wink in Miles's direction, which I saw Birdie catch from the corner of her eye, though she mercifully said nothing. "Whatever happens tonight," I continued, addressing my family but looking at Miles, "I've asked Miles to join us, stay with our party."

There was a beat of silence. Then Father, nursing a brandy he stole from the tray of a passing steward, gave a short, slightly cynical laugh. "Well, let's hope it doesn't come to swimming then, eh Mr. Force? Can you swim?"

"No, sir, I'm afraid not," Miles admitted sheepishly. "Terrible swimmer, actually."

"Lucky that you met our Benji then," Mother chimed in. "He's a champion swimmer. All through secondary and now at Yale."

"Is that a fact?" Miles looked at me, a genuine, warm smile finally breaking through his worry. "Very lucky indeed," he agreed, squeezing my hand briefly before letting go as we found seats together.

The conversation around us was a swirl of speculation and rumor. Some insisted it was merely a precautionary drill, others whispered about striking ice. Mr. Stead, seemingly unfazed, suggested this period of 'hurry up and wait' was an excellent opportunity to catch up on reading. "Margaret," he called over to Birdie, "perhaps now is prime time for another study session?"

Birdie shot him a look so cold it could have rivaled the iceberg itself, turning away without a word.

Just then, several stewards entered, led by perhaps the Chief Steward. He clapped his hands lightly for attention. "Ladies and gentlemen, may I have your attention, please!" The room quieted slightly. "We are preparing the lifeboats as a precaution. When they are ready, the order will be given for women and children to proceed to the Boat Deck first. I repeat, this is purely a precautionary measure," he stressed, though his face looked strained, "but please begin gathering your immediate parties together. The call to proceed to the boats will begin momentarily."

"Women and children first?" Birdie muttered beside me, her voice laced with indignation. "How perfectly antiquated."

"It's just a precaution, anyway, darling," Mother murmured, patting Birdie's hand. "There's no real danger."

"Still," Father announced, standing up decisively, "best get a head start, find a good boat before the crowds descend. Stay together."

Our party – Mother, Father, Birdie, myself, and now Miles – along with the Countess, Gladys, and Gracie who had joined our vicinity, agreed, gathering wraps and preparing to head towards the Boat Deck before the official call.

Mr. Stead, however, remained firmly seated, reopening his book. "If it's merely a precaution," he stated calmly to Gracie who urged him to come along, "then I prefer to remain here, where there's warmth. And perhaps," he added with a wry glance towards the bar stewards, "a final scotch." He settled back into his reading.

As the rest of the party moved towards the exit, Birdie hung back for a moment, watching Mr. Stead calmly turn a page. "I'll be right behind you," she called out to her mother. "It won't take but a minute."

Once the coast was clear, she walked back to the table where Stead sat reading, seemingly oblivious to the surrounding anxiety.

"Ah, Margaret," he looked up, apparently unsurprised to see her. "Decided to take me up on that study session after all?"

His calm demeanor, his pretense of normalcy after what Oliver had revealed, snapped something within her. "How dare you?" she whispered fiercely, leaning down so only he could hear, her voice trembling with rage.

Stead looked genuinely perplexed. "My dear girl, whatever is the matter?"

"Don't 'my dear girl' me," Birdie hissed. "I know everything. I'm not an idiot. Did you really think I wouldn't figure out your disgusting little game?"

"Game?"

"Using him! Using your puppet, to spy on my family! To try and dig up dirt on my father!" Her voice cracked with hurt and anger. "I can't believe I used to respect you, used to admire your work. Now...now I see you're just vile. Using people, manipulating them...taking their hardships to print to make yourself rich. How can someone like you have such a powerful voice, such influence?"

Stead's expression shifted from confusion to dawning comprehension, then to something like weariness. "Margaret..."

"You should be ashamed of yourself!" she finished bitterly. "I'll admit my father has his problems, more than you could possibly imagine, perhaps. But to print them for the entire world? What makes you think you have the right?" She turned sharply to leave, unable to bear looking at him any longer.

"You're wrong!" Stead called out, his voice sharp now, stopping her in her tracks. She turned back slowly.

He sighed, closing his book. "You're right about some of it, Margaret," he admitted quietly. "Yes, Oliver worked for me. Yes, I hoped to write about...certain societal hypocrisies, perhaps using your father as an example, though anonymously. But not for the reasons you think. Not for scandal, not for profit."

He looked at her earnestly. "You know of Oscar Wilde, yes?"

"Of course," Birdie scoffed dismissively. "Benji admires his writing."

"As do I," Stead nodded sadly. "Oscar was a friend. Years ago, I spearheaded an exposé...it led to legislation intended to protect young women. A worthy cause, I thought. But powerful lobbyists, against my will, inserted clauses into that Act...clauses that specifically targeted men like Oscar. Homosexuality became further criminalized, punishable by hard labor."

His voice grew heavy with regret. "Imagine my dismay, my horror, when my own friend, Mr. Wilde, was arrested, tried, and convicted, partly under the very laws my work had inadvertently strengthened. His health, his reputation, his spirit...they never recovered after prison. He died a broken, penniless man, his dignity stripped away, mocked by the press as a pervert or a laughingstock. And nothing I could do or say could fix the damage my 'crusade' had indirectly caused."

He looked at Birdie, his eyes filled with a deep, troubling sorrow. "Oliver...he was a young writer on my staff at the Pall Mall Gazette back then. He helped research those articles. We both felt...responsible...for Wilde's fate, and wondered how many other decent men might suffer because of those laws, because of the fear and ignorance they fostered."

"My hope, dear Margaret," he continued passionately, "in gathering material about your father, and others like him, was never to 'out' anyone. Names would never be mentioned. My aim was the opposite – to show the world how common homosexuality truly is, across all walks of life. To depict these men not as deviants or predators, but as ordinary people – loving, working, living alongside everyone else. Rich, poor, artists, businessmen, perhaps even royalty. If the world could only see them as people," his voice pleaded, "perhaps these antiquated notions, these prejudices born of fear and ignorance...perhaps they could finally begin to change. That was the goal. Humanization, not scandal."

Birdie stood frozen, absorbing the truth of his words, the unexpected depth of his motives, the weight of his past regrets. Her anger began to dissipate, replaced by a confusing mix of empathy and shame for her own assumptions.

Just then, the Chief Steward re-entered the Lounge, his voice louder now, more urgent. "Ladies and children, please! The order has been given! Proceed immediately to the Boat Deck! Please, this way!"

Stead looked up at Birdie, his expression calm again, resigned. "Well, my dear Margaret," he said quietly, gesturing towards the exiting crowd. "That's your cue." He reopened his book, settling back into his chair as if preparing to read until the very end.

CHAPTER 36

Captain Smith, flanked now by Chief Officer Wilde and First Officer Murdoch, stared intently off the port bow through the bridge windows. The earlier, almost blinding starlight seemed less helpful now, merely highlighting the vast, empty blackness surrounding them.

"There," Murdoch pointed, adjusting his focus. "Just off the port bow now. Those lights. Definitely a steamer."

Smith raised his own binoculars, followed by Wilde. "Aye," the Captain confirmed grimly. "Single masthead light and two navigation lights visible. Can't be far off if we can see her naked eye."

"Six, perhaps seven miles at most, sir," Wilde estimated.

"Right," Smith lowered his binoculars, turning decisively. "Mr. Murdoch, signal her with the Morse lamp. Tell her who we are. Tell her we've struck ice and require immediate assistance."

"Aye, Captain," Murdoch acknowledged, heading immediately towards the lamp station on the bridge wing.

Just as Murdoch exited, Harold Bride appeared again from the wireless room, looking pale but composed. "Captain," he addressed Smith directly, holding out another flimsy. "A response, sir. From the Cunarder Carpathia."

Smith seized the message, hope flaring briefly in his eyes before dimming as he read. "'Coming hard,'" he read aloud slowly. "'Expect reach your position in approximately four hours.'" He looked up, his face etched with grim reality. Four hours. He knew, Andrews knew, it would be far too late.

"Are they the only ones responding, Bride?" Smith asked quietly.

"Several others heard our CQD, sir," Bride reported. "Olympic, Frankfurt, Mount Temple... but they're all much further off. Carpathia is the closest by far."

"Thank you, Bride," Smith nodded wearily. "Keep transmitting. CQD and the new SOS. Keep giving our position. Let them know we are putting the women and children into the boats."

"Yes, sir," Bride affirmed, turning to head back to his vital post.

Smith's gaze drifted back towards the port wing, towards the distant, unresponsive lights of the mystery ship. So close, that steamer. Close enough to see. Yet, seemingly, a world away, deaf to their increasingly desperate signals.

The Boat Deck

We emerged from the relative quiet of the Grand Staircase landing onto the open Boat Deck, and the sound hit us like a physical force. A deafening, continuous roar assaulted our ears – the sound of immense volumes of excess steam being vented from the funnels high above. It made conversation impossible, adding a layer of terrifying, mechanical violence to the already confused scene. Stewards hurried past, trying to direct passengers muffled in coats and bulky life jackets. Crewmen struggled with unfamiliar ropes and pulleys, attempting to swing out the massive lifeboats under the harsh glare of the deck lights. The initial calm and disbelief I'd seen in the Lounge were rapidly evaporating, replaced by a growing, palpable fear. People were actually getting into the boats. This wasn't a drill. This was real.

Our family party, now including a pale but resolute Miles clinging tightly to my hand, huddled together near the forward port side boats, under the command of Second Officer Lightoller. Father, apparently deciding the truce with Mother extended to taking charge, immediately intercepted the officer.

"Officer," Father shouted over the thunder of the escaping steam, "surely my son and I can accompany my wife and daughter? We wish to keep the family together!"

Lightoller, his face grim and focused, barely glanced at him. "Women and children only in these boats, sir!" he yelled back firmly, his interpretation of the Captain's order absolute on this side of the ship. "No exceptions! Stand back, please!"

Just as Father began to protest further, Chief Officer Wilde appeared, clapping Father briefly on the shoulder and leaning in to whisper something urgently in his ear. I couldn't hear the words over the roar, but Father's expression shifted, his argument dying on his lips as he nodded curtly to Wilde.

And then, almost miraculously, the roar stopped. The venting steam abruptly cut off, plunging the deck into a sudden, almost shocking silence, broken only by the frantic shouts of officers, the creak of ropes, and the anxious murmurs of the passengers. A collective sigh of relief went through the crowd, everyone's nerves momentarily soothed by the cessation of the deafening noise.

Wilde checked in with Lightoller regarding the boat currently being loaded – Number 8, I think. "Capacity is sixty-five, Mr. Lightoller, let's try and fill them properly."

"With respect, sir," Lightoller replied, gesturing towards the new Welin davits holding the boat outboard, "I'm not familiar with these davits' tolerance under full load. I'd rather lower away with a lighter complement now, just to be safe. We can bring more passengers in through the gangway doors once the boat is afloat."

Wilde considered, then nodded. A reasonable precaution, perhaps, though it meant fewer spaces filled initially. "Very well. Find a few reliable hands – sailors, stewards, brave men, whatever – send them below immediately to get those D deck gangway doors opened and ready."

Father, overhearing the exchange, stepped forward instantly, seizing the opportunity. "Officer Lightoller! Perhaps I might be of assistance? Happy to volunteer to help organize things below decks, ensure orderly loading from the gangway." His voice rang with false bravado, the picture of civic duty.

Lightoller looked relieved to have a first-class volunteer. "Excellent, sir! Thank you. Stand by here, I'll gather a few seamen to accompany you down momentarily."

Mother looked momentarily worried, clutching Father's arm, but quickly masked it, resuming her role as the stoic society wife. Birdie, however, was less restrained. "But Father! Why should the men stay behind? It's absurd! We should all go together!"

"Now, now, Margaret," Father patted her hand condescendingly. "Someone has to remain. Ensure everything is managed properly. It's a man's duty to stay, just in case things become...dicey." He turned to Miles then, with a challenging look, perhaps testing him. "Well, then, Mr. Force, I suppose it falls to you and me to hold down the fort, eh old man?"

My blood ran cold. The thought of being separated from Miles now, here, like this, him staying behind with my calculating father. No, I wouldn't allow that. "And me," I stated firmly, stepping forward beside Father.

"What?!" Mother protested instantly.

"Benji, no!" Birdie cried out.

"You're only seventeen—" Mother began, her voice sharp with fear.

Miles's eyes widened beside me, the lie I'd told him about my age hanging exposed in the frozen air.

"Eighteen!" I corrected her sharply, meeting her gaze. "As of thirty minutes ago. I'm staying with Father." I glanced pleadingly at Miles, hoping he'd understand, hoping he wouldn't be angry about the stupid, pointless lie.

But the look on his face wasn't anger; it was a profound, weary disappointment, mixed perhaps with a dawning understanding of the complex, manipulative dynamic I was caught in. Without a word, he gently disentangled his hand from mine. "Excuse me," he said quietly, his voice flat, addressing the group but looking only at me. "I...I wish you all the very best. But, I'm afraid I have to go." And then he turned and walked away, disappearing into the anxious crowd milling near the stern.

"Miles!" I started to go after him, to explain, but Father's hand clamped down hard on my shoulder, stopping me. "Let him go, Benji," he murmured, his voice low. Then, louder, with a chilling smile, "Well, then. I guess it's just the two of us, son." The word son felt like poison.

"Look at this, Birdie," Mother said, her voice trembling slightly as she tried to rally, holding back tears, forcing herself to be brave for her daughter, perhaps for herself. "Our two brave men."

"Mr. Howell," Lightoller called out, returning with two sturdy-looking sea-men. "Ready to head down?"

"Indeed," Father replied briskly. "My son will accompany me."

Lightoller nodded, then turned his attention to loading Mother and Birdie, along with the Countess and several other women, into the waiting lifeboat. We watched them get settled, their faces pale and anxious in the harsh electric light. Mother blew me a kiss, her eyes pleading for me to be safe.

"Right this way, gentlemen," Lightoller directed us towards the entrance to the Grand Staircase nearby, just as the members of Titanic's orchestra emerged from the entrance, and began setting up their ensemble on the deck.

Father nodded curtly and started walking. I followed, my mind reeling from Miles's departure, my heart aching. Once inside, standing before the magnificent staircase, the sounds of the chaos on deck fading slightly behind us, sweetened by the haunting echo of the orchestra playing just outside, I started down the first few steps, expecting Father to follow. When I didn't hear his footsteps, I stopped and turned back.

He stood at the landing, watching me, a strange, almost pitying look on his face.

"Aren't you coming?" I asked, confused.

He gave a short, dry laugh, the sound echoing in the suddenly quiet stairwell. "Appearances, Benji, my boy," he said softly. "Always appearances."

"What... what are you talking about?"

He shook his head, as if disappointed by my naivete. "Benji," he sighed, "do you honestly think, for one second, that I intend to venture down into the lower decks of a sinking ship? With water pouring in? Use some sense, man."

"But... you told Lightoller... you volunteered..."

"I said what needed to be said," Father corrected, his voice cold, pragmatic. "To maintain our reputation. Your mother, the officers, they all think I'm bravely going below to help. That," he gestured vaguely towards the chaos outside, "is the important thing right now. Perception."

"I should have known," I said, shaking my head. "You never change."

"Look, Benji," Father stepped forward. "Wilde just informed me," he said, his voice low and urgent, dropping the performative facade instantly, "that an officer by the name of Murdoch is overseeing the boats on the starboard side. And apparently," he leaned closer, "he's being far more... sensible. Letting men on the boats, especially if they're escorting women or if space permits." He grabbed my arm. "We need to get over there. Now. Before all hell really breaks loose."

His words – the cold calculation, the immediate abandonment of the 'heroic' plan he'd just volunteered for – confirmed everything Miles had warned me about, everything my gut screamed. He wasn't concerned with helping others; he was concerned only with saving himself. And he expected me to follow suit. My heart sank even further.

Seeing the hesitation, the conflict on my face, Father's grip tightened. "I'm not asking you, Benji," his voice hardened, the earlier veneer of pride gone, replaced by cold command. "I'm telling you. We are going to the starboard side. Now." He gave my arm a sharp tug. "This isn't over, not by a long shot...I'll make a man out of you yet," he added, baring his teeth in a grimace that was far from a smile.

That phrase – make a man out of you – echoing the horrors of Paris, snapped something within me. Not only was he showing his true, selfish colors, but following him now, taking the easy, cowardly way out while others faced uncertainty, would mean sinking to his level. Becoming the man he wanted me to be. And worse still, it meant abandoning Miles, abandoning the fragile hope we'd just found. I had to find Miles, make things right, face whatever came together.

"I...I *can't*," I stammered, pulling my arm free from his grasp.

His eyes narrowed dangerously. "Maybe I didn't make myself clear—"

"No, you didn't make yourself clear!" I interrupted, finding my voice, fueled by a sudden surge of defiance, of Astor's advice resonating within me. "But I am making myself clear now. It's over, Father. All of it. The lies. The pretending." I took a shaky breath, the next words tasting like freedom and terror combined. "The controlling me, trying to force me into a life that isn't mine. I refuse to keep living your lie."

He stared at me, comprehension dawning in his eyes, followed swiftly by cold fury. He understood the insinuation.

"Miles isn't just a friend," I pushed on, the words tumbling out now, unstoppable. "We're...we're in love. And what's more," I added recklessly, needing to sever the tie completely, "we've already made plans. We're running away together.

Going to California. We're going to live our lives together, honestly, openly! We're going to be happy...the way I know you long to be happy but never had the courage!" I searched his face, hoping for a flicker of understanding, of shared experience. "Don't you see, Father? This is how it's supposed to—"

CRACK!

The sound echoed sharply in the stairwell as his open hand struck my face with vicious force. My head snapped back, stars exploding behind my eyes, the sting immediate, sharp. A few passengers lingering near the landing gasped, turning to stare.

Father's face was contorted with rage, his carefully constructed facade utterly shattered. He pulled me close again, his voice a venomous hiss, ensuring only I could hear over the distant sounds from the deck. "You are not my son," he spat, his eyes blazing with a hatred that chilled me to the bone. "You never were."

And with that, he released me abruptly, turned on his heel, and strode quickly across the landing towards the starboard vestibule entrance, disappearing without a backward glance, leaving me alone.

I stood there, stunned, trembling, my cheek burning, the imprint of his hand like a brand. A boiling pot of emotions – shock, pain, anger, betrayal, and a strange, terrifying sense of liberation – threatened to spill over.

"You know," a kind, calm voice said softly from behind me, "it seems to me that you might just need a drink, son."

I turned slowly. J.J. Astor stood there, his expression concerned, having clearly witnessed the exchange. He placed a gentle, steadying hand on my back.

The simple gesture of kindness almost broke me. Tears filled my eyes, blurring his face. I couldn't speak, couldn't move. I just shook my head silently, the single gesture conveying everything I couldn't put into words.

Early Monday Morning, Continued

The Boat Deck, Port Side

High above the dark Atlantic, the port side of the Boat Deck was a scene of organized, yet deeply unsettling, activity. Lifeboat No. 8 swung outboard in its davits, partially filled, while Second Officer Lightoller attempted to maintain order amidst the confusion. Nearby, inexplicably, the ship's orchestra played a surprisingly cheerful ragtime tune, a bizarre counterpoint to the palpable fear and the distant, chilling sound of steam still faintly hissing from the funnels. The roar had stopped, but the silence felt heavy, looming.

Seated in the lifeboat, huddled together against the biting cold, Birdie and Mother found themselves beside the Countess of Rothes and Gladys Cherry. The boat felt precarious, suspended high above the black water, waiting as Lightoller tried to persuade more women to board.

His current efforts were focused on a young woman near the railing, clearly terrified, clutching her husband's arm and sobbing uncontrollably, understanding nothing of Lightoller's clipped English commands to get into the boat.

"Sir, perhaps I can be of assistance?" The Countess of Rothes stood up gracefully within the lifeboat, drawing Lightoller's attention.

"Madam, please remain seated! It's safer in the boat!" Lightoller ordered curtly, distracted by the distressed woman.

"Nonsense," the Countess replied calmly, stepping deftly back onto the deck, ignoring Lightoller's frustrated sigh. "The poor thing is afraid. Can you blame her?" She approached the weeping woman gently, placing a comforting hand on her arm and speaking softly, "Parlez-vous français, madame?"

The young woman's head snapped up, her tear-filled eyes widening slightly with comprehension, with a flicker of hope at hearing, not her native tongue, but one she could understand and speak. The two women spoke in hushed, rapid French for a moment, the Countess listening patiently, nodding sympathetically. Then, the Countess turned back to Lightoller.

"She's newly married, Officer," the Countess explained quietly. "Her husband is here. She doesn't understand why she must leave him behind, why she is being put into this boat alone."

Sympathetic murmurs rippled through the women already seated in the lifeboat and those standing nearby. All eyes turned to Lightoller, waiting for his response. His stern face softened.

"Tell her...tell her it is merely a precaution, madam," he instructed the Countess, his voice tight. "Her husband will follow in a later boat. See if you can convince her for her own safety."

The Countess spoke gently to the young woman again in French. After a moment's hesitation, punctuated by a tearful glance back at her husband who nodded encouragingly from the crowd, the woman gave a small, somber nod.

"I shall see to her personally, Officer," the Countess assured Lightoller, taking the young woman firmly but kindly by the hand. Together, the two women climbed back into the lifeboat, the Countess settling the distraught newlywed beside her with reassuring words. A grateful Lightoller turned his attention back to finding more women to fill the remaining spaces.

"That's humanity," Mother whispered, leaning towards Birdie, clearly moved by the Countess's compassionate intervention. "You see, darling? Kindness, composure, helping others...that's what it is all about, even now."

"I agree, Mother, the Countess is very kind," Birdie said. "But she shouldn't have had to do that. If this rule weren't so barbaric...this ridiculous notion of separating families, of deciding who is more worthy of saving based purely on...on anatomy!" Her indignation flared again.

"Darling, please," Mother sighed wearily. "These are the rules. The Captain's orders. Perhaps someday they will change, but for now, why can't you simply accept them? Your father has accepted his duty. Benji has." Her voice softened with maternal pride. "You saw how bravely your brother stayed behind with him..."

Birdie scoffed, turning to face Mother fully in the dim light reflecting off the water far below. "*Bravely*? Mother, he didn't stay behind because of some silly rule or noble duty."

"What are you saying?" Mother asked, confused.

Birdie took a deep breath, the truth she'd been piecing together, the glances she'd intercepted, solidifying into certainty. "He stayed because of *Miles*."

Mother stared at Birdie blankly. "*Miles Force*? Birdie, darling, they barely know each other. Benji only just connected with him tonight after dinner. I hardly think that's any—"

"Oh, Mother, how can you be so blind sometimes?" Birdie interrupted, her voice low but intense. She took her mother's hands, forcing Mother to meet her gaze. "Mother, Benji and Miles are...*lovers*."

The word froze in the night air, stark and undeniable. Mother's face drained of all color, her eyes wide with shock, disbelief warring with a sudden, dawning horror of comprehension. Birdie watched as the pieces visibly clicked into place behind her mother's eyes – Benji's recent odd behavior, his insistence to include Miles in their party, perhaps even echoes of those rumors about her own husband...

"I mean," Birdie pressed on relentlessly, needing Mother to see, "can't you tell by the way they look at each other? The way they hold hands when they think no one is watching?" She paused, then added the final, cutting observation, "But...I guess...like *father*, like *son*."

The last words seemed to shatter Mother's remaining composure. Her breath caught in her throat. "It all makes sense," she whispered, her gaze distant, unfocused, speaking aloud thoughts meant only for herself. She looked back at Birdie, her eyes filled with anguish. "He tried to tell me...*tonight*...Benji... he wanted to tell me something, but I didn't...Oh, my Benji. Alone with him..." Her face hardened with sudden, fierce resolve. "No."

She stood abruptly within the swaying lifeboat. "I have to go to him. I have to tell him that...that it's alright. That I understand. That I love him, no matter what."

"Madam, sit down, now!" Lightoller commanded sharply, noticing her movement as the crew prepared the ropes for lowering.

"I can't!" Mother cried, stepping towards the edge of the boat. "I have to go! *Now*!"

Lightoller reached out to grab her arm, to physically restrain her. "Get your hands off me," she shouted, her voice laced with an aristocratic fury that made the seasoned officer momentarily recoil, "before I throw you overboard!"

Before Lightoller could react further, Mother scrambled deftly over the side of the lifeboat back onto the deck, smoothed her coat, and rushed past the startled orchestra, disappearing into the darkness of the Grand Staircase entrance.

Birdie watched her go, stunned. Then, her own thoughts raced. Her mother, running back into a sinking ship for Benji. Her father, somewhere below decks playing hero, or perhaps already seeking his own escape out of sight. Oliver, the liar, the spy, who had kissed her with such desperate intensity. Oliver, the man that she'd misunderstood. Misjudged. She hadn't seen a single third class passenger all night, where were they? Had anyone shown them how to get up top to the rescue boats? What was she doing here, sitting passively by, waiting to be saved while the men she cared about – Benji, Oliver, even her complicated father – remained onboard? Madeleine Astor's words echoed: Sometimes we just have to close our eyes and say, 'to hell with it,' and just jump.

"Not *again*," Lightoller sighed wearily as Birdie stood up purposefully within the boat.

"Miss, sit down! This boat is ready for lowering! It's not going to wait for you!"

"I don't want it to," Birdie insisted, stepping carefully onto the deck. She looked back at the remaining women in the boat, then met Lightoller's exasperated gaze. "Give my spot to a man," she stated simply, before turning and following her mother back inside the ship, towards the Grand Staircase.

Lightoller stared after her, dumbfounded, then shook his head, muttering to a nearby sailor, "I pity the *men* in that family." He turned back to the remaining occupants of the boat. "Right! Last call, any more ladies wishing to board? *Quickly now!*"

CHAPTER 37

The magnificent Grand Staircase, usually a stage for elegant promenading, was now a conduit for controlled chaos. Passengers, shuffling awkwardly in their life jackets, milled uncertainly on the landings or hurried towards the Boat Deck entrances, their faces etched with confusion and growing fear. Amidst the flow, Violet Jessop moved with purpose, an armful of spare life vests cradled against her stewardess uniform, pausing to help passengers secure their own vests or offering quiet words of direction towards the decks above.

Suddenly, a figure ascending the staircase caught her eye – J. Bruce Ismay, looking startlingly different from the confident executive she usually saw striding the decks. His face was pale, his eyes wide with a shock that seemed to have momentarily stripped away his usual arrogance. He wore his pajamas and robe, looking disheveled but strangely resolute. Some deep, perhaps primal instinct – that still, small voice even he possessed – seemed to be driving him now, compelling him to act, to help, to assert some control over the fate of his ship.

He saw Violet assisting an elderly lady with her life vest straps. As the lady moved on, Ismay approached the stewardess.

"Miss Jessop," he said, his voice strained but firm. "What are you doing lingering here? The order has been given."

"Just doing my part, sir," Violet replied calmly, holding up the remaining vests. "Ensuring passengers are prepared."

"I mean," Ismay gestured impatiently towards the Boat Deck, "why aren't you in a lifeboat? There's no time to waste."

Violet straightened slightly. "I'm crew, Mr. Ismay, not a passenger. My duty is here."

"Nonsense," Ismay retorted sharply. "You are a woman. That supersedes duty tonight. Captain's orders are clear. Go on now, find a place. Quickly!" He gave a curt nod, then turned, continuing his own progress up the stairs, perhaps intending to assist with loading on the Boat Deck himself, driven by some complex mix of responsibility and self-preservation.

"Well…I have to go back to my cabin and grab a coat—"

Ismay took off his own, wool overcoat, wrapping it around her. "Now, Violet."

He gave her a solemn nod, then departed.

"Yes, sir," Violet murmured reluctantly, watching him go. She knew he was right about the Captain's orders, but leaving felt wrong.

Just as Ismay disappeared onto the A Deck landing above, another figure came rushing down the staircase towards her – Birdie Sutherland-Howell, her face flushed, eyes bright with desperate purpose, her borrowed wool dress already looking out of place amidst the first-class finery congregating on the stairs.

"Violet!" Birdie cried out, relief flooding her face as she reached her friend, grabbing her arms.

"Birdie! What on earth are you still doing here?" Violet exclaimed, pulling her aside out of the main flow of traffic. "I saw your mother get into Number 8… I thought you'd be safely away by now!"

"I got out," Birdie said quickly, breathlessly. "Violet, I need your help. Now more than ever. I need to get down to third class."

Violet stared at her, aghast. "Birdie, are you mad? There isn't time! The ship…Mr. Andrews told the Captain…she hasn't got long! I'm supposed to be getting into a lifeboat right now, and so should you!"

"But Oliver—"

"This is about that grey-eyed fella again, isn't it?" Violet interrupted, her voice laced with exasperation and fear for her young friend. "Birdie, listen to me—"

"No, you listen!" Birdie insisted, her grip tightening on Violet's arms, her eyes blazing with conviction. "It's not just about Oliver! Where are the third-class passengers, Violet? Look around!" She gestured at the well-dressed crowd on the staircase. "Have you seen a single one up here? On the Boat Deck? They don't know the way! The gates might still be locked! They need someone to show them, Violet! To help them get to safety before it's too late!"

Violet hesitated, Birdie's impassioned words striking a chord. She hadn't seen many steerage passengers on the upper decks. Was it possible they were trapped below, confused, waiting for guidance that wasn't coming? The thought was horrifying. She looked at Birdie's determined face, saw the blend of personal desire and genuine altruism. She knew the lower decks could already be flooding near the bow, knew the danger was immense. But she also knew Birdie wouldn't be deterred.

"Violet, please," Birdie pleaded. "I'm going down there, one way or another. But if I want to be quick, if I want any chance of finding him or helping anyone else, I need your help. Your keys."

Violet chewed her lip, her mind racing. Ismay's order echoed – get to a boat. But Birdie's plea, the image of those potentially trapped below...She made a quick decision. Glancing around to ensure no officers were watching, she quickly unhooked a small ring of keys from her belt beneath her apron.

"Alright," she whispered urgently, pressing the keys into Birdie's hand. "Heaven help us both. Take the Grand Staircase all the way down to E Deck. At the very bottom there's a service door. It opens onto Scotland Road." She squeezed Birdie's hand. "That key," she indicated a small brass one, "should unlock it. No one will stop you, not tonight. Everyone's focused up here."

Tears sprang to Birdie's eyes. She threw her arms around Violet, hugging her tightly. "Thank you, Violet. Oh, thank you!"

Violet held her close for a brief, precious second, the unspoken fear of this perhaps being their final goodbye hanging heavy between them. "Best be going now," Violet whispered, pushing her back gently resolute. "I'll see you in New York?"

"It's a date," Birdie smiled.

"Good, because I'm gonna need that dress back, you hear?"

Both laughed, warming the tense moment.

"You haven't any time to waste. You be careful down there, Miss Birdie. Truly careful."

"And you, Violet," Birdie replied, her voice thick with emotion. "Find a boat. Be safe. Thank you. For...everything."

With one last, lingering look, the two women parted ways – Violet turning and resolutely heading up the crowded staircase towards the Boat Deck and the slim chance of survival, Birdie clutching the keys, turning and rushing down the magnificent staircase, towards the flooding lower decks, towards danger, towards Oliver.

Early Monday Morning, Continued
The First Class Lounge

Mother stumbled back into the First Class Lounge, leaving the relative order of the Grand Staircase behind, still able to hear the soft remnants of a stringed waltz. Her head swirled as she reached the center of the room, the large chandelier casting a cheery halo above her head. Yet there was nothing cheery about this moment. Benji. She had to find Benji. But where? The Lounge, once a picture of calm Edwardian elegance, now felt chaotic, distorted. Passengers huddled in anxious groups, some unnaturally quiet, others talking too loudly, their voices sharp with fear beneath forced composure. The lush carved paneling seemed to warp around her, stress and lack of sleep creating a disorienting tunnel vision. Stewards moved through the room with trays of coffee or brandy, their professional smiles strained. Where was Benji? Had he come back up? Gone to another deck?

"Caroline!"

A man's voice, low and urgent, called from behind her, near the revolving door she'd just come through. She spun around, half expecting, half dreading...

It was Bruce Ismay. He looked ashen, the confident facade she'd seen earlier on the promenade deck utterly gone, replaced by a raw, undisguised shock. He clearly knew more about the severity of the situation, and clearly, it wasn't good.

"Caroline... I..." He stopped, seemingly lost for words, his gaze locking with hers across the crowded room. For a long, charged moment, they simply stared at

each other, the noise and chaos around them fading, the unspoken history, the near-miss intimacy, the shared danger all hanging heavy between them.

He took a step closer, his voice barely registered above the anxious murmur of the room. "It's...it's all my fault," he choked out, the confession ragged, torn from him. "Everything. *This*..." he gestured helplessly around the tilting room, encompassing the ship, the situation, perhaps even the fraught connection between them. "You...me..."

His eyes seemed distant for a moment. "I can almost hear my father now," he murmured bitterly. "'I told you so, Bruce. You're not cut out for this, Bruce...You'll run White Star into the ground...'" He trailed off, lost in the specter of his father's judgment that seemed to haunt him even now. He looked back at Mother, a flicker of bleak understanding in his eyes. "Well," he gave a humorless smile, "I guess, try as we might, we can never quite live up to the impossible expectations of our parents, eh?"

His unexpected vulnerability, his echo of the very pressures she felt regarding her own children, resonated with Mother despite everything. She noticed tears welling at the corners of his eyes, a startling sight in the usually composed Managing Director.

"Well..." Ismay seemed to pull himself together with an effort, dropping his gaze, apparently unable to face her directly any longer. "I should...I should let you go. Find your family." He hesitated, then looked up briefly, his voice thick with emotion. "I just wanted to say...that I'm sorry, Caroline. For everything. I am so, very sorry." He dropped his gaze again, afraid, perhaps, for her to see the depth of his regret, the crack in his carefully constructed world. "Godspeed to you."

He turned abruptly, intending to leave, to escape the weight of her gaze, the weight of his own culpability.

"Bruce!" she stopped him, the word escaping before she could think. He turned back, surprised. "I suppose," she began softly, feeling an unexpected wave of empathy, of shared human frailty in this desperate hour, "if we're apologizing..."

He met her gaze one last time. She saw the tears brimming, the profound regret, the understanding of all that was lost, mirrored perhaps in her own eyes. He said nothing more, offered no further explanation or excuse, simply gave her a polite, almost formal, final nod – an acknowledgment, perhaps, of everything said and unsaid between them. Then he turned definitively and walked away, disappearing into the anxious crowd, leaving Mother standing alone in the middle of the grand, listing lounge.

Monday Morning, April 15th, 1912
Approx. 12:40 AM
The Bridge

Captain Smith and Chief Officer Wilde stood grimly side-by-side on the port bridge wing, their gaze fixed downward, towards the bow. Even in the stark, cold starlight, the horrifying progress was undeniable. The forecastle head, the very front tip of the great liner, was now barely above the waterline, waves occasionally washing over its deck plates. The ship's downward list by the head was becoming alarmingly pronounced. The tension on the bridge was thick enough to taste.

"She's going down faster now," Wilde observed quietly, his voice tight.

"Aye," Smith agreed heavily. He scanned the bridge behind them. "Have you seen Mr. Andrews recently, Chief?"

"Not since he gave his report, Captain. Though I heard a steward mention seeing him near the First Class Smoking Room a short while ago, urging passengers towards the boats."

"Find him, if you can, Mr. Wilde," Smith ordered. "I want to discuss something with him, something urgent." He paused, his gaze drifting back towards the unresponsive lights of the mystery ship, still visible several miles off the port bow. "And while you're at it," he added, frustration roughening his voice, "check in again with the wireless operators. See if they've had any response from that steamer, or any word on the Carpathia's progress."

"Aye, aye, sir," Wilde acknowledged, turning to head back inside.

"What are you," Smith muttered under his breath at the distant lights after Wilde had gone, "a bloody ghost ship?" He raised his binoculars again, searching fruitlessly for any sign of response to their signals.

Nearby, Fourth Officer Boxhall stood ready beside the distress rocket launching apparatus. "Rockets standing by, sir. Shall I fire?"

"Yes, Mr. Boxhall," Smith lowered his binoculars with a weary sigh. "Fire them at regulation intervals. One every few minutes. And keep a close eye on that vessel," he gestured towards the silent lights. "Let me know the very moment she responds."

"Yes, sir," Boxhall affirmed. As Smith turned back to his vigil, the sharp hiss of the rocket launching split the night air from the starboard bridge wing, followed by a low boom high above. A brilliant burst of white light momentarily illuminated the decks, warming the freezing air, before dissolving into a cascade of slowly falling stars, raining back down onto the doomed liner.

Simultaneously

The Starboard Boat Deck

From the relative calm of the Grand Staircase entrance, Ismay burst onto the starboard Boat Deck, immediately enveloped by a frantic energy far exceeding what he'd witnessed earlier. This side of the ship seemed much more crowded, a chaotic throng of passengers – men included – pressing near the lifeboats, their faces pale masks of fear in the harsh electric glare. Officers shouted orders, crewmen struggled with ropes, and the air buzzed with panicked questions and hushed prayers. It seemed Murdoch's reported leniency in interpreting "women and children first" had drawn hopeful crowds to this side.

Ismay pushed his way through the throng, his earlier sense of shock replaced by a desperate urge to do something, anything, to assert control, to expedite the loading.

"Look! Another one!" someone shouted nearby.

WHOOSH...

BOOM!

All heads, including Ismay's, snapped upwards as the second rocket soared into the black sky, bursting into its shower of ephemeral stars.

"Ooh, it's so pretty, Mama!" a small child's voice piped up nearby. Ismay turned to see a plainly dressed woman clutching the hands of two young girls, their faces upturned in innocent wonder at the deadly fireworks.

"Did you make a wish?" the other child asked her sister.

The sight struck Ismay to the core. Children. Still here. Why weren't they in a boat? He could see Boat No. 3 being prepared nearby, plenty of room still available, the loading stalled perhaps by passenger reluctance or crew confusion.

He strode over purposefully. "Madam, please," he urged the mother, his voice carrying authority, scooping the younger girl unexpectedly into his arms. "You must get your children into a lifeboat immediately! There's no time to waste! For your sake, and theirs!" He turned and practically deposited the startled child into the arms of Fifth Officer Lowe, who was overseeing the loading of No. 5. Ismay then turned back, firmly motioning the mother and her older daughter forward. "Come along now! Quickly! In you go!"

Startled into action by Ismay's decisive intervention, the woman obeyed, climbing into the boat with her remaining child. With several other nearby women encouraged by the sight, the boat finally seemed full enough.

"Alright then! That's enough! Lower away!" Ismay shouted commandingly to the crewmen handling the davit ropes.

"Excuse me!" A sharp voice cut through Ismay's command. Fifth Officer Lowe stepped directly in front of him, his expression furious. "Just what in the name of creation do you think you're doing, sir?"

"Getting this boat into the water, Officer," Ismay replied, slightly taken aback by Lowe's tone. "I'm only trying to help."

"Help?" Lowe scoffed, clearly not recognizing the Managing Director in his pajamas and dressing gown, or perhaps not caring if he did. "You'll 'help' by getting the hell out of the way so my men and I can do our jobs! Now stand down, sir," Lowe snapped, his hand hovering near the pistol holstered at his belt, "before your 'help' drowns the whole lot of them!"

Stunned by the officer's vehemence, Ismay automatically raised his hands in surrender. "I...I do apologize, Officer. Carry on." He stepped back quickly, melting into the swarm of nervous passengers on the deck, his authority completely undermined.

As he checked his surroundings, trying to regain his composure, he spotted a familiar figure nearby – Benjamin Sutherland-Howell, standing alone, looking pale and strained. Ismay felt a pang of guilt, the memory of his charged conversation with Mother in the Lounge returning vividly. Had she found her husband? Had she told him? He felt a sudden, overriding need to ensure Benjamin knew his wife was still aboard, possibly looking for him or their son. Her safety, in this moment, felt more important than pride, more important than whatever unspoken thing existed between them.

"Mr. Howell," Ismay called out, approaching him quickly.

Father turned, his eyes looking haunted.

"Mr. Howell... your wife... Caroline..." Ismay began, unsure how to phrase it delicately. "She's... she's still aboard, I believe. She came back inside earlier."

A look of sheer panic flashed across Father's face. "She what? Came back inside? Where is she?"

"I don't know," Ismay admitted helplessly. "She seemed distressed... perhaps looking for you? Or for Benji?"

Without waiting for another word, Father spun around and lunged back towards the Grand Staircase entrance, shoving his way through the crowd just as the third distress rocket hissed violently upwards into the night sky.

BOOM!

Early Monday Morning, Continued

Aft Grand Staircase & First Class Smoking Room

As J.J. Astor and I walked from the commotion near the Boat Deck entrance back towards the quieter aft end of the ship, towards the Smoking Room, I found myself still processing his unexpected offer and profound advice. He seemed to sense my lingering shock from the earlier confrontation with Father, steering the conversation towards his own recent encounter.

"Then...when Mrs. Astor was safely settled in her boat, I inquired if I might join her, given the circumstances, her condition...he wouldn't hear of it," Astor chuckled. "Quite adamant. 'Women and children only,' he said." He shrugged slightly. "Can't fault a man for following orders, I suppose."

"You? Really?" I asked, surprised. "Mr. Lightoller wouldn't let you board, of all people?"

"Well now, Benji," Astor replied calmly, "my life isn't worth more than anyone else's, is it?" We reached the aft Grand Staircase landing and continued towards the Smoking Room doors. "Besides," he added with another chuckle, "I don't think he honestly knew who I was."

We both laughed as he pushed open the door to the Smoking Room – a space I now realized, with a strange jolt of irony given my recent coming-of-age, I was finally old enough to enter freely.

As we stepped inside, the atmosphere was hushed compared to the decks, though not empty. A handful of men sat quietly at tables, seeking refuge, a stiff drink to take their minds away from outdated society protocols, and sinking ships. My gaze, however, was drawn immediately to the large, ornate fireplace on the far wall, its coals ablaze with comforting light. Standing just before it, their backs partially turned to us as they spoke quietly, were two figures. Thomas Andrews, seemingly in his favorite place before his beloved painting, his mind's eye undoubtedly traveling to the safety of Olympic, or the promised hope of Britannic. And beside him...Miles.

My heart stopped. Miles. Here. It felt like fate, like the universe conspiring, despite all the arguments and misunderstandings, to bring us back together one last time in this specific, meaningful place. This was where I was supposed to be. It was time to fix things, once and for all.

Miles and Andrews stopped talking when we entered, their eyes acknowledging our presence. As Astor and I strode over, the air thickened. Both Astor and Andrews immediately took note of the intense, unresolved energy stirring between Miles and me, the silent questions hanging in our locked gazes.

"Um...Benji," Astor cut in smoothly, ever perceptive, "I hate to run, but I just remembered a previous engagement. Urgent business." He winked playfully. "A mission of mercy, you might say. Seems someone forgot to release the hounds earlier. I think I hear Kitty calling my name," he said with a knowing smile.

"And," Andrews chimed in, picking up the cue instantly, his expression equally knowing, perhaps even gently amused, "it appears I'm needed up on the bridge. But," he glanced towards Astor, "I think I'll make a pit-stop with you first, Astor, if you'd care for a hand with those 'hounds'."

Astor nodded gratefully. The two men started for the doors, then Andrews paused, turning back briefly. "And...Benji..." he called out softly from across the room, "Happy Birthday." He offered a small, genuine smile. "And godspeed to you. Both."

And with that, they were gone, leaving Miles and me alone in the relative quiet of the handsome room.

Miles turned back towards the fireplace without a word, staring into the glowing coals, his eyes glossy, reflecting the firelight. Silently, my heart pounding, I joined him, standing beside him. The only sounds were the soft crackle and hum from the coal fire, the distant, muffled shouts from the deck, and the occasional ominous crash or groan from somewhere deep within the bowels of the injured ship.

After what felt like an eternity, Miles spoke, his voice low, heavy, sober. "You lied to me."

"Miles, I know, and I'm—"

"These past few days," he continued, cutting me off, still not looking at me, "all the talk about being open, about honesty, not living a lie. About trusting each other. And...still...you lied to me."

I said nothing. What could I say? He was right. In that moment, any excuse, any justification, felt utterly wrong.

"You're seventeen?" he asked quietly, thinking aloud, the question filled more with hurt than accusation.

"Eighteen now," I tried, weakly, attempting the same joke Birdie had made earlier, hoping for levity that wouldn't come. It didn't land.

"...And I..." he swallowed hard, "...we...You were just a child, Benji. When we..." He couldn't finish the sentence.

"Seventeen is still old enough for legal consent," I added quickly, defensively, foolishly trying to minimize the breach of trust with legalistic deflection. "So...it's no big deal, right?"

"It is a big deal, Benji," he said firmly, finally turning to face me, his eyes searching mine, filled with disappointment. "You knew it would be. Otherwise, you wouldn't have lied to me in the first place."

He was right. Completely right. My pathetic attempts at self-justification dissolved under his steady, honest gaze.

"Miles, look," I pleaded, taking his hand instinctively, needing him to understand, needing to bridge the gap between us. I turned him gently towards the large painting above the mantelpiece, Plymouth Harbour. I pointed his own finger towards the edge of the canvas. "Do you know what this is?"

He looked confused, skeptical. "A painting?"

"It's a continuation," I explained urgently, the metaphor suddenly clear, vital. "This isn't just one painting; it's part of a set. One for each sister ship. Where one harbor ends," I traced the edge of the painted sea meeting the frame, "the next begins."

"What are you getting at, Benji?" he asked, still wary.

"The point is," I met his eyes, pouring all my conviction into the words, "that, yes. I lied to you. I've done things this past year, things that were done to me, that I wish desperately I could take back. Things I'm ashamed of." My voice thickened with emotion. "But the one constant through all of it? The one thing that feels undeniably real, the one thing that resonates with that still, small voice inside of me, telling me everything will still be alright...is you, Miles. It's always been you, since that first moment."

I drew him closer, directing our gaze back towards the painting, towards the doomed ship it represented. "All of the emotional trauma that's haunted me,"

I whispered, "everything my father represents, everything that's ever made me second-guess being with you, wanting you...I want to leave it all behind. Right here. Right now."

I gestured towards the painting again. "Each of the Olympic-class liners has one of these paintings, representing their journey's beginning or end. In another hour, maybe less, this one," I indicated the canvas before us, representing Titanic, "will be sitting at the bottom of the Atlantic Ocean." The gravity of the words hit us both, stark and absolute. "But the other two," I insisted, turning him fully to face me again, holding his gaze, holding his hands tightly, "the Olympic, the Britannic...they'll live on."

I squeezed his hands. "Miles, all the doubt, all the fear, all the lies – fuck them, remember? Let's leave them right here, right now. Let my father's manipulations, Harper's dismissal, the ghosts of Paris...let it all go down with this ship." My voice grew stronger, filled with desperate hope. "Let's start our new life, our truth, together. Right here. Right now. Live in the moment. We are the other two harbors in the paintings, Miles. Connected. Surviving. Destined," I leaned closer, searching his eyes, "destined to see another sunrise."

CHAPTER 38

Ten miles, maybe less, across a freezing, flat-calm sea, the deck of the SS Californian felt like a separate, isolated world. Locked fast in pack ice that glittered faintly under the stars, her engines silent since late evening, the small freighter waited patiently for dawn. On her bridge deck, Second Officer Herbert Stone and Apprentice Officer James Gibson stamped their feet against the biting cold, their watch uneventful save for the baffling spectacle unfolding off their starboard quarter.

WHOOSH...

BOOM.

Another white rocket soared high into the black sky from the direction of the massive passenger liner they'd been observing for hours, bursting into a shower of brilliant stars before fading away.

"Another one," Gibson remarked, lowering the binoculars he'd been focusing on the distant ship. "How many is that now, Mr. Stone? Three? Four?"

"*At least*," Stone confirmed grimly, peering through his own glasses. "Firing them every few minutes now."

"So they're not distress rockets then?" Gibson mused, though doubt laced his voice. "Company signals, maybe?"

"Don't know of any company signals that look like bloody fireworks," Stone retorted dryly. "And a ship's not going to fire rockets at sea for nothing." He lowered his binoculars, shaking his head. "She was making knots when we saw her earlier, now she's stopped dead, same as us. And firing rockets."

"Maybe it's a party?" Gibson offered weakly, gesturing towards the blaze of lights that marked the liner across the water. "Look at her, she's enormous. One of those grand passenger ships, White Star maybe? Can practically see her sidelights from here."

"Party or not, rockets mean something," Stone stated decisively. "Right," he sighed, clearly reluctant. "Go and wake the Captain."

Gibson visibly hesitated. "Oh, it's my job now, is it?" he attempted a joke, pulling his collar tighter. "Just what I was hoping for. He fair loves being woken up in the middle of the night for a fireworks display."

The officers shared a brief, grim chuckle before Gibson turned and headed dutifully towards Captain Lord's chart room below the bridge. He knocked tentatively on the door, noticing a faint light appear through the shuttered window as someone stirred within.

"Come in," Captain Lord's voice grumbled from inside, thick with sleep.

Gibson entered the small cabin, cap in hand. "Sorry to wake you, Captain—"

"What is it, Gibson?" Lord interrupted curtly, propped up on one elbow in his bunk.

"That ship, sir," Gibson began. "The large steamer off the starboard. Can't be more than a few miles off now. She's acting rather...queer, you might say."

"Queer? How so?" Lord demanded irritably.

"Well, sir, we saw her lights approaching fast about an hour or two ago, looked like she was trying to pass us. Then she just...stopped dead. Went dark for a bit too, seemed like."

"Probably stopped for ice, same as us," Lord grumbled, already settling back down. "Sensible thing to do."

"I don't think so, sir," Gibson persisted. "Her deck lights came back on, brighter than before. But her position isn't changing, looks like she might be adrift. And now..."

"Now, what, man? Spit it out!"

"She's firing rockets, sir."

Lord sat up slightly again. "Rockets?"

"Yes, sir. White ones. Like starshells. At least three or four so far, at regular intervals."

"What kind of rockets?" Lord pressed. "Regulation distress signals? Company signals?"

"Not regulation distress signals, sir...not the ones we use, anyway," Gibson admitted. "Just...white rockets bursting into stars. Like I said, sir...she's acting rather queer. I'm not sure what to make of her."

Captain Lord considered this, rubbing the sleep from his eyes. A large steamer, stopped nearby, firing rockets that weren't clear distress signals. It was odd. But without the specific, internationally recognized distress pattern, he wasn't technically bound by maritime law to respond, especially given his own precarious situation. His mind immediately went to the treacherous ice field surrounding them – navigating it blindly in the dark to reach another vessel of unknown status was risky.

And then, more damningly, his thoughts turned to the cargo. The clandestine, last-minute addition overseen by that slick Mr. Y back in England. The crates filled with...well, he didn't know precisely what, only that his orders from the highest levels of the IMM, relayed through Mr. Y, emphasized absolute discretion and ensuring the cargo remained undisturbed, its presence unknown, at all costs. His career, his very stripes, depended on it. What would happen if he went alongside that liner? If he potentially had to take on hundreds of passengers? Where would he put them? They'd be everywhere, sleeping in corridors, perhaps even needing space in the cargo holds...nosing around, asking questions. The risk of discovery, of jeopardizing his secret charge, felt immense.

"I can wake Sparks, sir," Gibson offered tentatively, seeing his captain's hesitation. "Mr. Evans can try reaching her over the wireless—"

"That won't be necessary, Gibson," Lord cut him off, his voice dropping, his decision made, deflecting the logical next step. He couldn't risk it. Not with Mr. Y's cargo aboard. His orders were clear. "Just...note the rockets in the log as they appear. Keep trying her with the Morse lamp. If you get a distinct reply, or," he added grudgingly, "if you see her firing actual, regulation distress signals...well...then you let me know."

Gibson looked gravely at his captain, clearly understanding the implications of inaction, but knowing better than to argue further. The hierarchy was absolute. "Aye, sir," he swallowed hard, then turned to leave.

Stopping at the door, he paused, unable to keep the final thought unspoken, delivering it towards the closed wood rather than the Captain's face. "A ship's not going to fire rockets at sea for nothing, sir."

Then, he silently opened the door, left, and closed it softly behind him, leaving Captain Lord alone in his cabin. Lord lay back down, staring up at the dark ceiling, swallowing hard himself. His officer's words echoed his own instincts, his own seamanship. But the weight of his secret orders, the unknown contents of those crates below, pressed down harder, dictating a course of cautious, deliberate inaction.

Early Monday Morning, Continued
E Deck & Forward Third Class Open Space

Clutching Violet's keys, Birdie hurried down the majestic sweep of the forward Grand Staircase, pushing against the tide of anxious first-class passengers heading upwards. The ornate carvings and gilded details seemed almost obscene now, a mockery of luxury in the face of imminent disaster. Each step choreographing her footfall, as the forward pitching of the stairs made running down them an unrehearsed challenge.

Reaching the E deck landing – she quickly found the unmarked service door Violet had described. Her fingers trembled as she sorted through the keys, finally finding the small brass one. It slid into the lock and turned with a satisfying click.

She pushed the door open and stepped through, emerging onto the long, wide thoroughfare of Scotland Road. The contrast was immediate. The air was colder here, the electric lights harsher, the sounds different – not the strained politeness of the upper decks, but a low murmur of confused voices, interspersed with snippets of languages she barely recognized, and the ever-present, unnerving silence where the engines' thrum should have been.

Dozens of third-class passengers milled about, clutching children and meager bundles, their faces etched with bewilderment and fear. Few wore life jackets. They looked lost, uncertain where to go, cut off from the organized, yet chaotic, evacuation happening decks above them.

Seeing their confusion, Birdie's own fear momentarily subsided, replaced by a surge of adrenaline, of purpose. She propped the service door open, ensuring the route back to the Grand Staircase remained clear. Then, drawing on every language lesson she'd ever had, she began shouting, her voice surprisingly loud and clear in the corridor.

"Allez! Nach oben! Upstairs! Subito!" She pointed emphatically towards the open door, towards the faint sounds of the orchestra drifting down from above. "Les bateaux! The boats! Aufgang! Up! Go now! Presto!" She used her hands, gesturing upwards, pushing gently, urging the hesitant crowd towards the unexpected escape route.

Slowly at first, then with growing urgency as her commands registered, a stream of people began moving towards the door, towards the hope of the upper decks. Satisfied she had at least started the flow, Birdie turned and hurried forward along Scotland Road, towards the wide staircase she knew led up to the Third Class Open Space, the reverberant echo of her heels clicking on the pine decks, urgently chasing her the whole way. She had to find Oliver.

Ascending the familiar stairs, she braced herself. Would he even be there? Or would he have sought safety elsewhere? Stepping into the large open space confirmed her fears – and hopes. The room, usually teeming with life, was mostly deserted now. A few families huddled on benches, unsure where to go next, looking towards her with questioning eyes. And there, in his usual corner booth, seemingly oblivious to the crisis unfolding around him, sat Oliver, a book open before him, illuminated by the single bare bulb overhead.

Birdie quickly directed the remaining families towards the main staircase down to Scotland Road, pointing them towards the path she'd just cleared. "Down the stairs you just came up!" she urged them. "Through the door! Go up! Quickly!" As they hurried away, she turned her attention fully to the solitary figure in the corner.

She crossed the large, now echoing room, her footsteps loud on the wooden floor. The ship was groaning uncomfortably as it fought, trying hard to digest the unwanted Atlantic. Oliver looked up as she approached, his expression unreadable, perhaps resigned.

"You came back," he stated simply. It wasn't a question. His voice held a trace of something – hurt? Guilt that she hadn't heeded his earlier warnings? Or perhaps just weary acceptance?

"We have to go, Oliver," Birdie said urgently, reaching his table. "The ship...it's not good. They're loading the lifeboats. There isn't much time. Come on."

He didn't move, just looked back down at his book, turning a page deliberately.

"Oliver, please!" she pleaded, placing her hands flat on his table, leaning towards him. "Didn't you feel the impact? Hear the bells?"

"I told you, Margaret," he said quietly, not looking up, "I'm no good for you. You don't belong down here with someone like me. You don't know what I've done."

"I do know!" she insisted, needing him to understand, needing to break through his apathy. "Stead. He explained..." Her voice softened slightly. "Oliver, you cannot blame yourself for Oscar Wilde, for laws made—"

CRRAAASSH!

A deafening noise erupted from somewhere nearby – a violent, reverberant crash of metal or heavy cargo shifting deep within the ship, followed by the distinct sound of rushing water, closer now, perhaps just below the deck they stood on. The floor beneath their feet seemed to pulse with the impact.

"Oliver!" Birdie snapped back to the immediate danger, grabbing his arm. "Forget Stead! Forget the past! Look around! There isn't time! We have to go! There are still so many people down here, trapped, confused! We have to help them get out!" She held up Violet's ring of keys, shaking them slightly. "You know these decks better than I do! We can open doors, show them the way!"

She leaned closer, forcing him to meet her desperate gaze. "I don't care what you've done, Oliver! Or who you think you are! Helping these people now," she insisted fiercely, "that's what matters. This is what's right! And we can help more people...together." Her eyes pleaded with him, willing him to see past his own despair.

Another deep growl wailed through the ship's structure, longer this time, accompanied by a more pronounced tilt to the deck.

"Come on!" Birdie shouted over the noise, refusing to leave him. She grabbed his hand, pulling him forcefully to his feet. This time, he didn't resist. Together, hand in hand, they stumbled towards the wide staircase, descending back down towards the potentially flooding maze of Scotland Road, turning instinctively, urgently, towards the higher ground of the aft end of the ship.

Monday Morning, April 15th, 1912
   Approx. 1:40 AM
   The Boat Deck

The Titanic's Boat Deck tilted at an increasingly sharp angle, making walking treacherous. The ghostly sounds of the orchestra slowly fading into the frozen night. The lapping of water against the hull – closer now than seemed possible – sporadic shouts, and the occasional, terrifying groan from deep within the dying ship. Most of the lifeboats were gone, leaving stark empty spaces along the rails. Collapsibles C and D were feverishly being unlashed from the roof of the officers' quarters, so they could be prepared for launching.

Amidst the scattering groups of remaining passengers and crew, two men walked slowly along the deck – Thomas Andrews, his face drawn with exhaustion and profound sorrow, and John Jacob Astor, remarkably composed, holding his beloved Airedale, Kitty, securely in his arms. The nervous dog, sensing the tension, whined softly, licking Astor's face affectionately. They had just come from the ship's kennels further aft, having unlatched the cages, giving the dogs aboard at least a slim, desperate chance to swim for their lives in the freezing water. It felt like a small, necessary act of mercy in the face of overwhelming tragedy.

As they neared one of the final davits, which still held a boat, they passed a heart-wrenching scene. Officer Murdoch and one of his juniors were patiently, but firmly, trying to persuade Ida Strauss to step into the boat, while her husband, Isidor, stood beside her, his expression loving but pleading.

"Madam, please," the officer urged gently. "There is room. You must get in."

Astor and Andrews paused respectfully nearby, witnessing the quiet drama.

"I said no," Ida replied, her voice quiet but unwavering, clutching Isidor's arm tightly. Though frail, her dignity was immense.

"Ida, please, my love," Isidor implored, his voice thick with emotion. "For your own sake. Take your place."

She looked up at her husband, her eyes filled with a lifetime of shared devotion. "I am an old woman, Isidor," she stated simply. "We have lived together for almost all of our lives. Where you go, I go." Her resolve was absolute.

Andrews stepped forward impulsively. "Mrs. Strauss," he began gently, then turned to the officer, "...I don't believe anyone would object if an older gentleman such as Mr. Strauss were to accompany his wife in this instance?"

Isidor immediately shook his head firmly. "No, sir," he stated clearly. "I will not go before the other men."

"Then it is settled," Ida said, managing a faint, definitive smile, looking back at her husband. "We will stay together."

Isidor leaned down and kissed his wife tenderly on the cheek, a final, silent acknowledgment of their shared fate. The officer, moved after seeing their unshakable resolve, reluctantly turned his attention back to filling the remaining spaces in the boat.

Andrews watched them for another moment, his heart aching, before turning towards the bridge. Astor nodded solemnly, understanding Andrews needed to be with the Captain. "God be with you, Andrews."

"And you, J.J.," Andrews replied quietly, before continuing his difficult walk down the steeply tilting deck towards the officers' quarters and the forward bridge wing.

He found Captain Smith standing alone, gazing intently through binoculars at the distant, unresponsive lights of the ship they now knew to be the Californian. Smith looked older, smaller somehow, the weight of the unfolding catastrophe telling on his face. The forecastle deck, the entire bow section of his magnificent command, was now completely submerged, the dark water creeping steadily aft along the forward well deck. It was an eerie, terrifying sight – his worst nightmare made real.

"You wanted to see me, Captain?" Andrews asked quietly, stepping up beside him.

Smith lowered the binoculars slowly, his gaze distant for a moment before focusing on Andrews. "That ship..." he murmured, nodding towards the lights. "She can see our rockets. She must see us." His voice held a note of ragged disbelief. "Why doesn't she respond?" He seemed lost for a moment, overwhelmed by the inexplicable indifference of their potential rescuer, then visibly regained his composure, turning back to duty.

"The ship's log, Mr. Andrews," he said, his voice heavy now with the gravity of finality. "Before the ship..." Smith's words trailed off. He didn't finish the sentence. "I need your help. Going over a few of the particulars. For the ship's log. Ensuring everything is...in order. Ready for send-off."

Andrews stared past the Captain, down towards the bow, towards the black water inexorably swallowing the forecastle deck, the proud forecastle where he had stood just days ago during sea trials, filled with such hope. The eerie, slanting view of the deck, the water closing in... it was a horrifying validation of his calculations.

"Mr. Andrews?" Smith prompted gently, tearing him away from the grim spectacle.

Andrews turned back, meeting the Captain's weary eyes, understanding the final duty being asked of him. "Yes, Captain," he replied softly. "Of course."

The Titanic's bridge, once the ship's proud nerve center, now felt like a vigil station on the edge of eternity. The angle of the deck was severe, sending loose charts sliding across the tables. Outside, the water was noticeably closer, the stars reflecting on a black surface that seemed to be climbing the ship's hull. Captain Smith stepped with Thomas Andrews into the relative quiet of the chart room, the ship's logbook soon spread open between them under the dim emergency lights. They spoke in low tones, reviewing final entries, ensuring the official record was as complete as it could be before the inevitable occurred.

The door to the room opened, and J. Bruce Ismay stepped inside, looking utterly adrift. The earlier shock had given way to a hollowed-out despair. He approached the two men hesitantly.

"Mr. Andrews... Captain," Ismay began, his voice raspy, uncertain. "Might I have a word?"

Both Smith and Andrews looked up from their grim task, their expressions unreadable.

"I...I can't begin to..." Ismay stopped himself, the usual platitudes feeling obscene now. He swallowed hard, forcing the words out.

"Spit it out, Mr. Ismay, we haven't much time," urged Captain Smith.

"What I mean to say is..." Ismay continued, "I am sorry. Deeply. Regretfully sorry. For...for everything." His gaze flickered between the designer whose masterpiece was dying beneath them, and the Captain whose command was meeting its tragic end. He thought about his reckless desire and what role it might've played leading up to this moment.

Neither Smith nor Andrews responded immediately. They simply looked at him, the weight of the unsaid – the warnings ignored, the pressure for speed, the catastrophic consequences – hanging heavy in the air. Ismay stood awkwardly in the profound silence, unsure if he should say more, unsure if he should stay or simply turn and flee.

The moment was broken as First Officer Murdoch poked his head in briefly from the bridge wing. "Collapsible C is being prepared for loading now, sir," he reported quickly to Smith.

"Thank you, Mr. Murdoch. Carry on," Smith replied evenly. Murdoch gave a quick salute and disappeared back onto the chaotic deck.

The interruption seemed to signal the end of Ismay's attempt at confession. Without another word, Smith and Andrews turned their attention back to the logbook, their focus absolute, seemingly dismissing Ismay's apology, his very presence.

"Right then," Ismay murmured, his face falling, humiliation perhaps mingling with his despair. He turned quietly and walked out of the chart room, back towards the bridge door, intending perhaps to retreat to the rapidly diminishing safety of the ship's interior, or to try and save a few more souls.

As soon as the door closed behind Ismay, Captain Smith let out a long, weary sigh. He looked briefly at Andrews, a silent acknowledgment passing between them, then pushed himself away from the chart table and followed Ismay out onto the bridge, then onto the Boat Deck.

"Mr. Ismay." Smith's voice, quiet but firm, stopped the Managing Director near the davit where Collapsible C was being readied by a knot of crew and remaining passengers. The Captain closed the distance between them, keeping their conversation as private as possible amidst the surrounding noise and confusion.

The two men locked eyes – the Commander and the Owner. For a long moment, no words were spoken, only the sounds of the increasingly distressed ship groaning beneath them and the shouts of officers trying to organize the final boat.

Then, Smith spoke, his voice low, intense. "Someone needs to be held accountable for this, Mr. Ismay," he stated, the accusation clear despite the hushed tone. "When the inquiries begin...when the questions are asked...one of us has to be on hand to answer for this night."

Ismay stared back, absorbing the Captain's meaning.

Smith continued, his gaze unwavering. "The Captain," he said, the words heavy with tradition and finality, "is always the last man to leave his ship..."

"Any more women or children?" Murdoch's voice rang out nearby as crewmen helped the last few occupants into Collapsible C. "Any more ladies?"

Smith glanced towards the boat, then back at Ismay. "That boat, Mr. Ismay," he said deliberately, "might just be the very last one to leave the Titanic." His meaning was unmistakable. He held Ismay's gaze. "I think you had better be on it."

"But, Captain...I...I can't..." Ismay stammered, perhaps horrified at the implication, perhaps realizing the ignominy, yet trapped by the Captain's stare, by the weight of Smith's judgment.

"Anyone else then? Quickly now!" Murdoch urged again, preparing to give the order to lower.

Ismay and Smith continued to stare each other down, a final, silent battle of wills or perhaps a grim, necessary transfer of burden.

"Go, Mr. Ismay," Smith said finally, his voice absolute. "*Now.*" Murdoch glanced towards them, waiting for any final passengers. "That," Smith raised his voice slightly, ensuring Murdoch heard, ensuring Ismay understood there was no choice, "is an order!"

The command, shocking in its directness, broke Ismay's paralysis. As Murdoch shouted, "Lower away!", Ismay scrambled frantically towards the boat, climbing awkwardly over the rail and tumbling into the crowded collapsible just as it began its jerky descent towards the black water far below.

Captain Smith stood perfectly still, watching in stoic silence as the boat lowered away from his vantage point on the tilting deck, carrying the Managing Director of the White Star Line away from his sinking ship. Then, quietly, without a backward glance at the departing boat, he turned and walked steadily back to the bridge, back to his command, back to his fate.

CHAPTER 39

T he Titanic, mortally wounded, groaned under the immense strain, her downward angle by the bow growing steeper with each passing minute. Below decks, the lights had begun to dim, flickering ominously, casting long, haunting shadows. Up in the first-class areas, the carefully maintained illusion of order was fracturing. A frantic swarm of third-class passengers, having finally found their way from the labyrinthine lower decks, now surged through corridors and up staircases they had never been permitted to tread, their faces etched with a mixture of terror and bewildered awe.

One immigrant family – a husband, wife, and two small children clutching ragged dolls – stopped dead in their tracks at the entrance to the A Deck Lounge, staring wide-eyed at the sumptuous room. The carved oak paneling, the plush velvet, the glittering crystal chandeliers, even now askew and dimmed, were beyond anything they could have imagined. As the wife and children stood stock-still, momentarily mesmerized by the dying splendor, the husband, his face a mask of grim urgency, grabbed their hands. "Avanti! Avanti!" he hissed, pulling them onward, deeper into the first-class maze, desperately seeking the way up to the boats, towards an escape that seemed increasingly remote.

Nearby, on the steeply tilting expanse of the forward Grand Staircase landing, Hudson and Bess Allison stumbled, their faces fraught with a unique agony. Bess clutched their two-year-old daughter, Loraine, tightly in her arms, while Hudson scanned the remaining clusters of people with frantic eyes.

"Where can they be, Hudson?" Bess cried, her voice cracking. "Alice and Trevor...they have to be somewhere!"

"Come on, Bess, we have to keep moving!" Hudson pleaded, his own voice strained with unspeakable fear. "We need to get Loraine up to a lifeboat, now!"

Loraine, wrapped in her nervous mother's embrace, looked around at the evolving chaos – the strange angle of the floor, the anxious faces, the distant, haunting music – her small face a picture of confusion. She didn't understand what was happening, only that her parents radiated an almost unbearable tension. "It'll be alright, Mommy," she piped up, her childish voice surprisingly clear amidst the noise. "Mr. Andrews will make sure we're alright. He promised me a playroom."

Bess, caught in the maelstrom of her emotions, passionately kissed her daughter's hair, squeezing her even tighter, the innocent faith a sharp pang in her heart. The trio pushed their way out onto the port side of the Boat Deck, instinctively following the brave, incongruous sounds of Titanic's orchestra, still playing just outside the entrance.

The musicians, their faces masked in bravery, reached the end of a surprisingly jaunty tune. Wallace Hartley, the band leader, lowered his violin for a moment, his gaze sweeping over the remaining passengers, the grimly working crew, and landing briefly on the frantic Allison family as they hurried past, heading forward towards the bridge wing. The sight of little Loraine, her eyes wide with confusion, the utter desperation on Bess Allison's face...something seemed to crystallize for Hartley. The time for light airs was over. It was every man for himself, or perhaps, for something greater.

"Gentlemen," he addressed his small ensemble, his voice quiet. They all looked at their leader, instruments held ready. "You are, without a doubt, the finest group of musicians I have ever had the honor of playing alongside." He managed a small, sad smile. "And it has been a privilege. A real privilege." He gave a solemn nod, a silent release from their duties.

The men exchanged quick, knowing glances, some shaking hands briefly. One or two began to pack their instruments, ready to disperse, to seek their own slim chance. But Wallace Hartley remained fixed in place, his gaze following the Allisons as they finally spotted Captain Smith and Thomas Andrews on the port bridge wing. Then, lifting his violin to his chin, he drew the bow across the strings. The solo strain, sweet and achingly familiar, pierced the night: Nearer, My God, to Thee.

He carried the first measure alone, a fragile melody against the moans of the dying ship. Then, one by one, his bandsmen, moved by an unspoken accord, turned back. A cello joined in, then another violin, then the viola, the bass...until the entirety of the ensemble was restored, the swell of the poignant hymn stretching out across the steeply tilting, chaotic decks, a tender, heartbreaking closure to Titanic's final moments.

"Mr. Andrews! Captain!" Hudson Allison called out desperately as he reached the two men on the bridge wing. The deck slanted precariously here, and the gurgling, sucking sounds of water engulfing the forecastle just below were terrifyingly loud, vibrating through the very soles of their shoes.

"Mrs. Allison! Loraine!" Andrews exclaimed, his face wreathed with concern as he recognized them. "What are you still doing here?! I thought you were seen to a boat!"

"We're looking for my son, Trevor!" Hudson explained frantically. "His nurse, Alice Cleaver...she ran off with him hours ago, we think, and we've been searching everywhere!"

"We're going to stay and look for him," Bess chimed in, her voice trembling but resolute. "But we need to get Loraine to a lifeboat! Please, Mr. Andrews! Where is there a boat?"

Andrews's eyes, already filled with sorrow, became glossy as he looked down at little Loraine, then up at her terrified parents. He knew the grim inventory of remaining boats. "There are no more boats," he said, his voice barely a whisper, the words like a death knell.

"No more...?" Bess trailed off, her hand flying to her mouth, a sob escaping.

"But...there has to be..." Hudson stammered, his face ashen.

"I am so very sorry," Captain Smith said gravely, his voice heavy with the weight of their collective fate.

A moment of tense, unbearable silence hung between them, punctuated only by the final, fading notes of the hymn carried on the frozen wind.

"Mr. Andrews," Loraine piped up then, her small voice cutting through the despair, not an ounce of trepidation in her tone, only absolute, innocent certainty. "You'll think of something. Won't you? Like my playroom?"

The child's unwavering faith, her innocent reminder of a promise made in a different lifetime, seemed to pierce through Andrews's exhaustion. His eyes, initially crestfallen, raised to meet the mature, trusting gaze of the two-year-old girl still clinging to her mother's arms. Something shifted in his expression – a flicker of determination, a refusal to surrender entirely.

He gave a weary, but suddenly resolute smile. "The rafts," he said, his voice gaining strength, turning to Captain Smith, his gaze darting upwards. "The Engelhardt collapsibles! Up on the roof of the officers' quarters! There are still two on the port side, A and B!"

"Mr. Andrews, there's no time..." Smith began, knowing how difficult they were to launch. "The deck is already—"

"Nonsense, Captain!" Andrews retorted, his voice urgent now. "We have to try! For her! For all of them!"

A flicker of decisive energy returned to Captain Smith's exhausted face. He gave a curt nod. "Men!" he roared, his voice suddenly powerful again, cutting through the night. "Give us a hand here! To the roof of the officers' quarters! We need to get these collapsibles down...now!" He gestured towards any crewmen or able-bodied passengers standing nearby, urging them to assist in the desperate, last-ditch effort.

Monday Morning, April 15th, 1912
   Approx. 2:05 AM
   Marconi Wireless Room

The small Marconi cabin, high on the Titanic's rapidly slanting Boat Deck, felt like the last outpost of a dying world. Jack Phillips, his exhausted face streaked with sweat under the dimming electric light, still hunched over the Morse key, his fingers tapping out the distress call – CQD, SOS – with a desperate, almost mechanical persistence. The spark from the transmitter was noticeably weaker now, the hum from the motor-generator faltering as the ship's main power dipped precariously with each lurch and tremor from below.

Harold Bride stood beside him, looking wearily on, feeling the increasing tilt of the deck beneath his feet. "Jack, the signal's nearly gone," he said quietly. "She can't take much more."

"Damn it!" Phillips slammed his fist lightly on the table. "The backup set, Bride! Switch us over! Get the emergency dynamo powered up! We have to keep sending!" He knew, with a desperate certainty, that every fading dit and dah might be the one that made the difference.

"Phillips, you're talking to yourself, mate!" Bride pleaded.

A breathless Phillips looked at his partner, his gaze serious. "We have to try."

"Right, then," Bride nodded, moving quickly to the auxiliary transmitter and its independent battery power source, a small motor-generator in the adjoining silent cabin, hoping it could still punch a signal through the increasingly chaotic ether. As he worked, the door to the wireless room creaked open against the severe angle of the floor, and Captain Smith stepped heavily inside.

His uniform was immaculate, though his face bore an almost unbearable weariness. Yet, through the exhaustion, his eyes still held the dignity of a seasoned commander facing the ultimate test, refusing to give in until the very end. Phillips and Bride instinctively straightened, snapping to a semblance of attention despite the chaos.

"Gentlemen," Captain Smith said, his voice soft but carrying over the hum of the failing equipment and the distant, terrible sounds of the ship's final moments – breaking glass, splintering wood, the wailing churn of a leviathan giving up the ghost. "My officers and I thank you for your service. You have both done yourselves, and your company proud tonight. Beyond the call of duty." He paused, his gaze meeting each of theirs in turn. "But now...now it is every man for himself. I release you from your duties." He offered a faint, grim smile. "Godspeed to you both."

Both young operators looked at each other, the finality of the Captain's words sinking in. Phillips, however, turned back to the key almost immediately.

With that, Captain Smith gave a brief, almost imperceptible nod, then turned and exited the cabin, leaving them alone with the dying spark and the weight of his final command.

Phillips's fingers flew again, sending out another desperate call into the night.

"Phillips!" Bride implored, stepping towards him. "Jack, what are you doing? You heard the Captain! We haven't much time left! The power's nearly gone!"

As Bride pleaded for his partner to abandon the failing set and save himself, the cabin door, already ajar from the Captain's departure, met another unexpected guest. A soot-stained stoker, his eyes wide and desperate, poked his head inside, his gaze immediately fixing on a spare life vest lying on a chair in the small room.

"Hey! Get out of here!" Bride shouted instinctively.

But the stoker ignored him, lunging for the vest, grabbing it and hastily trying to pull it over his head, clearly intending to bolt.

Phillips was off his chair in an instant, all thought of Morse code vanishing, replaced by a primal fury. He slammed into the stoker, pinning the man against the wall. The stoker, desperate, shoved Phillips back hard, breaking free, and made a dash for the door, the stolen life vest half on. Phillips, with a roar of anger, launched himself after the man, delivering a hard, cracking blow to the side of the stoker's head. The man crumpled to the deck, unconscious.

"Blimey, Phillips!" Bride breathed, staring at the downed man. "I think you might've killed him."

"Serves him right, the bloody bastard," Phillips panted, retrieving his own life vest from where the stoker had dropped it. He pulled it on quickly, securing the straps. He looked at Bride, who was already wearing his. "Well, that's that then."

With a final, grim look around the small cabin that had been their world, Phillips reached over and decisively threw the main switch for the Marconi power unit, plunging the set into complete silence. The faint hum died, leaving only the groans of the ship and the distant, terrible sounds of its demise.

"Come on," Phillips said, his voice rough. Together, the two wireless operators turned and stepped out of the silent Marconi room, into the freezing, final moments of the RMS Titanic.

Monday Morning, April 15th, 1912
Approx. 2:10 AM onwards
Starboard Boat Deck & The Grand Staircase

The fragile peace we'd found in the Smoking Room shattered the moment we stepped back out onto the steep terrain of the Boat Deck. The chaos had intensified, the ship's downward angle by the bow now alarmingly severe. Water lapped at the forward end of A Deck below us, and the groans from the ship's structure were more frequent, more terrifying. There weren't many people left on this forward starboard side, near the officers' quarters. A little way off, J.J. Astor sat stoically in a deck chair, Kitty cradled in his arms, the dog whimpering softly.

Miles and I clung to each other, partly for warmth against the biting coldness of the dropping temperature, partly for the sheer terror that gripped us. We said little, the bond we'd just affirmed in the Smoking Room now a silent lifeline. We watched the stars, impossibly bright in the moonless sky, disappear with horrifying speed behind the raised davit of the forwardmost, now empty, boat station. It was our only gauge of how fast the ship was truly going down by the head.

"It's going faster now," I thought aloud, my voice merely a vapor amongst the distant, terrible sounds of the ship tearing herself apart.

Miles didn't respond. His silence, after the torrent of words and emotions we'd shared, caught my attention. I turned to him. "Miles?"

He looked at me, his eyes glossy with unshed tears, reflecting the faint glow of the deck lamps. He tried to muster a genuine smile, but it was a fragile thing.

"What are you thinking?" I whispered, my own fear momentarily overshadowed by his.

"I...I'm so scared, Benj," he choked out, the words quiet, raw. "So very scared."

"Miles, look at me..." I took his face in my hands, assertively, needing him to focus, to believe me. His skin was like ice. "I can't swim, Benji," he confessed, his voice trembling. "Not a stroke."

"But I can," I insisted, my voice firmer than I felt. "I told you. I'm an excellent swimmer, alright?" I held his gaze, trying to pour every ounce of conviction I possessed into my next words. "I am not going to let anything happen to you. I promise."

He searched my eyes, wanting to believe, perhaps. He nodded slowly, a single, almost imperceptible movement, trying to project a bravery I knew neither of us truly felt.

Suddenly, a hoarse voice roared from above us, near the roof of the officers' quarters. "That's it, men! Push! Heave!"

We looked forward. Crewmen, their faces contorted with effort, were desperately trying to maneuver one of the heavy, canvas-sided collapsible boats down from the roof, using oars propped against the bulkhead as makeshift ramps.

"Three! Two! One! *PUSH!*"

With a sickening *CRASH*, the heavy boat tumbled from the roof, sideways, toppling upside down onto the Boat Deck with a thunderous, splintering blast, scattering the men who had been trying to launch it.

I turned back to Miles, my heart sinking. That was one less chance. "They're not going to have enough time to right it, let alone launch it..." My voice trailed off. The water was visibly creeping up the forward end of the Boat Deck now.

"We... we should go further aft," Miles stammered, his eyes wide with terror. "The stern...it's still high..."

"No," I said, my mind racing, trying to think, trying to remember everything I'd ever read about sinking ships, about survival. "No, the suction will be worse there when the ship..." I couldn't bring myself to say the word. "It's better to jump from here. Closer to the water. Further from the propellers when she goes."

"Jump?" Miles whispered, his voice trembling uncontrollably. "Into that?" He gestured towards the black, freezing water that now seemed to be rushing up to meet us.

"Come on," I said, more forcefully than I intended, holding out my hand. Just then, a deep, violent BOOM erupted from somewhere deep within the belly of the ship, an ominous tremor rumbling up through the deck plates, shaking us both. An explosion.

Miles stared at me, his face a mask of terror, then his eyes found mine, a silent question, a plea. He took my outstretched hand, his grip icy, desperate. I helped him clamber over the slanting rail, then I followed until we were both standing on the narrow ledge, face to face with the empty, almost invisible void of the sea below. One hand holding his, one hand holding onto Titanic, freezing steel biting into my fingers. We stood there, balanced precariously, the chill biting at us, the sounds of chaos behind us, the black water beckoning below. Terrified anticipation.

"Benji...I..." Miles began, his voice choked.

I couldn't bear to hear his fear, couldn't bear to think of what was about to happen. I leaned in and kissed him, one final, desperate, loving kiss against the backdrop of silver stars and a dying ship. Then, urgently, pulling back, "On the count of three."

Our voices joined, thin against the rushing water and the ship's groans. "One... two..."

As we both tensed to say "three," to make that final, terrible leap, an ear-splitting *CRACK* from behind us, louder than any sound I'd ever heard, ripped through the night, pulling my focus involuntarily, fatally, away from Miles.

The braided steel cable stays supporting the massive forward funnel, pulled impossibly taut by the ship's increasing downward plunge, snapped like gunfire, one after another. Then came the sound of rending, splitting steel, another angry, guttural groan from the ship as the six-story funnel began to tilt, to fold into itself. Tons of metal flexing as if it were cardboard.

"Lookout!" someone screamed from further aft. Terrified shouts followed. People scrambled. The funnel dangled precariously forward.

The ship gave a sudden, violent lurch, sending a cascade of icy seawater surging up over the forward railing, washing across the already tilting deck towards us. Officers and men still struggling with the overturned collapsible screamed, trying to get clear.

The tsunami of water, a dark, unstoppable wave, caught the base of the brittle, weakened funnel, ripping it from its bearings with a final, agonizing shriek of tortured metal. It plunged into a horrifying freefall.

"Oh my god!" I cried, instinctively looking back towards the sea, desperately trying to spot Miles, but he was gone, vanished into the blackness. It hadn't even been ten seconds since we'd been together, ready to jump, but every second now felt like an eternity.

The funnel gave one final, mournful cry and dived towards the icy water where Miles had just been. I closed my eyes, took a desperate breath, and jumped – pushing myself as far out, as far away from the falling mass and the sinking ship as my terrified muscles would allow.

The impact with the freezing water stole my breath, a brutal, shocking cold that seized my very core. But worse was to come. The funnel hit the water with an apocalyptic splash, creating a furious surge, a deadly, irresistible wash that caught me in its undertow. Instead of being propelled away, I was swept violently back towards the ship, slammed with bone-jarring force against the steel hull, then dragged upwards against the windows of the A-Deck Promenade. The glass shattered around me, sucking me into the ship, back onto the enclosed deck, amidst a torrent of foaming, freezing surf.

The water was already climbing the steeply tilted promenade, a churning river of debris. It caught me, sending me careening, tumbling, towards the arch-topped windows of the forward Grand Staircase entrance. Again, the glass exploded inwards against the powerful force of the angry sea, the suction pulling me relentlessly in. I was spilled onto the polished floor of the landing, across the checkered patterns, slamming into, and splintering the level railing that connected this level to the one below, then immediately sucked downwards by the surging, breaching waves.

Down, down I fell, through the magnificent, open chasm of the Grand Staircase – my favorite view on the entire ship now a terrifying waterfall. A Deck, B Deck, C Deck, D Deck...I caught fleeting, nightmarish glimpses of horrified onlookers clinging to railings on the upper landings, their faces painted blurs in the amber warmth of dying electric lights, watching me fall as if in slow-motion.

Then, *SPLASH!*

I landed hard in the swirling, churning pool of icy water, the impact driving the air from my lungs, the shock of the frigid Atlantic a brutal awakening. Disoriented, in agonizing pain from where I'd slammed into the railing, I was submerged in the now-flooded E-deck level of the Grand Staircase. The muffled, groaning sounds of the dying ship vibrated through the water around me, a monstrous death rattle. Far above, the ornate dome was gone, replaced by a torrent of incoming sea, the lights submerged beneath the waves casting a sickly, spectral phosphorescent glow beneath the watery abyss.

For a moment, despair threatened to pull me under. The sheer force of the water, the crushing weight of the disaster, the knowledge of the ship's imminent end...what was the point? My survival instinct, battered and bruised, felt as weak as the wailing ship itself. Miles...was he safe? Had he made it? The thought of him, of the future we'd so desperately clung to just moments ago, a future now likely lost, was an unbearable ache.

Then, like a jolt of electricity, his face flashed in my mind – his smile, his eyes, his hand in mine. I'm not going to let anything happen to you. My own promise. And Astor's words: Never stop listening to that voice. That still, small voice inside, no longer a whisper, but a desperate shout: Live! For him! For yourself!

With a surge of adrenaline born of that thought, I pushed against the debris, fighting the current, kicking towards what I hoped was upwards. My head broke the surface, gasping for air, into a scene of nightmarish mayhem. I was at the E-deck landing of the Grand Staircase, the waist-deep water already drowning lower stairs and rising fast. Clawing at the banister, I pulled myself out of the churning water, collapsing onto the slanting, wet carpet of the Reception Room floor.

The vast room, usually a haven of light and elegance, was a dark, dying cavern. The main lights were out, but emergency lamps flickered intermittently, casting long, dancing shadows, creating brief, horrifying flashes of sickly green illumination, like looking up from beneath the waves. The air was filled with the heaving gulps of a dying monster – the Titanic herself – a sound that vibrated through my very bones, holding me captive in her belly. Then, another sound: a rushing, gurgling torrent as water poured in from broken windows and unseen breaches.

FLASH!

The emergency lights pulsed, briefly illuminating the tilting, water-slicked room. And in that faint, eerie green glow, I saw her. Standing near a doorway, clinging to the frame, her face a mask of terror but her eyes searching frantically.

"Mother!" I cried, scrambling to my feet, ignoring the pain.

"Oh, Benji! My Benji!" She saw me, her voice breaking with relief and anguish. She stumbled towards me, and I met her halfway, pulling her into a desperate hug. She kissed my wet hair, my cheek, clinging to me.

"Mother, what are you doing here? You were in a boat! Birdie—"

"I know, Benji," she whispered fiercely, her voice trembling against my ear. "I know. About Miles. About...everything. I know."

I pulled back slightly, staring at her, stunned into silence.

Her eyes, even in the dim, flickering light, burned with a fierce, unwavering love. "I am so, so proud of you, my son," she said, her hands framing my face. "So proud of the man you are. I love you so much, Benji. So much." She embraced me again, a warm, solid presence against the cold terror.

"Return the boats! Return to the ship!" a man's voice, tinny and distorted, suddenly echoed from somewhere outside, carried faintly through the darkness, amplified perhaps by a megaphone. "There are still people here! Row back!"

"What's that?" I asked, pulling away from Mother, straining to hear.

"They're calling back the boats," a familiar voice said from the shadows nearby. Father. He stepped into a flickering pool of light, his dinner jacket askew, his face grim, but strangely, surprisingly, sober.

"Your father is helping," Mother said quickly, a strained smile on her face as she looked between us. "He's been trying to direct people, find a way out for those still trapped down here." She managed a watery, almost manic laugh. "Look at us, Benji! Me and my men, together again." The words, meant to be comforting, perhaps, felt surreal, disconnected from the horrifying reality closing in.

The ship gave another violent lurch forward, the deck beneath our feet dropping sickeningly. "Come on!" Father urged, his voice suddenly sharp with urgency. "We haven't got much time. The gangway doors on the port side. They're open..."

Then, all at once, another deafening groan from the ship's core gave way to an ear-splitting tear – the shriek of massive steel plates twisting, buckling, surrendering. The floor vibrated violently, then seemed to drop, tilting even more steeply. Around us, the magnificent stained-glass windows of the Reception Room exploded inwards with a deafening crash. The emergency lights went out, plunging us into absolute blackness, then flared back for one horrifying, strobe-like instant.

"Benji!"

Mother's face, illuminated in that final, ghastly green glow, was wrought in an extremity of terror that made her features almost inhuman. Her eyes, her mouth, stretched to their absolute limit, a silent scream. Her eyes penetrated mine, pleading, desperate, begging me to help her, to save her.

Then the lights died completely, for good this time.

"Benji!" Her scream, no longer silent, ripped through the darkness, louder than ever, palpable with fear, with anguish.

And then, an explosive, cataclysmic rush of water. The D-deck Reception Room was instantly, violently submerged. I was thrown upwards, the buoyancy of my life vest a curse now, slamming me against the ornate plasterwork ceiling, pinning me there, unable to move, disoriented in the churning, freezing blackness.

This was it. The end. There was nothing I could do. I couldn't see. I was trapped. Utterly useless. Maybe Miles was already gone. Mother. Birdie. Perhaps it was better this way, to just let go...

No!

That still, small voice, Astor's voice, Miles's belief, my own desperate will – it wasn't just shouting now; it was pulling me, driving me. I wouldn't die here, not like this, not trapped in the dark heart of this dying beast.

My hands flailed in the darkness, feeling around, fingers tracing the cold, submerged plasterwork of the ceiling. I pulled myself against the vest's relentless upward pressure, fighting towards where I thought, hoped, a way out might be. A faint, distant glimmer of greenish light...the open gangway door further forward? It had to be.

I pulled, and pulled, dragging myself along the ceiling. My vest snagged on something sharp – the ornamental brass finial of a light fixture, the very one that had cast its approving radiance over me and Miles as we danced in what felt like another lifetime, only hours ago. It held me fast. Panic surged. I twisted, tore, felt the canvas rip, felt myself scrape against the metal, then I was free, propelling myself towards that faint, life-saving light.

Everything in the room seemed to conspire against me now, unseen debris swirling in the black water, pulling at my clothes, ghostly arms reaching viciously, trying to snuff the life out of me. But the light was closer. There. The door. Almost.

Reaching the upper frame of the open gangway doorway, I grabbed hold, pulling myself down against the vest's buoyancy, fighting to get through the opening. And then... *WHOOSH!*

The life-saving superpower of my vest, the very thing that had tried to trap me against the ceiling of the dying ship, now asserted its true purpose. It catapulted me upwards, out of the black, crushing confines of the ship's interior, through the open doorway, and into the freezing, star-dusted, terrifying expanse of the open sea, with a vengeance.

Monday Morning, April 15th, 1912
   Approx. 2:10 AM onwards
   Lower Decks, Aft Third Class

The lower decks of the aft third-class section were a cacophony of terror. The Titanic's great hull shuddered violently now, the walls trembling, quaking like a wounded beast, the sound thunderous, all-encompassing. Lights flickered ominously, dark shadows reaching down the narrow, pitching corridors, threatening to plunge them into absolute darkness at any moment. The once sturdy, mighty vessel felt like a fractured levee, living on borrowed seconds.

Birdie had managed to guide a small group towards a less-crowded aft companionway, pushing them upwards. She gave a final, urgent instruction to a young Swedish man, paralyzed with fear. "Gå nu! Snälla, gå!" she urged, pointing up the stairs. As he finally stumbled away, Oliver came running towards her from a dark adjoining hallway, his face serious.

"Birdie!" he shouted, his voice nearly lost in the reverberant echo of shivering steel and distant crashes, even though he was only feet away. He'd clearly been trying doors, rousing anyone left behind. "You must go, too! Quickly! There may be only minutes! The water is rising fast below!"

BANG!

A deafening explosion from somewhere forward thundered along the length of Scotland Road, the sound barreling towards them like an express train, followed by a fresh wave of screams from further down the corridor they'd just directed people through. The deck beneath their feet bucked violently.

"Alright! Come on!" Birdie cried, grabbing his arm, turning to run for the staircase leading up towards the aft well deck, towards open air.

CLANG.

The harsh, metallic sound of a closing gate rang out just behind her. She stopped instantly, spinning back. Oliver stood on the other side of a heavy, barred metal gate – one of the many designed to keep classes separate – his hand still on the latch he'd just thrown, locking himself in, locking her out.

"Oliver! What in God's name are you—"

"Go, Birdie, please!" he pleaded, his face faded in the flickering emergency light, his eyes dark with a terrible resolve as he peered at her through the cold metal grate.

"Oliver! No! Open this gate!" She rattled it furiously, but it was solid, unyielding.

"Birdie, I told you," his voice was quiet now, almost tender amidst the chaos. "You don't know the things I've done. The man I am. I don't deserve to live. But you..." He reached a hand through the bars, his fingers gently, reverently, stroking her hair back from her terrified face. "...you are the hope that I still have for the world. I know it'll be a brighter tomorrow, Birdie, if you're in it."

"Oh, Oliver," she whispered, tears streaming down her face, her hands gripping the cold bars separating them. She leaned her forehead against the grate.

He wiped a tear from her cheek with his thumb, his touch surprisingly gentle. "Take care of yourself, now. My dear, brave Birdie."

She surged forward, pressing her lips to his through the grate, a fierce, desperate, heartbreaking kiss – a goodbye she didn't want to accept, a finality that tore at her soul. The lights pulsed violently, then dimmed to a mere reddish glow, plunging them into near darkness, then flickered back, just barely enough to see the lines of his face.

"Go on, Birdie!" he urged, his voice cracking. "Live!"

She hesitated, her heart shattering.

"LIVE, BIRDIE!" Oliver screamed, his voice raw, desperate, pushing her away with his words. Just then, a new sound joined the dying throes of the ship – the horrifying, unmistakable roar of rushing water, churning down the once-swarming thoroughfare of Scotland Road, not far behind him.

That final, desperate command, the sound of the approaching water, finally broke her paralysis. With a sob that tore from her throat, Birdie pushed away from the gate, turned, and bounded for the stairs.

Level after level she climbed in the terrifying, flickering near-darkness, the steep, slanting angle of the stairways fighting her, tripping her at nearly every step. Debris rained down from above. The screams of those still trapped below echoed in the narrow passages, along with her own, uncontrolled breathing. But Oliver's final word – Live! – propelled her forward with an unbridled, desperate determination. Her lungs burned, her legs ached, but she forced herself on, scrambling over obstacles, pulling herself up by railings, driven by a primal need to survive, to honor his sacrifice.

Finally, gasping for breath, her clothes torn, her body bruised, she burst through a heavy door and stumbled out onto the open, steeply angled expanse of the aft well deck, greeted by the overwhelming, impossible beauty of an endless sky packed with cold, luminous stars. And the terrifying, slanting view of the Titanic's stern rising high into the night.

Monday Morning, April 15th, 1912
   Approx. 2:18 AM onwards
The North Atlantic

I broke the surface with a choked gasp, spluttering, spitting out freezing salt-water, my lungs burning. For a disorienting second, there was only the sting of the arctic air on my wet face and the overwhelming roar of what sounded like a thousand tortured souls.

Then I saw her.

The Titanic. Or what was left of her. Against the impossibly bright, watchful stars, her stern section loomed, a colossal, sharply angled silhouette, a long black finger pointing accusingly from the deep, reaching towards the heavens, momentarily blocking out a swathe of the cosmos. The water around me was a frenzy of struggling bodies, bobbing heads, screams of terror and pain, desperate prayers, choked sobs – a symphony of human agony.

"MILES!" I screamed, my voice raw, instantly swallowed by the deafening cacophony of the night. I thrashed in the water, searching wildly, desperately, for any sign of him, but there was only the churning, debris-strewn sea and the cries of the dying.

Then, a deep, violent rumble surged up from beneath me, an explosion from the ship's submerged depths, vibrating through the water, through my very bones. The Titanic gave a tremendous, sickening shudder. CRUNCH! CRASH! The sound of bending, twisting, shearing steel – tons of it – ripped through the night, a horrifying, metallic scream. Sparks, brilliant and incongruous, suddenly ignited along the lifeless, angled profile of the ship, a brief, ghastly fireworks display as her stern, overcome by the immense weight of her flooded engines, began to crush inwards, visibly contorting, breaking apart.

The unimaginable was happening. The great liner was splitting in two.

More shattering glass, the distant crash of china, a chorus of groans and tearing sounds – the ship herself seemed to cry out in agony as she was forced to accept her final, brutal fate. Bodies, tiny dark figures against the faint light, leaped from the still-rising stern section into the black water. Debris – deck chairs, planks of wood, unidentifiable wreckage – rained down around us. Geysers of water and steam plumed into the still night from within her fractured hull.

Then, with an angry, vengeful roar, the stern, now separated from the bow section already lost to the depths, seemed to crash back down into the water with an enormous splash, righting itself momentarily, as if it were all just some terrible, vivid nightmare, and she might yet float.

A nightmare, indeed. For a moment or two, I watched, treading water, numb with cold and horror, as she sat there, grotesquely upright, still impossibly huge. Perhaps... perhaps she could stay afloat, now that the deadweight of the flooded bow was no longer dragging her down?

But it was a fleeting, foolish hope. Slowly, pitifully, her stern began to dip into the water, head-first, once more. The angle increased, slowly, then faster, much, much faster she plunged. The screams from those still aboard, those clinging to her railings, intensified.

The black hull of the stern rose higher, pointing almost directly upwards now, perpendicular to the starlit sky, a ghostly, dark skyscraper looming impossibly against the constellations. She seemed to hang there for an eternal, suspended moment, poised between two worlds. Then, with a final, sighing surrender, she began to glide, smoothly, almost gently, like an elevator descending into the earth – down, down, down.

The remaining embers of light within her flickered, then died, plunging her into complete darkness. Silently, inexorably, she slid beneath the waves, until finally, every last inch of her magnificent, tragic form had been claimed by the vengeful sea.

The Titanic was gone.

CHAPTER 40

For one, single, lingering second, the entire world stopped. An absolute, profound silence descended, so complete, so unearthly, the only sound I could register was the ragged, shivering gasp of my own breath, loud in the sudden stillness.

Then, it began.

A low roar, like a monstrous intake of breath from the ocean itself, swelled from the darkness around me. It grew, moment by moment, into a sound I will carry to my grave – a chorus not of cicadas on a warm June night, as my disoriented mind first tried to grasp, but the collective, unbearable wail of the dying. Fifteen hundred souls, thrown into the freezing, black Atlantic, crying out, their moans, their prayers, their terrified screams merging into one continuous, deafening cry of human agony.

I squeezed my eyes shut, trying desperately to drown out the sound, trying to transport myself anywhere but here. Baker Bowl, I told myself frantically, the World Series, Phillies fighting for the pennant, the roar of twenty thousand fans cheering... "Yeah," I whispered, trying to convince myself through chattering teeth, "that's where I am, that's what's happening." This wasn't the sound of a thousand souls dying, the sounds of unimaginable pain, of fear and loss...

But no sooner had I admitted the horrifying reality to myself, I realized I too was screaming, or perhaps just whimpering, a raw, animal sound torn from my own throat, indistinguishable from the chorus around me. My body, my mind, no longer felt under my control. I was a puppet, its movements jerky and uncoordinated, pulled by the deadly, numbing chill of the icy water. Minutes. I knew I only had minutes if I wanted to survive. I had to get out of this water. But how?

All I could see in every direction, in the faint, cruel starlight, were scattered life vests, dark shapes in the black water, their inhabitants flailing desperately, thrashing, crying out, just as lost, just as terrified as I was.

"Miles!" I choked out his name, the sound swallowed by the overwhelming void. Where was he? Had he made it? The thought of him, the memory of our last kiss, the promise I'd made – I am not going to let anything happen to you – it was a fresh stab of agony, but also, impossibly, a spark.

Just then, a shrill sound pierced through the chaos – a whistle, perhaps. Muffled by the water frozen in my ears, it was more of a vibration at first, a distant, rhythmic disturbance, a realization that something, an object, was happening, moving, existing somewhere behind me. It drew me towards it, an instinct beyond reason.

I began to swim, or rather, claw my way through the water as best I could, my limbs heavy, numb, fighting for control of my own body. Sometimes I felt myself making progress, sometimes I felt the current pulling me back, but I never slowed, driven by that faint sound, by the desperate need to escape the open water. I pushed past debris, past the heartbreaking cries, fighting through the dark havoc, until I could feel the source of the sound coming closer.

Finally, my stinging eyes caught a glint of something – hazy, white, perhaps thirty feet away. An object. With the last dregs of strength I possessed, fueled by a desperate surge of adrenaline, I broke for it in a frantic, clumsy tear.

There it was. The overturned collapsible boat from the starboard deck, the one that had crashed upside down. Still belly-up, a dozen or so men teetered precariously on its slick, submerged hull, trying desperately to maintain their balance, outlined against the starlit sky.

"Help! Please!" I shouted, my voice a hoarse croak as I neared the swamped raft.

"There! In the water! Another one!" I faintly heard a familiar, cultured voice call out from the boat.

As I reached the edge of the overturned collapsible, a strong, vice-like grip seized my arm, hauling me unceremoniously from the freezing water, dragging me onto the slippery, unstable surface. I collapsed, gasping, shivering uncontrollably, water pouring from my clothes.

My eyes slowly focused on the distinguished face, the neatly trimmed mustache, the weak but kind smile of the Southern gentleman who had pulled me aboard.

"Ah, Benji, my boy," Colonel Archibald Gracie said, his voice strained but steady, already chafing my numb arms, trying to bring warmth back. "It'll be alright now. You're safe with us." He continued rubbing my arms and legs vigorously. "There we are, that's right. Deep breaths. Stay with us, son." His experience field dressing wounds on the battlefield was undoubtedly serving him, and now me, in this critical, desperate moment.

As I worked to keep conscious, my vision swimming in and out of focus, I scanned the other men crowded onto the precarious platform. Just behind Gracie, I saw him – young Harold Bride, the wireless operator, his face like a ghost. But he didn't see me. Like Gracie, he too was playing savior to a friend, cradling the hunched, unmoving form of Jack Phillips in his arms.

"Come on, Phillips! Stay awake, man!" Bride urged desperately, shaking his senior partner gently. "Come on, damn it! Wake up!" I heard him cry, his voice cracking with grief.

Second Officer Lightoller, who seemed to be organizing the men, trying to keep the swamped boat balanced, placed a gentle hand on Bride's shoulder. "I'm afraid it's too late for him, son," Lightoller said quietly, his voice heavy with sorrow. "He's gone."

"No!" Bride cried, a choked sob escaping him. "Phillips! Wake up!" he pleaded silently now, clutching his friend tighter, a part of him clearly dying along with the man in his arms, lost to the unforgiving cold of the North Atlantic night.

The initial, bone-deep chill began to recede slightly, replaced by a painful tingling as warmth, however slight, returned to my limbs. Colonel Gracie's vigorous chafing, and perhaps my own desperate will, had pulled me back from the brink of unconsciousness. I became more alert, the sounds of the night – Bride's quiet sobs for Phillips, Lightoller's low commands, the occasional groan from one of the other men – sharpening into focus. I realized, with a surge of returning survival instinct, that to stay still was to surrender to the cold, to the encroaching numbness. My best chance, for keeping my limbs, for staying alive, was to keep moving, to keep the blood flowing.

Carefully, I shifted, then managed to push myself into a standing position on the slippery, teetering hull. It made more room, a precious few inches on the crowded, precarious platform. In the faint, ghostly light of the stars, I saw other men doing the same, trying to help Lightoller and some of the crewmen pull another dozen or so souls from the black, freezing water. Each rescue was a desperate, gasping struggle, the boat tipping alarmingly with each new addition until it was terrifyingly clear we were at our absolute limit. Any more weight, any sudden shift, would capsize us completely, sending us all back into the unforgiving Atlantic. Lightoller, his voice hoarse but firm, finally called a halt.

Slowly, chillingly, the cacophony of cries that had assaulted my ears when I first surfaced began to die out. The desperate shouts, the prayers, the wails of fifteen hundred voices...they dwindled, one by one, into an eerie, profound stillness, broken only by the gentle, indifferent lapping of water against our swamped boat and the occasional soft moan from one of the men beside me. The silence, in its own way, was more terrifying than the noise.

As my eyes adjusted further to the darkness, I could make out the wreckage scattered all around us – pieces of wood, deck chairs, cork, unidentifiable debris...and darker shapes, still, unmoving, bobbing gently in the swell. Bodies. The stars above, ever brilliant in the clear, frigid sky, seemed to burn with an almost accusatory brightness, as if they were the countless eyes of heaven, silently gossiping to each other, bearing witness to the pitiful, tragic sight unfolding below them.

"Please!" A feeble voice, thin and reedy, suddenly echoed across the dark water nearby, startlingly close. "Help me..."

"There! To starboard!" someone on our boat called out, pointing into the darkness.

"We haven't any more room," another voice rebuffed immediately, flat with exhaustion and despair. "We'll swamp her."

"Please, sirs! For the love of God, help me!" The voice was closer now, the figure of a man, barely visible, swimming weakly alongside our overturned boat, his hand reaching out.

A grim silence fell upon our small, precarious island of survivors. Then, Second Officer Lightoller's voice cut through, strained but resolute. "Have we any dead aboard?" he asked, his gaze sweeping over the huddled forms.

A moment passed, then someone near Harold Bride spoke up, his voice hushed. "The wireless operator, sir. Mr. Phillips. He...he hasn't moved in a while."

Lightoller looked towards Bride, who was still cradling his senior partner, shielding him from the worst of the cold, his face a mask of grief. "Mr. Bride," Lightoller said, his voice surprisingly gentle. "We need the room. I'm sorry."

Harold Bride looked down pityingly at his friend, his shoulders shaking with silent sobs. After a long, agonizing moment of hesitation, he leaned down and pressed a final, solemn kiss to Phillips's cold forehead. Then, with infinite care, he gently guided his friend's body over the side of the boat and into the dark water, where it was silently reclaimed by the sea. He didn't watch it go, just turned back, his face buried in his hands, weeping without sound.

A wave of profound sorrow and respect washed over us all, a shared, silent acknowledgment of the sacrifice, of the loss. Then, duty, harsh and unyielding, called Lightoller back to action. "Right, men," he instructed, gesturing towards the struggling swimmer. "Let's pull him on. Gently now."

Several hands reached out, and the nearly frozen man was hauled aboard, collapsing onto the space Phillips had just vacated.

I timidly knelt beside Harold Bride, placing a comforting hand on his trembling shoulder. He looked up, his eyes red-rimmed, lost in the dim starlight. "Benji," he whimpered, recognizing me.

"Shhh," I said softly, not knowing what else to offer.

There was a slight, almost imperceptible shift in Bride's demeanor then. As if the ingrained habit of duty, like Lightoller's, could find its way even through the deepest grief. "I...I didn't get the chance to send your wires, Benji," he whispered, his voice hoarse, barely audible. "The power went out...just after the Captain...I...I'm so sorry."

I took this in. My words, Miles's words, our defiant declarations to our fathers, our desperate, hopeful plans...they had stayed on the Titanic, gone down with her. In that moment, I didn't know how I felt about the news. "It's alright, Harold," I reassured him quietly. "Just...rest now."

As the night wore on, an almost unearthly, ethereal glow began to paint the northern horizon. Soft curtains of light, shimmering in delicate hues of pale green, rose pink, and ghostly violet, watercolors dripping from the paintbrush of God, danced silently across the star-dusted sky. The Aurora Borealis. Despite the bone-chilling freeze that gnawed at our limbs, despite the ever-present, bobbing reminders of death surrounding us, despite the profound uncertainty of ever seeing another sunrise, the sheer, unexpected beauty of the Northern Lights took our minds off our plight, even if just for a few precious, awestruck moments. It felt like a message from another world, a silent, beautiful benediction from the heavens themselves.

Throughout the long, dark hours, Lightoller commanded our swamped, overturned boat with quiet authority. Floating upside down, without oars or any means of steering, we were entirely at the mercy of the sea. Our only means of survival was a constant, subtly choreographed dance of balance – shifting our weight minutely this way or that in response to the swell, a collective, unspoken effort to keep our precarious platform above the surface, to keep from being tipped back into the killing cold.

"Is any among us Catholic?" a voice, raspy with cold and exhaustion, spoke up from the huddled mass of men.

"What in God's name does that have to do with anything now?" another chided, his voice sharp with fear.

"I was just wondering," the first voice continued, undeterred, "if anyone might know the Lord's Prayer? I...I thought we might recite it. Together."

A hush fell over the boat. Lightoller, his face grim but moved by the suggestion, nodded slowly. "I think a good many of us, Catholic or not, know that one, friend. Why don't you lead us?"

The man cleared his throat, his voice trembling slightly at first. "Our Father, who art in heaven, hallowed be Thy name..."

One by one, other voices joined his – hesitant at first, then growing stronger, a fragile crescendo of shared faith, or perhaps just shared desperation, rising from the overturned boat into the cold, starlit night. English accents, Irish brogues, perhaps others I couldn't distinguish, all blending into a single, shared chord, a thread of humanity connecting each one of us – from pauper to millionaire, from stoker to officer. In that moment, all class distinctions, all earthly concerns, had vanished. We were simply men, clinging to life, united by a prayer, by the shared defiance of the odds. And in that unity, a sliver of hope: perhaps, just perhaps, we all might live to see another sunrise.

Monday Morning, April 15th, 1912
Approx. 3:30 AM – 4:00 AM onwards
The North Atlantic

The recitation of the Lord's Prayer, a shared murmur against the vast, cold apathy of the ocean, had brought a fragile sense of peace, a momentary respite from the individual terrors that gripped each of us. Now, an exhausted silence settled over Collapsible B. We were a huddled mass of about thirty men, soaked to the bone, teeth chattering uncontrollably, clinging to the slippery, awash hull, shifting our weight with minute precision under Lightoller's occasional, low commands to maintain our precarious balance. The immediate, frantic cries from the wreck site had long since faded into an unbearable, echoing silence, leaving only the gentle tap of water against our swamped craft.

Each man seemed to have fallen into his own silent rhythm of endurance, lost in the processing of the night's horrors, in the fragments of hope for a future that felt impossibly distant, in the haunting "what ifs" that gnawed at the edges of each of our sanity. I closed my eyes, trying to focus on Miles, on the feel of his warm hand in mine, on the defiant joy of our shared dreams, but the images were constantly threatened by the encroaching cold, by the memory of his face vanishing into the black water.

Second Officer Lightoller, his figure a steadfast silhouette against the star-studded northern sky, rarely took his eyes off the dark horizon, his gaze sweeping relentlessly, searching. The Aurora had faded, leaving the darkness even more profound before the first hints of dawn.

Time lost all meaning. It was an eternity of cold, of silence, of barely suppressed despair. Then, Lightoller stiffened.

"Mr. Bride," he called out quietly, his voice hoarse but carrying, careful not to startle the men, "are you awake?"

"Yes, sir," Bride's reply came, equally subdued, from where he huddled near the bow.

"You mentioned the Carpathia was making full speed towards us. Any idea...any estimate at all...when we might expect to see her?"

There was a pause. "She was making good time, sir," Bride said, his voice thin. "From her last signal...I should say another hour or so, sir. Perhaps less, if her captain pushed her hard."

Another hour. Could we last another hour in this killing cold?

Lightoller grunted, then raised his head again, his gaze fixed on a point far off our port side. "There's a light," he murmured, almost to himself. Then louder, "A light, men! Off the port bow!"

A ripple of hushed excitement, of desperate hope, went through our small band. I strained my eyes, following his pointing arm. At first, I saw nothing but the endless, dark water. Then, a faint, distant glimmer. Another. And another. Perhaps...yes, the distinct lights of a ship? Or another lifeboat showing a lantern? My heart leaped.

Lightoller fumbled in his pocket, producing his officer's whistle. He didn't want to get hopes up prematurely, not his own, not his men's. But that distant glimmer...it was too distinct to ignore.

WHEE! WHEE!

The piercing blast of his whistle cut through the pre-dawn stillness, sharp and commanding. He waited, then blew again. *WHEE! WHEE!*

"What's that then?" one of the men near me whispered, pointing now with a trembling finger.

"Look over there!" another called out, his voice cracking. "Another one! And another!"

The faint light we'd first seen seemed to steady, to change course slightly, as if responding. And then, from a different direction, closer, another light appeared, this one rhythmically waving, someone clearly trying to attract attention. It was another lifeboat, perhaps two, approaching.

"Be still, men!" Lightoller ordered sharply, though his voice held a new note of urgency, of hope. He blew his whistle again, a clear, strong signal across the water.

Slowly, agonizingly, the closest lifeboat drew nearer, its occupants pulling weakly on the oars. As it came alongside, its silhouette resolving in the dim starlight.

"Collapsible B, ahoy!" a voice called from Boat 4. "Officer Lightoller, is that you?"

"It is!" Lightoller called back, his voice strong. "We're swamped, barely afloat! Can you take some men?"

The transfer was a careful, perilous operation. Boat 4, already carrying many women and children, maneuvered as close as possible. One by one, with Lightoller supervising, the most exhausted and frozen men from our overturned craft were helped, half-lifted, half-dragged, into the relative safety of the other lifeboat. I found myself being pulled aboard along with Colonel Gracie and a near-catatonic Harold Bride, who still seemed lost in his grief for Phillips. The relief of being on a stable, albeit crowded, platform, out of the constant wash of the freezing water, was indescribable.

Our overturned collapsible, its duty done, was left adrift in the dark sea. I looked back at it as we rowed slowly away, a small, lonely relic, another piece of debris, rocking gently in the swell. A faithful, if unlikely, friend who had saved so many of us from the immediate terror of the Atlantic that night. My heart ached with a strange reverence for the battered, upside-down boat.

The time crept towards four o'clock. A pale, almost imperceptible band of pink began to wrap itself around the eastern horizon, hinting at the approaching dawn. The cold was still intense, but the promise of light brought a renewed flicker of hope.

Then, someone in our boat cried out, pointing. "There! Look! Masthead lights!"

"Pipe down," another voice scoffed wearily from the huddled mass. "It's likely just another lifeboat, man. Don't get your hopes up."

"No! It's not a lifeboat! It's a ship! A proper ship! Look!"

And sure enough, as the sky began to lighten further, there she was. Not one, but two masthead lights, clearly visible now, and below them, the distinct outline of a single-funneled steamer, making steady progress towards us. The Carpathia had arrived.

A ragged cheer went up from our boat, echoed by shouts from the other lifeboats scattered across the now visible, debris-strewn water. Men waved their arms, some produced flashlights, others tore strips from clothing, anything to signal their presence, to guide the rescue ship towards them. The Carpathia steamed valiantly onto the scene, her lone funnel casting a towering billow of black smoke against the paling sky, a symbol of salvation, her boilers clearly having been pushed to their absolute limit through the perilous night.

She slowed as she spotted the fleet of small, fragile lifeboats, her engines stopping. Her black hull became a beacon. One by one, the lifeboats began to coalesce around her flanks, gently encircling her as she prepared to receive us. Gangway doors were opened, ladders dropped, and the painstaking process of withdrawing the survivors of the Titanic from the frigid Atlantic began.

Now, in the growing, revealing glow of the early morning, a new, horrifying vista unfolded around us. As far as the eye could see, the ocean was not empty. We were surrounded. A vast, silent wall of ice – colossal bergs, smaller growlers, vast fields of pack ice – encircled us on all sides, glittering menacingly in the dawn light. The same ice that had not only taken everything from so many, but had also, with callous indifference, been watching us from the shadows all through that terrible, endless night.

CHAPTER 41

Our lifeboat, No. 4, was one of the last to reach the looming black hull of the Carpathia. As we drew alongside, her open gangway doors and cargo ports looked like welcoming mouths, lit by the warm glow spilling out from within. Sailors and stewards lined her rails, ready to assist, while passengers peered over her decks, a few taking pictures of the bizarre sight. The ship herself felt like a beacon of impossible safety in the vast, icy wilderness.

One of the first to be taken aboard from our boat was Harold Bride. The ordeal on Collapsible B had taken a terrible toll on his feet and legs, likely frostbitten, rendering him unable to climb. A makeshift canvas sling was lowered, and he was carefully seated in it, then hoisted gently up the side of the rescue ship like precious cargo. I watched him go, his face pale but relieved, finally safe.

Then, one by one, those of us who could manage it began the slow, arduous climb up the swaying Jacob's ladder that had been dropped down Carpathia's side. As I waited my turn, huddled amongst the other shivering survivors, I spotted Madeleine Astor being helped towards the ladder by a crewman. She looked fragile, her pregnancy evident even under her heavy coats, her face a mask of shock, perhaps unknowingly a widow now, but carrying herself with a quiet dignity. I thought of her husband, J.J., his unexpected kindness to me just yesterday afternoon, his wisdom about listening to one's inner voice. A fresh wave of grief, sharp and sudden, washed over me for his almost certain loss. I vowed then, if I ever had the chance, I would find Mrs. Astor, tell her about his final words to me, about the profound impact he'd had.

Finally, it was my turn. Hands reached down, gripping mine, steadying me as I made the clumsy, exhausting climb. As I was pulled over the rail onto the solid, steady deck of the Carpathia, the first thing that struck me was the smell – warm, comforting, almost overwhelmingly so after the sterile cold of the Atlantic. Hot soup, strong coffee, the hearty aroma of baking bread. Her galleys had clearly been working at full capacity for hours, preparing for our arrival, for the eager bellies and frozen bones of Titanic's precious, pitifully few survivors.

A line of Carpathia's staff – stewards, stewardesses, even some passengers, I thought – stood ready, offering sympathetic smiles that couldn't quite mask the horror in their eyes. They relied on their training, their sense of duty, to keep from cracking in the face of our collective trauma.

"There ya go, lad," a kind, gruff voice said, and a heavy, warm blanket was immediately draped around my shivering shoulders. I clutched it gratefully, the rough wool a welcome tether to this reality.

Since we were amongst the last of the lifeboats to be emptied, I looked around the now woefully crowded deck of our rescue ship. I took in the devastating tableau of survival. Carpathia's public rooms – lounges, Smoking Rooms, even corridors – were rapidly becoming makeshift dormitories, infirmaries. Survivors were everywhere, a fragile, dazed lot. Some sat in stunned silence, wrapped in blankets, staring blankly ahead. Others wept openly, men and women alike, their grief a raw, unabashed display. Some huddled in small groups, murmuring quietly, while others walked aimlessly, their faces distant, numb.

Several of Carpathia's crew, notebooks and pencils in hand, moved gently amongst us, taking down names, compiling the list that would eventually tell the world who had lived, and by omission, who had perished.

"Name, sir?" a young crewman asked me politely, his pen poised over a pad, his eyes kind but efficient.

"Sutherland-Howell," I managed, my voice still hoarse. "Benjamin Sutherland-Howell...the second."

"Thank you, sir," he replied, scribbling it down before starting to move on.

"Excuse me," I stopped him, my heart pounding with a new wave of anxiety. "Have you...have you by any chance registered a Margaret Sutherland-Howell? Or a...a Miles Force?"

He quickly scanned the pages he'd already filled. His brow furrowed in concentration, then he looked up, his expression apologetic. "I'm...afraid not, sir. Not on my list. But," he added quickly, offering a small, hopeful smile, "there's a good lot of us taking names all over the ship. Don't mean nothing yet, sir. She might be with another officer."

"Thank you," I said quietly, the hope he offered feeling thin against the weight of my fear. I watched him walk away to the next survivor.

"Mr. Sutherland-Howell, was it?" A man's kind, authoritative voice spoke beside me. I turned to see an officer with tired but compassionate eyes, his uniform denoting high rank. "I am Captain Rostron," he introduced himself, extending a hand. "RMS Carpathia. You have my deepest, sincerest condolences, son, for your loss and your ordeal."

"Thank you, sir," I said, my voice low, shaking his hand.

"The sea...she can be..." he began, then seemed to trail off at the sight of my undoubtedly red-rimmed, glossy eyes, perhaps sensing words were inadequate. "Well," he continued gently, "if there is anything at all you need, anything my crew or I can do for you..."

"Thank you, sir," I said once more, my gaze drifting back mindlessly to the scene of survivors before me – women weeping for lost husbands, children for lost fathers, all of us picking through the shattered pieces of our lives, trying to put them back together, going through the motions. I watched them, a dedicated spectator to their grief, assuming that, in time, I too would become one of them, alone, trying to piece together the remaining fragments of my own identity, my own future, without Miles.

"Some of my own passengers," Captain Rostron whispered, leaning closer, "have very generously offered up their cabins for those most in need of rest, son. If you'd like a quiet place...some privacy..."

"No, sir," I replied, shaking my head.

He looked at me, slightly disappointed, I thought, as if hoping I'd take immediate advantage of the special treatment, the comfort offered.

"Thank you, though. It's very kind." I looked around the crowded deck again. "I think...I'd rather stay out here, for now. See if the rest of my party...if they've made it aboard safely, sir."

Captain Rostron smiled then, a flicker of understanding, perhaps approval, in his tired eyes. "Alright, son. As you wish. If you change your mind," he winked innocuously, "just let one of my officers know."

I gave an appreciative nod. Then he was gone, moving on to offer comfort and assistance to other survivors, leaving me there on the deck of the rescue ship, wrapped in a borrowed blanket, the scent of coffee and hope mingling with the salt and sorrow, to begin the long, uncertain process of putting my broken pieces back together.

An hour or more passed. I walked the crowded decks of the Carpathia, scanning every face, checking every list posted by the diligent crew, searching the makeshift dormitories in the lounges and Saloons. Nothing. No sign of Mother, nor Birdie. No sign of Miles. The initial flicker of hope ignited by Captain Rostron's kind words and the crewman's reassurances slowly sputtered and died, leaving behind the cold, hard ash of reality. They were gone. All of them. I was utterly alone.

The thought was a physical blow, buckling my knees. I leaned against the ship's railing, the borrowed blanket suddenly feeling impossibly heavy. I didn't want the special treatment the captain had offered, didn't feel I deserved it more than anyone else huddled on these decks. But the need to escape the sea of weary, grieving faces, the scars of death reflected in every pair of hollow eyes, became overwhelming. I needed a quiet place. To cry. To pray. To simply stop seeing for a while.

I found one of the stewards who had been taking names earlier. "...Uh...excuse me, sir," I nearly whispered. "My name is Benjamin Sutherland-Howell. Captain Rostron mentioned...that perhaps there might be a cabin available...?"

"Yes, sir," the steward replied immediately, his eyes filled with sympathy as he recognized the name or perhaps just the depth of despair in my voice. "The Captain gave instructions. I was just about to take this breakfast tray to another of your...another Titanic passenger...in a cabin set aside. Why don't you follow me, sir? I'll drop this off on the way."

Numbly, I followed him through the crowded corridors, up a flight of stairs to a quieter deck where fewer passengers seemed to be stirring. A quiet wing, perhaps, set aside for those, like me, needing isolation.

"Here we are, sir," the steward stopped outside a cabin door. "I just need to deliver this tray, then I'll show you to your cabin just down the hall." He knocked softly. When there was no reply after a moment, he gently turned the handle and pushed the door open a crack.

"I said I'd rather not be disturbed...please," a muffled voice pleaded softly from within.

The voice was familiar. Strained, broken, but familiar. I stepped forward automatically, peering past the steward into the dim cabin. Sitting slumped in an armchair, still clad in last night's drenched pajamas, was J. Bruce Ismay.

"Mr. Ismay?" I said, surprised to find him here, hidden away.

He looked up sharply, his eyes red-rimmed, startled to see me. "Benji," he breathed, his voice hushed.

"My apologies, Mr. Ismay, sir," the steward interjected quickly, stepping into the room with the tray. "But the ship's doctor ordered that I deliver this to you. Said you need to keep your strength up. You don't have to eat it, sir, but I'm just following orders." He placed the tray on a small table, then turned back to me. "Alright, Mr. Sutherland-Howell. Let's carry on to your cabin, shall we?"

"Actually," I stopped him, an unexpected impulse taking hold. "If Mr. Ismay doesn't object...I'd like to stay. Have a word with him."

"Mr. Ismay is to be left alone, sir, doctor's—" the steward began protectively.

"It's fine, steward," Ismay cut him off, his voice regaining a fraction of its former authority, though still low and weary. "It's quite alright. Benji is...welcome to stay."

"Very good, sir," the steward nodded, backing out efficiently. And with that, he closed the door, leaving me alone in the dim, quiet cabin with the Managing Director of the White Star Line.

An awkward silence descended. Ismay stared down at his hands, seemingly unable to meet my gaze. He knew, I realized, that we would eventually have words, but clearly didn't want to be the one to initiate them. I decided to spare him the preamble.

"My mother's dead," I stated flatly, the words devoid of emotion, feeling strangely distant now that they were finally spoken aloud.

Ismay's head snapped up, his eyes instantly welling with fresh tears. He took a sharp, pained breath, absorbing the confirmation of what he likely already suspected after seeing her leave the lifeboat, after witnessing the ship's final plunge. "And...and the rest of your family?" he asked timidly, his voice cracking slightly. "Your sister? Your father?"

I just looked at him, letting my silence answer the question, letting him see the utter desolation in my eyes. He drew in a deep, shuddering sigh, burying his face briefly in his hands. "Oh, Benji. Dear God."

"Well," I said curtly, turning towards the door, the brief, strange encounter feeling suddenly pointless. "I just thought you should know."

"Benji! Wait!" Ismay called out, stopping me again as my hand reached the doorknob. I paused but didn't turn back immediately.

He hesitated, then continued, his voice thick with emotion. "I know what you must think of me, Benji." He took a shaky breath. "And...I also know this is hardly my place now...but...your mother...she spoke of your relationship with your father...how difficult it was..."

"You're right," I cut him off coldly, turning slightly. "It's not your place."

"Please, Benji!" he pleaded, desperation entering his voice. I stopped walking again, waiting. "Look...I...I know all too well," he struggled for the words, "what it's like. To have a father for whom... nothing you ever do seems to be enough." His voice trembled. "One minute you think you're charting your own course, finding success...the next you're pushing recklessly ahead through ice-infested waters, taking foolish risks, even when some part of you knows you shouldn't...because you're always trying to outrun that shadow. That disappointment. Trying to stay two steps ahead of it." Tears were openly slicing down his sullen cheeks now. "That voice, that judgment...it'll not only control you while they're alive, Benji, it'll continue to eat away at you, consume you, even long after they're gone."

I watched him, stunned by this raw, unexpected confession, this glimpse into the pressures that had driven him, perhaps to this very disaster.

"You have to let it go, Benji," he urged, his voice regaining a shred of conviction. "Before it destroys you like it destroyed...like it's destroying me." He pushed himself out of the chair, crossing the small space towards me, his eyes intense, pleading. "You are your own man now." He gripped my shoulder, his touch surprisingly firm. "You are the man of the house, now. The Sutherland-Howell legacy...the legacy you forge from this point forward...it is entirely your own. Not your father's. Do you understand?"

His words, echoing Astor's advice but delivered with the raw pain of lived experience, hit me with surprising force.

Then, as quickly as it came, the intensity seemed to drain from him. Without another word, he released my shoulder, dropped his gaze again, and stole back to his armchair across the room, fumbling for the cigarette case on the table, his hands visibly trembling as he lit one. He didn't look back.

I stood there for another moment, watching his hunched figure wreathed in smoke. Then, quietly, I left him alone in the room like that, him still looking away as I gently closed the door on him, perhaps for the last time.

CHAPTER 42

Leaving Ismay alone with his ghosts in that dim cabin felt like closing a chapter I hadn't even known I was reading. I needed air, needed to escape the confines of the ship, the suffocating weight of grief and revelation. I found my way back out onto one of Carpathia's upper decks. The rescue operation was largely complete now, the last of the lifeboats having been emptied hours ago. The morning sun felt surprisingly warm, a stark contrast to the deadly chill of the night, glinting off the calm, impossibly blue water that stretched to the horizon, now thankfully clear of the menacing ice field the dawn had woken to. Survivors still huddled under blankets, but a sense of weary, dazed routine was beginning to set in as the Carpathia steamed steadily towards New York.

As I walked slowly along the mostly empty deck, trying to process everything, I saw a familiar figure approaching, strolling slowly arm-in-arm with a uniformed maid or nurse. Madeleine Astor. Even pale and drawn, draped in borrowed wraps, she carried herself with that quiet, unmistakable dignity I'd noted when I first saw her boarding Titanic and again as she was rescued this morning.

An impulse, born of genuine gratitude and the need to share the unexpected kindness her husband had shown me, propelled me forward.

"Mrs. Astor," I began hesitantly as I neared them. She stopped, looking at me with tired, questioning eyes. "Forgive the intrusion. My name is Benji Sutherland-Howell. I...I knew your husband. Briefly."

Her face softened immediately, a deep melancholy clouding her eyes, yet tinged with a gentle appreciation for the acknowledgment. "Mr. Sutherland-Howell," she murmured.

"I just wanted to say," I continued quickly, before I lost my nerve, "that he...he was a very kind man, Mrs. Astor. Truly kind. Not at all like the intimidating figure one reads about in the papers." I thought of his advice, his encouragement, the simple gesture of giving me his book. "He spoke to me yesterday afternoon. Offered some...wisdom. And I don't believe," the words felt profoundly true as I said them, "that I would be standing here today if it weren't for his actions, his encouragement just before...well, just before."

Madeleine's eyes welled up with fresh tears, though she offered a small, grateful smile. "Thank you, Mr. Howell. That...that means a great deal to hear."

"Well," I felt suddenly awkward, having delivered my piece. "I just...I thought you should know." I gave a slight bow and started to turn away, not wanting to intrude further on her grief.

"So," her soft voice called after me, stopping me in my tracks. I turned back. "You're the famous Benji, then."

I looked at her, confused. "Famous?"

She crossed the space towards me, her steps slow but steady. "Louise," she said quietly to her companion, "would you fetch my small bag from the cabin, please? The leather one." The maid gave a shallow curtsy and departed swiftly down the deck, leaving Mrs. Astor and me alone.

"Your husband spoke of me?" I asked, astonished, a thrill running through me despite the circumstances. I'd made an impression on John Jacob Astor?

"He did," she confirmed with a gentle smile. "Mentioned a bright young man with ambitions, someone wrestling with expectations." She paused, her eyes softening even more, holding a different kind of knowing sadness now. "But J.J. wasn't the only one who told me about you, Benji."

My breath caught.

"Miles spoke of you," she continued softly. "Endlessly, it seemed. Said he'd met someone...different. Someone who saw the world in a unique way. Someone who made him think about the future differently."

The view of Madeleine blurred before my eyes, as tears instantly festered at the unexpected sound of his name spoken aloud, spoken of in connection to me. "Miles...he told you about me?" I whispered, my voice thick.

"He did," Madeleine affirmed gently. "I've known Miles since I was a young girl, my charismatic older cousin. Always saw him as...well, charmingly adrift. The type who might never put down roots, content to go wherever the wind took him. Never once, in all those years, did I hear him talk seriously about wanting to settle down, to build something real." She looked me directly in the eye. "Until he met you. You made quite an impact on him, Benji."

I stood there, mute, reeling from her words, afraid that any attempt to speak would betray the depth of my own grief, shatter the fragile composure I was barely maintaining.

Just then, the maid returned, handing Madeleine a small, handsome leather satchel – clearly men's luggage, not something belonging to Mrs. Astor herself.

"He gave me this," Madeleine said, holding the satchel, "just before I boarded the lifeboat." She managed another faint, sad smile. "He told me to hold onto it for safekeeping. Said if anything should happen to him...well, he said I'd know what to do with it."

She held the satchel out to me. "Here, Benji. It belongs to you now."

I stared at the bag, then at her, uncomprehending. "You...you want me to have it?" I managed to ask.

"Miles wanted you to have it," she corrected softly. "Benji, you did something for him that no one else ever could. Helped him see a different path, perhaps. A definitive future." Her gaze was kind, understanding. She pressed the bag into my hands. "...I just thought you should know," she added quietly, echoing my own earlier words back to me with gentle significance.

And with that, offering a final, small, compassionate smile, Madeleine Astor turned, rejoined her maid, and continued slowly along her walk, leaving me standing alone on the deck of the Carpathia, the unexpected weight of Miles's last message, his legacy, resting heavy in my trembling hands.

Monday Morning, Continued
  Aboard the RMS Carpathia

The steward showed me to a small but blessedly quiet passenger cabin that someone had generously vacated. He left me there with a final sympathetic nod, closing the door softly behind him. Alone, finally. The silence felt immense, heavy. I sat on the edge of the narrow bunk, the rough wool of the Carpathia blanket still draped around my shoulders. On the floor beside me rested the handsome leather satchel Madeleine Astor had pressed into my hands – Miles's satchel. His legacy. His last message.

I stared at it, my fingers tracing the worn leather. Inside, perhaps, were answers. Or perhaps just more questions, more pain. Some tangible, intimate piece of him to hold onto. But opening it...opening it felt like an act of finality. Like closing the door on hope. As long as it remained closed, some small, irrational part of me could pretend that Miles might still walk through the door, that Mother might appear with her honed smile, that Birdie might burst in full of indignation and life. Opening the bag meant accepting that they were likely gone forever, claimed by the freezing dark. And I wasn't ready. Not yet. The prospect of confirming I was truly, utterly alone wasn't something I could face.

A soft, hesitant knock sounded at the cabin door, startling me from my morose thoughts. It was the same kind steward who had led me into the room only moments ago. He poked his head in, his expression urgent now, yet respectful.

"Mr. Howell, sir," he began quickly, his voice low, "beg pardon for disturbing you again, but...well, sir, you'll want to come see this. Quickly, if you please."

His urgency, the strange look in his eye, sent a jolt of adrenaline through me, momentarily overriding my grief. "What is it? See what?" I asked, standing up.

"Just come with me, sir," he insisted, already turning back towards the corridor for me to follow.

My mind raced with possibilities – none of them good – as I hurried after him. We didn't head back towards the main passenger areas, but descended several flights of stairs, deeper into the ship, towards decks clearly designated for Carpathia's own steerage or perhaps where Titanic's third-class survivors were being housed.

"There was a young woman...pulled from the water by one of the last lifeboats, sir," the steward explained breathlessly as we navigated the crowded, less-appointed corridors. "Or perhaps found clinging to wreckage near a boat, accounts differ.

Barely conscious when they brought her aboard. Very nearly frozen." He glanced back at me. "We...well, based on her dress, sir, simple wool, no finery...we thought she was steerage. Took her down here with the others."

My heart began to pound with a sudden, illogical hope I hadn't dared to feel moments before. A simple wool dress...

"She's just come round properly," the steward continued, leading me around a final corner into a larger open space where dozens of survivors huddled, tended to by crew and Carpathia passengers. "Started asking...well, seemed to be asking for someone named Benji. We thought...given your name, sir..."

He led me towards a small group gathered around a figure lying on a makeshift pallet on the deck, covered in thick blankets. A ship's doctor knelt beside her. As we approached, one of the onlookers, perhaps a kind Carpathia passenger offering comfort, stepped back slightly to let the doctor work, revealing the survivor's face.

Pale. Exhausted. Lips tinged blue. Hair damp and matted. But unmistakably, miraculously...

"Birdie!" The name tore from my throat, a choked cry of disbelief and overwhelming relief. I pushed through the small circle, falling to my knees beside her pallet.

Her eyes fluttered open at the sound of my voice, hazy at first, then slowly focusing, recognizing me. She wasn't speaking yet, perhaps too weak, too shocked, but her eyes...her eyes held a universe of terror, survival, and profound relief that mirrored my own.

I reached out, taking her hand. It was ice-cold, frighteningly so, but she weakly squeezed my fingers. Tears I didn't know I still had streamed down my face, hot against my cold skin. I brought her frozen hand up to my lips, wrapping both of my own around it, trying to pour warmth, life, back into her.

"Oh, my precious Birdie," I whispered, my voice thick with tears. "My sister. You're alive. You're alive."

She looked up at me, a single tear escaping the corner of her eye, tracking a path through the grime on her cheek. In that moment, amidst the shared grief and loss aboard the rescue ship, finding her felt like finding an entire world saved from the wreck. We weren't entirely alone.

Tuesday Morning, April 16th, 1912
Aboard the RMS Carpathia

I sat up with Birdie all through that first long day and night aboard the Carpathia. Despite the bone-deep exhaustion that settled over me after the adrenaline faded, despite having gone nearly forty-eight hours without sleep, I knew that even if I tried, rest wouldn't come. My mind was too restless, replaying the horrors, searching the faces on deck, clinging to fragile threads of hope.

Birdie had eventually drifted into an exhausted, fretful sleep in the narrow bunk beside mine after the ship's doctor had checked her over. They had moved her up to the small passenger cabin the steward had found for me – it wasn't our usual standard, far from it, but it was quiet, private, warm. A haven. Miles's leather satchel still sat on the floor by the door, untouched, unopened. Looking at it felt like staring into an abyss. Opening it, acknowledging what it likely represented, would mean accepting Miles was truly gone forever, along with Mother, and almost certainly Father. But the prospect that Miles might still be alive, that perhaps another ship had picked up one of the unaccounted collapsibles, rescued survivors floating on a large piece of wreckage...it seemed impossible. Yet, here beside me, breathing softly now in sleep, was Birdie – pulled from the freezing water, mistaken for steerage, alive against all odds. She was the very impossibility that allowed me to hold onto that sliver of hope for Miles, however irrational.

The looming sunrise of Tuesday eventually began slicing brilliantly through the closed shutters of the cabin's porthole. Muted sounds filtered in – the distant wash of somewhat choppy waves against the hull, the creak of the ship's timbers. The Carpathia, smaller and certainly older than Titanic, rocked a bit more obviously as she pressed onward, carrying her precious, broken cargo towards New York. She felt less like a steady giant, more like a determined pony pulling a heavy load.

"Benji?"

Birdie's voice, weak but clearer now, startled me from my thoughts. She stirred, pushing herself slowly into a sitting position against the pillows. Her strength seemed to be returning, more than I'd seen since they brought her aboard.

"Careful, Birdie," I said gently, moving to help prop her up. "Easy now." A steward had left a tray earlier with warm broth and tea. "Would you like some broth?" I asked, holding up the steaming mug.

She shook her head slightly but didn't voice a refusal. I took that as a maybe, setting the mug down on the small bedside table within her reach, and waited.

We sat in silence for a moment, the only sounds the creaking ship and Birdie's soft breathing. Then, she looked at me, her eyes, though shadowed with exhaustion and trauma, holding a profound, searching question.

"What...what's going to become of us, Benji?" she asked, her low voice barely audible.

I almost asked her what she meant – us, the survivors? Us, the family? Us, the inheritors of a name now possibly synonymous with disaster? But I didn't need to ask. I knew exactly what she meant. I was wondering the same thing. Our lives, the ones we'd assumed stretched out before us just days ago – mapped, planned, secured by wealth and expectation – were gone, sunk beneath the waves along with the ship that carried them. Our parents were gone. The structure was gone. Now, nothing was certain. Everything was an unknown.

"Well," I began slowly, searching for words that felt true, words that weren't just hollow reassurances. "We're adults now, Birdie." I looked at her, meeting her gaze. "Or near enough. So, I suppose...I suppose we're going to have to learn to..." My mind grasped for the right word, the simplest truth. "...live."

Birdie looked at me, waiting for more.

"You know what I think I've learned this past year, Birdie?" I continued, thinking of Father's manipulations, Mother's hidden unhappiness revealed only at the end, Ismay's confession, Astor's surprising wisdom, Miles's defiant hope. "All the grown-ups around us – Mother, Father, Ismay, men like them...they always seem to have it all figured out, don't they? Confident, in control, navigating the world according to some secret map."

I shook my head. "But the thing about appearances, Birdie...they're rarely what they seem to be. I think every single one of them, no matter how successful or assured they appear, is just...taking life one day at a time, just like us. They may pretend to have it all figured out, pretend they know the destination, but deep down?" I leaned closer. "Deep down, I suspect they're just as scared and uncertain as you and I feel in this very moment."

A flicker of understanding sparked in Birdie's eyes.

"So, you know what we do now?" I asked softly.

"Live?" Birdie whispered, echoing my earlier thought.

"Exactly," I confirmed, finding strength in the idea, in the advice given to me by those I'd unexpectedly connected with. "Live in the moment. That's what Miles taught me. Because none of us are promised anything more than the breath we have in our lungs right now. The next minute, the next hour...it may never come. Worrying about the 'what ifs', trying to control a future we can't predict...it's useless." I looked at her and managed a small, genuine smile. "So, we just keep living, Birdie. Moment by moment." I reached out and took her hand, the one not quite so cold now. "...And maybe," I finished, echoing Astor's sentiment, "the rest will fall into place on its own."

April 16th - 18th, 1912

Aboard the RMS Carpathia

The days aboard the Carpathia blurred into a strange, suspended reality. Time moved differently now, measured not by clocks or ship's bells, but by the rhythm of grief, the slow return of physical warmth, and the endless, searching glances towards every newly-rescued face, hoping against diminishing hope.

We settled into a routine of sorts, Birdie and I, in the small cabin generously offered. Birdie's strength grew hour by hour, her resilience remarkable, though the shadows in her eyes spoke of the horrors she witnessed below decks, horrors she may never be ready to speak of fully. I sat with her, read to her sometimes, fetched broth, or simply existed beside her in silence. That silence, was so often the hardest part. When the immediate bustle of the rescue had faded, when the ship settled into its steady course for New York, the quiet became profound, oppressive, filled only by the internal echo of screams and the memory of the icy water.

Even young Harold Bride, his feet badly frostbitten and wrapped, couldn't bear the silence, couldn't bear the inactivity. Despite Captain Rostron's orders to rest, he insisted on being wheeled to the Carpathia's wireless shack each day. Their operator, Cottam, was overwhelmed, buried under the avalanche of official messages, survivor lists, and anxious inquiries from shore. Bride, knowing the vital importance of the work, lent his expertise, tapping out names, locations, reassurances, perhaps finding distraction, or maybe just solace, in the familiar duty amidst the wreckage of our voyage.

Birdie, too, found purpose quickly. Once back on her feet, some spark of her old crusading spirit returned. Teaming up with that force of nature, Mrs. Margaret Brown – "Maggie," she insisted we call her – Birdie began organizing. They moved through the first-class survivors, collecting funds, soliciting donations of clothing and essentials for the third-class passengers housed below, many of whom, as Birdie grimly confirmed, had lost literally everything but the clothes on their backs. Watching Birdie channel her grief into action, I felt a surge of pride, though her frustration that the considerable amount raised "wasn't enough" was entirely predictable. Some things, it seemed, even surviving the Titanic couldn't change.

Miles's satchel remained by the door, the entire time, unopened. The irrational hope I clung to in those first hours – that another ship might have picked him up – faded with each passing nautical mile. Accepting he was gone felt like another kind of drowning. Mother...Father...the confirmation of their absence on any survivor list is a stark, unavoidable fact. We were orphans now, Birdie and I. Heirs to a name and a fortune that suddenly felt alien, tainted.

April 18th, 1912

Arrival in New York

We steamed into New York harbor late that evening under a steady, dreary rain. The city skyline, usually a symbol of triumph, of arrival, felt different that night. Somber. Weighted. As the Carpathia glided slowly up the Hudson towards the Cunard pier at Chelsea Piers – Pier 54, ironically adjacent to the White Star berth where Titanic should have docked – Birdie and I stood together on the covered deck, watching the city lights blur through the downpour.

The rain felt...cleansing. A washing away of the salt, the grime, the lingering chill of the past few days. Preparing us, perhaps, for whatever came next. Standing there, watching the dockside crowds swell even at the late hour, I felt like an immigrant arriving, leaving an old world, an old life, irrevocably behind, bound for something entirely new, entirely unknown. The Statue of Liberty, held her torch aloft as we passed, usually a symbol of welcome, felt like a challenge. Liberty. What did that even mean now?

"The land of opportunity," Birdie murmured beside me, perhaps sensing my thoughts. "We can be anyone we want to be now, Benji. Reinvent ourselves completely."

She was right. Whatever path Father had laid out for me, whatever societal expectations Mother held – they were gone. There were no plans now. No predetermined course. Only the present moment, and the next, and the terrifying freedom to choose. We just had to live, moment by moment, see where the current carried us.

"Benji?" Birdie must've seen the distant look in my eye, that flicker of pain as my thoughts inevitably returned to the one person missing from this new future. She was reading my mind, just another one of her superpowers.

"Yeah?" I managed, my voice a little rougher than I intended.

She looked at me tenderly then, her expression not overly emotional, not pulling focus from the gravity of our arrival, just radiating genuine, honest empathy from her eyes. "I'm really sorry about Miles," she said softly.

A lump caught instantly in my throat, hot and sharp. I looked down at her, this incredible sister of mine. She offered a small, warm smile. There was no pretense in it, no pity, only understanding. She knew just what that moment needed, what I needed. She brought his name into this strange, new reality, pulling him from the swirling chaos of my internal thoughts, manifesting his presence here between us, acknowledging his loss without demanding I speak of it.

I didn't say anything; I didn't need to. I simply took her hand in mine, offered a weak, grateful smile in return, then looked back out at the blurred lights of the skyline that was swiftly approaching us, a future waiting, whether I was ready for it or not.

"You sure about this?" I asked, recalling the hushed, intense conversation we'd had earlier about the future, about the inheritance Father's letter had promised just before the end. I took her hand, meeting her determined gaze with a sly smile of my own.

She looked up at me, returning that smile, her eyes shining with a familiar fire, tempered now by loss but not extinguished. "Definitely."

The ship docked amidst a scene of pandemonium. Gangways were secured. And then, the disembarkation began. As expected, a throng of press surged forward on the pier, flashbulbs popping, reporters shouting questions, a clamoring wave held back by a line of police. They swarmed around the first few survivors coming down the gangway, hungry for an exclusive, for first-hand accounts of the tragedy, words raw from the mouths of those who had lived it.

"Mr. Howell!" a reporter shouted, spotting us as we neared the top of the gangway. He surely had gotten our names from the preliminary lists. "Over here!"

"Is it true you and your sister stand to inherit millions?" yelled another, pushing forward, notebook flapping.

"Can you give us a quote, Mr. Howell? A statement?"

The barrage was overwhelming. I stopped at the top of the gangway, taking a deep breath, Birdie steady beside me. I thought of Father's manipulations, the gilded cage his money represented. I thought of Miles, of Astor, of living authentically. I thought of the hundreds still lost beneath the waves.

"I will say this," I began, my voice carrying over the swell, amplified by the sudden, expectant hush that fell over the nearest reporters. "The sinking of the Titanic was an unimaginable tragedy. A loss that those of us who survived will likely never truly get over. I know that I won't." I paused, meeting the gaze of the reporters directly. "Yes, my sister and I have been informed that there is a sizable estate, a trust fund established just before...before the end." Another pause. "But as of this moment, I am hereby relinquishing my entire share. Every penny of it."

A collective gasp, a flurry of scribbling pencils.

"Every penny," I repeated firmly, "will be divided equally between the Seamen's Charity and a fund established for the survivors of the Titanic who have lost everything."

"Mr. Howell! A follow-up!" voices clamored.

"And!" I held up a hand, stopping them, a sudden, perhaps reckless, idea forming, a way to seize control, to truly start anew, fueled by Astor's belief and Miles's dream. "While I have nothing further to say about the tragedy itself tonight, I will offer my exclusive personal account of survival to the highest bidder. The proceeds," I added quickly, "will fund my future endeavors. Never let it be said," I allowed myself a grim smile, "that Ben Howell is not a self-made man."

And with that, I turned and began to descend the gangway, leaving the stunned press behind. Birdie squeezed my hand, then stepped forward into the flashbulbs.

"Like my brother, Ben," she announced, her voice clear and strong, echoing my own declaration, "I too will be relinquishing my inheritance. Every penny divided evenly amongst the Titanic Survivor's Fund..." she paused, then added with defiant conviction, "...and the National Women's Suffrage Movement."

More shouts, more flashing bulbs. "Miss Howell!"

"And!" Birdie stopped them coolly with a wave of her hand, a natural politician already. "...whomever comes in as the second highest bidder for my brother's exclusive story," she offered a wry, challenging laugh, "I'll gladly sell you mine. Never let it be said," she declared, her eyes flashing, "that Maggie Howell is not a self-made woman!"

And with that, she turned, took my arm, and together, leaving our old lives, our old wealth, our old names sinking behind us in the rainy New York night, we walked off the pier. We would use the money from our stories – our own self-made opportunity – to start anew.

So, we headed West, Maggie and I, to Los Angeles, each determined to forge a new life from the ashes of the old. She, of course, threw herself into politics – Councilwoman, then Attorney, eventually a formidable Congresswoman, always on the front lines, always championing her cause with that fierce, intuitive spirit. Her superpower, as she'd call it, always knowing just when to strike.

Me? I pursued the dream Miles and I had dared to speak of – the moving picture industry. Writing, directing, eventually producing. The world was new, the possibilities seemed endless, and for a time, I poured everything into creating the life we'd envisioned. Miles's satchel...I made the decision to keep it locked away. Some things are too sacred, perhaps too painful, to face immediately. I knew, deep down, that he was gone. That faint, desperate glimmer of hope that he might one day come waltzing back through the door, his smile as radiant as the California sun, faded with each passing year. But still, that unopened satchel...it felt like a vigil. As long as it remained untouched, some small part of him, of us, was still waiting. Just as I was.

Success found me, as it often does when one is driven by ghosts. But with it came a creeping unease. Little by little, I realized I'd stopped listening to that still, small voice J.J. Astor had spoken of, the one Miles had helped me hear again. I'd stopped truly living in the moment. Instead, I became obsessed with planning, with controlling, with building walls around a past that refused to stay buried. That voice would whisper sometimes, telling me I was veering off course, losing my way. But I didn't know how to stop, how to turn back to the boy who had stood on the deck of the Titanic and chosen hope.

That's when I met your mother, Will. My beloved Adelaide. She was a whirl-wind of life, a free spirit with an unapologetic zeal for living, for loving, without question or hesitation. I saw in her a light I thought had been extinguished in myself. I believed I needed someone like her to anchor me, to help me maintain that balance, to remind me when I was drifting too far towards the edge.

And then, of course, we were blessed. Four incredible children – you, Claire, Louis, and June. We vowed, Adelaide and I, to give you the childhoods we never had, to ensure you each felt free to choose your own paths, your own careers, your own partners, without the weight of expectation we had both known. And for a while, it seemed to work. I found fulfillment in my career, profound joy in my family. The ache in my soul seemed to quiet.

But the years, they have a way of ticking by, of eroding even the strongest defenses. That still, small voice, the one I'd once clung to, went silent once more, or perhaps I simply stopped being able to hear it over the noise of my own meticulously constructed life. And the old feeling returned, worse than ever: I felt like a fraud. My wife, my Adelaide, my forever leading lady... she loved me in ways I realized, with dawning horror, I couldn't fully reciprocate. Not in the way she deserved. And worse, far worse, I found myself lying – through smiles, through gestures, through silences – to convince her that I did.

That's when the thoughts of Miles crept back in, insidious at first, then over-whelming. Thoughts of what it felt like to be with someone who simply... fit. Who felt unequivocally right. A man. It's so difficult to explain, Will, especially when my love for Adelaide was, and is, so real, so true. But it was a different kind of love. The profound affection one has for their closest friend, their dearest family member. The love I felt for Miles... the love I still carry for him... it was a different element entirely. A different fire.

As more time passed, I became distant. Withdrew from your mother, from all of you. The fear consumed me – the fear that, like Dorothy, like Archie, like my own mother before me, you too would eventually see through the disguise, see the lie I was living. So I hid, no matter how much it hurt you, no matter how much it ripped me apart inside.

Then came the nightmares. Vivid, relentless. The longing for a past I couldn't reclaim, for a touch I'd never feel again. The memories, undying, unyielding, resurfacing with a vengeance that no success, no charitable act, no worldly dis-traction could quell.

That's when I finally opened the satchel.

Inside, untouched for decades, was Miles's camera. And a few dozen rolls of undeveloped film. Film he'd shot during our brief, incandescent time aboard the Titanic.

I had them developed. And suddenly, looking at those images – his eye, his perspective, captured moments of Birdie, of me, of the ship, of the sea – I was back there. On those decks. In that cabin. Reliving those moments, remembering our dream, the feel of his hand in mine. Remembering the ghosts I longed to be with, the ghosts who had never truly left me. But the camera, the film, they weren't the only memories locked away in Miles's bag. My journal, the one you're now holding in your hands, a relic of my former life, one I had tried to throw away, Miles had kept it, saving it for me so that the moment I decided to come back to it, I'd find it waiting.

Little by little, I lost myself in that past. I tried, Will. I tried so hard to come back, to find my way back to your mother, to you children. But the pull was too strong.

If you're reading this now, you'll know that I wasn't able to make it, son, even though, for a time, I truly wanted to. But if you've made it this far, through these pages, I hope you have a better understanding of me, of my silence, of the storm I was battling inside. Please know, it was never personal. Not with you.

I love you so much, Will. Just as I love your mother, my Adelaide. Just as I love Claire, and Louis, and June. And of course, your aunt Maggie, my indomitable Birdie.

And, as you will now truly know, I was in love with a man. A man named Miles. A man whom I had promised to save, but didn't. A man whose absence has been a wound that never healed. And that has never left me. And, until I am finally gone from this world, it never, ever will.

All because...*he jumped first.*

CHAPTER 43

I closed the heavy leather cover of my father's journal, the thud echoing in the sudden, profound silence of his study. For days afterward, I found myself adrift in that silence, the world outside muted, distant. I digested his words, my father's words, letting them settle, letting them reshape the landscape of everything I thought I knew. Just as his own young view of the world had been shattered by encountering its darkness, my view of him, the distant, enigmatic figure who was my father, had been irrevocably altered – not shattered, but...restored. Restored by seeing the good, the vulnerable, the loving heart that beat beneath the carefully constructed facade.

The bittersweet closure his truth brought was a heavy thing to carry, a secret I felt selfish keeping only to myself. Yet, he had chosen to keep it locked away, buried in the vault, and for a time, I felt bound to honor that silence, following his lead even in death.

Twentieth Century Fox, as these things go, eventually released their film, Titanic, without my father's name attached. The film, a spectacle of romance and disaster, brought the tragic story back into the public limelight. With it, that still, small voice, the one my father had learned about from J.J. Astor, the one he'd struggled to heed, began to whisper within me. It wanted to share his story, his true story. But still, I hesitated. The weight of his secrets, his pain, felt too personal, too raw.

It wasn't until months later, when I began the somber task of moving things out of his study – that sanctuary of silence and shadows – that everything changed. Tucked away in a drawer, almost forgotten, I found a large, thick envelope, its paper aged and brittle. Across the front, in a faded, elegant hand I didn't recognize, it was addressed simply: "To New Amsterdam." My heart stuttered.

The phrase from my father's journal – Mr. Stead's "inside joke" – resonated with sudden, chilling clarity.

With trembling fingers, I opened it. Inside, nestled amongst protective tissue, were photographs. Dozens of them. Developed prints, slightly sepia with age, taken with an artist's eye. Photos that, I realized with a jolt, no one but my father had likely ever seen since the moment they were captured in 1912. It was a visceral experience, surreal, like stepping directly into the pages I had just read.

There, in stark black and white, was the Titanic's Grand Staircase, just as he had described it – the soaring dome, the intricate ironwork, the clock honoring 'Honour and Glory.' Photos of the opulent Dining Saloon, the elegant Lounge, the sun-drenched Café Parisian where he and Miles had shared espressos and dreams.

Then, the people. Faces I'd only imagined. A candid shot of my grandmother, Caroline, looking regal, and a younger, spirited Birdie beside her – Aunt Maggie, as I knew her – boarding in Southampton, my father a handsome, hesitant youth beside them. There was a photo of J.J. Astor helping his beloved Madeleine into a lifeboat – likely the last photo Miles ever took before pressing his satchel into her hands.

And then...them. My father and Miles. Miles, a face I'd conjured in my mind, now real, vibrant, his smile as effervescent as my father had described. Photos of them in their separate cabins, leaning against railings on deck, laughing. The photo of my father, eyes shining, proudly holding the jeweled Rubáiyát in the dim cargo hold. Another of him leaning against the fender of that gleaming Renault motorcar, pulling a funny, uncharacteristically goofy face – a playful energy I had never witnessed in the man who raised me.

That's when it truly hit me, the full weight of the tragedy beyond the sinking itself. I had never seen my father like that. Even in his rare moments of genuine warmth, of unguarded smiles, he never carried that particular sense of...unbridled life, of lightness, that radiated from him in these photographs. It was as if "Benji," the boy in these pictures, the young man who had found love and dared to dream, had indeed died on the Titanic, alongside Miles, alongside his parents. The father I knew was a survivor, yes, but also a ghost, haunted by what might have been, by who he might have become.

More than anything, I realized, my father had simply wanted to live his life in the moment. Openly. Unafraid. In a profound sense, Miles was the only one who had ever truly seen him live that life, however briefly. And now, through the faded ink of his journal, through these astonishing, intimate photographs, I had been given the chance to see him too. To understand.

The decision, when it came, felt less like a choice and more like an inevitability. I spoke with Edie – my wife now, my partner in writing and in life, the one who had sat with me as I first navigated the labyrinth of my father's past. Together, we knew what had to be done.

Even though I was scared of tarnishing his carefully constructed public image, of destroying the legacy he had so painstakingly built, even though I worried that revealing such private truths might cause further pain, particularly to my mother, Adelaide, who had loved him so completely within the confines of what he could offer...I decided. The truth, his truth, was the only thing that could finally set him free. For too long, except for those few, incandescent days in April of 1912, he had lived his life as a prisoner of his secrets, of his fears. By keeping his story, the very essence of what had brought him so vibrantly, if briefly, to life, locked away, I would be the one destroying his true legacy. Because his truth is his legacy. *Dad... you're free.*

So, now you know. My father, Benjamin Sutherland-Howell – Benji, Ben Howell – was a great man. A complicated, flawed, deeply human man. A man that, perhaps, none of us who knew him in his later years truly knew until it was too late.

My only regret, the one that will linger, is that I never got the chance to tell him just how much I love him. To tell him that I understood. Because, to quote his own heartbreaking words about the love of his life, before I could...

He jumped first.